Also by Connie Brockway

Skinny Dipping
Hot Dish

Praise for the Novels of Connie Brockway

Skinny Dipping

"Realistically quirky characters, delightfully clever writing, and a warmly nourishing story about family, friendship, and love come together brilliantly." —*Chicago Tribune*

"Spiked with her addictively acerbic wit, Brockaway's latest beguiling blend of women's fiction and romance...unfolds into a richly nourishing tale of family, friendship, love, and laughter." —*Booklist*

"Bittersweet and touching . . . [a] most satisfying tale." —*Romantic Times*

"Just right for a long winter day." —*Minnesota Monthly*

"A witty, warmhearted novel that will keep the reader laughing. This hilarious, mysterious and romantic book is a keeper." —Romance Junkies

"An exquisitely rendered setting, an abundance of complex family dynamics, a story that explores what it means to belong, and a beautifully developed romantic relationship guarantee the appeal of this well-crafted tale for both romance and women's fiction fans alike." —*Library Journal*

Hot Dish

"Rapier wit and dazzling prose . . . Brockway writes sheer magic." —Elizabeth Bevarly

"A dazzling contemporary debut!" —Christina Dodd

"A hilarious, bittersweet look at going home." —Eloisa James

"Wry, witty, and wonderful! This cast of unforgettable characters will tickle your funny bone and your heartstrings." —Teresa Medeiros

"This combination caper and comedy-of-errors story is just wacky enough to keep you giggling. Brava!" —*Romantic Times*

"A smart and funny page-turner." —All About Romance

"Splendidly satisfying. With its surfeit of realistically quirky characters and sharp wit, *Hot Dish* is simply superb." —*Booklist*

continued . . .

The Rose Hunter Trilogy: *My Surrender*

"By brilliantly blending an exquisitely sensual romance between two deliciously stubborn individuals into a plot rife with danger, deception and desire, and then wrapping the whole thing up in wickedly witty and elegant writing Brockway deftly demonstrates her gift for creating richly imagined completely irresistible love stories."

—*Library Journal* (starred review)

The Rose Hunter Trilogy: *My Seduction*

"A well-crafted, engaging read." —*Publishers Weekly*

"A fabulous love story . . . wicked, tender, playful, and sumptuous. Too wonderful to resist." —Lisa Kleypas

The Rose Hunter Trilogy: *My Pleasure*

"This is why people read romance . . . an exceptionally good read." —All About Romance

Bridal Favors

"A scrumptious literary treat . . . wonderfully engaging characters, superbly crafted plot, and prose rich in wit and humor." —*Booklist*

"Never predictable, always refreshing, wonderfully touching, deeply emotional, Ms. Brockway's books never fail to satisfy. Connie Brockway is simply one of the best." —All About Romance

The Bridal Season

"Characters, setting, and plot are all handled with perfect aplomb by Brockway, who displays a true gift for humor. Witty and wonderful." —*Booklist*

"If it's smart, sexy, and impossible to put down, it's a book by Connie Brockway." —Christina Dodd

So Enchanting

CONNIE BROCKWAY

AN ONYX BOOK

ONYX
Published by New American Library, a division of
Penguin Group (USA) Inc., 375 Hudson Street,
New York, New York 10014, USA
Penguin Group (Canada), 90 Eglinton Avenue East, Suite 700, Toronto,
Ontario M4P 2Y3, Canada (a division of Pearson Penguin Canada Inc.)
Penguin Books Ltd., 80 Strand, London WC2R 0RL, England
Penguin Ireland, 25 St. Stephen's Green, Dublin 2,
Ireland (a division of Penguin Books Ltd.)
Penguin Group (Australia), 250 Camberwell Road, Camberwell, Victoria 3124,
Australia (a division of Pearson Australia Group Pty. Ltd.)
Penguin Books India Pvt. Ltd., 11 Community Centre, Panchsheel Park,
New Delhi - 110 017, India
Penguin Group (NZ), 67 Apollo Drive, Rosedale, North Shore 0632,
New Zealand (a division of Pearson New Zealand Ltd.)
Penguin Books (South Africa) (Pty.) Ltd., 24 Sturdee Avenue,
Rosebank, Johannesburg 2196, South Africa

Penguin Books Ltd., Registered Offices:
80 Strand, London WC2R 0RL, England

First published by Onyx, an imprint of New American Library,
a division of Penguin Group (USA) Inc.

First Printing, February 2009
10 9 8 7 6 5 4 3 2 1

🔵 REGISTERED TRADEMARK—MARCA REGISTRADA

Printed in the United States of America

PUBLISHER'S NOTE
This is a work of fiction. Names, characters, places, and incidents either are the
product of the author's imagination or are used fictitiously, and any resemblance to actual persons, living or dead, business establishments, events, or
locales is entirely coincidental.

The publisher does not have any control over and does not assume any responsibility for author or third-party Web sites or their content.

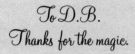
To D.B.
Thanks for the magic.

Chapter One

Mayfair, London
1892

When exactly had the mediums of London gotten together and decided that the afterworld reeked of san-
dalwood? Lord Greyson Sheffield wondered, taking a
sniff of the séance parlor. Because obviously they had,
for in every one of the séances Grey had attended—and
he'd attended many—the sickly-sweet stench inevitably preceded the resident spiritualist's declaration that
he'd made contact with the hereafter.

And sure enough, right on cue, Alphonse Brown's
eyes widened with childlike wonder.

In appearance, Brown was typical of male mediums: pasty complexioned, with white-blond hair, a
thin, downy mustache, and a slight build. His only remarkable features were his large, heavy-lidded eyes,
nearly imbecilic with guilelessness. Grey had been told
by several females who'd met the man that he was a
comely youth, even though he suspected Brown was

close to his own age of thirty-two years. To Grey, he'd looked like a dim-witted adolescent.

But then, Grey doubted two males could have looked more unalike than he and Brown. He was well aware that the combination of his swarthy complexion, the asymmetry of his features achieved by dint of a nose broken in a past altercation, and his perpetually beard-shadowed jaw only augmented his resemblance to a Welsh physical laborer. His burly physique didn't refute the similarity, either.

He was tall, broad-shouldered, and frankly muscular, all assets he'd used to his advantage in the ring, where he'd been his regiment's boxing champion for three years running. Happily, those days were done; he'd always disliked being hit. Currently his situation demanded he present a more refined persona to the world, since presenting a refined *appearance* was out of the question. As the son of a marquess, it was not too great a feat to pull off.

"I sense we are going to meet with success tonight," the medium now said aloud to the small group gathered in the dark room. "Can you not smell the perfume of the Other Side? Your loved ones are near."

A rumble of excited murmurs met this remark, followed by the usual round of barely voiced hopes, wet-eyed self-remonstrations, and eager questions, all of which Brown answered with vague assurances. The wealthy industrialist nodded emphatically, while a renowned M.P., recently knighted, swallowed convulsively, and his wife dabbed at her eyes. Next to Grey, a plump opera singer sucked in enough air to sing an aria, while on his other side an ancient German stared sadly at the ceiling above, waiting patiently for a glimpse of his lost love. There was only one empty chair at the table, that being directly across from where Brown sat, on the other side of the opera singer.

"The scent of the divine," the opera singer whispered raptly.

More likely a smudge pot. The only mystery was how Brown had introduced the scent into the room. Thick velvet draperies covered the walls from ceiling to floor, the only openings being the door through which they'd entered, another in the small cabinet in the corner of the room, and the small, unlit fireplace that Grey had surreptitiously examined while they waited for their host's arrival. The smell came from none of these sources.

"Mr. Kidd, you look dubious," Brown said, and Grey cursed himself. Spiritualists were successful because they read their quarry's every expression and word and designed their responses accordingly. And Brown was very, very successful.

"No. Just distracted," he said. It had taken him weeks to secure an invitation to this sitting. Brown was cautious. He invited only true believers, and only very wealthy believers. Grey had arranged an introduction to Brown by posing as a recently immigrated and immensely rich widower. "I don't dare hope too much," he added.

His answer must have succeeded in reassuring Brown, for he reached across the table and patted Grey's hand consolingly. Grey tensed as he fought to keep his face immobile.

He'd gotten very good at forgetting the events that had led him into his career as a special prosecutor for the Lord Chief Justice, exposing frauds and confidence tricksters, but every now and then the past awoke and ripped his heart anew before he kicked it back into submission. Just now, when Brown had patted his hand, Grey had been a boy again, quivering with impotent rage as his father fawned over a smug, sweating little toad of a man who'd hinted that he might be able to contact the marquess's long-dead daughter—Grey's half sister, Johanna. Grey had stood at his father's side, humiliated and impotent. The toad had noted Grey's revulsion and patted his hand in just such a manner, his hard eyes mocking him as he'd simpered, "Now, don't you worry, lad. I'll find your dear sister for your dad. No matter how long it takes."

It had taken two years, a huge portion of his family's heirlooms, and most of his father's unentailed properties. After his father's death, the recovery of each penny and every artifact had become Grey's raison d'être.

That, along with the complete annihilation of the toad.

But Grey hadn't stopped there. He found he enjoyed being the predator in this game, chasing his quarry to ground, dragging them into a court of law, where he exposed them as gimcrack charlatans, destroying their reputations and their livelihoods.

"Let us begin," the spiritualist now said, bringing Grey back to the moment.

Grey watched, interested. Brown rose and headed toward a cabinet in the back of the room. Though Grey had seen spirit cabinets before, he'd never seen a male simulate the effect. Generally, a female medium would enter the cabinet and forthwith fall into a "trance." Only in this state could she conjure up the "spirit guide," who would appear on the other side of the room. Should anyone open the door to the cabinet during the manifestation, however, not only would the spirit vanish, but the medium's very life would be imperiled. Or at least her credibility. Because inevitably the spirit was simply the medium herself, who, after circumnavigating the room through a hidden hallway, flounced about in the dark room in a bedsheet and a wig.

Grey hoped to God Brown didn't don a wig. Even a medium should draw the line somewhere.

But Brown simply opened the door, whispered something within, and turned with a tremulous smile. "My wife, Francesca."

A sylph entered the room. A creature of moonlight and shadows, wary, a hint of trepidation in the cant of her brows and the angle of her chin. That was his first impression of Francesca Brown, not of her beauty—he barely noted it at first—but of the isolation that surrounded her like an aura, a detachment that suggested she did not share the same air with mortal men.

He shook his head, troubled by such uncharacteristic fancifulness. She was young, perhaps not yet twenty, and luminous. There was no other word for it. Her eyes glowed like polished onyx. The sheen of the gaslight glistened on her flesh and caught in the inky coils of unbound hair that rippled down her back and around her breasts in a parody of innocence that verged on the indecent. Her gown of semi-transparent batiste revealed just enough of the figure beneath to ensure that the attention of every man in the room was focused on it rather than on Brown.

She hesitated as she came toward the table, her gaze sweeping over the sitters, catching on him before quickly passing on. Had he imagined it? She took her seat at the table without looking at her husband.

She shouldn't be here. The thought appeared out of nowhere with visceral certainty. *I need to get her out of here.*

He frowned, astonished and disturbed, first, because she was another's man's wife—though more likely she was his mistress—and second, because it was his self-appointed task to hunt her type, not to . . . get them out of here.

She was a fake, a sham. Everything about her had been artfully orchestrated for the purpose of deceit. He'd witnessed similar performances hundreds of times. Why, during Madame Blavatsky's séances, the "apparition" of a bawdy harem girl bounced from one delighted gentleman's lap to the next—a conjuration for which Blavatsky was handsomely compensated.

There was nothing unique about Francesca Brown. Except how she looked, how she moved, the midnight hue of her hair and the limitless depths of her eyes, the fullness of her lips and the exquisite sheen of her flesh. His body tightened in response, his reaction primal and uncomfortable.

"Too bright! Too . . . bright!" At the sound of Brown's groan, Grey's head snapped around.

The medium had taken his seat at the table and Grey hadn't even noticed, confirming his suspicions regarding Francesca's role as a diversion. Now Brown's eyes rolled back in his head. "The spirits cannot . . . find their way!"

The industrialist leaped to his feet and turned down the sconce, plunging the room into utter darkness.

Grey peered through the murk, trying to find Francesca, angered by his fascination, unable to help himself. He had just made her out, a slender shape dissolving into the darkness, when a sudden swirling pressure filled the room. He tried to pull his hands away, but the opera singer and the German held on with viselike strength.

"Angel wings," Brown whispered reverentially, and as quickly as the sound had arrived, it was gone.

Grey ground his teeth in frustration. He'd been caught off guard. Preoccupied with libidinous thoughts of Francesca Brown, he'd been unable to bring his full faculties to the task of identifying what sort of chicanery was going on. It was this specific effect that had won Brown his fame. Angel wings, the brush of a loved one's hand, the tug on a skirt—the witnesses Grey had interviewed claimed it could not have been possible for Brown or his wife to manufacture the effect from their positions at the table without the use of magic or the presence of a spirit.

Of course, they were wrong. There was no such thing as magic, and the world wasn't harboring ghosts. There were no mysteries, simply answers that had yet to be discovered.

Another memory sprang forth unbidden. He'd been seventeen, forced to endure yet another séance. This one would be different, his father had promised. This woman was authentic.

He could still see his father's expression as he watched a face "materialize" above a table in a dimly lit back room. It had been nothing but a plaster mask covered with luminescent paint and dropped from a box hidden in the ceiling. It was so pitiful, and yet his father had whispered, "Johanna." His father, someone he had once so admired and loved, had been reduced in that moment to a gullible buffoon.

Grey wished they'd just come one night and taken everything from him, every bit of silver, every family treasure, every stick of furniture and deed of ownership, every penny, painting, and promissory note, rather than take, as they had, that one thing no amount of effort on his part could ever replace: his respect for his father.

Grimly, Grey focused his attention on Brown, determined not to be distracted again. There followed the usual round of thumps, raps, and sighs, after which began a series of ear-offending twangs and off-key peeps. (Why had no one ever wondered why the entire population of the hereafter did not count amongst their members one passable musician?)

Francesca did not speak. She did not move. She did not, as far as Grey could determine, add anything to the proceedings besides her presence, which, he allowed, was addition enough.

Finally, after Brown had declared in a voice rife with wonder that the shriek of an ill-tuned violin was the spirit of Handel come to serenade them, Grey could stand it no more.

Jerking free his hands, he bounded to his feet and flung open the door to the séance parlor, flooding the room with light and exposing to view the five burly policemen he'd arranged to be waiting without. Then, as the séance party gaped, blinked, and gasped, he ripped the damask cloth from the table, revealing Brown's unclad right foot braced against a miniature violin, whilst the hoary toes of his left curled about a little bow. The trapdoor where he'd secreted his props still lay open beneath his chair.

"There's your spectral musician. No shade of Handel, just Mr. Brown's unwashed feet," he declared in disgust.

His pale mustache quivering like an albino rabbit's whiskers, and his large, soulful eyes narrowing to not-so-soulful slits, Brown sprang up, upending his chair.

Chaos erupted in the room. The opera singer collapsed in terror, and the other women screamed. Red-faced with outrage and, Grey hoped, chagrin, the gentlemen rose to aid the ladies and confront their deceiver.

Only Francesca remained motionless. Brown dove, seizing her by the shoulders and dragging her to her feet to use as a shield. She did not resist. She stood flinching in his bruising clasp, her expression contemptuous.

A red haze filled Grey's vision. He vaulted the table, jerking Francesca out of Brown's clutches, and thrust her behind him. Desperate, the spiritualist scuttled away, grabbing a nearby chair and flinging it. Grey knocked it aside, advancing relentlessly.

"Stay away! Stay away from me!" Brown shrieked, backing up.

Grey's right arm shot out, his fist landing squarely on the bastard's chin, knocking him off his feet and sending him crashing into the wall. Except it wasn't a wall.

The sound of shattering glass filled the room, and then Brown was swallowed by the velvet draperies and disappeared. The sound broke the paralysis holding the policemen, and they rushed to join Grey at the newly revealed window, just in time to see Brown pick himself up off the pavement ten feet below and flee across the street.

"Son of a bitch!" Grey shouted. He was every sort of ass. He should have tackled Brown, let the police tackle Brown, let the others tackle Brown, but because of some misplaced compulsion to beat the bastard senseless he'd allowed him to escape.

He spun around to glare at Francesca and found she had fallen to the floor and knelt in a pool of delicate batiste, her dark hair falling across her pale face. His curse died on his lips. He wanted only to sweep her up in his arms and take her away from here.

Madness.

She wasn't even looking at him. Her eyelids fluttered like those of a dreamer coming awake from a fantastical nightmare, and she gazed around her uncomprehendingly.

Then, slowly, she tipped back her head and laughed.

Chapter Two

SPIRITUALIST EXPOSED AS FRAUD!
EXCLUSIVE EYEWITNESS ACCOUNT!

"Scoundrel!" Lord Greyson's ringing denunciation followed the escaping villain. But, alas, all efforts to apprehend the fleeing criminal came to naught as Brown made good his escape.

"He didn't say *scoundrel*," Francesca muttered. He'd said something far worse, something unrepeatable.

She'd known "Mr. Kidd" posed a threat the moment she'd walked through the door. He'd no more in common with Alphonse's usual clientele than a bullmastiff did with lapdogs. A tall, powerful-looking fellow, dark complected and black haired, he'd looked like a Spartan entering battle, and just as harsh. Indeed, the only aspect of lightness about him had been his eyes, a unique, clear blue-green framed by banks of black lashes. They held no softness, no compassion, just hard brilliance, like gemstones.

The newspapers went on to say that he was a newly

minted barrister and special investigator attached to the Crown prosecutor. She hadn't realized Alphonse had been worthy of such exalted attention.

She went back to reading the newspaper, even though she had read very nearly the same article in several different papers every day since their dramatic exposure ten days ago. But today there was a new bit added.

Word arrived in this London office late last evening that Alphonse Brown, né Alfie Pudlik, died yesterday in a railway accident in Paris, where he reportedly fled. Brown's wife, Francesca, remains in London. The authorities have declined to charge her with any crime, deeming her involvement in her husband's schemes "undiscoverable."

She'd known Alphonse had died, of course. The police had told her. She was surprised she'd actually cried for him. He certainly didn't deserve her tears. Not after sending his mistress—"M'name's Dorothy, but Alf calls me his li'l Dot"—to demand Fanny pack his clothing so that she could take them to him.

"Alf also says to say you ain't to consider yerself married to 'im no more 'cause he don't," she'd announced. "Says to say he knows it ain't yer fault, but he can't abide sharing a bed wid' you no more, 'counta it gives him the creeping willies, you not bein' normal-like."

Well, at least that had explained the infrequency of Alphonse's conjugal visits. Even through her humiliation, Francesca had appreciated the irony. Just four short years before, Alphonse had talked her into eloping with him not in spite of her strangeness but because of it.

Dot cocked her head, eyeing Francesca from head to toe as she obviously tried to determine just what peculiarity Fanny was hiding beneath her clothing that could keep a man out of a woman's bed. "Oh, and you ain't to come after him."

"Tell 'Alf' he needn't fret," Fanny said, and slammed the door in her face.

Mrs. Brown is still reputed by a number of her husband's former followers to have occult powers. And, indeed, one might be forgiven for wondering if there is any fact behind the fancy, for surely if the old adage about a woman scorned is valid, the consequences must be doubled when the woman scorned is reputedly a witch. The question must be begged, did a hex end Alfie Pudlik's life?

No. It had been the morning train from Orléans.

Carefully, Francesca folded the newspaper and set it aside. She supposed she should be flattered. She was accumulating titles at an astonishing rate: confidence artist, oddity, spiritualist, and now witch. And one must not forget to add pauper.

She looked around the hotel room. She couldn't stay here long. The Savoy was expensive, but it was the only hotel she knew, and there was no one to suggest another.

Her parents were dead, having both fallen victims to a tin of tainted beef the year after Fanny had eloped. Her brother, Wesley, had blamed her, claiming they'd been so devastated by her disastrous marriage early that same year that they'd been too weak to combat the poison. But then, Wesley had been blaming her for everything bad that happened ever since The Incident.

She hadn't meant for anything bad to happen. There'd been no warning that her rapport with animals could have a dangerous side.

When she was three years old, the estate deer approached her; at five, wild hare suffered her touch; at ten, birds alit on her outstretched hands. But only when she was feeling some powerful emotion. And initially her family had been charmed by her affinity with wild things, her mother even claiming it was a family trait.

Until Wesley's "accident."

She'd been twelve, skinny, awkward, neither woman nor girl, but at that uneasy stage in between, oversensitive, overdramatic, and quick to talk back, as she had done at luncheon that day. She didn't even recall what she'd said that had her father sending her to her room. She just recalled marching out of the house and slamming the front door behind her.

Later, she learned that Wesley had been sent to retrieve her. He'd gone out the back of the house intending to intercept her at the stable. Wesley and she had never been close. Five years her senior, he was a bit of a snob and a bully who took himself and his position as his father's heir very seriously. The only value he found in her was as someone to tease.

Perhaps it was the desire for a spot of revenge over having to interrupt his meal, perhaps sibling rivalry, perhaps a little resentment that as the youngest, Fanny was babied. Whatever the reason, when he spotted her he'd waited in the shadows, and when she passed, he jumped out, shouting.

Terrified, Fanny screamed like a banshee.

Wesley laughed.

He held his sides, hooting and pointing at the tears streaming down her cheeks. She could still recall the fury rushing up in a molten streak. Unable to speak, shaking with anger and impotence, she'd glared at him as he continued laughing and doubling over with hilarity.

And then, as suddenly as Wesley had leaped from the stable door, a small dog shot from nowhere, snarling ferociously. Another joined it, this one larger, more muscular. Then another. And another. With single-minded intent, the estate dogs, the collies, and the hunting spaniels, the gamekeeper's mastiffs and the cook's little ratter, all came together like a pack and attacked her brother.

He went down shrieking amidst a flurry of snarling, snapping maws and slashing fangs. Fanny's fury vanished. For three breathless heartbeats she stared, stunned, before she started screaming. At once, as if answering some inner command, the dogs fell back, revealing Wesley where he'd fallen.

He lay on his side, bloodied and sobbing, his clothing shredded, in ten short seconds having acquired scars that would last his lifetime and an injury to his Achilles tendon that would cause him to limp for the rest of his days.

Fanny could not stop screaming. The dogs began to howl. In their stalls, the horses thrashed and kicked. Rats and mice streamed out of the barn in a panicked frenzy. Birds hurled themselves into the manor's windows, falling dead to the ground in little mounds.

Her parents came running.

Her life changed after that. The dogs, of course, were all destroyed, adding to her guilt and grief. Fear became her daily companion. How had it happened? What had she done? What if it happened again? What if next time it didn't stop?

The day marked the end of the garrulous, exuberant child she'd been and the beginning of the solitary creature she'd become. Her parents reassured her that they didn't blame her, as did her older sister, Jeanne— at least, for a while—but afterward there was always a certain watchfulness in their eyes.

Wesley made no mystery about his bitterness. Five years later, when Jeanne was to make her debut, he vehemently opposed Francesca's coming with the family to London. The scenarios he described had been so vividly appalling that Jeanne, always easily swayed by Wesley, had begged Fanny to ask to be left behind.

Fanny had been happy to oblige. She had no more desire to risk an "episode" than did anyone else in her family. It hadn't taken much to convince her parents to leave her with an elderly cousin that season.

It had all worked out well enough. Jeanne had met the baronet she later married. In fact, just yesterday Fanny had received a letter from her sister, the first communication since their parents' deaths three years ago. Jeanne had read about Alphonse in the penny press and sent a hundred pounds, along with a plea to keep silent on the matter of their relationship.

In a fit of prideful indignation, Francesca had sent

the money back—in retrospect a vainglorious gesture, because before he'd decamped, Alphonse had emptied their bank account.

Luckily, Alphonse had a taste for extravagance. The furnishings, the paintings, and the silver in their apartment had fetched a decent price from the reseller she'd summoned the day after the police raid. But that money wouldn't last long. Where would she go then?

A knock on the door interrupted her thoughts. She opened it to find an older gentleman standing outside with his hat in his hands, exposing a bald dome tonsured by a fringe of fading red hair. His ruddy complexion was blistered and freckled, the effects of prolonged sun exposure on fair skin, and he held his thin body rigidly erect. A military man, then, and, judging by the state of his skin, likely once posted in the East.

"Don't recognize me, do you?" he said.

She launched into her now familiar speech. "If you've come to demand I return the money my husband defrauded you of, I am afraid I cannot help you. He withdrew every cent from our bank account and took it to Paris with him, and now he is dead and I do not know where the money is."

She suspected Dot did, but Francesca hadn't the wherewithal to pursue the suspicion. "If I should ever receive any portion of it, I shall make whatever restitution is possible. If you could leave me your card and the amount—"

"You misunderstand," the gentleman interrupted. "I am Colonel Chase. Your family's estate in Surrey borders my own."

"Oh? Oh. Yes, of course." She looked closer, recognizing him now. The years had not treated him kindly.

She recalled him as a hearty, robust, red-haired fellow who'd married late, taking his wife to the fort in India where he'd been posted and where she'd died young. There had been a child, too. . . .

"I was wondering if I might have a few minutes of your time."

Oh, dear. She regarded him sadly. "I cannot contact the deceased for you, Colonel. Surely you've read the papers? It was all a hoax."

"Oh, no. I know," he said, worrying his hat between his gloved hands. "It's nothing like that, I assure you. If I could persuade you to accompany me, I have secured a table on the terrace of the hotel's restaurant overlooking the park."

He stepped aside hopefully. She hesitated, marshaling her courage. She couldn't hide in her hotel room forever. She took his proffered arm, allowing him to escort her down the grand staircase into the Savoy's lobby. As she descended the stairs, the murmuring of those scattered about sipping coffee and chatting faded to whispers.

"Witch, they're saying now."

"Just a trumped-up actress."

"Can't imagine the hotel would like knowing how she earned the money she pays her bill with."

"Earned? You mean stole."

"I wonder if she's a witch."

And then they were on the terrace under a bright April sun, alone except for another intrepid pair braving the chill of the morning in order to find some privacy. Colonel Chase ordered coffee and biscuits and, as soon they'd been delivered, began speaking.

She might not remember much about him, he said,

but he remembered her quite well, especially those things that set her apart from everyone. In fact, that was why he'd come. He'd seen her picture in the newspaper and recognized her.

"I have come here to speak to you about my daughter, my Amelie. She is like you. She is"—he looked around and bent over the table, lowering his voice—"touched by magic."

Chapter Three

Like her? Touched by magic? Francesca sank back in her chair, amazed.

For the next hour, she listened to Colonel Chase recount the facts of his daughter's life. Motherless since she was a toddler, Amelie had been raised in India until a few years ago, when the colonel had retired from the military, returning to England so that Amelie might become "a proper lady." Until recently their lives in England had been unremarkable. But this winter, around the time of Amelie's eleventh birthday, strange events had begun to occur in her vicinity: pictures flew from the walls, vases tipped over, and cutlery slid from its place setting.

Unfortunately, many of these incidents had taken place in the public eye. Rumors had begun to spread. Invitations had dropped off. Far worse, a sect of religious fanatics had denounced Amelie as being possessed by a demon, saying her father had sold her soul to the devil for the fortune with which he'd returned from India.

Colonel Chase, the recipient of many medals for courage, had been shaken to his core by an anonymous letter exhorting him to rid his house of the witch inhabiting it. Other letters had followed, the threats in them escalating.

"The last said that it is a sin to suffer a witch to live," he said.

"But you don't really think your daughter is in danger?"

His answer was unnecessary. His broad hand shook as he reached for his cup of coffee and took a sip. He returned it to its saucer before replying. "My dear, twenty years ago I would have said no. But that was before I witnessed firsthand what a mob is capable of when lashed into a frenzy of fear."

His gaze focused on the view across the river. "There was a girl who some villagers suspected had put a curse on their cattle." He shuddered. "She did not survive the mob."

"But that was in India," Fanny protested. "This is England. We are civilized here."

He shook his head adamantly. "There is no civilized place. Some veneers are just thicker than others. But they are all veneers. Beneath them lurks a mob waiting for an excuse to erupt into savagery.

"London is run amok with rumors of witchcraft and devil worship, exacerbated by the Whitechapel murders and that monster that dubbed himself 'the Ripper.' So, yes, I do think Amelie is in danger. I have gone to the police, but they either can or will do nothing."

He stopped, his jaw bunching with ill-controlled emotion. "Well, I *can* do something. I refuse to take chances with her life. That's why I'm sending her to Scotland as soon as possible."

He leaned forward. "I have a hunting lodge in the

Highlands, in as remote a location as one could find, surrounded by mountains and bordered by a river. The only population nearby is a tiny hamlet so small and isolated, one would immediately recognize a stranger. It is my intention to live there until I am confident there is no threat to Amelie here."

Fanny wasn't certain how to reply. "But why should you wish to tell me your plans?"

His gaze lifted to meet hers. "I was hoping that you would come with us. I came to offer you a situation."

He'd caught her completely off guard. "A situation? As what?"

"Well, officially as Amelie's governess, I suppose."

"But I—I haven't any qualifications as a governess," she stammered, nonplussed. She had no qualifications as anything, for that matter.

"Nonsense, Mrs. Brown," the colonel said.

"I prefer Mrs. Walcott, please." It was her mother's maiden name, and as there was no one left on that side of the family to protest her use of it, and she refused to use Alphonse Brown's, she'd adopted it as her own.

He nodded. "You are infinitely qualified, Mrs. Walcott. You have received a lady's education, you clearly have a cool and unexcitable nature, and you have polish and address," he said.

Cool and unexcitable. Yes. Of course, because she did not dare be anything else.

"Surely you ran your husband's household?" he suggested.

She had, actually. Alphonse had claimed he was too spiritual to deal with the mundane matters of daily life and so left them to her. She had enjoyed it tremendously, not only the managing of the household, but dealing with the tradespeople, who, being less gullible than their gentrified counterparts, assumed she was a fraud and treated her accordingly, with a knowing wink and an admiring grin for "tuppin' the toffs right smart."

Those had been her happiest hours as Alphonse's wife, because even though she knew the tradespeople thought she was a swindler, she was just a normal swindler. How wonderful it had been. Though she did wonder what *tup* meant. . . .

"Whatever else you need to know, I can teach you. I did have a garrison under my command, you know," Colonel Chase was saying. He studied her approvingly. "I suspect you would have made a first-rate lieutenant."

A lieutenant? The idea surprised a smile from her. Yes. She would have liked to be in a position of command, to have a say over the direction of her life. It would be a pleasant change.

"But most important, you are like Amelie."

Her smile faded. "No, sir. You are wrong. I am not like your daughter, and if you hope I can teach her how to control what power it is you imagine she has, I cannot. Inanimate objects do not take flight in my vicinity."

A trace of desperation flickered in the colonel's eyes, and Francesca noted how tired he looked. Her heart went out to him. He truly loved his daughter.

"The poltergeist activity is currently the only manifestation, but she is barely twelve, Mrs. Walcott. I do not know what the future holds. I need someone who is familiar with such things, who will not be unnerved by them. Someone with a good heart."

She looked away. It had been a long time since she'd examined the condition of her heart.

"I remember seeing you when you were a child," he said softly. "You always seemed such a happy, high-spirited girl. It was a pity. Not only what happened to your brother but what it did to you. Amelie is like you were before . . . before. I don't want her to change.

"I need someone who has insight into what my child might be experiencing, who can prepare her for the world before she is put into it."

The phrasing struck Francesca as odd, but she was too intrigued by his proposition to question it. She was so tired of being alone. Even married to Alphonse, she'd been fundamentally different, separate. *Lonely*, an inner voice whispered. Colonel Chase was offering her much more than employment. Still, she had to be forthright.

"I doubt I am the example for which you are look-ing," she said regretfully. "I have hardly made a smash-ing success of my own entrance into society."

He was kind, a little pitying. "You haven't been *in* society, my dear. You have been one of its many sideshows."

Well, that was bluntly spoken.

He heard her involuntary inhalation and reached out to pat her hand. It had been years since someone had offered her the comfort of a simple touch. "I am a confoundedly plainspoken man. I am sorry, my dear."

"Don't be." She met his eye. "I am sick to death of subtlety and equivocation."

She meant it. The colonel's candor was like a cleans-ing plunge in icy water. Every word Alphonse had uttered, both to his clients and to her, had been framed to suggest rather than affirm, to evade rather than illuminate.

"Allow me to return the favor," she said. "I was a willing participant in that sideshow. I helped my husband deceive his . . . *our* clients."

For a long moment, the colonel did not reply. He stared down at the coffee in his china cup. Fanny did not interrupt his thoughts, reflecting on her past.

She'd come to terms with her part in Alphonse's schemes. She'd been desperate to believe only good of the boyish-looking man who'd arrived at her family's country estate while her family was in London for Jeanne's debut. He'd claimed some nebulous family connection, and her elderly cousin hadn't questioned him too closely, but neither had she.

He began wooing her almost at once. He'd heard of her through mutual acquaintances and been struck by their similarities. He himself had the power to speak to the spirit world. She wasn't a freak; she was exceptional. She needn't hide her affinity with God's creatures; she must celebrate it. He would teach her how. Such abilities as they possessed were gifts to be used to serve mankind.

The idea seemed revelatory to Fanny. Here was someone who embraced his affliction, saw it as a boon rather than a curse. It never occurred to her that he was lying. How credulous she'd been at seventeen. Even though credulous, she hadn't been a fool. She knew her parents would never agree to the match. So they eloped.

Despite his promises, it was quickly clear that Alphonse had had no better idea than she of how to control her affinity with animals. He was disappointed when he realized that it was only when her emotions were completely engaged that creatures answered her call. He bullied, pestered, begged, and cajoled her to find some way to make use of her "gift." She owed it to him. She owed it to people "waiting for a sign of grace in this graceless world."

When she had finally managed the briefest of voluntary connections, Alphonse had been overjoyed. Within weeks he'd figured out a way to put it to use, having her call creatures to the room while he was holding séances, then suggesting to their credulous clients that the sounds they heard had otherworldly origins. A brilliant bit of marketing.

She hadn't protested when Alphonse had explained that they were simply aiding the faithless to believe what he knew for a certainty to be true: that angels surrounded the living. Why? Because she was a fool who had for four years pretended she believed him because she desperately wanted to think her life had value.

"There is no possible way anyone would willingly put an impressionable child in my care," she murmured. Looking up to find Colonel Chase's gaze on her, she added, "You should look elsewhere for your daughter's companion."

He studied her intently for a few moments before his expression relaxed. "I think not," he said. "I long ago discovered that experience is the best teacher. You have had experiences that can help guide my daughter. Imagine, Mrs. Walcott, if you had had the benefit of your current knowledge at Amelie's age. What would you do differently?"

Never, ever allow anyone to know what I am.

He saw her indecision. "You will be well compensated, I assure you. I am a very wealthy man, and when your term of employment is ended, you will have the wherewithal to do whatever you want with the rest of your life. Come now, Mrs. Walcott. You are still a very young woman. Barely a decade older than my daughter. Think of your future."

She was, but she also was thinking of Amelie Chase's future. "Colonel Chase, you cannot want your daughter's prospects tainted through an association with me."

"Bah." He waved his hand dismissively. "Give London a new sensation and you will be forgotten. Why, in a few years no one will even recall your name. Time will have its way, Mrs. Walcott. I guarantee it. I'm counting on it. Come, my dear. Name your price."

A few years? How dearly Fanny would like to have a reprieve from her past. Some time to figure out her options. Time to start again. She was still young. Barely twenty-one.

She hesitated. Colonel Chase's proposal had planted a seed of hope in her heart. *If* he agreed to her price.

"I tell you what," he cajoled. "Give me your terms and I'll consider them while we go meet Amelie. If, having met my daughter, you decide you won't suit, then that's the end of it. That's fair, isn't it?"

She nodded.

"Now, tell me what it is you want." His eyes were kindly interested, but there was a resolute determination there, too. He would have his way. "Anything. You have but to name it."

"A clean slate."

He blinked, then grinned broadly. "My dear, as far as I'm concerned the past few years never happened."

"No. I mean, a clean slate to present to the world. Should I agree, from this day on I am an unremarkable woman without a hint of anything unusual in my past. No one is to know to whom I was wed, my maiden name, or any part of my history other than that which I, and I alone, choose to disclose." The waiter came over to replenish their coffee. She waited until he'd left before continuing.

"So that *if* I accept your offer, when the time comes for us to part, I shall have established an identity that begins today, as . . . " She hesitated, making it up as she went along. "As the widow of one of your junior officers, Fanny Walcott. Francesca Burns, your neighbor's fey child, will be no more."

"Done!" he agreed, slapping his palm against the table. "You'll find Amelie a most discreet child."

She shook her head, holding his gaze. "The list of those exempt from knowing my past includes your daughter." She would not set herself up as some sort of mystical mentor, some Merlin in modern dress. If she were to have any chance for a normal existence, she must start now to re-create herself as a normal woman. She must *be* a normal woman.

He frowned. "But that will defeat the entire purpose of retaining you," he argued. "If she doesn't know that you share a similar condition to her own, how can you help her understand it?"

"I won't because I can't. Colonel Chase, you have been forthright with me. I will be equally so with you. I have no understanding of why animals respond to me. You want the advice that comes from experience? Your daughter should not seek to comprehend this thing that besets her, but ignore it and focus instead on those things she has in common with her fellow man rather than those that set her apart."

"But," Colonel Chase protested, "she'll wonder why I chose you to be her companion."

"Tell her you chose me because I am *not* impressed by evidence of the supernatural. Tell her I am a modern woman who assumes that once in a great while, through no offices of their own making, people are born with characteristics of an inexplicable nature. Such a happenstance of birth does not, however, give those people license to pretend to powers they do not have."

Colonel Chase's malleable face pleated with compassion as he read her guilt. "My dear, I did not know you well as a child, but I am a good judge of character, and I knew your parents. I would not seek to employ you had I any doubts as to your integrity."

She felt a surge of gratitude but waved aside his comfort. "I am not blameless. But I am guilty more of stupidity than of malice. Those are my terms."

"I don't know," Colonel Chase said, troubled. "I was hoping Amelie would find in you a unique confidante who shared her magical abilities."

Her lips twisted into a half smile. "There is no such thing as magic, Colonel Chase. Just outré phenomenon and curiosities. And those of us unfortunate enough to be oppressed by them."

But Colonel Chase was not ready to give up yet. "I have lived most of my life in exotic places, Mrs. Walcott, and I've seen things no proper Englishman would credit." He leaned forward. "There *is* magic in the world, my dear."

She regarded him pityingly. He wore the same earnest expression as did the visitors to her husband's salon, and spoke with the same heartbreaking need to believe. The same men and women who were convinced the mouse running over their sleeve was their son's hand, the brush of a bat's wing in the still air above the sound of angels, the clatter of the cat in the attic overhead the rapping of their ancestor.

In the end, he was simply another superstitious old man hoping to find some divine reason for his daughter's affliction.

There was no use arguing with him. "That may be, sir, but this is not India," she said gently. "No one in London wants to dine with a witch except those looking to entertain their guests with a curiosity. That's not the life you want for your daughter, is it?"

"I want her safe and happy. In that order," he said.

He did, bless him.

He searched her countenance and, finding nothing there to suggest she would reconsider, sighed. "Well, if those are the only terms under which I can persuade you, so be it. You and I will be the only ones who know you were once Mrs. Francesca Brown."

"Or Francesca Burns?"

"Or Francesca Burns." He stuck out his hand. "Agreed?"

But she'd learned caution over the last years, if nothing else. "I'll meet the girl first."

He laughed, lumbering to his feet. "Then our agreement is a fait accompli, m'dear. You won't be able to resist Amelie."

He was right; she couldn't.

Chapter Four

Six years later

It was noon in Little Firkin, Scotland. Not a traditional witching hour—midnight being considered more conducive to mayhem and maledictions—but as the townsfolk were always fast asleep by midnight and unwitnessed mayhem was generally acknowledged amongst witchly communities to be a wasted effort, it would have to do.

Besides, every indication suggested that noon was the new midnight. To wit: At exactly twelve o'clock a cock crowed, the bell tower clock struck *thirteen* times, and a weird sound (which later would be identified by a certain skeptic as the Bristol–Fort George train but right now was pretty much universally recognized as the cry of a soul consigned to hell) echoed mournfully through the tiny hamlet.

Otherwise it was a perfectly lovely spring day. The sun glimmered on the river dancing along the town's eastern boundary and shimmered on the snow-capped mountains encircling the small valley that sheltered Little Firkin.

Lovely day or not, what with the clock, the cock, and the eerie moan, the people of Little Firkin—no strangers to portents, portents being their bread and butter, so to speak—stopped what they were doing and paid attention. Those leaning over their back fence for their daily chin-wag hurried to the front yard, while those inside poked their heads out of their front doors. Half a dozen shopkeepers and an equal number of tavern owners—Little Firkians having long ago discovered that living in close proximity with the supernatural was a thirsty business—crowded their windows to see what Something Wicked This Way Came.

On cue, a wind nickered to life in one of the town's few alleys and skittered forth, kicking up a dust devil of leaves and halfpenny candy wrappers as a voice like a strangled cat pealed through the town center.

"Aieeeee!"

Little Firkin rubbed its collective hands together in anticipation. Women with small children shoved their tots behind them, while those with older brats squawked and flapped their arms, shooing them off the street like hens quarantining chicks before a storm. The old geezers in town towed their stools out to get a ringside seat at the anticipated proceedings.

They were not disappointed.

An ancient crone with a face like a withered apple appeared at the end of the town's main thoroughfare amidst a swirl of dust, her raggedy multicolored skirts shedding bits of decaying lace along with the crumbs from her morning's biscuit.

"Aieeeee!" The hag's screech broke into a coughing fit that ended only after she expelled a bit of cat hair.

She hoisted an oak bole over her head on stringy little arms and cried, "I come to take Little Firkin!"

A collective gasp of consternation and pleasure rose from the onlookers. A witch-off sounded just the thing for a fine spring day, and this promised to be a right doozy of a witch-off.

For half a dozen years, the old crone at center stage, Grammy Beadle, had been trying to lay her witchly claim over Little Firkin. She lived in Beadletown, twenty miles away up in the mountains, and not a town at all but a ramshackle collection of disreputable crofts populated entirely by Beadles—a race of cattle thieves and malingerers.

About ten years ago one of Grammy Beadle's grandchildren, in what was doubtless an attempt to find something other than her family with which to occupy the old hag, had convinced Grammy that she oughtn't hide her light under a bushel and should think of extending her reign of terror—or, more succinctly, reign of annoyance—to the other hamlets in the vicinity. It shouldn't be too hard, this same sanguine grandchild had explained, there not being many witches anymore. And as for the upkeep on Grammy's potential realm, it would involve only a bit of travel now and again to check up on the constituency.

Grammy Beadle liked the idea. Within a year, she was not only the Witch of Beadletown but the Witch of Ben's Tavern (Ben and his way station, even by Grammy Beadle's admittedly liberal definitions, not being worthy of hamlet status) and a year after that the Witch of That Pisshole East of Where All Those Damned Beadles Live.

From there she had turned her malignant gaze south toward the metropolis of Little Firkin, population 217, and it was here that her March of Irritation abruptly stopped. Coming out of the post office at the far end of town was the person who'd stopped her: a red-haired, very pretty, and very young lady dressed in the height of Parisian fashion.

Her appearance gave even Grammy pause. Hundreds of miles from the nearest city, cloistered by ringing mountains and raging rivers, marooned in a backwater of time and place while the rest of the world charged ahead with industrial fervor, a fashion plate was as unexpected as a kootchie dancer at a church social.

A rakishly tilted scrap of straw was perched atop an ingeniously arranged pile of flame-colored hair, while an ostrich feather, dyed to match the periwinkle braid edging a close-fitting velvet jacket, caressed a softly rounded cheek. Her skirts molded snugly about a womanly derriere before belling out into extravagant yards of green plaid that brushed the plank sidewalk. The open parasol resting on her shoulder dappled her pretty face with sunlight.

Grammy Beadle let out a shriek. "Stop, witch! I come to take Little Firkin from ye!"

The young lady, about to say something to her companion, a slender woman as arresting in her dark handsomeness as the girl was in her vibrant prettiness, turned around and faced Grammy.

"I come to take Little Firkin from ye!" the old woman repeated, hobbling down the center of the street.

"Why bother?" the very young lady asked, the lightest trace of a Highlands accent in her voice. "I'll just give it to you."

The old woman's lips compressed. "Oh, no, missy. I'll not have it said the Witch of Beadletown come by her dark empire through the pity of a young 'un."

"That's absurd."

"That's the way it be," grumped Grammy Beadle.

The girl cast an imploring glance at her sable-haired companion. "Just a few minutes?"

"Oh, ballocks," that lady muttered quite clearly. "But do try to hurry things up a bit, won't you?" And, taking the girl's parasol, she retreated to a bench outside the grocer's.

"Ye canna hurry dark magik," Grammy snapped, reaching into the tattered velvet bag hanging around her scrawny neck. With an evil cackle, she flung a fistful of something into the air—something that apparently had hard bits in it, because she yelped when the wind blew it back in her face. "Ouch!"

"What was that?" the young lady asked curiously.

"Magik! Magiks made with the feet of a white mouse born during the full moon."

At this, the young lady's hand flew up to cover her lips. "You chopped off a baby mouse's feet?" she whispered from behind her fingertips.

Grammy squirmed. "Well, maybe the mouse was stillborn. And maybe it weren't white but it were *very* light gray. But no doubt, 'twere a full moon."

"That's disgusting," the fashion plate said, setting her hands on her hips. "I am afraid I cannot allow someone who would chop off baby mice feet, even dead baby mice, to move into the neighborhood. You will have to go away."

"No, 'tis *you* who will have to go!"

"I am afraid not."

"I am afraid so—"

"Get *on* with it, will you?" someone shouted.

With a flourish Grammy whipped open her patched cloak and twirled around. "By the hair of Beelzebub's chin, by the cloven foot of Bacchus, I expel thee, oh, witch!"

The young lady remained unexpelled, but stood by politely. Finally, Grammy threw her hands up in frustration. "What are ye doin', you cluck? Spell me!"

"You're done?" the girl asked. "I assumed there was more to it than that."

Grammy's little sunken face collapsed in on itself even more. "Of course there's more. I was just giving you a chance to run away is all."

Once more, she hefted her stick over her head. "By Moobkamizer's black heart and Nimbleplast's hor—"

"Who?" the young lady interrupted. "I've never heard of those two."

Grammy's arms sank and she grinned, revealing a dimple of such unexpected charm that it went far in explaining the hitherto unsolved mystery of why there existed so many Beadles. "That's because they're brand-*new* demons."

"Really?" the young lady asked. "How frightfully interesting. Where did you find them?"

"Come to me in my dreams," Grammy said proudly, and then with a sly glance at the townsfolk added, "As an *incubus*. And I gots more, too. By Shillyman's wart and . . . and . . . Cobbiepouff's whisker, I take what was yers and make it mine. Begone." She spun around. "Begone!" She spun around again. "Begone!"

At the end of this last and most violent spin, Grammy pitched sideways, her hand outstretched and her eyes rolling. "I think I'm going to be sick," she said with a gasp.

The young lady grabbed the hag's arm, steadying her. "Sit down."

Gratefully, the old lady plopped down in the middle of the street, holding her side. "Yer turn," she wheezed.

"Come, now. This can wait until you are feeling more the thing—"

"Yer turn!" Grammy insisted.

"Very well," the young lady replied. She took a deep breath, lifted her hands, palms up to the sky, and pronounced in a loud, ringing voice, "Ipse dixit."

Grammy froze like someone who'd taken a spitball shot to the bum. "What? Who's that? What's that?"

"Ipse dixit," the girl repeated. She waved her hands in a circle. "Ipso facto. Ad hoc!"

Anxiously, Grammy patted herself down from head to foot. Upon discovering that everything was in the same place it had been that morning, she relaxed. "Yer magik seems to have left you, missy," she said.

The young lady very discreetly glanced overhead. Grammy Beadle followed her gaze. Directly above them two dark shadows were making slow, lazy circles in the tranquil blue sky.

"So what?" Grammy said. "A pair of birds."

Nonetheless, she scrambled up and surged forward on one foot, like a fencer executing a lunge, stabbing at the young lady with her bole. "By the Name of He Who Goes Unnamed and is Nameless, I take your power and your towwwwnnnnnn!"

The girl raised a slender finger to her mouth and nipped the edge of the nail off between her pearly

teeth. Again, her glance rose to the sky. Grammy's unwilling gaze followed.

The pair of ravens had been joined by a half dozen
others describing slow pirouettes. A distinctly uneasy expression crossed Grammy's face. As a witch,
Grammy Beadle was extremely conversant with all
things of the natural world, and the sudden appearance
of a host of silent ravens . . . well, it wasn't natural.

"Dark powers, unite! Heed me, Bacchus, Beelzebub,
Moobkamizer, and Nimbleplast, Shillyman, and . . .
and . . ." She trailed off as the young lady, examining
the torn nail on her left hand, made a slight indication
skyward with her right.

With a scowl, Grammy looked up.

Twenty ravens?

Furtively, she glanced around, gauging the Little
Firkians' reactions to the flock of malevolent death-
harbingers. If they had seen the ravens, they apparently didn't think much of them—except, that was,
for the girl's companion, who was leaning forward,
frowning up at the sky. The rest of Little Firkin was
watching Grammy, and their expressions were frankly
disappointed. Even a little pitying. And pity, Grammy
Beadle knew, was not a good foundation upon which
to build a witchly empire. She'd better get rid of these
heebie-jeebies and—

Caw!

The salutary sound sent her gaze overhead. A
single raven was winging its way to join the other—
Grammy's mouth gaped—forty ravens. All silent. Silent as the tomb. Grammy's skin crawled.

Maybe she didn't need to take over the town. Leastways, not today.

Still, pride kept her rooted. She'd never live it down if word got out that a bunch of birds had driven her off. Which meant she needed to provide a good reason for turning tail and running. And what better reason than—

"Is that all?" Grammy shouted. "Is that the best you can do? Come on, lass. Give it yer best!"

The young lady's face reflected a second of surprise before tightening. "No. That's not all. *Amo!*" she said, taking a step forward.

Gratefully, Grammy commenced quaking.

"*Amas!*"

Another step. This time Grammy's hand flew to her chest.

"*Amat!*"

Grammy staggered back as if impelled by some monstrous, unseen force. She whimpered for added effect.

The young lady, after a brief look of bewilderment, rubbed her palms briskly together as if preparing for some physical exertion and declared, "Per diem. Non sequitur." Her hand rose toward Grammy Beadle, who was now fully engaged in cringing backward.

"*E PLURIBUS UNUM!*"

With a shriek, Grammy Beadle lifted up her skirts, displaying a pair of crooked shanks encircled by improbable red garters, turned tail and shot off down the street, disappearing into a side alley.

The young lady, after a glance overhead at a sky now completely free of any shadows, ravenlike or otherwise, walked calmly over to her companion. The Little Firkians gave one another nods of approval and, without a single word to their champion and defender, went back to gossiping, eating, and drinking.

At the same time, a handsome and elegant young man let a curtain drop back down across the pub window through which he'd been watching.

"What an extraordinary creature. Whatever is she doing here?" the young gentleman asked, turning his bemused gaze to a man sitting tipped well back in the chair opposite him, a dark, broad-shouldered gentleman with sooty, overlong hair and piercing blue-green eyes currently riveted on the scene outside.

Before he could reply, the inn's rotund barkeep arrived at their table bearing two tankards of ale. "That be Amelie Chase," he said. "Our witch."

Chapter Five

"What do you mean by calling that delightful young lady a witch, barkeep?" Lord Hayden Augustus Collier asked, his gaze following the pert swish of plaid skirts down the street.

"I'm just stating what's fact," retorted the rotund barkeeper, Donnie MacKee. He plunked down their ale and a dish of beef and turnips and moved off.

Thoughtfully, Hayden lifted his tankard to his lips. This trip to the Scottish wilderness looked like it might have more to it than the trout fishing he had anticipated. Here was a mystery, by God. A cure for the ennui plaguing him these last few months, an ennui born of London's utter predictability: the same conversations, the same drawing rooms, the same music halls, the same women with the same goal to ensnare him in matrimony.

It wasn't vanity that led Hayden to this supposition. He'd only to look into the mirror to see a handsome face. Add to good looks an expensive education and pretty manners, and couple these with a future barony and the fortune that accompanied it, and only a dolt would fail to appreciate his desirability as a husband.

He had accordingly quickly agreed when his uncle had suggested a trip to the wilds of Scotland, where the renovations on his brother-in-law's hunting lodge had just been completed. Since his uncle's brother-in-law was also Hayden's father, and thus the lodge would one day be Hayden's, his curiosity was stirred. The old lodge had been uninhabitable since a fire some fifteen years earlier, and Hayden's memories of the place were vague. But the thing that made the trip irresistible was that it would be undertaken in the company of his uncle, Greyson Sheffield, a man one could never call boring. Exacting, intimidating, and unnerving, but never boring.

Indeed, Hayden considered it more flattering to be asked to join his maternal uncle on a fishing trip than to be chased around the London ballrooms by a flock of debutantes. At thirty-eight years of age, Grey Sheffield had developed a reputation for being notoriously picky about the company he kept.

Hayden glanced at Grey, balancing on the back two legs of his chair, his laced fingers cradling his head. The expression on his uncle's bold, angular face belied the insouciant pose. Something outside held his attention. His eyes had narrowed in intense focus.

"I'll be damned," he muttered.

"Grey?"

Grey shook his head slightly, his gaze never wavering from the view outside, staving off any questioning. Hayden knew better than to disturb him. He waited until the girl and her companion disappeared into the green grocer's across the street.

"What the devil is a beauty like that doing here dressed like a Parisian mademoiselle?" Hayden murmured, assuming he was echoing his uncle's thoughts. "And what the blazes did that fellow mean, calling her a witch?"

The intensity faded from Grey's expression. He let the front of his chair fall to the floor with a thump, swung his feet down, and applied himself to his food. "Don't be too harsh on the poor fellow, Hayden."

Hayden scoffed at such advice, coming from a man who took pride in being called draconian.

"I'm completely earnest," Grey said, stabbing a piece of beef. "The fellow is only speaking the truth. At least, such as he knows it. Who can do less?"

"You of all people don't mean to tell me you think that charming girl is a *witch*?"

"Please." Grey's lip curled at the suggestion. "I hope you know me better than that."

Hayden did, indeed. For fifteen years it had been Grey's vocation as a special adjunct working for the Crown prosecutor to expose dealers in supernatural phenomenon. Spiritualists, mediums, fairies, demons, haunts and hauntings, table rappers and mind readers, levitators and, yes, witches—he exposed them all as frauds and brought forth the necessary evidence to see them prosecuted as swindlers.

There had never been an instance where he could not reveal the science or trickery behind the supposed magic. He hated his quarry as much as he pitied their victims, and he claimed to despise them both.

"But simply because I do not believe the chit is a witch," Grey was saying, "doesn't mean our host doesn't. The poor bloke is a victim of his own desire to believe in something extraordinary, a curse caused by an excess of hope.

"No, Hayden, my lad. You can pity him," Grey said, waving his fork instructively. "You mustn't mock him."

"I've never noticed you refraining from mockery," Hayden said.

"That's different," Grey replied equitably, taking a swig of ale. "I am a lost cause. There is still hope that you shall grow a nicer view of your fellow man. At least, that is why I believe your father was willing to let you tag along. I am to provide a cautionary example of the wretched end to which a misanthropic worldview can lead."

"I don't need my father's approval to accompany you. I am, after all, twenty-one years old," Hayden said stiffly.

"Exactly," Grey said with a broad grin. "A babe. So, in keeping with my charge of educating you, eat up whilst I explain the amazing and monumental idiocy that has brought us here."

"I thought we were here to fish."

Grey rolled his eyes. "You didn't actually think I'd come all the way up here to dangle a string in front of some gaping piscatory lips, did you?"

"Fish don't have lips."

Grey sighed. "You have no romance in you, Hayden."

"And you do?"

Something flickered in Grey's gaze. It might have been amusement. Or regret.

"At one time." He shrugged. "But to answer your question, we are here precisely because of that young lady, Amelie Chase, who is, in fact, the town's witch."

At Hayden's look of astonishment, Grey laughed. "Though in all fairness, she belongs at least as much to your father, who is her legal guardian. At any rate, a few weeks ago your father received a letter from someone in this town stating, and I quote, 'Come quick. Someone is trying to kill our witch.' "

"Whatever are you talking about?" Hayden asked, bewildered.

"About six or seven years ago, Colonel Hubert Chase, the owner of the hunting land adjoining your father's here, moved to Little Firkin from London with his orphaned daughter, Amelie. He did so after unusual occurrences began happening in the girl's presence, occurrences for which society, being the credulous, dull-witted dolts they are, had, unsurprisingly, no explanation and therefore, as is the way of credulous, dull-witted dolts, seized on the most improbable explanation they could come up with: that the girl was possessed."

"That's ridiculous," Hayden declared. "What sort of occurrences?"

Grey took a deep draft of ale before answering. "The usual claptrap. Things moving about, flying off walls and tables. Plus, there were the feelings of unease and otherworldliness that are ubiquitous amongst believers. I wonder how many bowel rumbles have been attributed to the supernatural rather than indigestion."

"Was the girl responsible?"

"Someone was. But whether she purposely contrived these things as a childish prank or to attract attention—she was, after all, only about eleven—she hardly deserved to be labeled a witch."

"I find it hard to believe anyone could take such a thing seriously. This isn't the Dark Ages."

"All ages are dark, Hayden," Grey said gently, before continuing. "Unpleasant as society made it for the girl, it wasn't until a group of religious zealots began making threatening noises that Colonel Chase, reportedly himself a superstitious crackpot and having recently been diagnosed with a terminal disease, decided action was called for."

"*Zealots?*" Hayden breathed, his sympathies completely engaged. The poor girl.

"A pedantic little lot of posers who affected monks' garb. More like a masquerade party than a religion, actually, and mostly harmless. Mostly." Grey's expression briefly hardened.

"What did this Colonel Chase do?"

"He built a house just outside of town here, his old hunting lodge being antiquated and drafty, and hired a woman to act as governess and companion." Here, Grey's gaze moved back to the street outside. "He then installed the woman and his daughter here to keep Amelie out of harm's—" He abruptly stopped and leaned toward the window, staring outside.

Hayden looked to see what had arrested him. The girl and her friend had exited the grocer's and were moving slowly along the plank sidewalk.

"Is there more?" Hayden asked, eyes on the girl.

"Oh, yes. Much more even than I suspected," Grey replied softly before turning to regard him. "Don't stare."

Hayden bit back his protest that that had been precisely what Grey had been doing, knowing he'd never get the full story if he engaged in an argument with his uncle. The man loved to argue.

"Excuse me," he said. "Please continue."

"Colonel Chase then drew up a will, naming your father, the only friend from his pre-India days with whom he'd remained in contact, the girl's legal guardian should he die before she reached her majority. Shortly thereafter, he died."

"But?" Hayden prompted, reading his uncle's expression.

"But unofficially, Little Firkin is Miss Chase's guardian. At least physically."

"What? That's impossible."

"One would think. But apparently not. Colonel Chase's will states that when Miss Chase reaches the age of twenty-one *and* provided she is still living in the town of Little Firkin, she will inherit the bulk of her father's estate. Those who were residents of Little Firkin at the time of Colonel Chase's death and are still residents upon Miss Chase reaching her majority will divide amongst them one hundred thousand pounds."

"Dear Lord," Hayden whispered.

"That's quite an incentive to keep someone alive, wouldn't you say?" Grey finished the last of his ale and set the tankard down on the table.

"And after getting this letter my father asked you to come and see what's going on?" Hayden asked.

"Not at all. He told me about the situation, and I volunteered to come as his representative. How could I resist? Witchcraft, threats of dire doing, a positively Gothic will, and a beautiful young girl in need of protection. Or not."

"But there's no reason anyone would want to harm her," Hayden protested. "As you just pointed out, quite the reverse is true."

"Exactly," Grey said, nodding. "A delicious little mystery, is it not? Unless it's simply a prank."

"And you asked me to accompany you because . . . ?"

"As unlikely as it may be, I'm rather fond of your company. Besides, should anything happen to your father, you could inherit Miss Chase."

"How old is she?" He bristled inwardly at the thought of anyone wanting to harm the maligned beauty.

"Eighteen or thereabouts."

"Why doesn't she just leave?"

"The terms of the will make it impossible, barring a few exceptions. For instance, she can leave under a husband's care, but any husband would have to be approved by your father, and really, where is she to meet someone suitable? Or your father could remove her himself *if* he is willing to keep her under his direct supervision. Which means he would have to agree to let her travel with him, and we both know this is as likely to happen as pigs taking flight, which, by the way, a widow in Doncaster claims to have seen last week."

It was true. Hayden's father was constantly traveling throughout Great Britain and Europe. He wouldn't consider for an instant curbing his wanderlust in order to make a home for an orphaned girl.

"Not that the girl hasn't lately made the suggestion," Grey added, looking amused.

Hayden tilted his head inquiringly.

"She has written letters hinting she would very much like to spend some time with her guardian. Needless to say, she has been disappointed in the answer."

"How is it that this is the first I have heard of her?" Hayden asked.

"Your father probably just forgot to mention Miss Chase to you. It's not like she's had any reason to be forefront in his mind, and he does have rather a lot of things to occupy his thoughts," Grey answered, stabbing the last bit of meat in his bowl and lifting it to his mouth.

"Colonel Chase succumbed to cancer five years ago," he went on, "around the time your father became involved in the London dockworkers' strike. I suspect Miss Chase simply got lost in the shuffle. It's not as if she needed his immediate attention, in any case. And your father is always beginning some reform plan or other. Like the canal system on his estate. Or, for that matter, the pottery factory he meant to build here."

"Excuse me?" Hayden said.

"He came up here soon after Colonel Chase died, you know," Grey said, "to look in on the girl and to see if he could restore his hunting lodge. While he was mucking about, he discovered that Little Firkin's riverbanks are composed of some sort of extremely rare, premium goop that makes the crockery makers swoon.

"So, what with the guild movement becoming so popular, he decided to build a pottery factory here and turn the townspeople into self-sustaining craftsmen. He even went so far as to have a spur line run up here to build the factory and export the pots. Didn't you wonder why this little backwater was served by a twice-weekly train?"

Hayden hadn't, but he wasn't going to admit it. "Of course."

"Hmm. Well, as you can see, there's been more importing than exporting going on."

"What do you mean?"

Grey looked at him sympathetically. "Gads, boy. Look around. Little Firkin is living on expectations." Hayden looked back out onto the street. Grey was right. Neat, well-maintained shops lined both sides of the street, their glass display windows boasting stacks of pricey-looking goods being browsed by casual shoppers decked out in quality clothing, nary a patch to be seen. Even the dogs lurking about the back of the butcher shop looked well-fed and complacent.

His attention, however, did not stay long on the affluence of Little Firkin, because at that moment, across the street, the lovely Miss Amelie Chase had stopped. Sunlight spilled over her titian-colored hair and kissed an apricot blush on her smooth, round cheeks.

Hayden shoved his chair back from the table and stood up.

Grey looked up in surprise. "Where are you going?"

"Well, Uncle, you said that I might end up inheriting the care of Miss Chase someday. It only stands to reason that I ought to introduce myself."

Chapter Six

"Are you feeling all right, Fanny?" Amelie asked, the impish smile fading from her face. "You're quite pale."

No, Fanny was not feeling all right. Her brief encounter with Vicar Oglethorpe had shaken her.

The man had snuck up behind her as she watched Amelie and Grammy Beadle. "Wickedness!" he'd spat close to her ear. She'd jerked around to find his bland face suffused with purple and his small frame shaking as he stared out into the street.

"It's theater, Vicar," she'd replied with characteristic coolness, though inwardly disturbed by what, even for Oglethorpe, seemed unusual vehemence.

That "disturbance" had accounted for the ravens' reaction. Over the years, Fanny had learned to extinguish the communication she shared with animals by keeping careful control over her emotions. Only when she was overwhelmed by an unexpected reaction did she make an inadvertent connection. It had been nearly a year since the last such event.

"It's blasphemy," the vicar said. "I won't stand for

it." He leaned down until he was nose-to-nose with her. His eyes burned. "This *will* end! Mark my words!"

He stabbed a finger at her before spinning on his heel and leaving. Her pulse pattered in alarm as she watched him go. She'd always thought of Vicar Oglethorpe as negligible, a pedant whose superstition and fear, rather than any religious values, drove his hostility. But he'd never been this openly antagonistic before. It frightened her. *He* frightened her. And the ravens had felt it.

Of course, she couldn't tell Amelie this.

"Fanny?" she repeated, concerned.

"If I am pale," Fanny said smoothly, "it is the result of shock. 'Ipse dixit' and 'ad nauseam.' You grow more incorrigible by the day."

Her diversion worked; Amelie smiled.

"I was just having a spot of fun," Amelie said. "Though perhaps I shouldn't have spoken Latin. Suppose someone recognized one of the phrases and told Grammy? She'd be humiliated beyond speech."

"Oh, I think you underestimate Grammy's compulsion to speak," Fanny replied dryly. "Besides, given that I've yet to meet a native Little Firkian with more than a rudimentary knowledge of the English language, I sincerely doubt you need worry about any one of them identifying Latin idioms."

"What about Vicar Oglethorpe?" Amelie asked. "Didn't I see him stop beside you? He knows Latin, and he abhors anything to do with spirits and such."

"With the exception of the spirits that inhabit the bottle he keeps in his desk drawer."

Amelie gasped in delighted horror. "Fanny! Even if they're true, you oughtn't say things like that." She assumed a faux prim expression. "Please recall you are supposed to be my mentor."

Fanny raised a brow. "When one seeks to fill the post for a companion who must relocate to the Scottish hinterlands, one is bound to find the employment pool limited. As I've mentioned before, your father was forced to make do."

Amelie laughed and linked her arm through Fanny's. "Do not attempt to convince me you are anything but an aristocratic lady and entirely wonderful."

"Far be it from me to disillusion you," Fanny said, her alarm fading. Still, *something* was causing pinpricks of sensation, like kitten claws, to shiver up her spine and tickle the nape of her neck.

They continued down the sidewalk, unhailed by any of the other people on the streets. Not that anyone avoided looking at them or seemed in the least discomforted by their appearance. They simply paid no attention to them. *Like we're ghosts moving amongst the living*, Fanny thought, and not for the first time.

A thin, low-heeled border collie darted out from beneath a lorry cart and raced up to them, ears back and tail wagging. Amelie smiled and leaned forward, holding out her hand. Fanny stiffened. The last thing she needed was some dog leaping into her arms. Especially this one, an ardently affectionate female she occasionally petted, but only when no one was around to witness.

"Don't encourage it, Amelie," she said. "It's probably riddled with fleas and filth."

Amelie ignored her, reaching down to pat the dog's head. "I will never understand," she said, "how it is that the most kindhearted of women has an aversion to animals."

Of course, she didn't. But again, Amelie would never know this. For six years Fanny had lived as a forthright but unremarkable woman and still had fulfilled her duty to Amelie and Colonel Chase. As far as her situation had allowed, Amelie had grown from an exuberant girl to a charming (albeit guileless), uninhibited, and happy young woman. Even better, one free of any poltergeist association.

The phenomena had stopped shortly after Colonel Chase's death. Unfortunately, not before several Little Firkians had witnessed episodes, cementing the girl in the town's imagination as a witch.

"I'm not sure where you have come up with this notion that I am kindhearted, but as I hate to disillusion you, I shall forbear comment," Fanny replied.

Amelie laughed. "I know you. Beneath your self-contained facade you are most compassionate. You simply are not given to demonstrativeness. Like petting dogs."

Gads, she hoped not. Demonstrativeness for Fanny had potentially dire ramifications.

The mention of dogs brought Amelie's thoughts back to Grammy Beadle. "I don't believe I would regret it even if I did alarm the old witch today," she said.

"A deluded old woman," Fanny corrected her. "Not a witch. You should pity her."

"She claimed to have used mouse feet in one of her spells!" Amelie said, regarding Fanny with righteous indignation.

"She only made that claim to shock and discomfort you," Fanny said.

"Well, it worked," Amelie muttered darkly. "I say she deserved a taste of her own medicine."

Fanny stopped Amelie with a hand on her wrist. "To what exact medicine are you referring?"

"There were ravens in the sky. She thinks I sent them."

Fanny felt her pulse quicken. "*Dear* Amelie," she said, "it's all fine and good to tweak Little Firkin's nose a bit now and again. But someday you will leave here. You can't go about play-acting in London."

"What if it wasn't all play-acting?" Amelie said, glancing sideways.

Fanny started. She hadn't paid much attention to what was going on in the street between Amelie and Grammy Beadle; all her attention had been on Ogle-thorpe. Now she realized that Amelie had not only seen the ravens but felt that she'd somehow been responsible for them.

Fanny had spent years trying to convince Amelie that her childhood brush with the paranormal had been nothing but an unfortunate anomaly, a phase she'd gone through. She'd thought she'd succeeded. But she'd always suspected that Amelie had felt a little let down when the "magic" ended.

"Oh, don't look like that, Fanny. All pinched and disapproving."

"How else am I to look when you make such absurd statements?"

"They're not absurd." Amelie could not keep the excitement out of her voice. "Why do you always insist anything magical must act as a barrier separating me from the rest of the world?"

"Because, Amelie, your view of the world is skewed by having spent your early childhood in a part of India where magic is the norm and the inexplicable is acceptable." It was an old conversation. "But magic is not acceptable here. Just see how people treat us. If it weren't for the promise of your father's fortune we would be complete pariahs."

"This is Little Firkin," Amelie said. "The only way I would *not* be set apart is if I had been born here."

"But not to the same degree," Fanny insisted.

"I know!" Amelie said, uncharacteristically sharp. "Don't you think I know this? I am quite as aware as you of our segregation. And I am sure the people in London are not so prejudiced."

"My dear," Fanny said gently, "you *know* better. London's prejudice is precisely why your father came here with you."

Amelie shook her head, not about to be persuaded. "He was sick at the time. Mentally overwrought. He saw bogeys and threats around every corner. His illness made him paranoid."

Fanny thought so, too, but there was no use discussing it. They'd been here before. And they were in Little Firkin for another two and a half years, like it or not. "It is a moot point, anyway," Fanny said. "You have no special abilities and we are not in London."

Amelie wet her lips with the tip of her tongue. "Did you see the ravens? I . . . I think I *did* call them."

Fanny turned shocked eyes upon her, but before she could speak, Amelie rushed on. "And remember last fall, when Donnie MacKee's draft team bolted and they were heading for us? Your eyes were shut, but mine weren't. I was staring at them. I couldn't look away, and at the last instant they turned. I think . . . I think I turned them!"

Oh, dear God. She had no idea the girl had thought

anything of that incident other than that they'd had a near escape.

"They most likely shied away from your costume. You were wearing a shocking shade of crimson that day," she clipped out in a succinct, brook-no-argument tone. "And as for the ravens, I saw a flock of birds. Hardly a rare sight in the spring. In the sky. In Scotland."

"But they were silent," Amelie said meaningfully.

Damn it. A few slips in the course of all these years and Amelie would have to have witnessed them. How was she to come up with an explanation? And then abruptly she realized she wouldn't have to. She pointed behind Amelie. "You mean like those?"

Amelie spun. Scores of ravens were wheeling through the bright sky, congregating on the ancient oak tree that marked the end of the high street. They did not make a sound.

"Oh." Amelie sounded disappointed.

"If you waste your life trying to find mystical meanings in odd occurrences, at the end of your days you will find you've learned nothing and missed a great deal," Fanny said.

Abrupt as it was unexpected, Amelie's good humor returned. "Oh, Fanny. You're not yet thirty years of age and have spent the last six here in Little Firkin with me, so how is it you know so much about what one will and won't regret at the end of their days?"

The girl's amusement nonplussed Fanny. At some point during the last year or so, Amelie had gone from being Fanny's charge to being her peer, and the transition still startled Fanny.

Amelie regarded Fanny assessingly. "Sometimes

I am reminded how little I know about you. You never speak of the past, Fanny. You're something of a mystery."

"Nonsense," Fanny replied shortly. "You are romanticizing. I had an unexceptional childhood and was married young and widowed almost at once. Which you already know. I see no point in dwelling on the past when there is so much future to be had. For both of us."

Amelie sighed. "If it ever gets here."

Fanny laughed, glad to have the conversation turned. It always made her uncomfortable to evade Amelie's questions. If only Amelie were a child again, content to accept things for what they seemed, willing to live in the present. But over the last few months, as Amelie grew more restless with the constraints of life in Little Firkin, her questions regarding Fanny, her mentor's life before Little Firkin, and the great cities of Scotland and England had grown in number and frequency.

"Well," Fanny said, "I can't hasten the future, but I might be able to make the time pass more enjoyably."

Amelie looked over at her, interested.

"Mr. McGowan has returned from Edinburgh and sent word this morning that he has brought with him some newly published books. Should we stop at the bank now, or would you rather he send them over?"

"Oh. Let's stop now," Amelie replied excitedly. Amelie had recently developed a crush on Bernard McGowan, sole proprietor of the sole bank in Little Firkin, even though he had been in Little Firkin nearly as long as they had. Another sign that Amelie had reached womanhood.

McGowan had once been attached to Colonel

Chase's command, and after leaving the military he contacted the colonel soon after the colonel and his daughter had arrived in Little Firkin. In his letter, McGowan mentioned that he was looking to invest a small inheritance in the banking industry. Perhaps even open one himself, as his family had once owned a bank and he had some knowledge of them. Seeing a chance to keep his money near and help a former soldier, the colonel had suggested that McGowan consider opening a bank in the town. McGowan had not hesitated to do so.

By all appearances, the endeavor had been profitable, for it had not only allowed Bernard to buy Colonel Chase's old hunting lodge for his own, but to pursue his passion for stamp collecting. It was apparently a very expensive pastime. Bernard had once let slip how much he'd paid for a particular stamp—an ugly little pinkish mauve square—and it had been what Fanny considered a staggering sum.

However, it wasn't his wealth that Amelie admired. Bernard McGowan was a gentleman, the *only* gentleman in Little Firkin, and, therefore, the only gentleman of Amelie's acquaintance. In his early thirties, he was handsome and fit, and Amelie had once opined that with his quiet, deferential manner he reminded her of Jane Austen's Colonel Brandon—though Fanny had some trouble envisioning Colonel Brandon as a stamp collector. Still . . .

As they entered the bank, Bernard rose from behind a large, plain desk situated on the other side of a railed partition. His brown hair gleamed with pomade above his serious, intelligent face. His gaze immediately sought Amelie. Fanny suspected that

Bernard, too, had recently begun seeing Amelie in a different light, and she perceived that he might have begun a wholly diffident, respectful, and glacially slow courtship of the girl. At least, Fanny assumed it was a courtship. With such a very circumspect fellow, it was hard to tell.

"Miss Amelie," he said, coming around the desk. "And Mrs. Walcott. How nice to see you."

"It's been a long time, Mr. McGowan." Amelie dimpled. "You were gone for weeks."

He inclined his head. "I am flattered you noticed."

Amelie gave him an arch smile. "It would be hard not to notice. You're the only one who ever comes to and goes from Little Firkin."

"I stand chastised," he said, tilting his head. "But you are wrong, Miss Amelie. For only this morning Little Firkin is playing host to not one but two gentlemen. From *London*."

He spoke like an uncle bestowing a particularly toothsome candy on a favorite child, and Fanny wondered if Amelie might not resent such treatment from a would-be beau. But Amelie was too excited by the prospect of visitors to notice.

"I know!" she said. "The lads from that artisan's guild on their annual pilgrimage?"

Ever since Lord Collier had had analyzed the clay that lined the banks of Little Firkin's river, a group of investors had been badgering the residents to sell their property adjacent to it. But since the amount of money each resident would come into upon Amelie's reaching her majority exceeded anything the investors offered, and selling one's land ensured that one forfeited one's share of Colonel Chase's endowment, no one had taken the gentlemen up on their offer.

It didn't stop the guild from coming up here every year with fresh offers, and Fanny was grateful for that. It provided an opportunity to speak to someone new. And they always came for dinner, allowing Amelie and her to dust off their rusty social skills. Well, Fanny amended, it allowed her to dust off rusty skills. It allowed Amelie to develop some.

"No. Not this time," Bernard said, smoothing back his hair.

Amelie's eyes grew round. "No? Don't tease me so, Mr. McGowan. Do tell! Who are they then?"

" 'They,' " said an amused male voice from behind them, "are Lord Grey Sheffield and Lord Hayden Collier."

Amelie spun around, and Fanny followed suit. A handsome gentleman in an elegant lounging jacket stood inside the doorway, as well-knit as a young Apollo, his dark gold curls accentuating his hazel eyes, a cleft denting his strong chin. A dimple appeared in his smooth-shaven cheek as he smiled at her.

In contrast, the tall, broad-shouldered gentleman beside him looked as blasted and heavily muscled as Mars at his smithy. His black hair needed cutting, and his bold-featured, saturnine face stood in need of a shave. The only things pretty about *him* were his eyes: bright blue-green.

As pretty as they'd been six years ago, Fanny thought, and just as hard.

Chapter Seven

Fanny closed her eyes, praying they were deceiving her. The man who'd driven her from society could not be standing here in the company of a young man who simple deduction led her to suppose was Lord Collier's son. How many Lord Colliers with legal wards named Amelie Chase could there be? She opened her eyes.

God help her, there he stubbornly remained, still looking like thunder personified, big, broad, and powerful, his tousled black hair shot with charcoal gray, his rough-hewn features bold and arrogant. All he needed was a hammer and a bolt of lightning.

She had to leave before he recognized her. She'd spent six years re-creating herself. Surely Sheffield's presence here represented some breach of divine sportsmanship?

Her heart racing, Fanny slipped to Amelie's far side, away from where Sheffield loomed.

"Lord Hayden," Bernard said, shaking the younger man's hand. "It's a pleasure to meet you. I am Bernard McGowan, and I owe your father a debt of gratitude, for he has entrusted my bank with a portion of Miss

Chase's inheritance. He mentioned you in one of his letters."

She'd been right. Hayden was Amelie's guardian's son.

Bernard released Lord Hayden's hand and smiled at Sheffield. "And Lord Sheffield. It's an honor, sir. Even in Edinburgh we hear of your exploits."

Now, while everyone was otherwise engaged, she could mutter something about an errand and disappear. "Amelie," she whispered. "Amelie, we must go. Now."

She tugged on Amelie's hand, but the girl wouldn't budge. She was too busy staring at the young blond lordling with the sort of starry-eyed vacuousness that would make a rabbit look intelligent. Her eyes glowed, her cheeks glowed, her hair glowed. . . . God help her, the girl looked like she'd been dipped in Balmain's luminous paint.

"Amelie. *Amelie*," Fanny hissed.

Bernard heard her. "Ah, excuse me! Mrs. Walcott, allow me to introduce Lord Greyson Sheffield and Lord Hayden Collier."

There was no help for it. She stepped forward like a soldier being brought before a firing squad, forcing herself to meet Lord Sheffield's arctic gaze and . . . and . . . the world fell away, time stopped, and her heartbeat slowed in her chest to a single tolling beat.

She tried to look away but she was caught, held motionless in a blue-green gaze while around her the world continued spinning. Dimly, she heard others speaking, but she couldn't have repeated a word of what they said.

Time protracted and the chill assessment in his eyes thawed, leaving behind confusion. Vaguely, she noticed him frowning and tugging his shirt cuff up and laying his fingertips against the inside of his bare wrist. His gaze never left hers, and the world kept receding until it felt as though only the pair of them remained, time splitting and channeling around them. It was uncanny, unnerving . . . spellbinding.

Finally, he shook his head slightly, like a swimmer upon emerging from deep water, and so, broke eye contact. At once and with dizzying swiftness, the world telescoped back into focus, her heart thundered into action, and she released her breath, unaware she'd even been holding it.

"It's a pleasure to meet you, Mrs. Walcott."

The young man, Hayden, appeared at the periphery of her vision. Gratefully, she turned to him.

"Forgive my uncle," he said, casting an exasperated glance at Grey Sheffield. *Uncle? Uncle!* "We'd hoped by now that he'd mastered a few of the more rudimentary social skills. It appears our hopes were premature."

Greyson Sheffield was *related* to Lord Collier? God, Fanny decided, must be rolling on his celestial floor, overcome with hilarity at his jest.

Sheffield's smile was vulpine. "I warned you earlier that I was a lost cause. A tiger doesn't change his stripes, Hayden." He inclined his head toward Fanny. "Or her stripes, as the case may be."

Was he taunting her? He had to be, but his gaze seemed merely quizzical. She didn't trust that impression. Not for an instant. "Mrs. Walcott, did you say?" he asked mildly.

"Yes."

"Hmm," he said. "You look most familiar. We haven't met before, have we?"

Could he really not know her? But then, why should he? His affect on her life had been far greater than hers on his. He'd likely forgotten her the moment he'd walked out the door in Mayfair. Besides, it had been more than six years ago, and she was no longer a girl, and certainly no longer *that* girl.

"Have we?" he pressed, cocking his head.

She shook her head.

"No," he said. "Of course not." He looked at Amelie. "So, you are the witch, are you?"

Amelie's eyes grew round, Bernard started, and Lord Hayden made a tight, disapproving sound.

"Grey, that was surely uncalled-for," the young man said.

Sheffield made an impatient gesture. "But that is why we're here, Hayden. To see to the continued health of the town's witch. Besides, judging from the demonstration outside, it appears that Miss Chase has rather embraced the role. Tell me, Miss Chase, *are* you a witch?"

Fanny's protective instincts flew to the forefront, overcoming her desire to fade into the background. Her impulse wasn't the only one; Bernard's cheeks puffed out and Hayden flushed.

"See here, Grey," Hayden said. "You might speak to your music-hall charlatans in such a way, but this is an innocent young lady." He turned, flustered, toward Amelie. "My uncle is a barrister whose work for the Crown brings him into contact with very low company. I am afraid he has forgotten—"

"No, sir," Amelie broke in quietly, her dignity in no way compromised by her trembling lower lip. "I am not a witch."

"That's good, because I daresay there're a number of tutors who would be unnerved to learn they haven't been teaching Latin conjugations but dire incantations." At Amelie's look of confusion, Sheffield went on. " '*Amo, amas, amat . . .*'?"

The unexpected quip surprised Fanny. He'd sounded amused, almost friendly, and humor and kindness were characteristics she hadn't expected of him. She wasn't sure she liked finding them. He'd once swept into her life, shattered it, exposed it to be tarnished and tawdry, and then left her to pick up the pieces. She didn't want him to have any qualities she could admire.

She studied him as he continued speaking to Amelie. He looked older, she decided with uncharitable pleasure. The seams lining his lean cheeks were deeper, the crinkles at the corners of his exotic-colored eyes more marked.

Her pleasure faded. Being older should have made him less formidable. It hadn't worked that way. If anything, the additional years only made him seem more dangerous. Certainly more virile.

Even at their first meeting, he'd exuded more rough masculinity than any man she'd ever seen, and now that quality was magnified. He looked hungry. He looked predatory. In short, he looked more now that which he was in fact: dangerous. In spite of the humor.

"Sometimes I tweak a few noses." Amelie's admission caught Fanny's attention.

"Of course she does," Hayden interjected gruffly. "How could she resist taking to task those ignorant enough to think she's a . . . a witch? I can barely say it, it's so preposterous."

"Thank you." Amelie's shining eyes lifted Hayden atop a very tall pedestal. "As Fanny always says, 'There's no sense arguing with popular opinion, so one might as well have a bit of fun with it.' "

Please be quiet, Amelie, Fanny silently begged.

"Does she?" Lord Sheffield murmured.

"Oh, Fan doesn't encourage me, of course," Amelie said loyally. "I can behave quite naughtily without outside inspiration."

Hayden laughed as if Amelie had just made the wittiest remark imaginable. Amelie blushed, dimpled, lowered her eyes, glanced up through her lashes at the chuckling lordling, and blushed even deeper.

Oh, dear, thought Fanny. She should have realized what would happen the moment she'd laid eyes on Lord Hayden's strapping young figure, but she'd been too caught up in her own concerns to pay the girl and boy much heed. *Would* happen? *Had* happened. Amelie—dear, cloistered, inexperienced, and superlatively vulnerable Amelie—had taken one look at the golden youth and succumbed to a prodigious case of calf's love.

And Lord Hayden? His chest was puffed up and his eyes equaled Amelie's for brilliance. He had to be, what? Twenty? Twenty-one? Old enough to have known his share of debutantes, shopgirls, lascivious ladies, and manipulating mamas. Someone—Fanny darted an accusing glare at Sheffield—should have taught him by now that it wasn't nice to flirt with susceptible young girls.

But then, Fanny thought unhappily, he was just a young man, and young men did so love to be heroes. For him, Amelie probably represented the quintessential princess in a tower (or in this case, a town) guarded by a dragon (or in this case, 217 resident dragons) and thus needed rescuing. By a hero. Him.

"Lord Sheffield, what did you mean when you said you were here to look after my continued health?" Amelie tore her gaze away from Lord Hayden long enough to ask.

Grey Sheffield smiled pleasantly. In response, Fanny's nerves quivered a warning.

"Your guardian, who, despite the inexplicable posturing of this pup, is Lord Collier, not his son here," he said, "has received an anonymous letter asking for immediate assistance, as someone was trying to—well, why be shy?—kill you."

Fanny's concern about Sheffield's recognizing her vanished with his words. "What letter? Do you have it with you? Let me see it," she demanded, sticking out her hand as Amelie gasped.

"I don't have the letter with me," he replied, regarding her closely. *Let him.* "I have already spoken to the postmaster and he claims he does not recall it and that people often post their own mail and toss it in the mailbag without his knowing. It simply said, 'Come quick. Someone is trying to kill our witch.' "

Fanny frowned, more troubled than frightened.

"But," Amelie said, "why would anyone want to kill me?"

"Exactly," Sheffield declared approvingly. "Behold, Hayden. A young lady who cuts to the chase. How rare." He sat down on the railed partition dividing the bank's single room, swinging his leg casually. "So, what do you suppose this is all about then?"

"I haven't any idea," Amelie replied. Her eyes widened. "Do you suppose I am in danger? Have you come to take me out of Little Firkin?"

"Good heavens, no," Sheffield said. "Only your guardian has that power, and he is not currently in Great Britain, nor will he be back for some time. I am here as Collier's representative simply to assess the situation and make recommendations. Of course, if I felt you were in imminent danger, I would be forced to act, but I see that is not the case."

"Grey"—Hayden's voice held a warning tone—"do you think this is the proper place for this conversation?" He didn't look in Bernard's direction, but everyone—including Bernard—understood the implication. Well aware he was *de trop*, the bank owner had made a politic retreat to his desk, where he was now busily tidying and retidying a stack of papers, his gaze averted, his ear tips rosy with embarrassment.

"Why?" Sheffield looked around. "Might as well get to the bottom of this as soon as possible. And Mr. McGowan is bound to have some insight. What say you to this situation, McGowan? You seem a reasonable man."

Bernard looked up, pretending he'd just caught his name. "Eh?"

"Miss Chase. Do you believe her to be in physical danger? Because of being a witch and all?"

The way Sheffield said it made it sound absurd. Fanny could not disagree. First of all, why would someone want to hurt Amelie? She was worth a fortune to everyone in town only alive. Second, why would anyone want to hurt Amelie? She was as nice and agreeable a young lady as anyone might wish for. And finally, a note warning that someone wanted to hurt

Amelie meant that more than one person knew about it. A secret conspiracy? In *Little Firkin*? Where a dog couldn't pass gas in the middle of the night without its being noted and argued about for the next month? It made no sense.

Poor Bernard cleared his throat, visibly disconcerted, and Fanny's heart went out to him. He might be a little stodgy and his stamp-collecting mania a little peculiar, but then, she and Amelie might be considered peculiar, too. No, Amelie could do worse than Bernard for a husband. Besides, Bernard had the additional recommendation of not only being aware of Amelie's history but of always having treated her as though he weren't. Now *Sheffield* was forcing him to acknowledge what they'd all long since silently agreed to ignore. *Damn the man.*

"If Miss Chase is in danger, this is the first I have heard of it," he now said. "As far as Miss Chase being, er, atypical, that is the witless gossip of the ignorant."

"Hear, hear," Sheffield said, dropping lightly to his feet. He brushed his hands together. "Well, that's that then. No sense hanging about because of someone's notion of a prank."

"But . . . but . . . what if it *isn't* a prank?" Hayden hastily interjected. "That makes as little sense as a threat against her. What would be the object of such a prank, and who was its target? The postmaster? My father?"

The boy had a point.

"We should investigate," Hayden concluded.

The lad had positioned himself at Amelie's side, visually aligning himself with her. Amelie accepted his championship, her lashes fluttering like sheets on a clothesline. The girl's initial distress had faded. She gave every appearance of settling in nicely to her new role as damsel in distress.

"We? Oh, all right then." Sheffield sighed. "Has anyone threatened your life, Miss Chase? By either word or action?"

"No."

"And there has been nothing of a remotely suspicious nature which has in any fashion endangered you?"

Amelie did not answer at once, and he pounced on her hesitation. "I see there has been. Would you be so kind as to tell us what that was?"

"It's hardly worth mentioning."

"Indulge me. I am here as your guardian's representative. If you are in danger, it is my duty to see you are removed from it."

"*You* are Lord Collier's representative? But I thought Lord Hayden . . ." Amelie blushed again.

Hayden, displeased at having his shining armor brusquely repossessed by his uncle, moved closer. Fanny could empathize. Hayden's looks were better suited to silvery armor than Sheffield's, who would look more natural in, say, dented black.

"The decision of whether action is required may rest with my uncle," Hayden said in a tight voice, "but that does not preclude my concern in this matter. Rest assured, Miss Chase, I will not hesitate to act on your behalf and in your best interest should the need arise."

Oh, for the love of heaven. Are all young people so earnestly pompous?

"Yes, yes, Hayden, very pretty," Sheffield said dryly, clearly sharing her sentiments. "Now, can we get on with it?"

"Please tell us, Miss Chase," Hayden gently prompted.

"Well," Amelie said, "last winter I was crossing the river when the ice broke and I fell through."

Fanny recalled the incident. It had been an accident.

"Had I been a few feet farther out, where the channel runs deeper, I may not have been able to"—Amelie paused dramatically—"pull myself back onto shore."

Hayden dutifully gasped. Sheffield shot him an impatient glare.

Bernard stood up, startled. "My dear Miss Chase," he said, "why have I not heard of this before?"

"You were in New York City."

"Ice does on occasion crack," Sheffield said, ignoring the little byplay. "Especially if a spring is underneath."

"Indeed, yes, Lord Sheffield," Amelie said, returning her attention to him. "But this is a favorite place of mine where I often skate and picnic in the summer. I know the bottom well. There is no spring in that location."

"By the stand of oaks," Bernard murmured.

Amelie flashed a smile in his direction. "You know my habits well, Mr. McGowan."

The banker flushed.

"Additionally," Amelie went on, "I had crossed at the same spot only a few hours earlier and had been doing so regularly for some weeks. And the weather, rather than warming as it had for the previous few days, had once more turned quite cold."

"A bright day, was it?" Sheffield asked.

Amelie nodded. "I believe so."

"Expanding and shrinking ice would explain a weak

spot in its surface. Likely over a spring," he added with an air of finality. "Anything else?"

"Yes," Amelie said, a little huffy now at having her near tragedy so summarily dismissed. "There was an ax lying on the bank. I didn't notice it when I began to cross, but when I made it back to shore, I saw it tucked beneath a pile of brush."

"And the sight of this ax made you think someone had purposely chopped through the ice in order to lay a trap for you?" Sheffield asked, his tone sardonic.

Amelie snapped her mouth shut, doubtless feeling that since she hadn't wanted to reveal the story in the first place and had only been coerced into doing so by Sheffield, his manner was not only insulting but grievously unfair—all feelings Fanny assumed, because that was how she felt.

"No, she did not," Fanny said, unable to keep silent. "Amelie thought someone had been fishing from the banks and used the ax to break through a spot, thereby inadvertently weakening her crossing. You are the one who asked if anything imperiled her well-being. She was simply telling you what you wanted to know."

Sheffield's gaze shifted toward her. "So I did. I stand corrected, Mrs. Walcott. You play the part of fond companion most convincingly."

Play? Convin— Oh! Before Fanny could retort, he'd swung back to Amelie with an improbably charming smile. "Forgive me, Miss Chase, if I appeared to badger you. I am a barrister by training and I am unused to dealing with *innocent* young ladies. Now, has your health in any other way recently been jeopardized?"

Amelie concentrated, her brow puckering prettily.

"Well," she finally said, "it wasn't just me, but shortly thereafter both Fanny and I were taken terribly ill. We were bedridden for two days." She paused to cast a shy glance at Hayden. "Fanny was quite worried."

"Worried enough to send for a physician?"

"The nearest physician is in Perth. And poor Fan was even sicker than I." Amelie glanced at her. "She was beside herself. She finally resorted to procuring some sort of tisane from . . . a local woman."

"I could have gone," Bernard announced. "You should have sent for me."

With all the overpowering male personalities filling the room, Fanny had momentarily forgotten Bernard, still sitting at his desk.

"We appreciate the sentiment," Fanny answered, "but you would have been in the middle of the Atlantic, returning from your trip."

"Ah, yes," Bernard said, musing. "The Shield, Eagle, and Flags thirty-cent. Original paste." Bernard kept track of the past by the dates on which he'd acquired specific stamps.

"Perhaps it was just a bad bit of fish," Sheffield suggested, regarding Bernard oddly. "Or a rancid twist of cheese?"

"Possibly," Amelie allowed, once more looking slightly peeved that another life-imperiling incident was being dismissed.

"On the other hand," Hayden put in, "someone is concerned enough about Miss Chase's health to have felt it necessary to alert my—alert us. I think it would be very irresponsible to discount the warning without at least making some inquiries."

Sheffield nodded thoughtfully. "You think it our duty, then?"

"I do."

"And you, Mrs. Walcott," Sheffield suddenly asked, his brilliant eyes lancing toward her. "What do you think?"

Fanny didn't hesitate. "I think it a great lot of tommyrot, but mysterious tommyrot. I do not think Amelie is in any danger, but I dislike mysteries and I should like this one cleared up."

"Then I suppose we must," Sheffield said. "Never let it be said we shirked our duty."

Hayden blustered. "It will, of course, also be an honor."

"Oh, *thank you*, Lord Hayden," Amelie breathed.

Involuntarily, Fanny rolled her eyes, and in doing so caught a glimpse of Sheffield doing the same. He saw her. For a second, his generous mouth quirked in a conspiratorial smile and they were comrades-in-arms, reasonable adults forced to deal with the exaggerated emotions of the very young. Then he appeared to recall his dignity and looked away.

He strode across the room and secured Hayden by the elbow. "Come along, Hayden. We have yet to settle in at your father's lodge, and besides, there is only so much gallantry I can stomach in a single morning."

"But," Hayden protested, "shouldn't we arrange a meeting with Miss Chase? And Mrs. Walcott, of course. To talk about . . . things and discover . . . things?"

"We'll make arrangements later."

"Might I suggest dinner at my house? What is today? Monday? What say Thursday evening?" Bernard asked. "I'd be delighted to have you all as my guests. I don't employ a chef, but there's a local woman makes a passable roast when called upon to do so."

"But, Mr. McGowan," Amelie inserted hastily, "do you think that's wise? I mean, what about Brutus and Caesar . . . ?" She referred to Bernard's two monstrous hounds. The poor beasts had been imported already trained to attack trespassers. "You recall Fanny's apprehension about them."

"My guard dogs," Bernard explained, then added, "I am a keen philatelist, and often away on trips adding to my collection, which I am humbled to admit is accounted one of the most extensive in Great Britain." He dipped his head in a modest gesture that had the effect opposite of conveying modesty.

"You will doubtless think it silly, but there are people who would travel great distances and commit the gravest of crimes to acquire an Inverted Head Four Annas. Brutus and Caesar dissuade such types from carrying out any mischief whenever I am gone."

Sheffield regarded him blankly a second before saying, "You're right. I do think it's silly." Again, Fanny had to catch herself from laughing.

Uncertain how to take this, Bernard instead looked at Amelie. "Your concern does you credit, Miss Chase. I had forgotten abut Mrs. Walcott's aversion. Perhaps my invitation was ill-considered. "

Good. The last thing on earth Fanny wanted was to be stuck at a dining table with—

"I know!" Amelie exclaimed. "We can dine at Quod Lamia!"

Fanny briefly closed her eyes. *Oh. Damn.* Amelie might as well have handed him an announcement:

"This is Francesca Brown, whom you exposed as a fraud six years ago."

Sheffield's head snapped around, Bernard looked frankly uncomfortable, Hayden seemed fascinated, and Amelie, being long familiar with the name with which Fanny had dubbed their house, suddenly recalled the meaning and blushed.

" 'Which . . . witch'?" Sheffield mused interestedly.

"Fan named the house when we moved in."

Be quiet, Amelie! Please. Before he remembers.

"You might not warrant it, but she has a naughty sense of irony." Amelie twinkled, the supposed threat to her person completely forgotten. *Ah, youth.*

"Oh, I can quite believe that," Sheffield said, smiling sunnily in return. He didn't glance at her. She was safe.

For the time being.

"What say you, Fan?" Amelie asked eagerly. "We could host a small party. Our Miss Oglethorpe is a fantastic cook. Please."

What could she say? It was Amelie's house, and Fanny was, when all was said and done, a paid companion. She could acquiesce gracefully or she could provoke speculation by refusing.

She smiled weakly. "Lovely. Shall we say Thursday at eight o'clock?"

Chapter Eight

If she married Lord Hayden it went without saying that their children would be exquisite-looking, Amelie mused, sauntering along beside Fanny as they made their way back to Quod Lamia. But would they have red hair? Or red-gold? Hazel eyes . . . perhaps blue? They would be not overlarge—unless by some fluke they ran to Lord Sheffield's massiveness—but be very nicely proportioned. Very nicely.

She was being silly, of course. She supposed many young ladies had indulged in just such daydreams after meeting Lord Hayden. The thought made her frown. Three whole days before she could see him again . . . Well, she'd just have to see about that.

"You're upset," Fanny said abruptly.

Amelie glanced over at her friend. "Pardon me?"

"You were frowning. You're worried. I knew it. I *knew* your pose of insouciance was feigned," Fanny declared, her brow puckering.

Amelie blinked, uncertain what Fanny meant.

"Amelie." Fanny touched her arm. "My dear, I sincerely do not think anyone is trying to, er, do you a misdeed."

Oh! Fanny was referring to the anonymous letter. But . . . misdeed? In spite of herself, she laughed. Which only made Fanny study her more closely and, indeed, Amelie knew her amusement was inappropriate. But that blunt, plainspoken Fanny should resort to vague euphemisms struck her as funny.

Now Fanny would take her laughter as a sign that Amelie was putting on a brave face, and she really wasn't. Sure enough, Fanny was studying her worriedly. Amelie did not want Fanny to fret a moment over her. She sobered.

"I'm sorry, Fan," she said, "but to hear you pussyfooting around a subject when you have never been anything but frank with me is so ridiculous. And the only reason I *am* diverted is because I am *not* worried."

"Really?" Fanny said, clearly wanting to be convinced. "You aren't curious about where this letter came from?"

"Of course I am," Amelie replied. "I am also curious about the fairy Grammy Beadle claims to have caught. It doesn't mean I believe she actually has a fairy stashed away somewhere in Beadletown in a pickle pot. I suspect both Grammy Beadle's fairy tale and the writer of this letter are simply people seeking attention by saying ridiculous things."

"That's awfully insightful of you, Amelie," Fanny said.

"Well," Amelie said, adopting her "reasonable" voice, one—had Fanny but recognized it—she'd learned from Fanny herself, "what other explanation is there? Am I supposed to believe that someone actually wants to kill me? Pshaw. On the other hand, if Lord

Sheffield thinks it best for me to leave here and go with him to my guardian's house . . ."

At this, Fanny smiled and shook her head. The reappearance of Amelie's desire to leave Little Firkin reassured Fanny that her unconcern over the letter was real and not bravado. "Don't waste much hope there, Amelie, m'girl. You heard him. He's here only to assess the situation and make recommendations to Lord Collier."

"Do you think he might ask us to go to London?" Amelie asked.

Fanny shrugged. "If nothing is resolved about that letter, perhaps. But in the meantime you'll simply have to wait. Though I must say, you quite impress me, my dear. I was concerned you would be frightened, and here you are trying to figure out some way the situation might be worked to your advantage. When did you become so Machiavellian?"

Amelie gave a wan smile. "Oh, a long time ago. Too long. Not that there's anyone here to notice, let alone appreciate, my deviousness, or anything else about me, for that matter, other than my"—she glanced at Fanny—"*supposed* special powers. Except," she continued, smiling apologetically, "for you."

She went on. "What's the use of having one's wardrobe created by the House of Worth when the only ones around to see you are sheep?" She sighed deeply. "I'll be an old maid by the time I am free to enter society again."

"Twenty-one is hardly an old maid," Fanny said, in that "reasonable" tone. "And there's no sense grousing about it."

Fanny was always telling her one must accept the

things one could not change. Perhaps that was what came from having a cool temperament. Amelie was not so fortunate. She railed against the well-meaning tyranny her father's will imposed, at times coming close to hating him for it. Of course, she didn't. She understood he'd simply been trying to protect her. But that she should have to remain exiled because of her father's belief in hobgoblins was just *so* unfair! And that was exactly what the supposed "dangerous factions" in London that had driven them here were: hobgoblins out of the tormented imagination of a dying man.

During all her years in India and later in London, Amelie never felt a moment's unease. She recalled both her former homes as places of excitement and color, movement and vibrancy—the antithesis of life in Little Firkin, which was frankly as boring as a place could get. Lord, she disliked living here!

But now, amazingly, fantastically, the immediate future glittered with promise. She would not let a letter cast a pall over it. Or allow anything else to dim *his* light.

"Do you not think him the *perfect* gentleman?" she asked, clasping her hands and whirling around in the center of the road. "Such address! So debonair! Such refinement! And did you *see* the cut of his coat? I am convinced it was tailored in Bond Street. I have an eye, you know, and I not only study the ladies' fashion magazines, but the gentlemen's too."

Fanny did not reply.

"What is it, Fanny? Do not say there is something about Lord Hayden of which you disapprove."

Fanny glanced at her. "Good heavens, was I just commending you on your maturity?" she asked. "You

sound remarkably like you did the morning your pony
was delivered."

Amelie felt too deliciously euphoric to take offense. "Then you *do* approve!" she said. "Is he not
smashing?"

"Smashing?" Fanny repeated. "I see I shall have to
review the amount of sensationalist fare entering the
house."

"You can't distract me by putting on that govern-
essy tone." Amelie ground to a halt, putting her hands
on her hips and tapping her toe. "I insist on knowing
your opinion of Lord Hayden."

Fanny threw her hands up. "All right. He's a very
handsome young man." She began walking again.

Amelie did not. "Is that all you have to say?"

"He's a very young man," Fanny said.

"He's older than me."

Fanny looked over her shoulder at Amelie. "*You* are
a very, *very* young lady."

"But you concede he has address."

Finally, Fanny stopped. "Fine. He has address."

"And polish."

"Yes, yes. He positively gleams."

Amelie pouted. "Now you are being sarcastic, and
you always told me that sarcasm is the province of
mean-spirited journalists and vulgar politicians."

At this, Fanny grinned. "I always fancied I'd make
a good politician." She turned her head forward again
and continued on her way, Amelie behind.

There was no use for it; Fanny would not be persuaded to enthusiasm. Even over a paragon like Lord
Hayden.

Fanny was a darling, but without a single excitable

bone in her body. If Amelie could wish one thing for her friend, it would be that she had a more passionate nature.

Not for the first time, Amelie wondered what Fanny's marriage must have been like, and if Mr. Walcott had been as cool a customer as his wife. She supposed it was so; otherwise Fanny would have spoken of him more often. As it was, Amelie couldn't help but feel sorry for poor, dead Mr. Walcott, who, in his short time as a husband, had made so little an impression on his wife that she seemed to have more or less forgotten him.

But she felt even sorrier for Fanny, who, she assumed, had known love only as a tepid, placid sort of affection. Amelie was certain that when *she* fell in love it would be spectacularly intense and all-consuming. As well as tender, noble, and enduring, of course. She wouldn't have it any other way, and, as Fanny often pointed out, she generally got what she wanted.

They'd just reached the steps leading up to Quod Lamia's long, deep porch when the front door opened and Vicar Oglethorpe stomped out, slamming it behind him. He stopped, snapping his hat viciously against his knee.

"Dirty," he muttered angrily.

"Excuse me," Fanny said, her voice an arctic blast.

Amelie fell back a step. The vicar intimidated her. From the moment they'd arrived in Little Firkin, he'd accused her of willfully conspiring at witchcraft, and nothing her father or Fanny had said could persuade him otherwise. As luck would have it, he had actually witnessed a plate flying from the table. It had flown straight at his head.

She knew his fixation on what he'd seen disturbed

Fanny, too, for once she'd said, "The man must not be right in the noggin. Here he insists that all signs of the preternatural in our house desist, and for years now they have, and still he natters on about all the dark deeds occurring at Quod Lamia."

"I suspect you shouldn't have named the house Quod Lamia, then," Amelie had offered, and Fanny had given way to one of her unexpectedly roguish and wholly delightful grins.

"I suspect not."

They hadn't discussed the matter again, but as time went on, the vicar's mania became more pronounced. Amelie supposed it had something to do with his sister having left his house to come to work for them. Not that the vicar especially liked his sister—Amelie decided he didn't like anyone—but he viewed her decampment not only as a personal affront, but as a sure sign that the two women at Quod Lamia had used unnatural influence to tempt her into their midst. In actuality it had been much simpler: They'd offered her a wage.

Fanny had stopped at the bottom of the stairs and was glaring up at the vicar, even from the disadvantage of her inferior height appearing far more commanding.

He looked up from swatting at his trousers and his lip curled. "Your *house* is dirty, Mrs. Walcott. You ought to teach that slatternly creature you call a maid how to use a feather duster and a mop."

He was talking about Violet Beadle—though using the term *maid* in reference to the girl was stretching the definition of the word a bit. He started down the steps.

Fanny held her ground. Fanny always held her ground.

"Though," he intoned darkly, "I think we both know that the furnishings are not the only unclean things about this household." He stopped a few steps above her.

For a long moment, they locked gazes, but then Fanny smiled and began calmly mounting the stairs, deliberately heading straight to where the vicar stood. He had no choice but to move or risk being knocked aside. And both Amelie and the vicar knew Fanny was quite capable of such an act.

With an angry sputter, he leaped out of her way just in time to avoid a collision. Fanny sailed past with regal disregard, turning at the top of the stairs.

"I'm surprised you'd sully yourself by entering the house," she said.

"I have a duty to the sister who has chosen to dwell in this—"

"Den of iniquity?" Fanny cut in.

"Insolent, irreverent wench," the vicar shouted. "How *dare* you mock me?"

"Well, why not go for broke, Vicar?" Fanny drawled in that scornful manner with which she verbally lashed anyone who dared speak rudely to either her or Amelie. "If you must be a caricature, you might as well speak in clichés."

Despite knowing Fanny could handle the vicar, Amelie fidgeted. She wished Fanny would not bait the man. He'd turned an alarming shade of red and actually stomped his foot. His hand clenched into a fist. Fanny yawned, delicately hiding her mouth behind her hand.

"You needn't worry about Miss Oglethorpe," Amelie offered, trying to console him. He looked like he might strike Fanny. "She dislikes us, too. And she is a most devout . . ." Oh, Lord, what denomination *was* Vicar Oglethorpe? She wasn't sure she even knew. . . . No. She didn't. "Whatever it is you are."

His eyes bulged and she hurried on, at the same time backing up. "She is always praying over us. I hear her in the kitchen . . ." She trailed off.

Her attempt at conciliation had been in vain. Oglethorpe raised a shaking hand and pointed a finger at her.

"You. *You* are the root—"

"Of all evil?" Fanny again cut in. "No, that would be money. Though Amelie does look to come into scads of that someday."

"Quiet, Lilith!" the vicar thundered, and stormed past Amelie without glancing at her, which, Amelie suspected, had been Fanny's goal all along. They watched him go, sending up little puffs of dust.

Fanny was a genius at deflecting the vicar's attention from her. Indeed, Amelie was not sure whom the vicar considered the greater threat to his flock—assuming he had one somewhere—the witch or the witch's keeper.

"It's a good thing you're not the witch, Fan," Amelie said, winning a startled glance from Fanny, "or the vicar would have had you burnt at the stake by now."

"Yes," Fanny agreed in an odd tone. "It is, isn't it?"

Chapter Nine

It was her. Francesca Brown.

Grey's pulse was still racing from the initial shock of recognition. He almost laughed at the absurdity of it, of finding her here after so many years. He'd thought it was her when he'd spied her across the street, but there had been something unfamiliar in the way she walked: open and relaxed, the angle of her head high. Quite unlike the tremulous, wraithlike girl in the Mayfair apartment.

But then, he reminded himself, con artists were chameleons, adapting to their environs. The only quality Fanny Walcott shared with Francesca Brown was the intangible sense of separateness he'd noted so long ago. As though she were only second cousin to mankind, and not an immediate relative. No matter. It was just another illusion.

"I should have let my valet come along," Hayden suddenly blurted out, catching Grey off guard. He hadn't been attending his nephew, immersed in his own thoughts as they made their way on foot to Bernard McGowan's house, having accepted an invitation to lunch so that they could see his stamp collection.

"I told him his services wouldn't be required up here in the wilds of Scotland," Hayden said disconsolately. "I told him we would make do with the servants that had gone ahead to air out the place. Ha."

Grey nodded. Hayden didn't need a response. In fact, no conversation had been required of Grey since they'd left McGowan's bank, for the simple reason that Hayden was quite content to carry on a monologue—mostly about what a pretty and pleasant young woman Amelie Chase was, and how could anyone imagine she was a witch? An angel? A stunner? A charmer? Yes and yes and yes. But a witch? Most definitely not. And why hadn't his father told him about her?

Grey had told Hayden that the last time his father, Lord Collier, had seen Amelie, she'd been a pimply-faced adolescent, but his remark fell on deaf ears. Hayden ignored him, babbling on.

So it went. They walked along the road following the river's bank as it left town and climbed into the foothills of the surrounding mountains. Past the blue disk of an inland lake, they reached a drive marked by two mossy boulders. The low stone house McGowan had described stood at the end of it, an iron fence surrounding it.

"Colonel Chase's old hunting lodge," Grey said. "Dour sort of place. Though I suspect the fish in that lake we passed are attractive."

Hayden wasn't attending. "Damn."

"Some new crisis?" Grey asked mildly.

"No. The same one, as you'd realize if you'd only been listening. What am I going to wear?"

"Wear?"

"Oh, it's all very fine for you to go about looking

like you do. No one expects anything of you anymore. But there are those of us who seek not to offend every time we appear in a drawing room."

Grey regarded his nephew in amused surprise. He was more used to hero worship from the young man than criticism.

"I must go immediately to the lodge and unpack and see if I have anything suitable in which to appear at a young lady's table."

"We're not dining there until Thursday."

Hayden's young jaw set stubbornly. "I shall not feel comfortable until I am assured I can present myself to Miss Chase—and Mrs. Walcott—in an acceptable fashion. I may have to hire a mount and ride to . . . the nearest town that offers gentlemen's collars or stockings."

"Yes," Grey said, knowing that to argue would be futile. "You'd best plan to do that."

"Give my apologies to the Scotsman," Hayden said.

"McGowan."

"Yes, that's it. Tell him I'll look at his butterflies some other time."

"Stamps."

"That's right. Stamps. Thank you. I'll meet you at the house later." Hayden's handsome face finally relaxed. "And don't worry, Uncle. I shall look for something suitable for you to wear, also."

"Too kind," Grey replied.

Hayden strode off, leaving Grey to continue on to McGowan's house. He was not unhappy. As diverting as it was to see Hayden go all mooncalf over a slip of a girl, it was the girl's keeper who interested Grey. More than interested him, in all truth. But then, she always had.

Six years ago, he'd left her husband's apartments vowing he would return later to confront her. But by the time he had, she'd disappeared. He'd been confounded by his reaction to her, knowing his attraction was unworthy of him—not only because she was, presumably, a married woman, but because she was a cheat, a petty criminal, and a seductress. The exact type who'd ruined his father and come close to bankrupting his family.

Soon after, word reached him of Brown's death in a French railway accident. Driven by an unexplored urgency, he'd used his contacts to find out more. Specifically, whether or not *she* had been with him and hurt as well. She hadn't. His relief had been as palpable as it had been inexplicable. He'd been unable to discover anything else.

Now, he smiled. He'd always known their paths would cross again.

The gall of the creature. To imagine she could deceive him with her straight-backed hauteur and her purloined respectability. She could have worn sackcloth, shaved her head, and donned dark spectacles, and he would still have recognized her.

Soon enough she'd learn better than to underestimate him. For the time being, let her think she'd fooled him, because only then would she go forward with her scheme, and he had no doubt there was a scheme. It was what she did, who she was.

Oh, he knew about Colonel Chase's bequest to her. His brother-in-law had shared with Grey the terms of the colonel's will. Once the terms of the will were met and Amelie turned twenty-one, Fanny would be well compensated for her years here. Enough to live comfortably for decades. But confidence artists did not ply their trade for mere comfort; they did it for wealth.

As Alphonse Brown's wife, Fanny had once been well on her way to being truly rich. Would a woman like that have hidden herself up here for six long years with the only payoff in sight being *comfort*? He did not think so. Not from what he knew of professional frauds. No. There was a scheme.

She must have added a mesmerist's tricks to her arsenal of weapons since they'd last met. What else could account for the suspension of time, the impossible sense of affinity with her he'd felt? He'd even checked his pulse to ascertain whether he was having some sort of physical event.

Anticipation uncoiled in his veins, as intoxicating as those moments in the bank when their gazes had locked. Whatever her game, he would discover it. He only needed to ascertain what she was playing for and determine whether the girl was victim or coconspirator.

By God, it ought to be fun, he thought, arriving at McGowan's house. He passed the heavy gate, to be greeted by an explosion of ferocious barking. At the side of the house, two enormous brown dogs flung themselves against the thick links of the chains tethering them. They had heads the size and shape of anvils, massive jaws, and thick, muscular bodies. They did not appear happy to be receiving company.

"Brutus! Caesar! Quiet!" McGowan shouted, emerging from the front door. With grumbles of discontent, the beasts ceased barking and settled into pacing at the end of their chains, digging further into the well-worn track that marked the limit of their range.

"Please come in, Lord Sheffield," McGowan welcomed him, stepping aside. "I hope the dogs didn't alarm you?"

"Damn right they did," Grey said. "Quite some pets you have there."

McGowan smiled. "Oh, they're not pets. Not at all. They protect my collection."

"They must do one hell of a good job. I can't imagine any sane man challenging those beasts for the sake of a stamp," Grey said, following McGowan into the hallway.

McGowan laughed. "Clearly, you're not an enthusiast. Brutus is a replacement for an earlier guard dog, one shot by a rival collector who thought I didn't deserve the cover I outbid him for."

Grey had no reply for such inanity. He liked dogs. He did not like fanatics. He looked around. There was little furnishing and less decoration in the halls or to be seen through the open doors leading to cavernous rooms. "You have spartan tastes for a banker, McGowan."

"Oh, I have expensive taste, I assure you. It's just that I limit my extravagances to one area: my stamps." His smile was self-deprecating. "But where is the young man?"

"My nephew sends his apologies, but I'm afraid a sartorial crisis has claimed the rest of his day."

McGowan accepted the excuse with good humor. "He's very young."

"Yes."

"It will be good for Miss Chase to be with someone of her own age for a change."

"I'm sure my nephew thinks so."

McGowan's expression grew faintly melancholy. "She's an enchanting young lady."

"So I've been told." Good God, was he to be forced to listen to yet another simple-minded sot drone on about Amelie Chase's virginal perfection? He decided to pre-empt the possibility. "Did you know her father well?"

"I was in his command for a short while in India. After I left the service I contacted Colonel Chase and we began a correspondence. In one letter he mentioned the need for a bank in Little Firkin and encouraged me to look into it." Bernard smiled. "Ironic, when you think of it. I originally wrote him because I'd hoped he might have kept some uncanceled Indian stamps."

McGowan had been a soldier in India? Grey would never have tagged him as such. He seemed too fastidious, too prim.

"I wish I could arrange for her to leave here so that she would not have to put up with such ridiculous slander," the banker fussed.

"You could always marry her."

The man blushed, and Grey, who'd been speaking ironically, felt his interest sharpen. Well, of course, it made perfect sense. A lovely, extremely wealthy or-phan ripe for the matrimonial plucking? Of course.

"Oh. My," said McGowan. "I don't know that I dare have hopes in that direction. I mean, perhaps I am too old for her? Too stodgy?"

Well, there was that.

McGowan waited for Grey to contradict him. He didn't.

"Besides, I could not ask her to enter into a marriage without her first experiencing something of the world. It would be unfair."

And there was that, too. "Most levelheaded," Grey said. "Unfortunately, levelheadedness is the one quality the young never seem to appreciate."

McGowan nodded gravely. "Your years have given you wisdom, Lord Sheffield."

Years? Wisdom? The ass. He had less than a decade on McGowan. Any latent tendency to goodwill toward McGowan vanished.

"Clearly, you are a man who could appreciate the sublime beauty of everyday objects," McGowan went on.

So much for McGowan's discernment. Grey had no more of an artistic sensibility than he did a sartorial one.

"Come, let me show you my collection," McGowan said.

Seeing an opportunity to interrogate McGowan about Francesca Walcott, Grey followed him down a bare hallway to an equally bare room, its only furnishings three neat rows of glass-covered cabinets. A sheet of white paper had been rolled down the center of each display, and each sheet of paper held a single widely spaced row of stamps. Above these had been positioned magnifying glasses so that a viewer, gazing through the glass top, would be able to see the most minuscule detail of the stamp below.

McGowan stood aside, his face alight with pride. "Look around. Take your time. There are stamps here that are unique."

Dutifully, Grey approached the nearest cabinet and peered down at a little brown rectangle.

"A Dove," McGowan informed him, shaking his head mournfully. "Alas, canceled."

"Alas," Grey agreed. "Do you know Mrs. Walcott well?"

"What?" McGowan asked in surprise.

"Mrs. Walcott," Grey said impatiently. "Do you know her well?"

"I'm not sure what you mean."

"What do you know of her? Her character. Her temperament."

"She's a fine woman." McGowan must have read Grey's dissatisfaction with the answer, for he went on. "Very, ah, forceful. I mean resourceful."

Oh, Grey already knew that. The sound of "angel wings" that she and her husband had somehow produced was one of the few effects he'd never been able to debunk. How had they achieved that? The question had plagued him for years.

"Of course, she has had to be," McGowan went on, as though worried that being resourceful was a feminine shortcoming. "Colonel Chase did not live long after coming to Little Firkin, and he was weak. A good deal of the overseeing of the building of Quod Lamia fell to Mrs. Walcott. Yes, indeed, an extremely efficient woman."

"Anything else? Anything, say, a detractor might mention?"

McGowan looked mildly affronted but replied, "Some might find her brusque and perhaps unapproachable, but I think her candor is quite bracing and her self-containment laudable."

"She's intolerant?"

McGowan scowled. "She is not shy about offering an opinion, and she does not use emotion in place of reason. Before he died, she and Colonel Chase had some spirited debates."

"Cold, is she?" Of course she was cold. Cold-blooded. As were all her type.

"I would say aloof," McGowan said, clearly disliking the conversation.

"A woman like that would find the society in a place like Little Firkin most confining," Grey said. "She must resent that the terms of Colonel Chase's will make it impossible for her to leave here before Miss Chase without forfeiting her bequest."

At this, McGowan laughed. "No, I'm afraid you have it wrong, Lord Sheffield. Mrs. Walcott wouldn't leave without Miss Chase regardless of the terms of the will. She may not be the most demonstrative woman, but her devotion to Miss Chase is unquestion— Oh! I see you've spied the Neubaum cover. Three Hawaiian Missionary one-pennies."

"Fascinating," Grey said, a little disappointed that his working theory regarding Fanny's presence here was being challenged. *Hmm.* But then, McGowan could be wrong. How well could he know her, after all? *Very well.* Grey frowned. "What do you know of the woman herself? What do you know of her history?"

McGowan didn't bother to tear his gaze from the envelope in the case below. "Little enough," he said. "But I am not one to pry. I believe her husband was under Colonel Chase's command and died on foreign soil."

"But as you, too, were in the colonel's command, surely you knew Mr. Walcott?"

Ha! He had the slippery vixen. How could she have been so careless as to create an alias that could so easily be discredited? And by her one and only neighbor?

"I'm afraid not," McGowan said. "I was attached to his battalion as a member of a sharpshooter corps for only a few months. I didn't meet any of the regular army chaps."

The soldiering made sense now. The precision with which McGowan spoke, the neatness of his nails, the extreme polish of his boots all indicated the sort of exacting nature required of a marksman.

And Fanny Walcott hadn't made a blunder.

"Why do you ask after Mrs. Walcott? You don't suspect *her* of wanting to harm Miss Chase?" McGowan said. "If you do, I won't believe it."

"Not at all," Grey denied. "I'm a very uncomplicated man. When I see a handsome woman, I am interested in why she is unattached. And she is a very handsome woman."

"She is in all ways admirable," McGowan said softly.

Grey's eyes narrowed. Practicality might insist that a chap set his sights on one matrimonial prize, but that didn't preclude him from appreciating another. A sharp jolt of something—he wasn't sure what, but he knew it wasn't jealousy—lifted Grey's lip in a curl of derision. Abruptly, he decided that they'd spoken enough about Mrs. Walcott.

"But enough about Mrs. Walcott. She is not the reason I am here." *Not the reason that brought me here*, an inner voice amended. "Miss Chase and this threat against her are. I assume you would like to help me get to the bottom of this little mystery?"

McGowan nodded.

"Then let us deal in hypotheticals for a moment, shall we? Suppose someone were trying to harm Miss Chase. Who would it be?"

Bernard thought a moment. "I don't know," he finally said. "I can't imagine."

"What about the old woman?"

"Grammy Beadle? Harmless."

"Anyone with an ax to grind or who bears Miss Chase, or Mrs. Walcott, a grudge?"

McGowan brooded. "Well, there is Vicar Oglethorpe. Admittedly, he is of a hellfire-and-brimstone mentality and can be rather alarming. But his parish is over thirty miles away, and he visits here only sporadically."

"Perhaps in one of his more impassioned sermons he alarmed someone and they now feel obliged to send a warning?" Grey suggested.

McGowan shrugged.

"What about the money? If Miss Chase dies before she reaches her majority, what happens to the money that was to have been divided amongst the townspeople?" Of course, Grey already knew the answer; he wanted to see who else did. In particular the banker.

"Every cent goes to charity," McGowan answered without pause. "The Benevolent Officers Fund for Military Orphans."

Grey nodded. So there was no ostensible motive for anyone to want Amelie Chase dead.

"Do you think the threat is real?" McGowan asked, gnawing his lower lip.

"No. I suspect it was sent out of sincere, if misplaced, fear for Amelie Chase's life," Grey said. "Perhaps now, with just a few more years left before the terms of the will are met, an overly concerned citizen saw something dire in the recent illness Miss Chase told us about. Or someone overheard a bit of drunken bluster."

"Doubtless you're right," the banker said, following Grey down the row of cabinets.

The matter having been handled to his satisfaction, Grey allowed his interest to be awoken. Not by the stamps, but by the sort of man who would collect them.

"Stamp collecting is more than a way of passing the long Highland winters for you, isn't it?" he asked.

McGowan nodded, his face alighting with more animation than Grey had seen since they'd met. "Oh, yes. I admit I am a full-blown zealot. I've been collecting stamps since I was a boy. Truth to tell, I asked to be posted to the Indian frontier not because of the adventure, like the other lads, but because I saw it as an opportunity to come by some very rare stamps."

Good God. The man must be as mad as a March hare.

"But why?" Grey asked, sincerely puzzled. "What about these little squares of paper engenders such fascination?" He'd been about to say *fanaticism*, but thought better of it. He didn't want to alienate the fellow.

McGowan regarded him with a touch of exasperation. "I don't know. They just do. I suppose you find it ridiculous?"

Grey wasn't going to lie. He hated liars and deceit in any form; it was the essence of his nature. "I find it incomprehensible."

McGowan shook his head. "Why does anyone find anything fascinating? Why is a musician enthralled by a passage of music? Why does a horticulturist go into transports over a type of rose? Why does a man obsess over a certain woman?"

Because she is a mystery, and he had devoted his life to unraveling mysteries.

"It is because it is a passion with them," McGowan said when Grey remained silent. "Passion is a gift, Lord Sheffield. It doesn't matter what the object of that passion is. If we are lucky enough to find something that stirs and entrances, fascinates and beguiles us, we would be fools not to give ourselves wholly to the experience. It is how we know we are alive."

Not merely mad, but mad north by northwest, with a great deal more insight into his own nature than most men had. Perhaps including Grey. Besides a devotion—some would say obsession—to bringing down frauds and cheats, what stirred Grey's emotions, excited and captivated him?

An image flashed through his thoughts, startling him: dark eyed and black haired, an elegantly crafted face along with a slender, fine-boned form. He banished her.

"Lord Sheffield?" McGowan said. "Would you agree?"

"What? Oh. You are quite right, McGowan." He was a private man who rarely confided in anyone. He kept to himself, presenting a face to the world that was urbane and indifferent. He always had. It had been his way of dealing with the ridicule arising from his father's well-publicized ghost chasing.

They had moved along the line of cabinets as they spoke and stood in front of one devoted to stamps from the exotic East.

"Why have you left a place between these two stamps?" Grey asked.

McGowan brushed his fingers lightly over the glass surface protecting the empty sheet of paper.

"That's where I hope to one day exhibit a Two-Hump Yellow Wrong-Kneed Camel. Should I do so, I would be the only collector in the world to have representatives of each color incarnation. It is accounted one of the rarest stamp runs in history." McGowan's eyes had taken on the dreamy look of a lover.

"Well, someday perhaps you'll find one."

McGowan laughed bitterly. "One doesn't *find* a Two-Hump Yellow Wrong-Kneed Camel. One bids for it, buys it, steals it." He laughed again. "Or inherits it. The fact is, one is reputed to be about to come on the market. Not that I stand a chance of getting it. It will go for far more than I could ever pay."

McGowan ushered him to a single small cabinet set apart from the others in a place of honor. "Here. This is what it looks like. This is the Two-Hump Yellow Wrong-Kneed Camel. A facsimile, I'm afraid."

Grey peered through the magnifying glass at a homely little mustard-colored stamp with a cartoonish-looking knock-kneed camel in its center. "I spent five thousand pounds for that, thinking I'd just acquired the greatest bargain in philatelist history," McGowan said, without rancor. "It isn't worth the paper it's printed on."

Five thousand pounds on a swindle.

Grey felt a surge of pity for McGowan. His father had done the same thing time and again, the only difference being that he never had understood that what he'd purchased had been fake.

"Why do you have it here?" he asked curiously.

"I put it there to remind myself how easy it is to be duped into believing a counterfeit is real, especially when you want it very badly."

Grey did not reply. His thoughts once again turned to his father and then, unaccountably, to Fanny Walcott. He feared he understood all too well.

Chapter Ten

"You are quite sure I can't escort you somewhere?" Bernard McGowan asked Amelie again, appearing in the doorway to the bank as she hurried past on her sixth circuit of Little Firkin's main thoroughfare. He'd also peeked out on her third.

"Yes, quite sure," Amelie answered brightly, wishing the banker would just go back inside. "I'm just enjoying a stroll."

Bernard looked at her quizzically but was too much a gentleman to point out to her what everyone had noticed: that she had spent more time on the streets of Little Firkin in the last two days than she had in the last six months. She'd begun to feel a little silly window-shopping, particularly as there were only twelve windows to shop in. But if she wasn't on the streets of Little Firkin, how else was she to "run into" Lord Hayden?

"Well," Bernard said reluctantly, "if you are certain I can do no service for you . . . ?" He brightened. "Perhaps you'd join me in a cool beverage at MacKee's?"

Amelie caught back her start of surprise. Bernard had never asked her to accompany him anywhere without Fanny. Last week she would have been delighted. Today she had in mind another companion.

"Oh, no. No. But thank you for asking."

"Then may I escort you back to Quod Lamia when you've finished your business here?" he asked hopefully.

"That won't be necessary. Fanny has insisted Ploddy accompany me whenever I leave the house," she said. Ploddy was Quod Lamia's only real servant, an elderly gent who'd once served as her father's batman. "I'm to fetch him from Mr. Davies's establishment when I'm ready to go back." She only hoped he wasn't too inebriated at that time. Ploddy had something of a problem.

"I see," Bernard said.

"Yes," Amelie said. "I think it's all a bit silly. But Fanny will not be gainsaid."

"She is taking this letter seriously then?"

"She says not, but that we might as well not take unnecessary chances."

"And you, Miss Chase?" Bernard gazed earnestly into her eyes. He was not so tall as Lord Hayden. "Are you worried?"

She shook her head, trying to sort out her feelings. "Not really. I suppose I ought to be, but it is hard to imagine someone would want to harm me, not when I am so valuable to everyone here, and all that value rests on my being, well, alive. I am most unhappy this has caused so much consternation for Fanny."

His smile was tender. "You are precious to some for more than the reasons you outline."

Oh, dear. Oh, no. She should have felt flattered, or at least a tiny bit pleased by his words. Instead, she only felt uncomfortable.

"Too kind," she chirped, as if people told her she was precious on a daily basis. "Well, I'd best be on my way. Good day to you, Mr. McGowan."

He looked disappointed but smiled. "And to you, Miss Chase. I look forward to dining with you tomorrow."

"And Fanny. And Lord Sheffield. And Lord Hayden," she said.

"Of course."

She sailed on, knowing full well that her walk was causing Bernard much speculation. She refused to feel ridiculous.

Besides Bernard, who was there to care? The locals were concerned only that she didn't get herself killed before they collected their money. And that she didn't conjure up something she couldn't unconjure. She supposed in an odd way it was a testimony to their tolerance that soon after she'd moved here, a delegation of Little Firkians had arrived on their doorstep, pushing forward their ambassador, Donnie MacKee.

Her father had already been too ill to attend the little meeting on the porch, but Fanny had stood in for him. Hands clasped primly at her waist, she'd blocked the doorway as Amelie watched from behind her. Fanny had eyed the townspeople with clinical detachment, as though they were Gypsies pedaling suspect tin.

She greeted them in her most quelling tone. "Yes?"

Donnie cleared his throat. "I come to say what needs to be said."

"Yes?"

"Aye."

"And that is?" Her politeness was as formidable a weapon as any Donnie would have ever encountered.

"Now, then, missus, we don't think as yer lass here be a bad lass. But a witch she be, and bad or good, a witch is trouble."

"Really?"

Donnie nodded. "Aye. There's a witch lives up Beadletown and she's come over a right pest."

"Amelie will not be a pest."

"That's good 'n' all fer ye to say." He hesitated. "But when ye come right down to the matter—"

"Please do."

"When ye come down to the matter, we ain't sure how bright a lass she be, and what with magik bein' dangerous 'n' all, well, we're thinking it be best if she give up conjuring altogether." He paused. "Leastways long as she's here."

Amelie could still see the twinkle flashing into Fanny's eyes and the irrepressible twitch at the corner of her mouth. Fanny had had to look away a moment, but when she turned back, she had regained her composure.

"Fear not. She's a bright girl."

"That may be, but still . . ." Donnie waggled his red brows suggestively.

Fanny capitulated. "I promise you, you have nothing to worry about."

It seemed to have appeased them, for no one bothered them after that. No one really bothered *with* them, either. Except to make deliveries and the usual daily sorts of business exchanges. If her father had chosen a place for its population's placidity, he couldn't have chosen better than Little Firkin.

The townspeople were by nature sedentary, by temperament lazy. Which was why to a man (and

woman) they were content to sit around and wait for
her to grow up and move away, rather than endeavor
to make something of Little Firkin, with industry and
businesses and a future that did not depend on a girl
reaching her twenty-first year.

Lord, she would be happy when she was finally free
to leave here. If she'd voiced that desire once, she'd
voiced it a hundred times. Unfortunately, as Fanny
pointed out just as often, no good came of complaining. Certainly nothing but polite refusals and inquiries
as to her health had come of the letters she'd written
the senior Lord Collier. No. There was nothing for it.
Her father had determined that until she reached the
age of twenty-one, one way or another, she would be
attended twenty-four hours a day, be it by Lord Collier (who had already made clear his unwillingness to
assume the task), Little Firkin, or a husband. A husband . . . She smiled, her good mood restored.

"Miss Chase!"

At the sound of Lord Hayden's voice, Amelie twirled
around. *Finally* she'd managed to orchestrate a chance
encounter with the elusive young gentleman.

"Miss Chase!"

He trotted out of the post office, hat in hand. As
soon as he made her side, he swept a hand though his
golden locks and donned his hat. "How are you?"

"Very well, Lord Hayden. Thank you. And yourself?"

"Very well," he said, beaming down at her. He
glanced around. "Very well, indeed. Is Mrs. Walcott
with you?"

"Oh, no," Amelie said. "She is more likely fishing or
bicycle riding or lofting golf balls into the loch. She's a
rather solitary lady."

"But don't say you are unattended!"

"Why, yes. Well, not completely. Ploddy walked with me here and shall walk me back. But until then I am completely on my own," she said. Too late, Amelie recalled that unmarried ladies in society did not leave their homes without a chaperone. What rubbish. For the first time it dawned on Amelie that the society she longed to know might not be everything she liked. "Do you disapprove?"

He looked taken aback by her question. Had she made another faux pas?

"You oughtn't," she said, a little stung by his continued silence. "Who is supposed to attend me when Fanny is unavailable, and what purpose would they provide? I do not require a keeper, Lord Hayden. I am not a toddler."

He continued to regard her with slack-mouthed wonder. Was she so very odd then?

"Please say something, Lord Hayden."

He blinked, coming out of whatever trance held him. "Excuse me. You're just so . . ."

She braced herself to hear the word *unpolished* or worse.

". . . refreshing!"

She relaxed, her face blooming in a wide smile. "Refreshing?"

"Yes." He nodded vigorously. "I am sorry you could think I was such an old fogey. I could never disapprove of a young lady I only wish to impress favorably."

He wished to impress her favorably? How utterly lovely! "Really?"

His boyish smile took on a more debonair cast as he looked deeply into her eyes. "Really."

She blushed.

He offered her his arm. "May I accompany you to wherever it is you are going?"

Oh, blast. What to say now? They could go to Donnie's tavern, but she doubted even the most relaxed gentleman would like to think a young lady passed her free time in a pub. Then she recalled that Johnston had recently installed a liquid carbonic tank in his inn. Surely an inn wasn't the same as a tavern, even an inn that was in actuality a tavern (seeing how no one but the very incidental traveler ever stayed there).

"I was shopping but I find I am quite thirsty. I don't dare go into a tavern by myself." She glanced sideways to see if he was impressed by this show of maidenly modesty. "But the inn has recently had a soda fountain installed." She let the implication dangle.

"You've never had a soda drink?" he asked.

"No."

"Well, we shall have to rectify that straight off. Which way is this inn?"

She nodded down the street and tucked her hand in the crook of his arm as he led her forth.

"If you weren't thinking you disapproved of me," she said, "what were you thinking?"

"How intrepid you are," he answered.

"Intrepid?" Now she was surprised.

"Why, yes. Here you endure under an unknown threat and yet there is nothing about you to suggest an ounce of anxiety. I call that intrepid." He leaned a little closer. "That isn't to say I approve. I don't know that I like the thought of you all alone in this town, without anyone to watch over you."

She felt a thrill run through her, but her innate honesty forced her to reply, "Really, Lord Hayden, I am sure there is no need for alarm. I may not be the most popular person in town, but I am the most important, and there is no one in Little Firkin who isn't well aware of it."

"What remarkable clearheadedness," he said admiringly. "So few of the young ladies I meet would be capable of such reasoned thought. Or even want to attempt it. You almost convince me."

She blushed again. He was too wonderful! "Please do be convinced. I should hate to have a pall cast over your visit here."

"Then there won't be," he avowed. "I hereby declare our visit here a holiday."

"And what are we celebrating?" Amelie asked, charmed.

"Why, my meeting you, of course," he said.

And the day only got better from there.

Chapter Eleven

The day of the dinner party, Fanny awoke to the sound of pots and pans crashing, a young girl squealing, and an older woman shouting: Miss Oglethorpe and Violet engaged in battle.

The day only got worse after that.

Amelie was still not speaking to her after she'd roundly chastised the girl for disappearing into Little Firkin yesterday, only to return hours later glowing like a candelabra. Fanny had been about to start down the road to Little Firkin when she'd spied Amelie and Ploddy making their way back to the house. When they'd reached her, she'd given the girl a sharp dressing-down, even though she knew she was being unreasonable. Amelie had always enjoyed free rein of the town. What could she do—keep Amelie prisoner at Quod Lamia until the author of the letter had been revealed? And what if that never happened? The letter had been dated three weeks previous, and in the interim nothing unusual had happened.

But as she performed her morning's toilette, she kept seeing Oglethorpe's livid face. Could Oglethorpe have gone dotty? Reportedly, in the last few years his sermons had grown even more rabid. And really, he needn't have gone dotty to be at the root of this mystery; he needed only for someone else to think he was dotty. Perhaps Miss Oglethorpe, after hearing his spittle-attended sermon, had decided that he was crazy and so written that letter. Not so much out of fear for Amelie, but out of fear that if her brother killed Amelie, she'd be out of a cushy job. By the time Fanny went downstairs, the musing and worrying had started her head aching all over again. She found Miss Oglethorpe waiting for her at the bottom of the steps, her round, flat face set in a pugnacious expression.

"There's nothing fer to make a decent dinner this evenin'," she declared in her thick Highland brogue. "Tha' slattern Violet hae left the door open ta the ice chest and the eel's spoiled."

"Miss Oglethorpe," Fanny said, "did you write a letter to Lord Collier saying that Amelie's life was in danger?"

Caught off balance by this unanticipated sally, Miss Oglethorpe rocked back on her thick heels. "Why would I do a fool thing like tha'?"

"Someone did."

"Well, weren't me."

"Do you have any idea who might have?" Fanny asked.

Miss Oglethorpe bent a cold eye on her. "No. I don't and I don't care to. Whatever troobles ye and tha gel hath broot down on yer heads is nae concern of mine," she said, and then, the matter settled, she asked, "Wha' would ye hae me do aboot dinner?"

Fanny wasn't sure whether she believed the woman

or not but recognized that asking further questions would be a waste of time.

"Well?"

"I'll send Violet to town for a nice joint of beef," she said.

Miss Oglethorpe crossed her arms over her broad chest. "There'll be no joint. I had me plans and they'll stay as is or I'll no' be cookin'," she said. "Dinner was to be fish, and I already made those things best with fish, and I'll not change me mind cause some wee scrawny slut canna shut a door proper."

In the end, Miss Oglethorpe ruled the day; Fanny would have to go fishing.

Even though she resented having to fish for Grey Sheffield's meal, generally Fanny would have looked forward to a morning spent knee-deep fly fishing in the crystal-clear waters of Quod Lamia's small loch. But today, she hadn't time to enjoy the beauty of the dark water or the thrill of flicking the mirrored surface with her fly line.

Instead, she would need to drag Amelie's little dinghy into the lake, row out a hundred feet or so, dump a hook over the side, and wait for some stupid pike to take it. She had no doubt it would. The loch was teeming with pike. She just hoped it didn't take too long.

She changed into a dark serge skirt and plain white shirtwaist, donned sturdy shoes, and tucked her hair beneath a soft cap before heading to the loch. There she found Amelie's dinghy overturned on the shore, where it had been left since last fall, chained and padlocked to the end of the dock. The boat had been Fanny's present to Amelie on her sixteenth birthday, her attempt to encourage the girl to partake of more physical exercise. Fanny smiled. Amelie loved the dinghy but was more likely to be found floating in it about the loch, her hand drifting in the water, than actually rowing it.

She unlocked and overturned the boat, loaded her fishing kit and the new fishing rod, and looked about. The water level was low, half the short dock on land. She would have to wade in, shoving the boat ahead of her until its keel cleared the rocky bottom. That was just the way the day had gone. Sighing, she resigned herself to wet feet. Luckily, her garments were made for practical outdoor use and not fashion.

Once in the dinghy, she rowed toward the center of the loch, where a submerged rock shelf often attracted decent-size fish. It didn't take long to reach her destination. The loch wasn't very big. She threw the anchor overboard and dropped her line, noting with dismay that she'd hauled a fair amount of water in on her skirts. She lifted her feet out of the water pooling in the dinghy's bottom and onto the bench in front of her.

A pleasant breeze ruffled the loch's sapphire surface, and the scent of flowering plums wafted gently across the water. The bright sun dazzled her eyes. She stripped off her jacket and tucked it in the boat's prow, then leaned back, using it as a pillow. She looped the fishing line loosely around her fingers and, tipping the brim of her soft cap forward, closed her eyes. The spring sun toasted her cheeks and soaked through her cambric shirtwaist. . . .

With a start, she came awake, her fishing line cutting into her fingers. She bolted upright and her feet landed in cold water. She jerked them up and stared.

Water had filled the bottom of the dinghy. Far more than she'd brought in on her skirt.

She looked over the gunwales. There were mere inches of freeboard. The boat was sinking. She stared, looking for something with which to bail out the boat. There was nothing. She wasn't afraid; she was a first-rate swimmer. She was mostly angry—angry at the loss of her boat, her fishing rod, and her dinner.

"No!" she shouted, standing up. The water swirled, her hem floating around her calves, and the boat, already unsteady, wobbled. She sat back down and, muttering curses Amelie would be shocked to learn she knew, wrenched off her shoes and socks. She had just reached behind her waist to unbutton her skirt when a gush of water erupted from the middle of the boat. With nary a whimper, Amelie's dinghy headed for the bottom of the lake.

The shock of the icy water took her breath away. For the first time, a tendril of unease touched her. She struck out for shore, and the movement jerked the fishing pole from her hand. Freed, it started sinking slowly away from her.

Without thinking she dove after it. Ten feet below, she snatched the fishing rod and jackknifed around, kicking hard against the drag of her sodden clothing. Unease jettisoned into fear. She was a strong swimmer, yes, but the water was ice-cold, far colder than any water she'd ever been in before, and her skirts felt leaden around her.

She dropped the pole and raised her arms, spearing upward. Kicking violently, she broke the surface, choking and gasping for breath and—

Something snatched her around the waist.

She cried out, thrashing.

"Don't struggle!" a deep voice commanded.

She jerked her head around and found herself staring into the beautiful blue-green eyes of Grey Sheffield. She nearly sank again then, out of pure amazement, but he held her.

"No . . . I . . ." She tried to tell him she could swim, but her lips had grown numb.

"Stop trying to swim. I've got you," he growled. He looped his arm around her chest and headed toward shore, her body supported atop his.

It took only a short while for him to swim to shallow water. Once there, he stood up and effortlessly plucked her from the loch's chill embrace into his much warmer one. Without thought, she curled into that warmth, wrapping her arms tightly around his neck as she instinctively sought to steal his heat.

Since she was a child, she had not taken refuge in another's strength. But Sheffield was so strong, and she was so cold, and she wanted to be comforted. She pressed her eyes shut and drank in the sensation of being cared for . . . safe.

Too soon he dropped to one knee and gently laid her on the ground. He pulled her sodden cap from her head and carefully brushed her wet hair from her face. His touch was immeasurably gentle, his fingertips as light as a kiss.

She opened her eyes. He was bending over her, his dark head backlit against the brilliant sky, his black curls sparkling with water. She could not see his face.

"Mrs. Walcott?" he asked.

"I'm fine," she said through chattering teeth.

"Right. I, too, consider blue lips and an opalescent

complexion fine." His voice was dry, but she thought she heard relief there, too.

He reached behind himself, then eased his arm beneath her shoulders and wrapped his jacket around her. It was dry and warm. He must have shed it before swimming out to her.

"Better?" he asked.

She nodded, shivering. "Thank you. I don't think I would have been able to swim to shore. My skirts . . . were so . . . heavy."

"Well," he said gruffly, "we shan't ever know." Then, without asking permission, he sat down next to her and gathered her close, her back against his chest, tucking her head beneath his chin. It was an oddly natural act of charity from a man whom the penny press claimed had none. It was even more oddly easy for her to accept it.

"There, now," he murmured against her hair. "There."

He gathered the collar of his jacket high under her chin and cupped her cheek with his broad palm, urging her to lay her head against his chest. It was a wonderfully broad chest. It didn't take much urging. Even though he was as wet as she, he still exuded a wonderful heat.

He gathered her hair in a thick coil, held it away from them, and wrung it out. She didn't protest. She couldn't have found the breath to do so; his ministrations had stolen it away. She could not remember the last time she'd experienced such casual intimacy.

He dug in the outer pocket of the jacket and withdrew a folded silk handkerchief and, with that same devastating familiarity, dabbed her face dry.

"There," he murmured again, finishing.

Warily, she nestled closer, relaxing slowly when he didn't tense.

"Now, what the hell were you doing in a leaky boat in the middle of a freezing cold loch?" he asked mildly, reaching around her and tugging on the boots he'd apparently shed somewhere along the way.

She didn't take exception. She was far too comfortable. She could rest like this forever.

"Well," she began, "I was—" She bolted upright.

"What is it?" he asked in alarm.

"My fishing pole!" she said. "My brand-new fishing rod and reel and all my tackle. It's gone. Sunk. And the fish, too."

"The fish?"

"The pike I'd caught for dinner this evening."

He took her shoulders in his big hands and gently pulled her back, rumbling, "Stay put. There's nothing to do about it now, and you're white as chalk and shivering like aspic on a ship captain's table."

She made no attempt to resist. He was right. The rod, the reel, the fish, and the boat were all lost causes.

"So, you were fishing for dinner," he said, "and the boat just capsized?"

"No," she answered. "There must have been a leak in it. I had set the anchor and dropped my line, and I must have dozed off for a few minutes. I woke when I felt a tug on the line and found the boat half-submerged."

"You didn't notice anything before today?"

"No. But I wouldn't. No one has used the boat since last fall. Normally I would have made sure everything was in proper working condition before I let Amelie . . ." A terrible thought seized hold of her. She came upright out his arms again, and this time he let her go.

She turned to him, only half-aware that she braced a hand on his thigh as she did so.

His blue-green eyes scoured her face questioningly. "Amelie?" he repeated.

"The boat is hers."

He frowned. "You think someone purposely damaged Amelie's boat, hoping she would drown?"

Fanny gazed helplessly at him. "Amelie wears far more elaborate clothing than I," she said, unable to keep the quaver from her voice. "In her usual skirts or dress she would have been so weighed down she would have sunk like a rock."

His dark skin turned ashen. "Thank God you dress more sensibly than that."

"Do you think this could have been an attempt on her life?" she asked. He might consider her his enemy if he knew who she was, but she knew he was good at what he did, and she respected his opinion.

His frown deepened as he thought. "You just said you would normally inspect the boat before she put it to use. I assume you take equal care with her safety in other areas?"

She nodded.

"And this is well-known?"

She flushed. "I take my responsibilities quite seriously," she admitted.

Did a smile flicker over his stern face?

"And does no one but Miss Amelie and you use the boat?"

"Sometimes Ploddy. And I suspect Violet's filched the padlock key now and again for her relatives." At his quizzical expression she explained, "Violet is one of our servants. In a manner of speaking."

He let that pass. "You say you suspect, but do you *know*?"

She was reminded that by training Sheffield was a lawyer. "I know," she admitted, and then she added, "There are few secrets in Little Firkin."

He regarded her for a long moment before finally speaking. "I don't think this was an attempt on anyone's life. The method is too sloppy, too reliant on chance and happenstance for its outcome. The boat might be inspected beforehand, or tied in the water at the end of the dock and seen to be sinking. The occupant might not be the intended victim. The boat might sink too fast, or within wading distance of the shore, or sink too slowly, allowing the victim time to return. Indeed, had you not dozed, you probably would have seen the water early enough to row back to shore"— a smile flickered across his hard face—"with your pike."

Warmth and gratitude filled her responding smile. She was more worried about this letter than she'd realized. "Thank you," she said earnestly. "You've put my mind considerably at ease."

"I am happy to oblige," he responded.

She hesitated, then said, "Please, can we keep this between us two? What with the letter and everything, I don't want Amelie jumping at shadows or seeing threats in every corner. I think one of us doing that is sufficient," she finished ironically. She turned her head and was surprised to discover they were smiling at each other.

"You don't strike me as the type to jump at shadows."

She sighed. "I wouldn't have said so, but apparently my imagination isn't always at my command." The realization alarmed her. One good episode of uncontrolled histrionics and voilà! The animals would come running and she could become the Pied Piper of Little Firkin.

"You said you take your responsibility for Miss Amelie seriously, but I think it is more than duty that motivates you," he said in an odd tone.

She saw no reason to deny it. "Amelie is as close to a family as I know. I love her."

He cocked his head. "You have no one else?"

"I have a brother and sister, but . . . we do not speak."

She expected him to say he was sorry. It would be the acceptable response, but then, this was Sheffield. "What of your parents?"

"Deceased."

"And your husband's family? Or is the title 'Mrs.' an honorary one?"

"No. I am a widow," she said, stiffening. "And he had none. At least that I am aware of."

"How is it you came to work for Colonel Chase?"

"His country house was close to my family's," she replied shortly.

"Oh?"

He was asking too many questions and her wariness, absent for a short while, rushed back. "So many questions, Lord Sheffield. Should I be seeking counsel?"

She had tried to make the reprimand sound light-hearted, but his eyes narrowed. "I don't know. Have you done anything wrong?"

"Oh, doubtless many things," she said, donning once more the armor of insouciance.

"Then best pray I don't discover them," he advised.

"Well, then I shan't answer any more questions, lest you lure me into revealing my dark past."

It was a high-stakes game she played, hoping to divert his suspicions by inviting them, and she could not tell whether she succeeded. She moved away from him, putting distance between them. Having done so, she could for the first time see more than his shoulders and face.

His wet shirt clung to his upper torso, molding tight to the planes and angles of a brawny chest, flat, corrugated belly, and muscular arms. Water made the fine cloth transparent, revealing the dusky hue of his skin and the black hair covering his chest.

She looked away, praying her flesh was still too cold to raise a blush. He leaned toward her, bracing his weight on one fist planted on the ground between them. The movement did fascinating, subtle things to the muscles along his rib cage and shoulders. No wonder he'd handled her weight so easily. He was composed of nothing but brawn and bone and dark, bronzed skin. Like some dangerous predatory animal.

And that, she reminded herself, was what he was: a predator focusing his sights on anyone stupid enough to attract his notice. A bird of prey set loose in the skies above London to rid it of vermin. Like Alphonse. And her.

Caution and common sense came crashing back.

Divert by invitation? The man was a seasoned investigator and a renowned barrister. She'd been an idiot to think to play games with him. She had only one hope of coming out of any encounter with Lord Sheffield unscathed, and that was not to have any encounters.

"Good God, you're shaking like a leaf. We have to get you warmed up." He stood and scooped her up again into his arms. This time she was not nearly so comfortable. She was aware of each shift of tendon and sinew against her body, of the breadth of his hand spanning her waist, the rise and fall of his chest with each breath he took.

"You can put me down." Her voice was chill with fear. "I can walk."

"Nonsense. You don't weigh more than a drowned cat."

"*Put me down*," she said, taking refuge in flinty imperiousness. "I am not a sack of flour to be manhandled about at your discretion."

Spots of dark bronze appeared high on his cheeks. Without another word, he set her on her feet and stepped away.

"I shall send someone with your jacket as soon as I return to Quod Lamia," she said.

"It can wait until this evening." He looked embarrassed, angry, and confused by her abrupt coldness. Which was good. She knew it was good. But it seemed a poor sort of way to thank him for rescuing her and reassuring her and holding her and making her remember how it felt to have someone take care of you rather than always being the one to take care.

"Thank you," she said, hating the stiff formality in her voice.

"My," he said. "If that didn't sound like it cost you a pint of blood."

She flushed, pretending not to hear. Could he never act in the prescribed manner? Why didn't he just bow and go away, like a normal man? She fought back a retort and instead turned away. She heard his footsteps behind her. She looked over her shoulder.

"Please. It isn't necessary for you to come with me.

Quod Lamia is only a quarter mile through that pine wood," she said, nodding toward the wood's edge. "In fact, I insist."

There was nothing he could do but acquiesce, but this he did with poor grace.

"Fine," he said, crossing his arms over his chest. He just stood there.

"Are you going to just stand there and watch me?" she asked.

"Unless you object to that, too," he said.

Oh, she wanted to. She wanted to stay, too. She could feel the heat of battle rising in her veins, a singing sort of vibrancy she had come to feel comfortable with. From the pine wood, some gray jays began squawking loudly.

Oh, God. They felt it, too.

"Good-bye, Lord Sheffield," she said, and hurried away, all too aware of his eyes on her.

And the scolding chatter of a dozen jays.

Chapter Twelve

Grey watched Fanny stomp her way into the pine grove and disappear. Only then did he turn.

Dictate to him where he must go and whom he could watch, would she? The sun and the brisk breeze coming off the mountains had nearly dried his shirt, but his trousers and socks were still wet. And cold. And bloody uncomfortable. All of which he deserved for acting like such a raw, heated, untutored boy.

By God, he couldn't believe the woman had actually made him blush. *Blush.* He hadn't blushed since he was sixteen and a doxy purporting to be Cleopatra's "spirit" had landed in his lap hands first. There had been nothing spectral about her fingers.

Now, let Fanny Walcott imply that he was reluctant to let her go and he pinked up like a virgin. Because he had been reluctant, damn it. Even though his ministrations had begun innocently enough, there had been little innocence left by the time she demanded he put her down in that crushing tone of voice.

His actions had started out noble. He had been walking past the small loch on his way to Little Fir-

kin to further his "investigations" when he'd spied
the dinghy bobbing low in the water. Thinking it had
come loose of its mooring, he'd wandered down to
offer his assistance, arriving at the shore just in time to
see Fanny shoot to her feet in the center of the boat, sit
down again, and promptly sink.

He'd shed boots and jacket and been in the water
before he even realized what he was doing. His heart
had thundered in panic as he swam, matching an
inner litany suspiciously like a prayer. *No. No. Please.
Not after I've finally found her. Please. Let me be in time.*
And when she'd disappeared beneath the water, then
abruptly resurfaced, and he'd snatched her to him,
nothing save death could have wrested her from his
grip. His preoccupation with the woman had become
something more, something . . . potentially dangerous.
He could not remember the last time he'd felt this sense
of jeopardy. But jeopardy from what? And threatened
by whom? That slender black-haired tartar? Though
he periodically kept company with one of several intelligent and lovely ladies, not one of them had ever so
fascinated him.

There was only one viable explanation: The excitement of the moment had led him, the least fanciful of
men, to succumb to a fit of fancifulness. That was it.
Her narrow escape from tragedy had produced in him
a heightened emotional state. There was probably even
some sort of biological imperative that could have explained why. There. A rational explanation. He liked
rational explanations. He depended on them. He lived
by them.

Satisfied, Grey turned back to Collier's lodge. He
doubted he'd have discovered anything about the

threat to Amelie Chase in Little Firkin, anyway. But because he'd promised his efforts and he did not lie, he would go tomorrow.

He entered the lodge through the kitchen and met the startled stares of the middle-aged cook and her husband, both peeling vegetables at the sink. The pair, who worked for His Lordship, had come ahead of Grey and Hayden to open Collier's newly refurbished lodge.

Grey stripped his jacket off and tossed it across the table. "Twinnings, isn't it?" he asked the man, hopping on one foot as he took hold of his boot heel.

"Yes, milord," Twinnings said, setting down his carrot. "Can I be of service, milord?"

"Indeed you can, Twinnings." Grey grunted as he tugged on his boot heel. "You and Mrs. Twinnings have been here a few weeks now. You must have had conversations with some of the locals."

"Of a limited variety," Twinnings intoned.

"What is the general feeling toward Miss Chase and"—he jerked the boot free and sent it spinning across the tile floor—"Mrs. Walcott?"

Twinnings, bless the man, was far more astute than McGowan. He understood at once what Grey was after.

"Resignation, sir. Nothing more, nothing less."

"That ain't so, Mr. Twinnings," Mrs. Twinnings said. Not to be outshone by her husband, she spun around, a half-peeled potato in her hand. "There is also a dollop of chagrin about Miss Chase and a heaping spoonful of umbrage with regards to Mrs. Walcott."

Ah. Culinary metaphors. He liked the woman at once. "Why do you think that is?" Grey asked, yanking off his other boot.

"They've no doubt Miss Chase is a witch, but it makes them feel at odds with themselves. Not because she's a witch, as they say there's always been witches hereabouts, but because they must *harbor* her."

"Harbor?" Grey handed his boots to Twinnings.

"There's a line between 'coexisting' with a witch and 'harboring' a witch, and it's clear it's one they feel they've crossed," Twinnings explained, patiently waiting for Grey to strip off his sodden socks. "But they're practical folk, and the economic advantages to harboring witches are apparently considerable." He waited for Grey to divulge a bit of gossip. Grey disappointed him.

"Still, makes their consciences wiggle a bit," Mrs. Twinnings insisted.

"Wiggly enough to try to get rid of Miss Chase?"

"Get rid of Miss Chase?" Twinnings breathed, shocked.

Grey, who'd been musing over the matter on his way back to the lodge, held up his hand. "Do not let your imagination run away with you, Twinnings. I mean 'get rid of' as in frighten the girl away."

This explanation for the letter struck Grey as being far more reasonable than the idea that someone actually meant to kill an innocent girl. Or even an innocent witch.

Mrs. Twinnings answered. "I don't think so, sir. I'd say most of the folks hereabouts is too lazy to kill the goose what laid the golden egg. They been expectin' a nice little golden egg for years, and with only a few more to go, it don't make sense someone would choose now to get all morally affronted, like."

"Morally affronted," Twinnings scoffed. "How would you know?"

"I know people," Mrs. Twinnings stubbornly declared.

"Then what is your opinion of Mrs. Walcott?" Grey said.

"Never met the lady," Mrs. Twinnings said, adding before Twinnings could speak, "Neither has he.

"But," she went on, "from what I hears tell, she's a lady keeps her own company, has a right sharp tongue, and doesn't take no guff from no one." Mrs. Twinnings's expression grew sympathetic. "Course, bein' a woman alone up here and head of a household and then havin' to get these Scottish heathen men to do for you would be a trick and a 'alf 'less you did have a tongue like a razor."

"Anything else?"

Mrs. Twinnings shrugged. "A bit flinthearted. Won't even let Miss Amelie keep a pet dog."

"She's unkind to Miss Chase?"

"No, you misunderstand. She's loves that girl. It's just not her nature to be all lovey-dovey. Why, from what I hear, this spring the girl and Mrs. Walcott both come over sick, and even though she were the sicker of the pair, Mrs. Walcott gets out of 'er bed to tend the girl through that night and the next. And when they're well, she makes sure the girl has anything her heart desires. Anything money can buy. 'Ceptin' livestock in the house. Can't say I blame her. My sister had a rat terrier once that she kept in the house, and that dog peed all over—"

"That's enough," Twinnings said, returning from laying Grey's socks by the stove. "Excuse her, Lord Sheffield. She forgets to whom she's speaking."

But Grey wasn't paying attention. Another idea had

occurred to him. Two pieces of information kept being repeated from various sources: Fanny Walcott was devoted to Amelie, and Fanny had been "beside herself" when the girl had fallen ill this spring.

If nothing else, he was convinced that Fanny's affection for Amelie was real. And though logically he knew that affection did not preclude one from using another for one's own purposes, he knew Fanny would never put the girl in harm's way. He did not even pause to consider why he felt so strongly or even if it was rational. It was just true.

When Amelie had grown so gravely ill, Quod Lamia's isolation and the town's dearth of qualified medical care must have been borne in on Fanny with frightening significance. Had the episode so shaken her that *she'd* written the anonymous letter in the hope that Amelie would be removed from Little Firkin before something even more dire occurred?

Grey considered. The hypothesis fit with the known facts. It made sense. It even allowed for his unprecedented feeling that Fanny Walcott was not a heartless cheat and a fraud. True, she would still in effect have been perpetuating a deception, but at least her motive had merit.

But then he thought of her expression as she'd begged him for reassurances that Amelie Chase's boat had not been sabotaged. Could she be *that* good an actress? He did not know.

He did not trust his own judgment where that woman was concerned. He was too close; there was too much past between them; she engendered too many things for Grey, and most of them at odds with one another: disapproval, empathy, condemnation, excitement, challenge, camaraderie. Desire.

Whatever was going on here, he knew in his bones that Fanny Walcott was at the center of it. But what was it? Only she knew. He had one thing working to his advantage: She still did not know that he recognized her. If he could provoke her enough, she might give herself away and in doing so reveal her plan.

It was worth a shot.

"Will there be anything else, milord?"

"What?" Grey looked up to find Twinnings waiting attentively.

"Can I be of further service, sir?"

"No, that will be—" Grey stopped and considered Twinnings.

"Milord?"

"Twinnings," Grey said, "do you fish?"

Chapter Thirteen

It took Hayden two hours to find and dress in an outfit he deemed suitable for an evening in the company of an angel. It took Sheffield fifteen minutes. Which was, Hayden noted, ten more than he usually spent.

Bernard McGowan picked them up from Lord Collier's hunting lodge in his carriage and conveyed them past the small loch where Grey had found Fanny earlier, and a short distance up the mountain.

They arrived at a large, many-cornered, various-storied house built of quarried stone. The broad porch spanned the entire front before wrapping around the west facade, while the east corner of the house sported a fat tower irregularly punctured by oriel windows and capped by a slate roof. In short, it was as modern-looking a home as any found in London's more fashionable suburbs, made doubly incongruous by its wild backdrop of mountains.

"This is Quod Lamia," McGowan said as they descended from the carriage. "A handsome place, isn't it? I believe in America the style is known as Queen Anne."

Before McGowan could knock, the massive front

door swung open, revealing a crooked old man exuding a strong scent of whiskey. He waved them in with an air of resignation, taking their coats before leading them down a broad hallway cluttered with tables, statuary, and various unrecognizable contraptions and thingamajigs into an even broader and more cluttered drawing room.

"Ploddy was Colonel Chase's batman," Bernard explained as the old man shuffled off. "Poor chap has a bit of drinking problem. Mrs. Walcott does well to keep him sober most days. It looks as though this isn't one of them."

Hayden looked around in fascination. The room resembled a magpie's nest, overflowing with gimcrack and gewgaws. Having learned yesterday—and what a wonderful day it had been!—the history of those who lived in the house, he found it odd that every surface bore evidence of exhaustive travels no one living here had ever undertaken. There were bell jars encasing exotic butterflies, etchings of noble edifices in Greece, leather-bound tomes in Arabic script, delicate ivory oriental figurines, hand-colored daguerreotypes, and brightly feathered examples of the taxidermist's art. Unfortunately, a fine layer of dust covered much of these treasures. Hayden sneezed.

The room stood in need of a thorough cleaning and some sort of attempt at organization. Stacks of newspapers and journals jockeyed for space on tables already littered with books and clippings. Had he thought it a magpie's nest? More like a tinderbox. God help them if a fire ever broke out.

"Gentlemen." Mrs. Walcott appeared in the doorway, her hands folded at the waist of a modest pearl gray gown, a few touches of lace discreetly embellishing its neckline. She surveyed them with much the same look an iron-fisted governess might wear upon being presented with a trio of pupils whose reputations as troublemakers had preceded them.

She'd be a stunning woman, Hayden thought, had she worn a softer, more feminine expression instead of such a sardonically assessing one. It unnerved a chap. It also reminded him of someone. . . .

"Amelie will join us momentarily. In the meanwhile, may I offer you something to drink?"

Hayden was just about to accept when a light, feminine voice hailed, "Good evening, gentlemen."

"Miss Chase . . ." Hayden's words trailed off into love-struck silence.

Amelie's soft lips parted as though she were going to speak, but instead they curved into a shy and radiant smile.

Hayden never would be able to recall exactly what she wore that evening, only that it was something pale, frothy, and light, a cloud of shimmering lace and tulle that rustled when she moved and revealed the sweet swell of her bosom, the slope of her shoulders, and the tiny span of her waist. She looked like a fairy-tale princess come to life.

Hayden gaped at her. In London, had he become so completely speechless, he would have felt gauche. But this was not London, and besides, he'd never been rendered speechless by the sight of a young lady before. But it wasn't simply the sight of her that beguiled him; it was Amelie herself.

She was utterly unlike any young lady he knew. Her enthusiasm for, well, everything was infectious. Her eagerness to experience and enjoy things was contagious. When he was with her, even the most mundane things seemed interesting. *He* felt interesting.

So, abandoning himself to his newly besotted state, Hayden wallowed in his intoxication. A rosy hue washed up Amelie's neck and into her cheeks. But she did not look away.

"Lord Hayden," she said, her voice a little husky.

"Yes, yes. And I am Grey Sheffield, and this is Bernard McGowan, and we did this all the other morning, did we not?" Grey's impatient voice broke their subtler communication, and for the first time Hayden found himself in accord with those social hostesses who, when informed by their husbands that Greyson Sheffield would be on their guest list, silently wished the ill-mannered fellow to perdition.

The color deepened in Amelie's cheeks. "Of course. Excuse me for being late."

"No need to apologize," Grey said, deciding to be magnanimous. "Every deb in London considers it her right to be late in order to make an entrance. No reason you shouldn't, too."

"Greyson!" Hayden breathed, appalled.

"What?" Grey asked, looking around. "Am I wrong? No. Then why are you glowering at me? You don't really believe every young lady in London is constitutionally incapable of telling time, do you, Hayden? Of course not. Their tardiness is orchestrated. No harm to it. Just a bit of showmanship, eh?"

Grey's jocularity was suspicious. What the hell was his uncle up to?

"Necessary for any sale, like . . ." Grey waved his hand, searching for an example. "Oh, what is that amusing term the Americans have for it? Ah, yes, like a snake-oil salesman hawking his magic cures. One wants a bit of a song and dance to make the wares more intriguing."

"Amelie is *not* wares," Mrs. Walcott declared icily. Until this moment, she'd been motionless and silent, her dark eyes fixed on Grey.

"Of course she is." Grey wheeled on her. He'd been waiting to engage her, Hayden realized. In fact he'd likely been deliberately provoking her to achieve this very result. There was an eagerness to his stance, a keenness in his gaze, that hadn't been there a second ago. "As is any young lady in society. Why else would they call it the 'marriage mart'?"

For a long moment no one spoke. Amelie flushed, Bernard fidgeted, and Hayden joined him. Mrs. Walcott stood rigidly. Then, abruptly, as though she had come to some decision and it had lifted a great weight from her, she took a deep breath and raised her chin. Her left brow climbed in an attitude of mockery.

"*They?* Oh. You mean your contemporaries. I fear you are dating yourself, Lord Sheffield," she said. "Your ideas are so clearly those of a previous generation. But then, you are Lord Hayden's . . . uncle, did you say? Or was that *great*-uncle?"

Hayden fought back a surprised bark of laughter. *Gad!* She'd scored a proper hit.

She continued, her tones unctuously kind. "But I suppose there's really no need for you to try to keep current with the attitudes of younger people. Many older men cling to their preconceptions. I suppose prejudices offer some comfort in a world that is changing at such an alarming rate." She regarded Grey with a sort of bland pity, making it clear she placed him amongst that company.

Good Lord. Hayden's amusement turned to awe laced with trepidation. He believed this paid companion living in a backwater hamlet in the middle of nowhere had just called his sophisticated, thoroughly au courant uncle an old mossback.

"Why, you baggage," Grey uttered in a hushed and wondering voice. "You incorrigible bit of *baggage.* What cheek!"

Hayden started, shocked speechless by Grey's rudeness. Even for his uncle this was extreme.

"Do not dare call my dear friend such a terrible name!" Amelie said, her lower lip quivering.

Grey ignored her, his gaze still on Mrs. Walcott.

"Greyson!" Hayden found his voice. "We are here as these ladies' guests."

"*Ladies,*" Grey intoned righteously, still locked in a battle of stares with Mrs. Walcott, "do not insult their guests by implying that they are ridiculous old fossils."

"*Gentlemen* do not call young girls 'wares'!" Mrs. Walcott shot back. She did not look offended. She looked angry. Grey looked angry, too. And both of them looked oddly exhilarated.

Outside, a dog began yapping.

Amelie moved closer to Hayden, as though seeking safety from a brewing storm. He understood the impulse. The atmosphere was thick with the promise of disaster. At any moment, he expected spontaneous combustion to consume them—

"I believe I would like that drink, after all." Bernard McGowan gulped.

Chapter Fourteen

Grey, along with the rest of the company, turned to McGowan. The banker stood beside the decanter, an empty glass in his hand, smiling anxiously.

For several minutes Grey had forgotten he was there, so engaged had he been in his verbal skirmish with Fanny. The audacious creature had actually been *baiting* him, thinking to best him. Damn and blast McGowan's ill-timed thirst. He'd been enjoying himself.

He glanced disgustedly at the banker, who was being soothed by a contrite-looking Amelie Chase.

"Poor Mr. McGowan," she said, laying a hand on his forearm. "What terrible heathens you must think us! Forgive us for making you uncomfortable."

McGowan flinched, doubtless at being called *poor* by the woman he'd seen as a prospective mate. "No cause for an apology, Miss Chase. None at all. Really—"

He was spared from making further reassurances by the arrival of what appeared to be a London guttersnipe. Dressed in an ill-fitting and not particularly clean uniform, a condition shared by her small, wizened face, a child stalked into the room.

"Food's waiting and getting cold," she announced.

"Ah. Thank you, Violet," Fanny said with regal aplomb.

Violet stomped off.

"Shall we?" Fanny asked, and, without waiting for a response, sailed majestically from the room.

With a relieved smile, Bernard offered Amelie his arm and followed, leaving Hayden to fall into step beside Grey.

"I am mortified to call you my uncle," Hayden murmured.

"Then don't. Grey will suffice," Grey replied.

"I am serious. Miss Chase is embarrassed, and you are the author of her discomfort. I will not—"

"Oh, for God's sake, Hayden." Grey stopped and regarded his nephew with unusual irritation. He was generally the most equitable of men. "If you're going to call me out over some imagined insult, have done with it so that I can refuse and we can carry on."

Hayden remained stubbornly mute. Grey studied his nephew in exasperation. "Do the young ladies of London really find this sort of overreaction attractive? Because if they do, I cannot help but feel pessimistic about the fate of society."

"I am sorry if my attempt to shield an innocent from your bad manners strikes you as being excessive," Hayden clipped out.

Grey clapped Hayden on the arm. "Apology accepted, old son."

"I was being sar—"

"Still," Grey interrupted, "perhaps you ought to

spend less time at the theater this year. I fear all that histrionic claptrap has inspired in you an unfortunate tendency toward melodrama."

Hayden sputtered. "You are the most im—"

"Ah, here we are." Grey shoved Hayden into the dining room, looking around expectantly, his good mood restored. Hayden, spying Amelie waiting while Bernard seated Mrs. Walcott, hurried to hold her chair. She smiled up at him. "Thank you, Lord Hayden."

"Please. I would be honored if you would use my Christian name."

She dimpled. "I thought I had."

"Without the title," Hayden said, twinkling.

God preserve us, Grey thought, watching the little by-play. Surely he'd never been so wet behind the ears, so painfully obvious?

Grey secured a seat beside Fanny, eager to renew their conversation. Hayden took the chair next to Amelie, opposite McGowan.

"Well," Grey said, as soon as they'd all been seated. "Now, about this death threat. I assume you've all spent the last few days considering any possibilities. Whom do you consider most likely to have sent the letter?"

Though he was watching for Fanny's reaction, he couldn't help but note Amelie's. The girl gasped and visibly blanched before turning huge, reproachful eyes on him. He had the uncomfortable sensation of having kicked a kitten.

"Please, Lord Sheffield. It is such a fine evening. Cannot this wait for some later time?" Amelie said.

"But the purpose of this dinner was to—"

"Of course it can," Hayden blustered manfully, his

chest puffing and his eyes flashing in the approved hero manner. "Can't it, Grey?"

"Well," Grey grumbled, caught between Amelie's reproach and Fanny's unconcealed glee. "I suppose it can."

After that the meal, punctuated by brief appearances by Violet bearing various dishes she unceremoniously slapped down in front of them, dragged on with disappointing geniality. Hayden and Amelie chattered without the apparent need to breathe, and Francesca and McGowan rattled on, too, mostly about golf, a game at which Fanny apparently excelled. Along with bicycling, tennis, and ice-skating. The woman must be a bloody Amazon. At least the food was good.

"Mrs. Walcott, have you visited London?" Hayden finally tore his attention away from Amelie long enough to ask.

"Oh, yes. At one time, Fanny lived in London with her husband," Amelie said.

Grey mentally rubbed his hands with anticipation. This was more like it. Let Fanny try to slip and slide her way through this interrogation. She hadn't the excuse of wet clothes to aid her flight.

"Did she?" Hayden asked eagerly, willing to find anything Amelie said riveting.

Amelie nodded. "When she was young."

A crocodile smile spread across Grey's lips. "*Young*, did you say?" he asked casually, leveling a pointed glance at Fanny. "And how long ago was that?"

"Oh, quite a while," the girl said, unconsciously but effectively relegating her sainted companion to the land of dodderers, where he, according to said companion, also resided. He raised his brows.

Fanny caught his glance and, rather than glowering, actually looked like she might laugh. A shock of magnetism raced through his body.

He'd always appreciated people who could laugh at themselves, and a beauty who could laugh at herself was immeasurably more attractive. And a beauty whose dark eyes invited him to share her humor was . . .

He looked away, annoyed with himself. She was not at all what he expected, the usual toadying variety of confidence artist, with facile charm and ingratiating manners, but with a dearth of wit. Fanny had no charm, facile or otherwise, her manner distanced rather than ingratiated, and her wit was as sharp-edged as a Japanese sword.

What a fascinating creature she was. How unique. On whose unfortunate hide had she honed that tongue? Had necessity made her acerbic, or was it, as Mrs. Twinnings had suggested, her nature? And was it her *true* nature? Or was this persona simply another skin she wore, like the one of Alphonse Brown's sylph-like wife?

Abruptly Grey's pensiveness vanished, replaced by chagrin.

"Before her husband . . . departed," Amelie was explaining.

"Departed?" Grey snapped, ill temper arising from his preoccupation with . . . No. From his *attraction* to Fanny. It was not only a betrayal of his father's memory but of his own logic. "Where did the fellow go?"

"To that country from which no traveler returns,"

Bernard answered with pious dignity. Grey glanced at him. Once more, he'd almost forgotten the banker, he'd been so quiet.

"Oh," Grey said flatly. "There."

He faced Fanny. "Despair not, Mrs. Walcott. I have it on great authority that even though a chap may not return to this sphere *in corpus*, he may well still be floating about nearby, sight unseen." He waved his hand at the ceiling. "Indeed, there are people who claim they can put you in touch with the dearly departed. For a certain financial remuneration. But if you'd care to take a stab at contacting the chap without one of these professionals present, I'd be more than happy to oblige. I feel certain you have the necessary sensitivity to make a go of it."

Her dark eyes shot sparks. "Thank you for your concern, Lord Sheffield, but I don't require their *or* your services."

"Why? You don't miss your husband?" he asked innocently.

"Grey!" Hayden said from the other side of the table. He tossed his napkin down and rose dramatically from his chair. "Mrs. Walcott. I am so sorry. Please accept my sincere apologies."

Fanny, who'd been grimly studying Grey, looked up at his nephew, her expression baffled. "For what?"

"For what?" Hayden echoed, nonplussed.

Grey threw an arm over the back of his chair as he watched disgustedly. Of course, Fanny wouldn't be offended by mere verbal swordplay, he thought. He would wager a year's salary that being used to fighting her own battles, she resented interference.

"Why . . . why . . . my uncle's regrettable . . . insensitivity. Regarding your bereavement," Hayden stammered.

Fanny waved a dismissive hand. "Lord Sheffield isn't the only boor I've ever encountered, young man. Nor will he likely be the last."

He watched her approvingly. He'd known he was right.

She turned her black eyes on him. "Regardless," Fanny continued, "it isn't your place to apologize for your uncle. He ought to be able to do that for himself."

If she thought to embarrass an apology from him, she would have to think again.

Hayden's eyes rounded, but he gulped and plowed on. "You are too gracious, Mrs. Walcott."

Grey snorted. Hayden shot him a glare but went on. "But I do not want you to think that I am unconscious of his earlier . . . unpleasantness, either."

"What earlier unpleasantness?" she demanded peevishly. "Lord Hayden, what are you talking about?"

He blinked.

"Yes," Grey put in, scowling. "What the blazes are you nattering on about, Hayden?"

Hayden looked from Fanny to Grey, his confusion growing. "I was concerned that you would take exception to my uncle's manner. I . . . I must have been mistaken," he finished lamely.

"Indeed, yes," Grey said. "If you'd unglue your gaze from Miss Chase and attend the conversation at the table, you wouldn't be making odd statements like this. Mrs. Walcott and I are getting along famously." He issued her a challenging glance. "Aren't we, Mrs. Walcott?"

She met it by tilting her chin up another degree and blasting him with a smile. "Indeed, we are, Lord Sheffield," she said. "Famously."

Seconds stretched into an interminable minute. Bernard shifted in his chair, Hayden tossed down the rest of his wine, and Amelie began studiously cutting the last piece of beef on her plate into minuscule portions. Once more, Violet saved the day.

"Dessert'll be in the library," she announced from the hall without bothering to enter. "Pudding."

"Lovely! I adore a good pud!" Amelie declared, overly bright.

"Me, too!" Hayden said.

"A sweet sounds just the thing." Fanny set her napkin down preparatory to pushing herself from the table, but Grey gainsaid her efforts by shoving his chair back with so much force he nearly upended it and leaping to his feet to assist her. She accepted his ministrations with a noblesse oblige reserved for royalty, the hoyden. One would think she were a queen, not a second-rate trickster.

But then he gazed down at the elegant column of her slender throat, her polished ebony hair, and the snowy sheen of her pale skin. There was nothing second-rate about her.

Someone coughed, recalling him to the present. *Damn.* She'd done it again! Used her mesmerist tricks on him. He looked around. Hayden and Amelie Chase were gaping at him.

"What?" he demanded. "Can't a fellow offer a lady a service without occasioning comment? I wasn't raised by wolves, you know."

It was only later that night that Grey realized he'd called Fanny Walcott a lady. And meant it.

Chapter Fifteen

After such a promising beginning, the evening was quickly heading toward disaster, Hayden thought, following McGowan and Amelie into the drawing room. The blasted Scotsman had taken advantage of Hayden's momentary amazement at his uncle's claim of good manners to offer his arm to Amelie. Of course, she hadn't any choice but to take it.

And what *had* Grey's bit of chivalry been about, anyway? All through dinner Grey had been variously angry, amused, and contemptuous, only to cap it all by bolting into uncharacteristic gallantry.

Once in the room, McGowan secured a place next to Amelie on the divan and commenced chatting her up with the comfortable familiarity of an old friend. A very old friend, Hayden thought, dragging an armchair next to Amelie's unattended flank. The banker had to be on the far side of thirty.

The girl, Violet, materialized. "Pud'll be late. Ploddy needs me help gettin' to bed 'counta bein' whiffed, and Miss Oglethorpe ain't willin' to serve," she announced, and vanished.

Mrs. Walcott took this news without a hint of embarrassment but with a certain degree of irritability. "He will be useless tomorrow," she muttered.

"You have an interesting staff," Hayden said conversationally.

"Servants are hard to find. Especially those willing to work at Quod Lamia," she replied, moving a stack of newspapers from a lumpy-looking armchair and taking a seat.

Grey alone remained standing. Looming, actually. Over Mrs. Walcott. Who, it must be admitted, didn't appear to notice or, if she did, didn't particularly mind.

"Colonel Chase's will might oblige Little Firkians to live in the vicinity of a witch," she elaborated, "but they refuse to enter service to one. Besides, why work when you can muddle along on credit?"

There was more than a hint of bite in her voice. She was an uncomfortable sort of woman, Hayden decided.

"We have tried importing help, but those few servants sent up from the agencies in Edinburgh rarely last out the month," Amelie put in.

"Once they discover their employer is a witch they flee?" Grey suggested.

"No. They become bored and flee. Can't say I blame them," Mrs. Walcott replied. "Little Firkin is exemplary only for its inhabitants' xenophobic attitudes. It's not fear so much as disapproval."

The conversation was getting a little stuffy as far as Hayden was concerned. "Well, I think it's wonderful you're able to make do with the elderly fellow and the girl," he said, smiling at Amelie. She pinked up delightfully.

"We have Miss Oglethorpe, too," Amelie said.

"Miss Oglethorpe?"

"She's the vicar's sister." Amelie nodded. "She cooks."

"Little Firkin has a vicar?" Hayden asked, surprised.

"Oh, no. It's far too small," McGowan put in. "The vicar lives in Flood-on-Blot, thirty miles away. It's the nearest town with a proper church."

"How ever did you convince the vicar's sister to work for you when no one else would?" Hayden asked.

"God's will," Mrs. Walcott explained, favoring them with an unexpectedly impish smile. It was a pity she didn't smile like that more often. She was really quite young, he realized.

"Though I suspect Miss Oglethorpe had a say in it, too," she continued. "Working for us, she not only gets paid but can also bring salvation into our humble lives."

Amelie's brow puckered adorably. "We are not entirely sure how our salvation is to be accomplished, however, as Miss Oglethorpe rarely speaks to us. It is a matter of some debate between us."

"She prays over the potatoes and calls good enough done," Mrs. Walcott said.

Hayden couldn't tell if she was attempting to be amusing or not, and so wasn't sure how to react. McGowan appeared to be slightly embarrassed, but Amelie didn't seem aware of anything odd about the conversation. Grey looked highly amused. "You approve of such sophistry?" he asked Mrs. Walcott.

"How can one help but approve of sophistry whose sole goal is to happily delude oneself?"

A shadow crossed Grey's face. "Delusions are never happy, because they are not real," he said bluntly.

"Only someone who has never been displeased with his reality would say that," Mrs. Walcott rejoined with equal force.

Once more the two were engaged in an invisible battle. Hayden regarded them in dismay. Frankly, all the innuendos and undercurrents between the pair were becoming tiresome. He much preferred things to be pleasant. Oh, a bit of wordplay was fine, but all this Sturm und Drang? *Bother.* Worse, Amelie had begun to feel the effect of their contentiousness. The poor darling looked unhappy. He *must* do something.

"Tell me, Mrs. Walcott," he said with determined cheerfulness, "is your Violet here under similar circumstances as Miss Oglethorpe?"

Mrs. Walcott regarded him blankly before breaking into a broad grin. "Good heavens, no. Quite the reverse," she said. "Violet is Grammy Beadle's great-granddaughter."

"Grammy Beadle?"

"The old woman in town the other day," Amelie put in helpfully.

"Violet is our resident spy," Mrs. Walcott elaborated. "She was sent here expressly to ferret out the secret of our dark power. The only trouble is, she wasn't a terribly good ferreter. Always popping up in the shrubbery, hanging upside down from the rooftop to listen in on our conversations, clamoring about in the trees to get a better look inside . . . We were terrified the lass was going to fall on her head and we'd end up being responsible for her care for the rest of her days."

"Terrified," Amelie agreed, nodding vigorously. "She's not very agile."

"Yet, no matter how many times we confronted her, she refused to desist with her lurking and go home." Mrs. Walcott paused thoughtfully. "I suppose in that she and Miss Oglethorpe are not so dissimilar."

"So we hired her," Amelie finished happily.

"She arrives at first light and goes home when she's through spying," Mrs. Walcott said. "And with whatever cleaning we can convince her to do. All in all it works out nicely."

Grey regarded Mrs. Walcott oddly. "You felt hiring the child was your only choice?"

Mrs. Walcott lifted a shoulder. "It was either that or never see another untrampled pansy again. Violet exhibits an impressive degree of determination. She is convinced that it is only a matter of time before she surprises us in the midst of performing some occult ritual."

"And will she?" Hayden drawled, hoping to achieve some of his uncle's sangfroid.

Mrs. Walcott turned her dark, implacable gaze on him. Her smile was very slow, very knowing, *very* enigmatic. A shiver touched the base of his spine.

"Oh, we're not so imprudent as that," she said. "Violet would be off to Beadletown as fast as her skinny little shanks could carry her, and we'd be fresh out of a maid. No, indeed, there's little chance of *that* happening."

Hayden's smile froze. She *must* be joking. Unless his ears were deceiving him, Mrs. Walcott had just insinuated that if Violet were more clever she might surprise them in some . . . mystical performance. He glanced at his uncle to see his reaction. Grey's complexion had grown darker. *Oh, dear.*

She'd gone too far. Grey had no patience with people who pretended to occult knowledge. Even dabblers incurred his wrath and contempt. If Hayden didn't do something, Mrs. Walcott might continue teasing and provoke one of Grey's infamous tongue-lashings, and after that . . . well, there would be little chance of Hayden seeing Amelie in a congenial setting again.

"Pray allow me to explain the reason for my uncle's purple complexion, Mrs. Walcott," he blurted out before Grey could snarl something inexcusable. "He's no sense of humor about the supernatural."

"You seem to spend a great deal of time apologizing for your uncle, Lord Hayden," Mrs. Walcott said, turning toward Grey and looking him over carefully, like a suspect bit of beef she was having second thoughts about purchasing. "Do you always?"

"Yes," Hayden breathed at the same time Amelie gasped, "Fanny! Your manners!"

"Oh, rubbish," Fanny said, reminding Hayden forcibly of Grey, then, "Fine. Forgive me, Lord Sheffield. I didn't realize you were the sensitive type. Have a bad taste in your mouth from some experience with the Unknown, have you?"

Grey replied in arctic tones, "I've never had *any* experience with the Unknown, madam. I have always known exactly with whom and with what I am dealing. Indeed, I have a reputation of making mincemeat of those pretending to an otherworldly knowledge.

"It is my vocation to bring to justice those defrauded through fakery and tricks. It is my *avocation* to make those who perpetuate cruel hoaxes suffer whilst I do so. And, lest you worry yourself needlessly over my palate, I assure you I find the taste of their humiliation quite delicious."

Worse and worse! Grey sounded like half a madman, and a very nasty sort of madman to boot. Mrs. Walcott might think twice about allowing further acquaintance between Amelie and anyone sharing Grey's bloodlines, and he couldn't say he'd blame her. If Amelie were in his care, he would certainly be discriminating about the young men he permitted near her. And while any potential suitor for Amelie's hand needed his father's approval before she was twenty-one, Mrs. Walcott had the power to ban anyone from this house.

Amelie looked positively stricken, Grey's smile looked positively feral, and McGowan looked positively ill. Only Mrs. Walcott appeared unaffected, though he could see her hands were clenched so tightly the knucklebones shone through the skin. Her cool gaze traveled lazily over Grey.

"I see," she said.

"I don't think you do, Mrs. Walcott," Hayden said desperately. "My uncle's zeal for exposing frauds has its roots in a tragic past," he rushed on, aware of his uncle's betrayed expression. Grey was an intensely private man.

"My mother was my grandfather's only child by his first wife. After my grandmother died, my mother became doubly dear to him. Even later, after Grandfather remarried and had three sons, my mother retained her position as favorite. Not only with my grandfather but with her half brothers, too. Including Grey, who was the youngest."

Hayden risked a glance at Grey. He was staring at the tips of his boots, his legs stretched out in front of him in a nonchalant attitude. Hayden knew better. He'd thrust his hands in his pockets. Like Mrs. Walcott's, they would be clenched.

"She died giving stillbirth to my brother when I was but one. It caused the entire family a great deal of pain, but none more than my grandfather. He could not bear to think he'd lost both his wife and his daughter for the rest of his life. He thus began an unhappy quest, seeking reassurance that she still lived on in some other plane and was safe and happy and awaiting him."

Mrs. Walcott's expression had not changed, but he thought he detected a flicker of some deeper emotion in her eyes. "Grey was only a boy of seventeen at the time of my mother's death. He, in particular, felt most keenly the crimes committed against my grandfather, being an unwilling participant at the séances his father forced him to attend."

"That's enough, Hayden," Grey said.

Hayden hesitated. Amelie was regarding him somberly, her eyes shimmering with unshed tears. He went on. "It has made Grey loathe what most of us would consider a harmless evening's entertainment. Not only did he witness his father's descent into despair, but he watched without recourse as his father lost most of the family's fortune to spiritualists and table rappers."

"How terrible," Amelie whispered. "I am so sorry, Lord Sheffield."

"Don't fret, my dear," Grey drawled. "After my father's death, I made sure I recovered most of it."

He turned to Hayden. "Now look what you've done. You've made poor Miss Chase weep." His gaze shifted toward Mrs. Walcott. "Thank heavens Mrs. Walcott is made of sterner stuff. Such a rarity these days, an un-sentimental lady."

"Thank you," Mrs. Walcott replied evenly. "I've found sentiment is best left to those who can afford the luxury."

"You look to have plenty of luxuries here, Mrs. Walcott," Grey said. "Foodstuffs from Harrods, Mr. Eastman's new camera, fine wine, a telescope . . . Indeed, a nicely feathered nest. Surely you can spare me one small tear?"

"A gilded cage is nonetheless still a cage."

Hayden glanced at Amelie to see how she reacted to Mrs. Walcott's statement. She was nodding in agreement. *The poor darling. The lamb.* How terrible for her. Something must be done.

"Are you asking for *my* pity?" Grey was saying to Mrs. Walcott. He sounded flabbergasted.

"Surely you can spare me one small tear?" Mrs. Walcott echoed his earlier words. Her tone was not precisely sarcastic, but neither was it sincere. She was a hard woman to read. Harder to understand. Hayden didn't even want to try.

"I fear we are both doomed to disappointment," Grey said softly.

"You can't be disappointed in not receiving what you don't expect."

Their gazes tangled and held tight to each other, bright blue-green and inky black.

Blast and bloody hell, Hayden thought. He'd had enough. If Grey and Mrs. Walcott wanted to waste precious hours embroiled in some ridiculous and overly intricate verbal fencing match, they could bloody well do so without an audience.

He stood up.

"Miss Chase, I imagine the view from the terrace is most wonderful. And I see you have a telescope out there. Might I impose upon you to show it to me?"

"I'd be delighted!" Amelie said, jumping up and taking the arm he offered. She did not look to Mrs. Walcott for permission.

Hayden did not waste time wondering whether he was being circumspect.

They fled.

Chapter Sixteen

"I had best say good night. I still have quite a bit of unpacking to do," McGowan explained a little too heartily, his gaze on the couple standing together on the terrace outside the drawing room.

In disgust, Grey noted the poor fool's bewildered expression. Here in this backwater, the banker apparently had thought his suit all but guaranteed, and so had neglected to court the girl. And now her interest had turned elsewhere.

"Must you, Bernard?" Fanny asked.

Bernard?

"I'd hoped to show you an anomaly amongst the stars that I've spotted through the telescope," she said. "It's out on the terrace. If you'd join me?"

What was she up to? She was practically purring at McGowan, who was going as red in the face as if she'd propositioned him. *Bloody ass.* She just wanted to show him a star . . . Didn't she?

Or maybe she saw an opportunity to inveigle McGowan for herself now that Amelie's fancy had turned, at least temporarily, elsewhere. Though even with a fortune attached to her, why McGowan would prefer a girl to a woman was a mystery. But no greater mystery than how a woman like Fanny could even consider McGowan a potential . . . anything. She could cow him by asking him to pass the butter. He was simply not her match.

"Thank you, Fanny. But I am not feeling quite the thing. Perhaps tomorrow?"

Tomorrow? Did the bloody man intend to live in the woman's pocket?

"Of course, Bernard." Her smile was filled with all the tenderness that had been so notably lacking when Hayden had recounted Grey's family's history—which reminded him to have a conversation with the lad about keeping the family skeletons firmly interred. Of course, had she turned those dark, luminous gems on him with any vestige of pity he would have been furious.

No. You'd have been shattered by mortification.

Had she known about his father? Had she suspected? Was her seeming indifference an act of charity? Of . . . compassion? He shook off the odd notion. It was hardly the point.

"Well, if you must, you must," she was saying. "I'll just go fetch Lord Hayden and the *three* of you"—she paused for emphasis—"can be off."

She started toward the terrace doors, but McGowan stopped her. "Oh, no! Don't spoil the evening on my account. I will send the carriage back for your guests."

"No, no. No need for that," she clipped out.

"Please," McGowan said, all earnestness. "I would never forgive myself for depriving Miss Amelie of company. She so seldom gets the opportunity to socialize with young people."

Fanny gave a start, though McGowan didn't seem to realize he'd implied she was not "young people." The man really was an imbecile. Fanny couldn't be thirty yet.

"Your generosity is heartwarming." Fanny's tone had notably cooled. "We'll see you tomorrow, I hope?"

McGowan's gaze drifted once more toward the terrace. "If I'm feeling better," he said.

"Certainly you will be well enough to—"

"For the love of God, let the poor chap go home," Grey broke in.

Like those of an infuriated cat, Fanny's eyes narrowed into slits, but she refused to look at him. Well, she couldn't avoid making eye contact all evening. Was she going to stare at the wall once McGowan shoved off?

"Of course," she said. "Good evening, Bernard."

McGowan did not need any further encouragement. He shot one more yearning glance at the terrace, tendered a tremulously brave smile at Fanny, nodded at Grey, and strode manfully from the room. Or as manfully as a fellow who wore his heart on his sleeve could manage. Which, to Grey's mind, wasn't much. Not manfully at all, actually. Fanny *couldn't* be interested in him.

Fanny watched him go.

"He seems a nice enough fellow," Grey commented. Finally they were free to return to their conversation. "Bit of a ponce, though. Were I to encounter a rival for my lady's affection, I would hardly stand aside and let it happen."

"Oh?" Fanny's tone was remarkably mild. She was still looking at the door through which McGowan had left, waiting for something. "You are not sympathetic to his situation?"

"Not in the least. But should you be, you could always present him with some sort of love charm," he said slyly. "If you only knew a witch who could make one."

She didn't reply.

"Mrs. Walcott?"

Nothing.

"Fanny?"

The sound of the front door closing behind Mc-Gowan broke the spell holding her in place. She swung on him, her skirts belling out and a long tress of black hair flying free of its tidy constriction.

"Oh, for the love of God, Sheffield," she declared. "*Do* cease with the heavy-handed innuendo. You don't honestly think you are being subtle with all those gibes and taunts, do you? I have rarely met a less subtle man. Honestly." She *tsk*ed lightly. "You ought to be ashamed of yourself."

Grey gaped at her, for the first time in his adult memory completely at a loss for words. He scrambled for a comeback. "So, you admit you are Francesca Brown?"

"Yes, yes, of course I am," she said impatiently.

"But—" He was still scrambling. "If you knew I'd recognized you, why did you not say something earlier?"

"Because," she said, gesturing toward the terrace. "Amelie doesn't know. No one does."

"You must think ours is a terribly odd household." Amelie shook her head, and the light spilling out of the open terrace doors caught on her fiery locks.

"No," Hayden whispered, transfixed by the beauty

of her profile against the majestic lilac and indigo twilight.

She gave a little laugh, unconvinced. "I must strike you as being quite uncouth. Not at all smart and dashing, like the young ladies of London." She glanced at him from beneath her lashes.

"I think you are absolutely enchanting," Hayden breathed. And he meant it.

The time they'd spent together yesterday afternoon had been the most enjoyable of his life. She was jolly and sweet and altogether swell. She had no idea of how to flirt, and so everything she said was fresh and genuine. After all the posturing and studied manners of his London set, she was like a breath of fresh air, and he couldn't bear the thought of going back to the stale confines of society.

She frowned. "I am sure you would not be speaking so boldly to one of those London young ladies."

"I wouldn't," he admitted, "but only because I would never want to say such things to them. I have never said such things to anyone before. Because I have never been enchanted before."

He heard the quick intake of her breath. "Lord Hayden!"

"Tell me you feel the same!"

And now a trill of laughter. "Enchanted? So, I am a witch after all."

He caught her hand in his, even though they stood within easy view of the open French doors. "You're quite right to laugh. I said 'enchanted' only because I am afraid of what your response would be if I were to name my true feelings."

"Are they so frightening, then?" she asked shyly.

"They are to me."

"Why is that?"

"Because once spoken, I entrust them to you and am at your mercy."

"And you think I am cruel and would abuse them? Then perhaps you'd best remain silent. Or not." She was playing the coquette, he realized in astonishment. But when she did it, she did it adorably. He wanted to seize her hand and kiss each finger from its tip to its base and then her palm and wrist and on and on . . .

"I have no choice," he declared. "I must speak!"

"You admit that you inveigled yourself into an ailing gentleman's household as a companion to his child under false pretenses?" Disappointment made Grey's voice gruff.

"No," Fanny denied flatly. "Colonel Chase knew my history. It is only Amelie who remains oblivious." She leveled him with a haughty look. "Did I say 'only Amelie'? How remiss of me."

He would *not* let her assume the role of the injured party. "That's an easy enough claim to make," he said. "Colonel Chase can hardly vouch for you, can he? Lest you intend to call up his spirit to do so. That ought to prove interesting. Perhaps you can call up a few angels to flutter about the room, too. That was your specialty, wasn't it?"

Finally, he'd managed to bring a flush of color to her cheeks. It wasn't nearly as satisfying as it ought to have been. This was what he'd wanted, he reminded himself, to catch her in her pretense and then, while she was off balance, push until she revealed her plan. Whatever that might be.

He knew she was hiding something. His instincts in this had never failed him. Whether her plan was motivated by greed or other reasons, he did not care. He cared only that she hid something from him, that some deceit was going on, and it was his avocation to uncover that which was hidden, expose lies, and reveal deceits.

"Will you tell Amelie?" she asked. The dark eyes meeting his were stricken but unwavering.

"Is there any reason I ought not to?"

When she finally spoke it was in a voice so low he had to strain to hear it. "I would not want her to think less of me."

The admission was so poignant, the explanation so simple, he almost believed her.

"And," she went on, "there is no reason to tell her. My past has nothing to do with my life now. Or with that letter. Or you. Or Lord Hayden. Or Lord Collier." She lifted her head, meeting his gaze directly. "Please."

Reason demanded he ignore her plea. He'd heard scores of the convicted ask for mercy in just such a tone. Few, if any, deserved it.

"You are claiming that after making a fortune as a sham spiritualist in London you assumed a new name, a new identity, and have hidden yourself away up here for the last six years as companion to a purported witch and kept your identity secret from everyone, with no other reason than that you wish to remain in your charge's good graces?"

"Yes!" she declared hotly. "What do you *think* I'm doing up here?"

"I'm not sure. Perhaps grooming Miss Chase to take your place in London's spiritualist salons?"

Fanny snickered. "Amelie has no psychic abilities, nor does she pretend to have them—except when goaded by the local population into putting on a show. And even if I wanted to train her as my protégée, why ever would she agree to such a thing? Money?" Her laugh was scornful. "She will be wealthy in her own right soon enough."

True. But it wasn't the only possibility. "Then perhaps you have in place a scheme to secure some of her wealth for your own?"

"And why would I do that? You certainly must know the terms of Colonel Chase's will. You seem to know everything else," she said sarcastically. "I shall be handsomely rewarded for my service here."

"Handsomely," he sneered. "Your husband stole twice the sum you've been promised from the men and women he duped in the course of four years. Such a 'reward' would seem paltry in comparison."

"I see. I am insatiably avaricious. Fine. And what is this scheme you think I have to extract more money from my situation?"

"I'm not sure. But it would rely on Miss Chase's remaining ignorant of your past."

Her skin paled. He disliked himself intensely at that moment, but then he reminded himself of all the people Brown had victimized. He did not want Amelie to be another. Still, he had to give her a chance to explain herself, even though he knew she would just spin some credible tale. It was what a confidence artist did best. But he had always been just that much better at discrediting them.

"If you are virtuous, why the assumed name? Why pretend we had never met? Why accept a position so far from that which you'd previously known?"

She cast around the room. For a moment he thought she might refuse to answer. But then she swung toward him.

"Can't you understand? Don't you see?" The words came from deep within, vibrant and intense. Outside dogs began to bay.

"I didn't want to be *her*. If I'd stayed in London, if I'd kept my name, there would be no escape from people like you! With your suspicions. Your prejudices. Your grievances."

He started to speak, but she shut him down with a burning glance. How could anyone think this woman cold? She breathed fire.

"Do not mistake me. You are entitled to your acrimony. But that doesn't mean I have to bear it willingly." Her voice broke, and he'd taken an involuntary step toward her before stopping himself.

"I saw the chance to rid myself of my past and I took it," she said. "If that makes me a coward, then that is what I am."

She waited, breathing heavily but silently, only the rapid movement of lace above her décolletage testifying to her agitation. He wanted to believe her. Like his father had wanted to believe a dozen like her. But he wasn't like his sire: an easy dupe, a prime mark, always getting his heart broken, always willing—no, always *eager*—to have it broken again until there'd been nothing left to break. He would not blindly accept the assurances of his heart.

He was made of sterner stuff than that. Tougher stuff than those who'd broken his father. Than her.

He had only history and experience to use to guide him, and her history was as an admitted bunco artist, and his experience was that cheats cheated. He owed it to his father's memory not to follow in his footsteps.

"You will forgive me if I doubt you?"

He might have slapped her. Her chin snapped up. "I don't really care what you believe," she said. "Just *please* do not tell Amelie. She wouldn't understand."

She would not let this point go. He vacillated. He could think of no reason not to keep her secret. "Unless it becomes clear it is in Miss Chase's immediate and best interest to know, your secret is safe."

She took a deep, shuddering breath. "Thank you."

"Of course," he said, his voice gruff. "And . . . don't worry." The words came out of nowhere, surprising them both.

She glanced away, confused.

Whatever she saw caused her eyes to widen. She turned back. "The only thing I am currently worried about is out there," she said, the familiar suaveness back in her voice. "And I want to know what *you* intend to do about it."

She pointed out at the deepening twilight, where Hayden had—Grey leaned forward and peered more closely—secured Amelie Chase's hand. Fanny was right to be indignant; Hayden should know to be more circumspect. But then, Hayden was naive (as only those convinced of their worldliness are naive,) and, more important, susceptible to playing Sir Galahad (as all men are susceptible, even, at one time six years ago, Grey).

Still, there was no cause for alarm as far as Grey was concerned. Hayden might be young, romantic, and enamored of his role as white knight, but he had also already spent several seasons successfully eluding the machinations of marriage-minded debutantes—a danger-fraught journey that, Grey flattered himself, his own excellent tutelage in such matters had helped pilot the boy through. Hayden might fancy himself in love with Amelie and flatter her a bit, but he would *never* raise her hopes by declaring himself.

"I love you!" Hayden declared passionately. "I love you!"

Amelie didn't swoon.

This rather disappointed Hayden, who'd been looking forward to holding her in his arms, if only to carry her back inside.

Instead, she bit her bottom lip and regarded him with a probing gaze. "You do?" she asked.

This response made him uncomfortable. Generally, when one told a girl one loved her, one anticipated an encouraging response, not suspicion. Not that he'd told other girls he loved them. True, he might have occasionally—and, in hindsight, imprudently—insinuated something similar to love, but only to be polite.

Girls, in Hayden's experience, dearly loved being loved, and occasionally, just to bring that special glow to their adorable faces, he might encourage them to hear in their imaginations what they wouldn't with their ears. But it went without saying that he would never feign a deeper affection for Amelie Chase than he felt. He could never be dishonest with her—though *dishonest* seemed a rather harsh indictment of the harmless flirtations with which he was now, and forevermore, done.

He truly, sincerely, and most ardently knew himself to be in love with Amelie, and it wounded him that she doubted him. It also presented him with a delicious challenge. He would *prove* his love and make her love him in return.

"I do love you! Please. I beg you, tell me there is hope that you could return my feelings. If not now, on some day in the future. And tell me what I can do to make myself worthy in your eyes!" he demanded, though he was having difficulty imbuing his voice with the ardency such sentiments deserved, circumstances forcing him to whisper.

"How can you love me on so short an acquaintance?" she replied. "How do I dare believe you? I may lead an isolated life, but I assure you, Fanny has seen to it that my mind has roamed free. Far freer, I warrant, than those of many of the young ladies you know. I have read all about young swells and how they like to trifle with girls' affections," she finished darkly.

"I am not a young swell. I don't trifle." He caught the hard glint in her eyes. She'd heard the hint of hesitation in his voice. *God!* It only made him love her all the more! Already she knew him better than any woman ever had. She would be the making of him. He was sure of it.

"I'm not trifling now. Not with you. And never again. You are unlike any woman I have ever met, and yet I feel I have known you forever. You are clever and artless, vivacious and adorable, unspoiled and elegant."

"You really think I'm elegant?" she asked.

"Intensely." He seized on the slight advantage, tugging her gently away from the doors.

"I say," he announced loudly. "Is that a cat down there, do y'suppose?"

Clever girl, she understood at once.

"Perhaps. Or a fox. Let us try to get a closer look, shall we?" she answered in a carrying voice. "You'd best stay inside, Fanny!" Amelie called over her shoulder. "I think there're some foxes out here."

She looked up at him from the shadows. "Fanny doesn't care for animals," she whispered. "They unnerve her."

He didn't care what unnerved Mrs. Walcott. He had Amelie well away from the door now, her small hands still clasped in his. All traces of the unsettling skepticism in her face had vanished.

"Say you can love me."

"I dare not."

"Why?" He'd meant to sound commanding; he feared he sounded petulant.

"You don't know me."

"I do. I know you in my heart. My soul is mate to your own. I was unwhole until now. I did not know how bereft I was until I looked into your eyes and—"

"But, Hayden, you don't understand. I really may be a witch."

Chapter Seventeen

Anxiously, Amelie twisted her hands together. Hayden did not look quite so dashing with his jaw hanging open, though in his defense surprise hadn't opened it. It had opened when he'd begun his wonderful, romantic speech. Surprise had simply kept it open.

To his credit, Hayden didn't actually stutter or squint or flee, all of which Amelie considered very good signs. Especially since she had fallen head over heels in love with Hayden and decided that since he loved her (and not for one instant did she believe otherwise, at least not after she'd caught him fudging a bit and he'd staunchly forfeited his part in any and all future flirtations), it would be smashing if they were to wed. She felt confident she would be the perfect wife for him.

But first, while there were some things she had no intention of revealing, she felt strongly that she must tell him about those things that made her unique. It only seemed cricket, and despite Fanny's adamancy that she ignore her exceptionalness, she knew otherwise.

Being different was what, well, made her different.

As a child on the Indian frontier, she'd gained notoriety as a good-luck talisman because of her bright red hair. She'd quite liked it. And later, in London, she'd never been frightened of the odd falling picture or sliding vase. It had been a wee bit exciting, truth be told.

She had no choice but to tell Hayden, really. It would be dishonest to do otherwise. Besides, if he could not love her as she was, then it really wasn't love, was it? She might as well know now, when the blow would be only devastating but perhaps not fatal. But, oh, she so hoped it was true love! She waited in breathless anticipation.

His smooth, manly brow wrinkled in consternation, he tipped his head to regard her soberly, cleared his throat, and said, "Ah . . . come again?"

She took a deep breath, telling herself she had nothing to fear. Love would conquer all. Even witchhood. Or whatever it was. "Well, not a witch, exactly, but I have certain attributes other young ladies do not."

"Most decidedly," he averred at once. She sighed. He was so lovely.

"Not *those* sorts of attributes. I do things. Or, rather, affect things."

He'd released her hands, she noted, and clasped his own behind his back. *Oh, dear. Not* a good sign.

"Such as?"

"Well, objects occasionally have moved when I am nearby. Without my touching them." At his expression, she hurried on. "But that sort of thing hasn't happened in, oh, years."

He stayed silent.

"Lord Hayden?" she ventured worriedly. "Hayden? Please. Say something."

"What sorts of things do you affect now?" he asked.

"Animals," she replied weakly. "I . . ." She searched for the appropriate word but couldn't find it, so she made do. "Sometime in the last six months or so, I have acquired the ability to talk to animals."

His smile faltered, true, but then he drew a deep breath, expelled it, and, without a blink, said in an almost normal voice, "How unusual. Pray, what do they have to say?"

"Well, what do you have to say about that?" Fanny repeated, glaring out toward the terrace.

"Calm yourself, madam," Grey said. "They are simply viewing the wildlife."

"Oh, for the love of all that's sacred. They most decidedly are *not* viewing the wildlife. They are canoodling."

"Canoodling," Grey repeated blankly.

"There's hanky-panky going on out there, mark my words."

"Are you under the delusion that you are speaking the King's English? Do you think you might communicate without resorting to vulgar slang?"

She set her hands on her hips, looking magnificent. She had buried her momentary vulnerability and was once more ready to do battle. He had never met a woman more bracingly audacious. . . . *Be damned.*

"Perhaps this is clear enough," she said now. "Your nephew is outside dallying with Amelie."

"Well, yes. I expect so. Strapping, red-blooded young man, pretty girl. Natural as breathing."

Her jaw slackened before snapping tightly together. She covered the distance between them with one long stride that sent her skirts swirling, giving him a glimpse of slender ankles and shapely calves, before stopping just short of him.

The scent of her surrounded him, disturbing and breath-stealing . . . *Aha! That* was why he found her so formidably distracting. Some opiate in her perfume coupled with her mesmerist's tricks would account for his inability to concentrate on anything important when she was close, like discovering what she was up to, and who—if anyone—was threatening Miss Chase.

He wouldn't have it. He would overcome this irrational fascination with the woman. He was a man of reason. She was all about illusion and deception. Why, even this persona, this formidable, dazzling hellcat, was probably just another construct.

But what to do about it? And what to do about *this*?

Whatever accusation, demand, or protest she'd been about to make had died on her lips. Her head had tipped back so she could look him more directly in the eye, and hers had grown luminous. Her lips softened, parting slightly, releasing on her breath. It carried the slightest hint of cloves. She blinked, like a sleeper trying to rouse herself from a dream but without much success.

"I will not have it," she whispered, echoing his thoughts. For a fateful instant, he thought she'd read his mind. From outside came the distant sweet, trilling song of a nightingale.

"Won't have what?" he asked, struggling to retain his composure. But he could see the pulse shivering in the elegant niche nestled above her collarbone, almost feel the velvet-silk texture of her fine-grained flesh, the silkiness of her glossy sable locks. "A bit of dalliance? Pray, do not act the prude with me, *Mrs. Walcott.* I recall quite clearly the interesting dishabille in which you displayed yourself in your husband's salon, even if you choose not to."

"I was fully clad," she said with a gasp.

"Your *hair* was down, madam," he said in his most quelling tones. Ever since he'd seen her wet hair hanging down her back, he'd been haunted by the idea of her long black tresses rippling across his palms. And every other part of his person.

An expression of befuddlement replaced her ire. More nightingales added their voices to the first. "What?"

"Don't play the innocent with me, madam. Your appearance was planned to distract men's attention whilst your husband plucked violin stings with his toes. And a damn good distraction it was. Who could spare a glance for a whey-faced spiritualist when a dark beauty was disporting herself so decorously?"

"You cad!"

"If stating a fact makes me a cad, I plead guilty," he said, feeling like an utter cad but refusing to back down. If she gained the upper hand for one instant, she would take advantage of it.

He'd known dozens of charlatans and frauds and confidence tricksters. He'd hunted them, exposed them, chased them from their dark salons and séance parlors into the merciless light of public scrutiny. He'd broken more of them than this woman had years. They were all the same, preying on grief and tragedy, exploiting their fellow man when he was at his most vulnerable. Her husband had been one of them, a pale, effete poseur with no more blood in him than a blancmange.

But she . . . ? A volatile, passionate nature roared for release beneath her icy exterior. A Valkyrie—

"Please leave."

"What?"

"Are you deaf as well as—" She bit off the last word. A dog outside began snarling. A cat answered with a hiss. "I am asking you— No. I am *telling* you to leave. Now."

Good Lord. She was throwing him out.

Now, Grey had been thrown out of places before, but never a private home. At least, not in recent history. And most certainly never by a confidence artist.

"Why are you looking at me like that? You cannot really expect to remain welcome in this house after saying such things?" She gave a short, astonished laugh. "By God, you do. You are beyond amazing."

Hurriedly, he regrouped. He wasn't ready to call it quits yet. The battle had barely begun. "You are only throwing me out to evade detection."

"Detection? Of what?"

"Exactly," he said. "Why all this hand-wringing and drama over a little—what was that word? Canoodling? Miss Chase is obviously languishing for want of some male attention, and if all she's been offered is that stick McGowan, I daresay Hayden's gallantries will do her a world of good. That banker reeks of postage paste."

"Oh!" Fanny huffed as the dog outside began his barking more emphatically. "Mr. McGowan is *not* a stick. And he does not smell like paste! He is a gentleman. With excellent manners. And refinement. He wouldn't appear at a dinner table in a—" Her scathing gaze raked over his person. "Rumpled shirt and limp tie."

Involuntarily, his hand rose toward his collar. He snatched it back.

"Nor would Bernard McGowan ever, *ever* say reprehensible things to me," she continued.

McGowan's name on her lips sent a rush of unreasonable jealousy rippling through Grey. Unreasonable, but irrefutable. And ungovernable. He spoke before he could think better of it. "Doubtless true. But neither would I. To Francesca Brown, however . . ."

Her hand shot out to strike him across the face. He didn't move, didn't flinch, the feeling that he deserved being slapped eradicating any satisfaction at having scored a point. But then, at the last instant, she jerked her hand away, staring at it in horror. Outside, another dog joined in the barking. A fox must be skirting the property.

"I will never forgive you," Fanny whispered with shaming dignity.

Luckily, Grey was not easily shamed.

"For reminding you of your former trade?"

"No. For nearly making me forget I am a lady and lowering myself to your level." It would have been fine had she stopped there. She didn't. "*And* for offending our good, our only friend here, Mr. McGowan."

Why the bloody hell did she have to keep bringing up McGowan?

"You cannot really have set your sights on that monosyllabic stamp collector?" he asked. "One would think you'd had enough of milquetoasts. Or is that the reason you don't want Hayden flirting with Amelie? Are you jealous that she might experience something you have never known?"

He waited for her to refute any attraction to Mc-

Gowan. Instead of firing back a response, she narrowed her eyes, and just as he was about to ask her what she was thinking, she muttered, "To hell with being a lady," and took a swing.

Had Amelie declared herself a leprechaun, the Queen of Siam, or an American sharpshooter, Hayden would have supported the notion. Therefore "not a witch exactly" and "certain attributes" seemed relatively minor obstacles for his love to overcome. Besides which, she'd said that the objects-moving-about thingy hadn't happened in years. Perhaps it had been nothing but idiosyncrasy, simply a phase. As for talking to animals, well . . . he liked animals.

"Oh, it's not exactly like that. There's a connection between us. I have always been fond of them, but I understand now that the affinity is closer. Last fall, I diverted a team of horses from running Fanny and me down, and . . . well, did you see the ravens in Little Firkin?"

Ravens seemed harmless enough. And as for diverting stampeding draft teams, well, one couldn't object to that. "Can you read their minds?" he asked.

"Oh, no. I don't hear anything or see anything. I don't even feel much of anything. I just have witnessed how they react to me."

"Amazing! Anything else?"

"Once in a while, when I am feeling very sad, like when I've had words with Fanny, a vixen comes and stands beneath my window and whimpers."

"That's extraordinary. You are extraordinary," he said, looking down at Amelie.

She gazed at him as though he had just ridden on his white steed over the ogre guarding her moat. She gave him a radiant smile, and his heart thudded in response. "Thank you."

"Thank me? For what?"

"Most people would have said, 'Coincidence,' 'It's your imagination,' or something like that. But you didn't. You believed me. *In* me."

"Of course I believe you. That's what people in love do. Believe in one another," Hayden replied, quite sincerely. "Besides, why ever would you lie about something like that?"

"Oh, I wouldn't exactly *lie*," she said, pinking up prettily. "But you might think I was deluding myself."

"Why would you do that? Clearly, you are a stable, levelheaded sort of girl. Normal as pie. Not at all the type to go all vaporish over some silly story she'd invented to make herself interesting. Believe me, I know."

She smiled tremulously. "Oh, Lord Hayden, *Hayden*, I do believe I love you, too!"

Hayden regarded her in bewilderment. Paeans to her beauty and first-rate declarations of love had pried only amusement from her, but tell her he didn't think she was a liar and her expression filled with as much rapture as any heartsick swain could want. Nonplussed he might be, but Hayden was no Johnny-come-lately, either. He came out of his bemused state quickly when he realized Amelie's piquant face was raised to his.

Eagerly, he raised his hands to draw her into his embrace, but then . . . then he realized that this was no ordinary girl, no society coquette, no diversion at a ball. This was the woman he loved.

Reverently, he placed his hands on the lace covering her shoulders, being careful not to touch her skin with his bare hand. Just as reverently, he stepped closer while still maintaining a respectful distance between his chest and her soft, milky— No, no. Such thoughts were inappropriate for now. Then finally, adoringly, he lowered his face to hers and, with the most reverent touch of all, pressed his lips to hers.

Grey caught Fanny's wrist before she could land the blow and tugged her off balance, tumbling her forward. Using her momentum, he spun her around, looped an arm around her waist, and pulled her back against his chest. Every detail of her form thus pressed against him awoke excruciating desire. He was aware of every soft swell and winsome valley: the glide of her hair beneath his chin, the imprint of her shoulder blades against his chest, and the lush mounds of her buttocks snuggled intimately against his groin.

"You seem to have a penchant for manhandling me, Sheffield," she proclaimed. But her voice was breathy and the chill hauteur a wafer-thin veneer. "Let me go."

He had no intention of letting her go. He'd been cowed by that tone once today. It wasn't going to work twice. He wheeled her in his embrace, one hand encircling her throat, the other tipping her chin up.

"Not this time, Fanny," he muttered as his mouth descended hungrily on hers.

For a heartbeat she froze, and then she flung her arms around his neck and was kissing him back, her mouth opening with delicious surrender, her body arching up in passionate response as he fell forward with her to the couch so conveniently at hand there. He loosed one arm and swept books and magazines from the cushions, sending them flying across the room as, lips locked to hers, he gently laid her down. Bracing a knee next to her hip, he lowered himself over her.

Her body trembled. Urgently, he combed his fingers through her black hair. A cascade of pins skittered across the floorboards as the thick, glossy veil fell free. He groaned deep in his throat, twisting a rope of the satiny tresses around his palm and pulling her head gently back.

He released her mouth, and she made a soft sound of protest before his lips fell on the smooth column of her arching neck. Through the cobweb-fine lace, he kissed her, dampening the cloth. She gasped and sighed, her arms traveling restlessly around his waist, her hands roving over his back, settling on his shoulders, only to jerk away, return, wrap tighter, release him once more, and then come back again, destroying his reason.

She seemed to have no idea how to move or where to go. Her mouth remained sealed, almost prim, but then would open intuitively, her untutored tongue devastating in its unskilled ardor. Slowly, a din of sound penetrated his conscience. Loud, caterwauling cries came from outside, where Hayden— *Good God*. If they came in, Fanny's reputation wouldn't be—

It took every bit of his effort to do so, but he tore his mouth from hers and rose, stepping back, his chest heaving like a bellows. They stared at each other, the only sound the duet of their labored breathing. Her lips were rosy and swollen from his kisses, a small piece of lace dangling loose from her collar.

He saw the self-awareness seep slowly into her onyx eyes. She scooted up on her elbows, going bright red, and touched her cheek with shaking fingers. "Don't you own a decent razor?"

A series of bloodcurdling screams splintered the still night air.

"What was that?" Hayden asked, straightening abruptly.

"A cat," Amelie said, annoyed. "Or rather, cats, from the sound of it."

"Cats?" Hayden asked, looking confused—in an entirely noble manner.

She smiled shyly. "It is, after all, spring."

"Oh? Oh!" Hayden smiled rakishly, and Amelie's cheeks warmed. He reached for her—

"Hayden! Hayden, we're leaving! At once!" Lord Sheffield bellowed from inside the drawing room.

Hayden looked over his shoulder, his face darkening thunderously.

"You'd best go," Amelie said, unable to keep her disappointment from her voice.

"I'm my own man, Amelie."

"Yes," she agreed. "Of course you are. But I am not my own woman. I am under Mrs. Walcott's care and guidance. Should she decide not to allow you into the house—and she can, you know. My father gave her authority over the household—I would have no recourse but to . . ."

She let hang in the air the suggestion that she would be forced to sneak from the house and meet him. Of course, if it came down to it, she would. One did not abandon the love of one's life over a set of unreasonable dictates. But she loved Fanny, and so would rather not deceive her more than absolutely necessary.

"You would not ask me to do anything against my conscience?" she asked, fairly certain of his answer. Still, she appreciated his insulted expression.

"I should say not! I'll go, but I'll be back tomorrow. I promise."

"I will look for you."

"Until I see you again, every second shall seem an eternity." Gracefully, he fell to one knee, securing her hands in his and gazing earnestly up into her face. "I will not be able to eat or drink. I can only hope to sleep away each hour that separates us so that I will not know the torment of—"

"Hayden, you young bounder! Now!"

Amelie, though quite liking Hayden's protestations of love, was, as he'd so discerningly pointed out, a practical girl. She grabbed hold of his arm and urged him to his feet, swiping at the dirt on his knee.

"Best go," she whispered, and then, because even though she was practical, she was also eighteen and in love, she rose up on her tiptoes and butterflied a kiss against his lips.

At once, he responded in kind. She was gratified to find this second kiss even more wonderful than the first, a fact that gave her great hopes for the third and fourth and all subsequent kisses.

Then she shoved him gently, nodding encouragingly. "Until tomorrow, then. Good night."

Chapter Eighteen

A fist hammering on her bedroom door awoke Fanny the next day. Fanny knew that hammering.

"What is it, Violet?"

"The lord from the new lodge is downstairs asking fer you," Violet yelled through the closed door. "Ye want I should send him on 'is way?"

Fanny bolted upright in her bed. "What lord? Which lord?"

"The big black-haired one."

Grey was here? What could he want? Had he come to apologize, or . . . Why even bother guessing? Grey did not follow any pattern. It was impossible to predict what the man would do or why.

"Well? I ain't got all day."

"Come in here! Stop bellowing!"

"Can't. Me arms're full of laundry," Violet replied. "Now, should I send 'im on his way or not?"

"Not! Have him wait . . ." Not the drawing room. The memory of last night was too fresh. "Have him wait in the library."

"Fine." Violet's heavy-booted tread began retreating down the hallway.

"Wait!"

"What now?"

"Has he asked for Miss Chase, too?"

"No," Violet snapped. "Now, if you don't mind . . . ?"

Fanny didn't bother replying. She looked at the mantel clock. Eight o'clock? The man had come calling at eight o'clock in the morning? He deserved to wait for his audacity. Let him wait all morning.

She flung off the blankets and hurried over to the armoire. What to wear? What to wear? Something that bespoke seriousness. Something flattering but serious. Seriously flattering. She was in a dither and she knew it, and it didn't help.

Why should she worry about impressing Grey Sheffield? He did not trust her, he thought the worst of her, and he was suspicious of her.

Lavender. The pale lavender kerchief material with the coffee brown knot design. Just the thing! Feminine but not frivolous.

She tossed the dress on the chair and flew to her dressing table, already unbraiding her hair. Last night, Sheffield had caught her off guard when he'd scooped her up in his arms as easily as if she'd been a doll. She hadn't had time to throw up defenses.

And then she hadn't wanted to.

She stared into the mirror. A stranger looked back, one with sparkling eyes and rosy cheeks, her lips swollen from kisses. Wonderingly, she touched her reflection. Was that her?

She couldn't seem to catch her breath. Sheffield had

stolen it, just as he'd stolen her peace of mind. He'd stripped away the immunity she'd spent six years perfecting. He provoked her, frightened her, amused her, incited her . . . even moved her.

She knew who'd sent the fish that had saved their dinner last night. It was an unaccountably gentlemanly gesture, and since he was, by his own admission, no gentleman, that meant his action had been inspired by something else.

What in blazes was she thinking?

She jerked her brush through her hair and wrapped it into a loose coil on the crown of her head. She didn't know whether she was a bigger fool now than she was. At least with Alphonse she'd had the excuse of being young and lonely and naive. And Alphonse Brown had been beautiful, with his delicate features, limpid brown eyes, and slender physique. Everything about him had been celestial.

There was nothing beautiful or in the least celestial about Greyson Sheffield. He was striking, imposing, disdainful, and unrepentantly earthy. Mars convicted to a sentence on earth. Her eyes drifted shut as she called up the memory of how he'd braced himself over her as he ravished her mouth.

Hers had been a nearly celibate marriage. Alphonse had claimed they risked compromising their respective "gifts" through too much carnal exercise.

Carnal exercise.

Abruptly, Fanny stood up and pulled the ties holding her nightgown at the neck so that it fell in a pool around her feet. She couldn't imagine Grey Sheffield using a term like *carnal exercise*. Something raw, offensive, and forthright, yes, that she could imagine him saying. Like the man himself, his speech would use a dizzying mixture of polish and roughness, bluntness and then refinement.

Oh, God, what was she thinking? She slipped on her undergarments. He was an *impossible*, rude, arrogant bully. But there had been instances when she'd glimpsed something else beneath his rough demeanor, a sensitivity he kept buried. A pain and even a vulnerability he went to great lengths to conceal.

She understood. She'd lived a similar life, keeping her emotions at arm's length, never daring to be spontaneous, avoiding the heights and depths of human feeling. Her brother, Wesley, and the rage that had led to his crippling was always in the back of her mind. And yet, yesterday when Grey and she had been sparring and the cats and dogs and all those dratted birds had responded, nothing terrible or dangerous had happened. And she was older now. If nothing else, her experience as Amelie's governess had taught her that pubescent girls were passionate, frenzied, liable creatures. It was perhaps her adolescent emotions that had run out of control rather than her odd . . . influence on animals.

She did not think she could feel rage in the same way anymore. She had no doubt she could feel it to the same degree, but not as something so immediate, uncomplicated by experience or conscience.

She pulled the dress over her head, trying to analyze her anticipation and, yes, undeniable pleasure. Sheffield didn't believe in anything he couldn't see, hear, or explain. To him, she was a normal woman: exasperating, vivacious, unfathomable, impertinent, if she'd correctly heard the words he'd uttered under his breath as he'd waited for Hayden, but normal, nonetheless. And the final epithet he'd muttered last night had held a quite different connotation from any of the other times it had been attached to her.

He'd called her a beguiling witch.

Her mouth curved into a smile as she opened her bedroom door and hastened down the stairs to the library. At the bottom, she counted to twenty. It would never do for him to see her out of breath.

"Good morning, Lord Sheffield," she said, entering.

He was bent over a table, scrutinizing a small figurine. He did not straighten or turn his head. "What is this thing?" he asked without preamble.

No manners at all. She sighed loudly, letting her disapproval be known, and then moved to his side to see what he was frowning at. "That is a Japanese netsuke."

"It looks like Donnie MacKee in diapers."

She stifled the impulse to laugh. "I believe it is a type of athlete known as a sumo wrestler."

"What is it doing here?"

"Excuse me?"

"Why do you have it? How did you—" He'd started to turn to look at her and seemed to have forgotten what he'd been about to say. His gaze swept over her. He swallowed.

"How did I what, Lord Sheffield?" she asked, a little breathlessly. She must have taken the stairs faster than she'd realized.

"How did you come by it?"

She studied him a moment. His hair was shaggy and touched by charcoal gray at the temples. He looked . . . perplexed. "Do you always ask so many questions?"

"Always," he replied.

"I had it sent here from an antiquities dealer in Edinburgh. I acquired it to provoke conversation and inquiry into that country's history. That's the how and why for most of the things you see in the house. I've considered it part of Amelie's education," she said.

"Now it is my turn. Why do you want to know?"

"You have never been to Japan, and neither has Miss Chase. You have no occidental blood, and neither does Miss Chase."

"That is not an answer."

"I am curious about you."

She started. Had he been referring to her alone or the plural that would include Amelie?

He smiled. It reached into his eyes and lit them from within, and she realized that though he might not be beautiful, when he smiled like this, he was undeniably handsome. "You, Mrs. Walcott," he said, reading her thoughts.

She didn't know what to make of that. It flustered her. Which may well have been his intent. Her eyes grew round. Had kissing been an attempt to fluster her, too? *Oh!*

She stepped away from his side, uncomfortably aware of how much space he filled and how his masculine heat disturbed the air.

"Why are you here?" she demanded.

His smile faded. Consternation took its place. "Two reasons, actually."

"Yes?"

"The first has to do with . . . well . . ."

"What are you waiting for, Sheffield?" she asked, her curiosity aroused. "Get on with it."

He scowled at her. "Do not try to bully me, Fanny

Walcott. The matter I wish to speak of requires some diplomacy, and I am trying to think how to phrase it."

So, he *was* going to apologize. Her mouth must have dropped open, because his frown deepened.

"You needn't look like that. I am fully capable of diplomacy. Just . . . wait a moment, won't you?"

He looked vastly uncomfortable. And after a few more minutes of waiting, when it became obvious he hadn't made much progress, she decided to take matters into her own hands. It was her usual response to any given situation. "Let me help you, Sheffield," she said. "You have come to apologize for accosting me."

He gaped at her, frozen in place.

"Don't worry. I accept your apology." She gave him a kindly smile.

It had the effect of breaking his paralysis. "I most certainly am not here to apologize for kissing you. Why should I? There's nothing to apologize for. You enjoyed kissing me as much as I did you."

Heat piled up her chest, into her neck, and up to her face. "Oh! Bounder!"

He made a dismissive gesture of disgust. "Ach. Tell me you did not enjoy our kiss. I dare you."

"That is not the point!" she said, growing flustered.

"I think it very much is," he countered.

"You did not ask permission. You . . . you took me by storm!"

A slow, amused smile spread over his dark, bold face. "Oh, my dear Mrs. Walcott, I assure you, you were not taken by storm. Should that have happened, you would not now be standing here berating me for kissing you."

"Then where would I be?" she demanded, setting her hands on her hips.

"Still abed. With me."

She gasped, more from the immediate carnal images his few words conjured than the embarrassment she suspected she should be feeling. In bed with Grey after an entire night of his mouth, his hands . . . She gasped again.

"All right," he muttered. "I concede *that* warrants an apology. Forgive me."

"I should say so!" Fanny huffed, with more indignation than she felt.

"You provoke me."

"*That* is not an adequate defense," she replied.

"No. It's not," he said, and grinned. "You would have made a good barrister."

Her lips quirked in response, but she stomped out the impulse. "Do you think so? Perhaps I shall pursue your profession someday after we leave Little Firkin. Who knows? We might meet in court to argue opposing sides of a case."

"I should welcome the opportunity to have you under oath, Mrs. Walcott," he said, his gaze lazily tracking her movements.

"Oh, but I wouldn't be there as a witness," she replied. "I would be there as council."

"But council is always under oath, Mrs. Walcott. Didn't you know that? Perhaps you'd better rethink law as a career option after all."

She felt herself flush. "Why? Because you think I am constitutionally incapable of the truth?"

He shook his head slightly. "No. I am not sure what I think about you."

He abruptly clasped his hands behind his back and took a broad stance before her. "That is the other reason I came."

"Ah, we're back to it, are we? Yes. Do tell me why you are here."

He frowned at her, but then cleared his throat. "First, to reassure you that Miss Chase and her heart are perfectly safe with Hayden."

"What do you mean?"

"The boy might be a bit of a bounder, but not where young ladies of quality are concerned. He is well aware that Miss Chase is required to live in Little Firkin for over two more years and therefore any relationship between them would be curtailed by both time and distance. Consequently, he would never encourage her to think of him as anything more than a casual friend. A *very* casual friend."

"But he held her hand," Fanny protested, at the same time all too aware of the incongruity of her protest. Grey had done far more than hold her hand, and she didn't think of him as even a friend. But then, she was not eighteen.

"And I daresay she liked it. But that is hardly a declaration of undying devotion, is it?"

Unhappily, Fanny agreed. "No." Perhaps she was overreacting. "I do not want her hurt, Sheffield."

"No one does. Including Hayden. The boy would never do anything to hurt her. I guarantee it."

His guarantee did make her feel better. There was no reason Amelie shouldn't enjoy the company of an attentive young man. It would be good practice for when she did enter society. "If you say so," she told

Grey. "You know the lad well enough to make such an assurance, so I will accept it."

"I do."

She nodded. "And now, what was the second reason for your visit?"

He shifted uncomfortably on the balls of his feet, then took a deep breath. "To tell you that I may have misjudged you."

She blinked. It was the last thing she expected to hear.

"I spent the evening assessing everything I know of you and Colonel Chase and his daughter and his will," Grey went on. "Despite intense scrutiny, I cannot discern how any conspiracy you could concoct would benefit you more than you will be simply by staying the course here. Especially since you have already put in six years of hard labor. You see, I was not deaf to your gilded-cage allusion." He regarded her with obvious satisfaction.

Fanny stared at him in bemusement. Why, the arrogant bastard actually believed himself to have delivered her a compliment by telling her he didn't think she was scamming anyone.

He waited. "Well?"

She pulled herself out of her astonished state. "Would you like me to thank you?" she asked.

"No. That won't be necessary."

He was amazing. "Good." *The ass.* She fixed him with an enigmatic smile. "But what if you're wrong?"

He met her gaze. His expression subtly, almost imperceptibly softened. "It's a possibility I'm prepared to risk," he said.

The wind abruptly ran out of Fanny's sails. *The bastard.* He'd confounded her again. Just when she'd been about to verbally rip him to shreds. Because he'd meant it.

This hard, clinical logician was willing to take the chance that she might not be a cheat and a fraud and a schemer, and it melted her heart. He must be crazy about her. She must be going daft. On the face of it, it didn't seem all that momentous. Or flattering. But it was. Because Grey Sheffield didn't know how to trust anything other than his reason, any more than she knew how to trust anyone but herself.

Time and experience had set them deep into their molds, and fighting free was a difficult and risk-laden proposition.

A terrified squeal rent the silence.

It was Violet. Chances were she was just squealing. She did that when she came upon a spider unawares. Still, Fanny could not ignore the fear in her voice.

"Excuse me," she said to Sheffield, and hurried from the room. At the end of the cluttered hallway, Violet hung from Mr. Oglethorpe's grip, her face ashen. Fanny stopped, collecting herself.

Even at a distance, Oglethorpe's eyes looked bloodshot and wild. He glared at her.

From the door at the end of the hall, Miss Oglethorpe emerged, drying her hands. Her small eyes darted from Violet to Oglethorpe to Fanny. Fanny welcomed her with relief. She had no standing with Oglethorpe, but his sister would.

"Miss Oglethorpe, please tell your brother to let go of Violet."

Miss Oglethorpe's pinched face twisted in disapproval, but she remained silent.

Oglethorpe gave Violet a shake. The girl went as limp as a rag doll, scaring Fanny.

"I'll teach you, witchling!" he ground out.

"Please, Miss Oglethorpe," Fanny pleaded.

The woman regarded her with mute obstinacy. "He's a man of God. Not fer me to tell him what to do," she clipped out. And with that, she wheeled around as though afraid she could be pressed into service against her will.

"Vicar. Whatever Violet has done I am sure she is sorry for it."

"Done? I'll tell you what this devil brat has done!" Oglethorpe sputtered. "She cursed me!"

"Oh, Violet." Fanny had no doubt he spoke the truth. Violet was always casting spells. What Fanny couldn't believe was that the girl was so stupid that she'd cursed the vicar right to his face.

"What the bloody hell is going on out here? Who are you, and what the blazes do you think you're doing?" Grey spoke from behind her. "Let that girl go."

Instant relief and gratitude washed through her. Oglethorpe took one look at the giant behind her and released Violet.

The girl threw herself against the wall and edged away from Oglethorpe, tears streaking down her dirty little face.

"Say you're sorry, Violet," Fanny said. Even though he'd released her, Oglethorpe still looked capable of violence.

"I ain't going to!" Violet shook her head. "He come in the kitchen and says 'ow I'm goin' to hell, along with Gram and all me brothers and sisters and uncles and aunts, and then he goes on to say 'ow everyone in this

house is cursed, and so I says he might as well join the
party, and I puts the curse on him. And I ain't takin' it
back!"

Fanny stared, uncertain how to proceed. Violet
sniffed, Oglethorpe frothed, and suddenly Grey burst
into laughter.

"Good God, Fanny, I see why you keep the chit
around! Well done, Violet!"

Oglethorpe's countenance turned an alarming shade
of purple.

"Best go, Oglethorpe, before you grow horns or cloven feet or . . . What sort of curse did you say you put
on the vicar, Violet?" Grey went on to inquire.

"Bowel troubles," she intoned darkly.

"Good God," Grey said, feigning shock, "then you
really had better be off, old chap."

Fanny couldn't help it. She started laughing and,
once started, she could not stop. The vicar, reduced to
being the butt of a ribald joke, trembled in impotent
rage.

"And, Vicar," Grey said, still smiling, even though
all warmth had left both his eyes and his tone, "do not
come back. You are not welcome here."

"I think it got stuck up in those shrubs," Amelie
called to Hayden.

Her handkerchief had pulled free of her sleeve when
she'd responded to Hayden's gentle—if frustratingly
respectful—embrace. A flirtatious wind had blown it
into the slow-moving river, and Hayden had leaped to
rescue it and disappeared in the undergrowth beside
the bank.

Now she waited patiently for her lover to return.

This was her favorite place in the world, a verdant patch of velvety grass spread beneath the emerald bower of ancient oaks. The ground was soft, the light ephemeral, a moss-covered boulder angled just so for leaning against. She always came here when she wanted to think. Or dream.

She'd been engaged in the latter when Hayden had hailed her from the road. She'd looked up to see him at a short distance, silhouetted against the dawn sky, his hair gleaming like liquid gold. He might have walked straight out of her daydreams.

Upon arriving, he'd explained that he'd been searching for her, hoping that she, like him, had been unable to sleep after the wonder of the night before. When she asked how he'd known to find her here rather than at the house, he smiled—he had a dimple!—and explained that he'd been attending carefully when Bernard had mentioned her favorite place at the river's bend. Eyes twinkling delightfully, he'd told her he'd counted five bends in the river before finding her. He was so romantic!

"Miss Amelie! I say, Miss Amelie!"

At the sound of Bernard McGowan's voice, she spun around. Bernard pulled his pony cart to a halt by the side of the road and jumped out, striding down the embankment toward her, his handsome faced wreathed in smiles. He was a fine-looking man, Amelie thought, but nothing about him stirred her heart. She'd given it to another.

"Hello, Mr. McGowan. You're up early today?" It was a question.

"Yes," he said. "I had a post yesterday that I was eager to share with you. And Mrs. Walcott."

"Yes?" She inclined her head, wishing Bernard would share his news and go away. She was suddenly very conscious of the fact that she was alone in the wilderness with Hayden. While she did not mind for herself—after all, she already had the stigma of being a witch to contend with, so being considered a bit of a romp didn't seem too terrible by comparison—she understood that Hayden might feel awkward. Or, even worse, embarrassed.

"Yes. A representative from the Glasgow Art Workers Guild is arriving in Little Firkin next week. Mr. Edgar Rennie. I recall he quite fascinated you on his visit here last fall."

"Mr. Rennie is coming back?" Amelie asked. "But he swore never to set foot in Little Firkin again after the townsfolk refused to sell him their mud."

Bernard chuckled. "Clay, Miss Chase," he said indulgently.

Hayden never looked at her indulgently. He mostly looked awed. Amelie decided she much preferred awed.

"They didn't refuse to sell him the clay, just their land. He did not want to transport the clay; it's too expensive. He wanted to build a factory here," Bernard continued. "His letter says his conscience will not allow him to live with the knowledge that the best clay in Scotland is daily being swept down a river."

"He was rather frighteningly fervent, don't you think?" Amelie asked.

"Most visionaries are," Bernard said. "At any rate, I thought you might enjoy his company again at a little dinner I am hosting. And Mrs. Walcott, of course."

"Got it!" Hayden's voice arrived a moment before his hand emerged from the shrubbery, waving about her kerchief. A second later he broke free of the thicket, twigs and leaves in his hair, his collar askew, and a tear in his tweed jacket. He looked extremely virile, even with the handkerchief. "Little blighter was hiding behind some lily— Oh. I say. Hello, McGowan."

Hayden came up to Amelie's side and, with a theatrical little flourish, twirled the kerchief and bowed, presenting it to her. "Milady."

She giggled, taking it from his outstretched hand. "Thank you, sir."

Only then did Hayden return his attention to Bernard.

"Out for a morning jaunt, are you, McGowan?" he said pleasantly, not in the least ill at ease.

Bernard glanced back and forth between Hayden and her, clearly uncomfortable. "Not exactly. I was coming to extend an invitation to Miss Chase and Mrs. Walcott and thought I saw Miss Chase here. I didn't realize you were with her."

"Didn't you?" Hayden asked casually.

"No."

"Ah."

The two men sized each other up.

"Well, Mr. McGowan," Amelie said to break the silence. "Thank you for the invitation. I am sure Fanny and I would be pleased to accept." She glanced at Hayden. "Perhaps Lord Sheffield and Lord Hayden . . ." She let the suggestion hang.

"Of course!" Bernard said, color rising in his face. She shouldn't have done it, but she would have breached any line of etiquette to spend another entire evening with Hayden. "I assumed our current visitors would be gone by next week. Apparently I am wrong?"

Hayden shrugged, tucking his hands into his vest pockets and striking a noble pose. "Can't say."

"Then your investigations into the anonymous letter have not met with success?"

"No," Hayden said. "We have no idea."

"Please, Mr. McGowan," Amelie said. "We have made a pact, Lord Hayden and I, not to spoil our conviviality with speculations about nonsensical and unpleasant things," Amelie cut in swiftly. She did not want to talk about that letter. It could only ruin her pleasure.

Bernard blinked at her. "But that is the purpose of his trip—"

"No buts," she said firmly. "We are determined to be jolly. Are we not, Lord Hayden?"

Hayden turned his warm gaze on her. "How can I be anything else when I am with you?"

Chapter Nineteen

Grey stood on the banks of the creek meandering through his brother-in-law's property, his hands on his hips and his shirtsleeves rolled up over his forearms. He'd forgotten how bracing the Highland air was. A crisp afternoon breeze riffled his hair as he lifted his chin and drank in the springtime elixir. By his feet lay a tackle kit, the contents a jumble of jigs and lures, flies and feathers. It was a perfect day to go angling for a pretty little trout.

The sun spangled on the creek, and the rush of springwater escaping the mountains played backdrop to the sound of birdcalls. Beyond, the orchid-tinted Highlands rose against a clear blue sky, bracing and valiant.

Like Fanny Walcott. He liked it. The way he liked Fanny Walcott. He liked her prickliness, her independence, her courage, and her coolness under fire.

He'd witnessed it yesterday, when she'd stood in the hall before that idiot vicar. He'd watched her gathering her courage to confront Oglethorpe, and he'd been visited by a sudden insight: She was this little makeshift family's knight in shining armor, because there was no one else to be. And just like six years ago, the compulsion to go to her rescue, like his own daft version of a knight errant, had swept over him. He'd indulged the compulsion, a simple enough task, given that the vicar was just a common bully.

When he'd heard her laughing at Violet's curse . . . Well, it had been the sweetest sound in his recollection.

"Is that you *humming*?"

Grey jumped at Hayden's sudden appearance.

"What's that?"

"I asked if you were humming."

"What of it?"

The lad lifted one brow at his tone. "Nothing. I've just never heard you hum before, is all."

"Balderdash. I'm an inveterate hummer. Hum all the time," Grey said without the least bit of guile, despite the fact that this was an out-and-out lie. He wasn't in the mood to be interrogated by someone with only one foot in the realm of manhood.

"It's the scenery," Grey said, waving his hand toward the mountain. "It's inspiring."

He turned his attention to the tackle box. His fingers moved idly over the surface of the lures: hare's ear, ginger quill, red spinner, stone fly, and greenwell. Behind him, he heard Hayden take a deep breath.

"Grey," he said, "I am in love with Miss Chase."

"Hmm?" Which lure to use? It was early in the season, so something bold would be called for—

"I said I am in love with Miss Chase."

—a challenge as well as a lure, something to awaken her fighting instincts as well as her appetite. He hummed another snatch of a music-hall ditty.

"Aren't you going to say something?"

The question really wasn't what lure to use, he realized; it was how to present it. As in much of life, enticement was all a matter of presentation—

"Well?"

"Yes, yes, I heard you," Grey said, snapping down the lid of his tackle box. The boy was not going to leave him alone until he'd spilled his heart out. Youth. They could not resist sharing every page of their internal diaries. "You're in love with Miss Chase. I heard you the first time. That's splendid."

"You mean, you approve?" Hayden asked, wide-eyed. Quickly, he regrouped. "Not that I need your approval."

"Of course you don't," Grey agreed, fervently wishing the boy would go moon about under Amelie Chase's window. He had important matters to consider, a slippery little fish to entice.

"You don't seem very surprised."

"Not in the least. Of course you're in love with the girl. What red-blooded young man wouldn't be? A pretty princess ensconced in a tower—I realize their house is hardly a tower, but you see what I'm getting at—by a dastardly father—though, in all fairness to Colonel Chase, I wouldn't call him so much dastardly as a world-class crackpot," he finished. "Indeed, I should have been surprised if you hadn't fallen in love with her."

Amelie marched down the hall toward a familiar whooshing sound coming from the breakfast room. It was eight o'clock in the morning, and she'd been up two hours preparing what she would say. Because she knew that at the first opportunity, Bernard would tell Fanny about seeing her and Hayden at the river's edge. He would doubtless consider it his "duty." She needed to prepare her response to Fanny's hearing of this news.

And Fanny, being Fanny, and therefore overly cautious of intense emotion and mistrustful of spontaneous attachments, would object and caution and fret and stew and perhaps even turn Hayden away. Which wouldn't do a thing to dampen Amelie's love or keep her from seeing him, but would cast a pall over her romance. It was time Fanny abdicated her role as teacher and caretaker, and assumed one of friend. In Amelie's mind, they were peers, no longer pupil and instructor.

Bolstered by these thoughts, Amelie opened the door to the breakfast room to the sight of Fanny taking practice swings with her golf club, her head bent over an imaginary ball. She was humming.

"Fanny," she said firmly and without prelude, "we need to talk."

Fanny didn't look up. "Must we?" she murmured.

"Yes. About the night before last."

Fanny blushed.

What did Fanny have to blush about? Unless . . . Could Fanny have witnessed the precise five seconds (after hours of reliving the event, Amelie had determined that it had lasted exactly five seconds, no more, no less) when Hayden had held his lips to hers? Heavens, how embarrassing! Heat welled up into her cheeks.

"I'm sorry if you are shocked, Fanny," she said, "but I feel no remorse, nor can anything you say induce me to regret one second of those lovely five seconds, and they *were* lovely, Fanny. Truly."

"Five seconds?" Fanny raised her head from scrutinizing her imaginary golf ball. "What five seconds?"

Ah! Fanny hadn't seen The Kiss. "Never mind. I have something important to tell you."

"By all means, proceed," Fanny said, returning to her phantom golf shot.

"Fanny, I am in love with Lord Hayden Collier."

Fanny swung through, barely brushing the thick pile of the oriental carpet beneath her, her head lifting to follow her shot and her gaze fixed on an imaginary ball flying over an imaginary lawn. "I see."

She reset her golf club's head on the carpet, adjusted her stance, and was about to take another swing when Amelie said, " 'I see'? That's all you have to say about—— Would you *please* stop swinging that golf club? This is important."

Fanny straightened and leaned nonchalantly on her club like a dandy on his walking stick.

"You must have some opinion," Amelie said plaintively. She'd expected Fanny to raise objections, to caution against hasty attachments, at the very least to question the legitimacy of a love formed in the course of one short evening. Had their roles been reversed, *she* certainly would have.

"Well, Amelie," Fanny said mildly, "you're a healthy young woman. He's a very comely young man, and he has that knight-in-silver-armor effect working for him, doesn't he? Quite dashing, and a bit of a young blade if I read him correctly. If I were of a romantic disposition, I might have fallen in love with him myself."

"You misunderstand me, Grey. I am not only *in* love with Miss Chase. I *love* her. Truly," Hayden said somberly.

"But," Grey said slowly, his attention finally engaged, his left eyebrow arched, "you haven't said as much to her?"

"Of course I have."

"You think I'm just a child, Fanny, but you are wrong," Amelie said forcefully. "I love Hayden and he loves me. And should he ask me to elope, I would do so in an instant, even knowing that I risked my inheritance."

"What?"

Chapter Twenty

Grey pounded on Quod Lamia's front door. Beside him Hayden beamed like a coal miner's lantern. Hayden caught his eye, and Grey manufactured a weak smile. Damn Collier for allowing him to bring the boy here. Now he was obliged to play surrogate papa, and he was ill-equipped for the job. Besides, he was furious—at her, at Hayden, at the girl, but most of all at himself.

He'd believed Fanny Walcott had no ulterior motives in her dealings with them. *Ha!* He'd believed she was simply the affectionate friend of a lively young girl, concerned for Amelie's poor heart. And while he'd been so solicitously reassuring her, Amelie had been with Hayden, inveigling him.

She must have known. Fanny'd been up and about when he'd arrived at her house. No woman got dressed in ten minutes.

She'd betrayed him. She'd led him down the garden path and he'd followed like a puppy. Like a besotted, eager, gullible puppy.

Grey banged on the heavy door again, rattling it on its hinges. Luckily, Hayden was too lost in a walking daydream to note. Poor Amelie's heart? What of poor Hayden's? The boy was moonstruck by the girl.

Had Grey ever imagined he'd have to pilot his nephew through the first throes of love, he would never have brought him along. But who in his right mind would expect to arrive in the hinterlands of Scotland and find an attractive, vivacious girl who liked music-hall tunes and was au courant with the latest Parisian fashion? In other words, a pretty pitfall for a like-minded young man.

He pounded savagely on the door, this time winning a surprised look from Hayden. "I think the old duffer who acts as butler might be a little hard of hearing," he explained with feigned composure. The door swung open, revealing Violet's grubby little face.

"You back agin? Wot is it wid you showin' up so blinkin' early? Not that I'm unconscious of the service you done me. But still, it ain't even nine o'clock."

"What is she talking about?" Hayden asked.

"Who can say?" Grey answered, before turning to Violet. "Kindly inform Mrs. Walcott and Miss Chase that we are here."

"Are you expected?" the girl asked suspiciously.

"No, but I am sure we will be welcome," he said, impressed at how genial he sounded, "if you would only inform Mrs. Walcott of our presence."

"No need to shout. I'll see," grumped the girl. "Wait out here." The door slammed shut on them, leaving them waiting outside.

Grey continued to smile, inwardly seething.

Hayden's arrival here must have proved an irresistible opportunity for Fanny. Amelie Chase was, if not precisely unweddable, an undesirable match. Her childhood had been fraught with peculiar incidents that had led to an unexpected departure from London amongst rumors of witchcraft. From there, she'd spent her entire adolescence in exile to a tiny, Gothic Scottish village. No. She was hardly the ideal wife for a baron.

She was lovely, yes, and heir to a respectable estate, but that couldn't compensate for the rest. Not amongst the elite set where she might have done her husband-hunting. And none knew this better than Fanny, who'd experienced the vagaries and closing ranks of the upper class after her husband had absconded. But then Fate—with a nudge from Grey—had dumped a viable matrimonial candidate in Fanny's lap (and he assumed it was her plan, because he simply could not picture Amelie Chase having the cunning necessary to devise an impromptu scheme).

Collier would never stand for it. Watching his father-in-law come apart under the influence of table rappers had left him with his own strong distaste for anything supernatural.

By now Amelie would have informed Fanny that she'd extracted a vow of love from Hayden. She would be celebrating. At least the young jackanapes hadn't offered marriage.

"I swear, Uncle, I have never felt like this before. I am an entirely new man."

"Ah, love!" Grey ground out. Luckily, he knew his nephew like he knew, well, himself. Any hint of disapproval and Hayden would be hell-bent on securing that which was denied him. So, after his initial involuntary outburst, Grey had been careful to project nothing but congeniality. He planned to convey something entirely different to Fanny Walcott.

"Have you ever been in love?"

God, deliver him. Was he to be reduced to trading girlish confidences with his nephew?

"I'm sorry—it's none of my business," Hayden apologized, exhibiting the sappy hypersensitivity people who supposed themselves to be "in love" often did.

"Not at all," Grey said. "I was just trying to recollect."

"Then you've never been in love," Hayden pronounced with the sanctimonious certainty of the love-enlightened. "Because if you had been you would never need to pause to recollect."

"Ah! How instructive. Thank you."

The door swung open again, and Violet reappeared. "You kin come in. Follow me. The ladies is out on the terrace taking tea. I suppose you'll be wanting some, too?"

"That would be lovely, Violet," Hayden said, bestowing such a dazzling smile on the girl that her grim expression dissolved under its power.

Grey grasped his nephew by the elbow and marched him past the smitten maid.

He had no trouble navigating through the cluttered hall and rooms filled with what the other day he'd perceived to be nothing but toys and indulgences. Today he saw them as the attempts of an intelligent and inquisitive mind to reach out and connect to a world beyond her prison.

Grey frowned. What else would you call a place you could not leave? What must it be like for an intelligent, agile-minded individual to be stuck here, knowing the world was transforming daily with advancements and new discoveries and that she could not be part of it? He had to admire the efforts she had gone to in order to stimulate her charge's mind and bring what she could of the world to Little Firkin.

Yes, fine. The woman was not entirely without merit, but that did not excuse her from attempting to ensnare Hayden for her charge.

They exited through a set of French doors that led onto a stone-lined terrace directly below a second-story balcony. Grey looked around. The terrace had been as carefully staged as any fakir's parlor, and very prettily done, too. Flowering chestnut trees spilled their petals onto the flagstones, and urns teeming with sweet peas and carnations lined the edges of the terrace. A wrought-iron table situated at the edge of the terrace overlooked a meadow beyond, its lace tablecloth billowing gently in the mild air.

But the pièce de résistance of the pretty vignette was sitting gracefully upright on a small, wrought-iron chair in profile to him, calmly sipping tea from a china cup, her face shaded by the brim of the most enormous hat he had ever seen. The straw confection of pale ribbons and mounds of brilliantly colored silk flowers sat at a pert angle atop hair piled into the most glorious disarray of black curls he'd even seen. Adding to the remarkable and unexpected allure of the thing, a single fluttering ribbon swept down off of the broad brim, brushing her cheek.

A snug, figure-revealing sheath of white lace eyelet covered her from neck to toe. She was utterly feminine, lovely, ravishing.

His eyes narrowed and he mentally rubbed his hands. She'd donned battle gear. *En garde.*

"What is that on your head? It looks like you ran amok in your greenhouse," he said, striding forward.

She slowly turned toward him, lifting one dark, winged brow in his direction. "Ah, Lord Sheffield."

Her gaze climbed his form with the negligible interest of the casual buyer. "Gracious as usual, I see," she murmured softly. "This is a hat. It is au courant in Paris. Not that I would expect you to know that."

"It"—he paused—"is strangely becoming." He took a seat, crossing his legs. "Indeed, most captivating."

Her eyes widened in confusion at his compliment. She wasn't alone. That hadn't been what he'd meant to say. From a nearby flowering tree birds began to warble, adding their melodic charm to the scene.

He recollected himself. He was not here to pay this woman compliments. "I expect you know why I am here?"

"To thank us for dinner the other night?" she asked sweetly. "I'm afraid I didn't receive your note."

He blinked, caught off guard.

"No?" she said. "Well, then as this is not a courtesy call, why *are* you here?"

"Look, Grey!" Hayden called. "Miss Chase has been painting a watercolor."

Grey turned toward his voice. He'd all but forgotten about Hayden and Amelie. The pair was standing a short distance away, Amelie looking coy and Hayden holding up an indifferent study of a rabbit and a pink flower.

"Most delightful, Miss Chase," Grey called back, and then, still smiling, muttered, "If you think you are going to manipulate my nephew into a situation where he has no choice—"

"You are truly becoming quite an artist, Amelie," Fanny shouted sunnily, interrupting him. "I've never seen a prettier carnation."

"It's a *rose*. Like all the rest!"

"Ah, yes. I see it now. And speaking of which, darling, why don't you show *dear* Lord Hayden the other pictures you painted? They're on the table."

Dutifully, the pair drifted off, Hayden's head bent attentively over Amelie.

Fanny watched them with all the appearance of a fond doyenne—if one's doyenne happened to be a ravishing beauty with flashing eyes and a figure that would tempt a saint—while the birds in the tree redoubled their singing efforts.

As soon as the couple was out of earshot, Fanny turned to him. "*Me*, manipulate *your* nephew into a situation?" she said. "*You* guaranteed *me* that your nephew would not act the cad! And here he's making declarations of love to the girl!"

"Don't pretend you aren't pleased. You have been contriving from the moment we arrived for a match between your charge and my nephew."

"Oh!" she huffed, her black eyes snapping. "I assure you I have no wish to see Amelie jeopardize her future for the sake of a pretty-boy layabout!"

He gaped at her. "Hayden is *not* a layabout."

"Ha!" she countered. "Has he an occupation, a career? What has he done of merit or value for anyone other than himself?"

Damn the woman, she had a point. She made him feel as if he were applying for the queen's blessing to a very questionable union, one she had no intention of bestowing. She should be the one trying to win points for her suit.

"He's young yet," he countered, for in truth, Hayden didn't have a career or employment, or a vocation, or even an avocation—except for impeccable grooming—nor any desire to have any of the afore-mentioned, as far as Grey could tell. Still, Grey had hopes that in spite of his not needing to make a liveli-hood, Hayden would develop purpose and ambition as he matured. He was still young. Which would be a strong objection to Hayden's wedding to this or any other girl.

Hayden wasn't ready to take a wife. Why, in Grey's opinion he himself was barely of an age to consider matrimony. Not that he was considering it. He might end up married to a termagant like Fanny. And what would that be like? To see the battle lights gleaming in the seemingly cool depths of her eyes? Each night to stoke an altogether different fire. . . .

The woman had him at sixes and sevens. He turned away to collect his thoughts and saw a pair of rabbits frolicking on the spring meadow beyond, a calming sight. They were obviously a fond pair, close enough to— *Damnation.* Why, the rabbits were copulating like . . . like rabbits.

He looked away. *Bloody hell.* Under the chestnut tree, another pair of the beasts was having at it. Wherever he looked was he fated to be reminded of his celibate state?

"How long will it last, do you suppose?" Fanny asked.

Grey's head snapped around. "Excuse me?"

"I asked how long Lord Hayden intends to use youth as an excuse for idleness." She looked him over. "Apparently one can do so for quite some time."

He was awed by her nerve. No one of his acquain-tance had ever dared to question his value, either materially or socially. He wasn't applying for some position. He didn't owe her one word of explanation. "Madam, as you well know, I have an occupation."

"Oh, yes. I recall. You annoy ghosts. No, that's not exactly right. You annoy people who annoy ghosts. How could I forget, when the world is so much safer for your efforts? Indeed, your very name must be anathema to the criminal underground."

Again, she dumbfounded him. She was mocking him, suggesting his avocation was petty and unimportant.

"Has anyone ever told you that you are the most sarcastic woman they have ever met? No. Wait. Don't answer that. I already know the answer," he said. "No. But that would be only because you haven't *met* anyone in what? Six? Seven years? At least, no one who'd dare stand up to you. You've gotten too comfortable playing lady of the manor. It's made you feel important. It's given you airs."

"I do *not* give myself airs."

"You do," he said succinctly. He'd segued into a smooth, kindly manner, such as one might employ in giving advice to some pathetic soul incapable of following it. It would drive her crazy.

"Perhaps acquiring a caustic tongue is inevitable living out here, but, my dear, before you return to society, *should* you return to society, do endeavor to control yourself lest you end up wanting for dinner invitations."

"Oh!" she breathed.

He smiled. Her affronted expression gelled into a cold, superior smile. He waited, eager to pounce.

"Happily, my dietary companions, or lack thereof, are no concern of yours. Nor will they ever be."

His blood stirred. How dared she tell him what was and wasn't his concern? The moment he heard she was in London, Paris, or wherever she chose to live after leaving here, he would find her and ask her to dine. Force her to dine, if necessary. Pick her up, throw her over his shoulder, and march her straight into Escoffier's dining room.

"Would you care to wager on that, my darling?" he asked softly, and immediately regretted the impromptu endearment, though it was, of course, ironically meant. Luckily, the sound of the birds in the nearby chestnut had increased to a din, masking his words.

"Come again?" she said, frowning. "I didn't hear you."

"What *are* those bloody things?" he asked over the birds' racket.

"I think they're larks," she said, staring in bewilderment at where the chestnut tree was dropping a blizzard of petals as birds crowded its branches, bellowing at a stentorian level.

"What the devil are they doing?" he asked. How were they to have a sub-rosa conversation with all this noise?

She frowned at the tree. "I have no idea."

He picked up an apple from the bowl on the table and hurled it at the tree. The flock within took flight, leaving them in relative quiet. Relative, because the birds simply moved their noisy chorus to the next tree over.

Amelie waved from the other side of the terrace. "Is everything all right, Fanny? Lord Sheffield?" she called anxiously.

"Right as rain, dear!" Fanny called back. "Just a bit of a problem with all those larks."

"Oh, let them sing! They know it's spring and they want to shout their joy!" Amelie called, and blushed.

Grey shifted his chair closer to Fanny's so she could hear him more easily.

"If you are set against that pair furthering their acquaintance," he said, "why are you so honeyed in your interactions with them?"

"I might ask the same of you, Lord Sheffield, and I suspect the answer would be identical," she replied. "Amelie can be stubborn, romantic, and intractable, especially when she perceives herself as being thwarted. I might as well throw her into Hayden's arms myself as deny her his company."

She was right; that was exactly how Hayden would react. "That may be true, but it is the same answer you would have given if you wanted to deflect my suspicions."

"Give me strength," she muttered in disgust. "Tell me, Lord Sheffield, *are* your suspicions deflected? *Have* I persuaded you of my pure intentions? No?" Her mouth flattened. "I thought not. At least give me the courtesy of assuming I know exactly where I stand with you, sir. I'm not a dolt."

She seemed angry. One might even think hurt.

"And you still haven't found your razor," she continued tartly. "I refuse to listen to someone who can't be troubled to shave before visiting a lady. I refer, of course, to Miss Chase," she ended bitingly.

"Don't worry, madam. My unshaven face and I will be offending you only until I can find some way to wrest Hayden from Miss Chase's company without doing something rash."

At this, she blanched. "No. You can't go," she said. "You can't go until you have found out who is trying to harm Amelie."

Back to this. How disappointing.

"I insist that as your brother-in-law's representative you either discover for a certainty whether Amelie is in danger or remove her from here to her guardian's home."

"Where Hayden just happens to live."

"He said he lived in London."

"Immaterial. When his father is in the country, Hayden is often at the family estate."

She gave an exasperated sigh. "Lord Sheffield, I do not care if Hayden lives in London, Paris, or Calcutta. The one and the only concern I have is Amelie's welfare, for which *you* have assumed temporary responsibility. As a gentleman—assuming you still have some pretensions in that direction—of honor—again, perhaps presumptuous, but still supposing your passing acquaintance with the concept—it is your duty—I won't even trouble to speculate here, but remain naively hopeful—to protect those under your care."

If she'd been a man, without a doubt they would have come to blows by now. As it was, he was forced to simply sit and marvel. "You have the most audacious tongue I have ever heard a woman employ."

"Why? Because no woman has ever had the temerity to question whether you're qualified to use the title 'gentleman'?" she challenged.

"Oh, no," he said honestly, "women are questioning that all the time."

Ah. Finally. A point for his side. Her spectacular eyes widened, and he'd be damned if the corners of her mouth didn't quirk upward. She turned her head, stifling a laugh, but not before he'd heard it.

"No," he continued, "I refer to your insistence on pointing out my lack of skill with a razor."

This time she did laugh outright, and he smiled broadly in response, even as he asked himself why he found such pleasure in the sound of her laughter.

He watched her, bemused and confused, trying to analyze his response to her. Beautiful as she was, she still wouldn't be to most men's tastes. She was too opinionated, blunt, autocratic, and peppery. She would never be a comfortable sort of companion or a comfortable sort of anything else.

A man would never have the luxury of taking Fanny for granted, ignoring her opinions, or having her dutifully agree with his own. Particularly if they were contrary to hers. He would always need to be alert, nimble of mind and spirit, constantly reevaluating his beliefs and attitude to make sure they would stand if challenged, or she'd cut him to shreds.

It would be exhausting.

It would be exhilarating.

"You are a very difficult young woman, you know," he said.

"You are a very difficult man," she returned, the shadow of a smile still hovering on her soft lips.

"You didn't say 'young.' "

"So I didn't," she agreed.

"You want me to stay?"

The lightest flush of pink spread up her neck and tinted her cheeks. "You *have* to stay until you discover the would-be assassin or else remove Amelie from Little Firkin. Amelie might make light of this threat. Indeed, I seem to be the only one who takes it seriously. But I do."

It was too bad, but this part of the game had reached an end.

"There is no assassin," he said, watching her closely. "You wrote the letter claiming someone was trying to kill Amelie Chase."

Her eyes locked with his.

"You wrote it assuming that Collier would simply send for the girl and your term of imprisonment here in Little Firkin would be ended. There is no threat to Miss Chase's life, nor has there ever been, has there?" he asked, his voice softening. "I don't blame you, Fanny."

The color had leeched from her face as he spoke, but her eyes held his steadily. "No. That's preposterous."

She stared at him white faced, but before he could respond a movement behind her caught his eye. He looked up to see one of the urns balanced on the balcony rail teetering precariously right above where Hayden and Amelie—

He leaped past Fanny and lunged forward, thrusting Hayden and Amelie under the balcony as the urn crashed to the ground at his heels.

"Devil take it!" he swore as Amelie collapsed into Hayden's arms.

Above her brilliant red head, Hayden's eyes, dark in his ashen face, met his. "She could have been killed," he whispered.

"I know," Grey said, moving out from under the

balcony. "I don't see how the damn thing could have just fallen like that."

He peered up in time to see a dark shape moving on the balcony overhead, and then an object was hurtling down at him. He dodged but too late. Pain exploded on the side of his head and he fell, a single thought following him as he dove into blackness: Fanny might not have written that letter after all.

Chapter Twenty-one

Fanny's heart stopped as the second urn struck Sheffield. At first, his face betrayed only astonishment, and then he collapsed onto the flagstones and she was on her knees at his side, staring in horror at the gash oozing blood near his ear, matting the dark hair.

"Oh, dear God, dear God. Please, dear God," she murmured, laying her fingers against his throat. His pulse beat strongly beneath his beard-rough skin. She closed her eyes, relief making her hand shake, and brushed the hair from his forehead.

Grey's eyes fluttered open. "Lord, Fan . . . you're . . . weeping. How . . . touching."

"I am not," Fanny declared, Grey's face shimmering before her suddenly blurred vision.

"What can I do?" Hayden asked gravely.

Fanny looked up. Hayden and Amelie stood beside her, Hayden's face pale with concern, Amelie's hand tight in his.

"Amelie, fetch some water and bandages."

"And some whiskey," Grey muttered thickly.

"*No* whiskey. Water. Go, Amelie. Get Violet and Ploddy, too. We need to get Lord Sheffield inside."

"Of course," Amelie said, releasing Hayden's hand and hurrying away.

"I'm going to go have a look around on the balcony," Hayden declared, avoiding looking at Grey. "That was no accident."

"Of course it was," Fanny said, relief making her sharper than she'd intended. "A cat probably knocked the urn over," she said. "I saw something moving about up there."

"Then it was a damn big cat," Grey mumbled, gritting his teeth. A stream of blood had begun trickling down the side of his face.

"We have lots of big cats here. Feral ones."

"But what if it wasn't a cat?" Hayden insisted, his eyes scanning the balcony. "Amelie might have been killed."

"And what of your uncle?" Fanny snapped. "He could have been killed, too."

"Exactly. I'm going to look," Hayden said, and took off.

"No!" Grey protested, struggling to rise on his elbows. His eyes promptly rolled back in his head and he fell back unconscious in Fanny's arms.

Fanny didn't care where Hayden went, as long as Amelie got her water and bandages and some aid. But from where was that aid going to arrive? There was no doctor nearby to help, only Grammy Beadle. Oh, Grey would love that.

She shifted his head into a more comfortable position and bent to examine the wound. It bled freely, a pool already forming on the terrace. She wadded up as much of the hem of her skirt as she could and pressed it against the gash. He moaned, twisting in her lap, and she winced.

He was a big, rude, tactless, unkempt brute. True, he was attractive in a rough, elemental sort of way. Like the mangy old tomcat that lorded it over the others in the carriage house, perhaps a shade past his physical prime, but still more vital, more powerful, and more dominant than any of the others' current best.

Yes, Greyson Sheffield was definitely a dominant sort. And she had never felt more alive than in his company. Combat, she supposed, did that to a person. Which only made sense. In order to survive one would need to be aware of one's enemy on an almost cellular level. Certainly, that was so for her with Sheffield.

Not only did her mind seem more agile when she was with him and her anticipation sharper, but all of her senses seemed heightened, too. Her skin tingled with sensitivity, her vision seemed keener, her hearing more acute. She swore she could tell his proximity from his scent alone.

It was an ungodly provocative scent, uniquely Sheffield's. Even now she wanted to move closer to him to capture every nuance. Of course, one didn't go around sniffing unconscious men. It just wasn't done.

She shook off the nonsensical impulse, studying the way the shadow of Grey's lashes formed a crescent on his cheek and the interestingly asymmetrical line of his nose—had it been broken at some point? Relaxed, his mouth lost its characteristic curl of derision. In fact, he looked quite handsome.

She was being ridiculous. He thought the worst of her, suspected she was hiding something dire from him. And she was: She was hiding her strangeness. The difference that set her apart from everyone else. But mostly, especially him.

A bee, mistaking the bloodstain on her skirt for a flower, wandered over to investigate. She bent forward to whisk it away and caught a hint of that fascinating scent. Her eyes drifted shut and she sank closer, inhaling deeply. Warmth. How could a man *smell* warm? And virile. Virility was not a scent. Fascinating.

"Please, Fan, take off that hat . . . before it falls off."

Her eyes flew open. Grey was regarding her in a woozily amused manner, his blue-green eyes lambent. "Having survived an urn, it would be too lowering to succumb to a hat."

"Are you all right?"

"No," he said, squinting up at her. "I have a god-awful headache and the sun is in my eyes."

She leaned back over him, her hat shading him.

He relaxed. "Too kind."

"Should I send for Bernard? He's not a physician, but he's a very capable man."

"To hell with Bernard," Grey muttered. How he managed to sound so vigorous when his skin was the color of wet ash was beyond Fanny. "I'll be fine. Had worse. Probably won't be the last time, either. "

"True," she said thoughtfully. "I suspect there are an awful lot of people who want to hit you."

"They try." He smiled with a touch of conceit she found bizarrely endearing.

"Close your eyes." He obliged, though she thought he had no choice, as his eyes had rolled back again before his lids fluttered shut.

Ridiculous waste of sooty lashes on a man like Sheffield. Black as his hair, thick as a painter's brush. Tentatively, she brushed a few locks from his brow with her free hand. He didn't move. Emboldened, she gingerly combed the hair from his uninjured temple.

She'd never touched a man with this much latitude before. It was quite . . . stirring. In unexpected contrast to the warm scalp beneath, Grey's hair was thick and glossy and cool. A nice clip would do wonders for his looks. And a shave.

She was still toying with Grey's hair when Amelie reappeared carrying a tray, Violet and Ploddy trudging dolefully in her wake. Guiltily, she snatched back her hand.

"Here, Fanny." Amelie set the tray down, her eyes locked on Grey's face. "Is he dead?"

"No, he's not *dead*," Fanny replied, shocked by Amelie's unhealthily fascinated tone. "He's simply passed out."

"What do you want us to do about it?" Violet asked, nodding toward the blood next to Fanny. "I s'pose I will 'ave to clean up that mess, won't I?"

"Yes," Fanny said, eyeing Grey's wound. The bleeding had slowed, and she was relieved to see that the cut wasn't very deep, though still long and with a jagged edge. It was a pity, but he'd have a scar. On the other hand, he'd probably like that.

She dampened one of the bandages in the bowl of water Amelie had brought and dabbed gingerly at the cut. His continued unconsciousness worried her. What should she do if he didn't wake on his own? Should one attempt to rouse the insensate?

She didn't know. A sense of powerlessness and ineptitude filled her, bringing with it feelings of frustration and helplessness. And fear. She'd felt the same way this winter when Amelie had fallen so ill.

She finished cleaning his wound and began dabbing it with iodine.

His eyes shot open. *"Bloody hell!"*

Ah! She smiled down at him, relief washing through her. He sounded almost like his old self. "You oughtn't swear."

"Bloody. Hell," he repeated succinctly.

Ah, yes, quite himself. She eased his head from her lap and stood up. At the chorus of gasps greeting her, she looked around. Her companions were staring in horror at her.

She looked down at her skirts and sighed. She had to admit there was a lot of very red blood on her very white dress.

Amelie was blinking as though she had sand in her eyes, and even Ploddy had turned a distinct shade of green.

She didn't have the patience for such nonsense.

"If any of you faint, I will cradle your head in this very same lap," she warned.

Both Violet and Amelie gulped and stared resolutely at a place on her forehead. Ploddy slunk into the background.

"Come, Fan," Grey said. "Don't threaten them. You look a horror. I've seen battlefield surgeons covered with less gore than you."

"Hmm," she said, unconvinced. "What good in an emergency is a person who cannot stomach the sight of a little blood?"

"I don't intend to be in no emergencies, thank you very much." Violet sniffed with the peculiar dignity with which she occasionally armed herself. "Now, what do you want us all here for? I hope you don't think we're going to lug the likes of him anywheres. I don't get paid for 'eavy lifting."

"You don't get paid at all. You get meals and the opportunity to lurk to your heart's content," Fanny reminded her.

"Not content enough to break me back over," she declared stubbornly. Fanny's gaze slewed toward Ploddy.

"Don't look to me," Ploddy said. "My sciatica's been a bastard these past weeks. Besides, I'm an old, old man, and he must go fourteen stone, lad his size."

"Thirteen, actually," Grey said. "And no one need worry about hauling me anywhere." Before Fanny could stop him, he'd rolled over and climbed to his hands and knees. "For the love of God, Greyson, sit back down at once!" she said, alarmed.

This command achieving exactly the result she expected—none—she crouched down beside him and, linking her arm around his waist, helped him stagger to his feet. She angled her shoulder beneath his arm, taking as much of his weight as he'd allow. He didn't object, and this, coupled with his deep, ragged breaths, told her the price rising to his feet had cost him. He was a cursedly independent man.

He looked down into her eyes. "Thank you."

"I didn't find anyone, but there was some sort of large beast in the shrubbery beneath the balcony." Hayden appeared breathless at the bottom of the stairs leading up to the balcony. His gaze swept past his uncle, found Fanny, and dropped abruptly to her skirt. He stopped dead in his tracks.

"Dear Lord," he muttered thickly. "Is all that . . . Grey's"—he stopped, swallowing audibly and continued— "blood?"

Fanny didn't bother to answer.

Hayden had already fainted.

Chapter Twenty-two

Amelie looked up at Fanny, Hayden's head in her lap. "You'll have to change your dress before he wakes up, Fanny," she said. "Hayden is obviously more sensitive than the rest of the common herd."

Fanny, still supporting Lord Sheffield, regarded her narrowly. "While I understand that certain sentiments raise the consequence of another in our eyes," she said, "I draw the line at being grouped with the bovine community. Pray remember yourself, Amelie. And I see no reason why I should change my garments in order to attend Lord Sheffield."

The resurrection of the pontifical tones Fanny had once used when Amelie was in the schoolroom made her flush with resentment. She was not a child. She had always ceded to Fanny's opinions and looked to her for counsel as someone wise and worldly. But in reality Fanny was not so much older than her, and having been in Little Firkin as long as Amelie, Fanny's knowledge of the world would have to be somewhat curtailed.

Amelie regarded her with the bittersweet sensation

of stepping across a line that could never be recrossed, one separating her childhood from adulthood. It was difficult to be at odds with one you loved, to realize she was not the paragon you'd always imagined her to be. But it was time Amelie established herself as Fanny's equal, and one who would not hesitate to go her own way. As long as it was the same way as Hayden's.

"I'm asking you, for Hayden's sake, to change out of that dress before he awakes."

Fanny hesitated.

"And do *not* look at him so," Amelie said, straightening his limbs. "It's not his fault you're covered in blood. And I'm certain most decent, civilized people would be appalled at such a spectacle as you are at present. It's not as if it were a spot of gravy. "

She couldn't help but cast an accusing glance at Lord Sheffield, who'd shed all the trouble-causing blood. He was still leaning heavily on Fanny, a situation neither seemed in any hurry to remedy, Fanny because she was stubborn, and Lord Sheffield because he obviously delighted in making others uncomfortable. Well, he had his work cut out for him with Fan. She'd be driven three feet into the ground beneath his weight before she'd give a hint of discomfort.

Amelie supposed she was being ungrateful. Lord Sheffield *had* saved her from being squashed by the urn. But that had been trumped by bleeding all over Fanny, thus causing Hayden to faint. When Hayden awoke, he would likely feel something of a weak sister. And he wasn't!

She'd been quite thrilled at the heroic way he'd raced to the balcony to do battle with her phantom enemy. And lots of fine people couldn't abide the sight of blood. In fact, she wished she were so afflicted. It only bespoke a lofty nature. She sniffed.

"Please, Fan. I'll wait here with Hayden. And Lord Sheffield."

"Best do as she says," Grey agreed. "She won't stop until she's had her way. She has been under your influence for too long. You've only yourself to blame."

"Oh, all right." Fanny agreed. "Violet, bring a chair over here. Ploddy, help me get Lord Sheffield into it."

Violet dragged a wrought-iron chair screeching and bumping over the flagstones. "There," she said, puffing. "Now I'll gets the garden cart and we can haul him—"

"I am not sitting in a garden cart to be lugged about like an enormous cabbage," Lord Sheffield said, making no visible effort to transfer his weight from Fanny's shoulders. "Or a turnip. Or a marrow."

Violet's face puckered with contempt as she shoved the chair behind him. "We don't use the cart to haul marrows. We use it for dung."

For a second, no one said a word; no one moved. Then Fanny burst out laughing.

Amelie stared at her in shock. Lord Sheffield was about to collapse from a head wound, Hayden was still unconscious, Fanny was covered with blood, and she was *laughing*. And Lord Sheffield, taking one look down into Fanny's upturned face, began laughing, too.

The exertion proved too much. His eyes rolled back in his head and he slumped in Fanny's arms, abruptly ending Fanny's hilarity. Ploddy grabbed Lord Sheffield about the waist and together he and Fanny lowered him into the chair.

"Knock on the noggin like that," Violet said, putting her hands on her hips. "He ain't going nowheres today. Likely should stay abed tomorrow, too."

"You know something about medicine?" Fanny asked interestedly.

Violet snorted. "I'm Grammy Beadle's granddaughter, ain't I? Course I do. Any self-respecting witch knows a bit of physicking. Don't you?"

"No," Fanny answered. "But then, I'm not a witch."

"Her ought to, then." Violet jerked her chin in Amelie's direction.

"She's not a witch, either."

Violet snorted again, one of her favorite conversational rejoinders, as Hayden began stirring.

"Fanny, please," Amelie said, "before he sees you and we have two men once again unconscious on our terrace."

"Well," said Fanny, "since you put it that way. It does seem a little outré, even for a witch's house."

Without further comment, she piled the tea things from the table onto the terrace, whisked the lace tablecloth off, and tied it neatly around her waist. One could still see the red stain under the openwork pattern, but at least it wasn't so obvious.

"There. This will do for now. I promise to change into other garments as soon as we've seen to the fallen. Now, wake the boy up, Amelie, so he can help us walk Lord Sheffield into the house."

"Throw a cup o' water on 'im," Violet suggested.

"Smell of cat piss'll wake 'im up without soaking 'is clothes," Ploddy added.

"And where we gonna get cat piss, you disgusting old wart?" Violet demanded. "Mrs. Walcott won't abide the things anywhere near the house, let alone in't. Throw water on him. It's a warm day. His clothes'll dry."

"No!" Amelie said forcefully. "No one is going to throw anything on him, whether from a well or a cat."

"Didn't say nuthin' about throwin' it on 'im," Ploddy grumbled. "Use it in place of smellin' salts—"

"That will be enough," Fanny said. "Amelie, wake him or I will."

Amelie bent over Hayden and softly blew into his face. "Lord Hayden. Lord Hayden? Please wake up."

She heard Ploddy make some sort of vulgar sound, and Violet muttered, "I'll fill a cup, just in case."

"Wake up, Hayden," she whispered. "The nasty bloody lady is gone."

She heard the sound of fluttering wings and looked up to see a bird—a plump rock dove, it looked like—land on a flagstone terrace halfway between Fanny and her. The bird cocked its head inquiringly. Pretty thing. "Look," she told Hayden. "Even the dove is wondering what you're about."

"Amelie?" he said, his eyelids opening.

He was so handsome. So perfect. She secured his hand tightly in hers, giving it a squeeze. She didn't care who was watching. *Fie on decorum!* She *loved* him.

"What happened? Oh. Oh!" He scrambled upright, his face red. "I am mortified. But ever since I was a child—"

Unfortunately, in rising he'd faced Fanny. His gaze fell unwillingly to the red-and-white pattern on her skirt. He teetered once, then slowly, but exceedingly gracefully, slid back to the ground.

"Oh, for the . . ." Fanny muttered, shaking her head. She looked around and found Violet hovering hopefully beside the water carafe. "Violet, get the garden cart."

Chapter Twenty-three

"What a wonderful day," Hayden said, drawing Amelie's hand more closely into the crook of his arm. They strolled along the footpath bisecting the small kitchen garden next to the house.

"Except for your nearly being hit by an urn, of course," he hastily added, sobering. If anything happened to Amelie . . . he couldn't bear to think of it. Thank God, from the look of things the urn falling had been an accident.

He'd not only been quick to look around the house, but afterward he'd questioned Ploddy, Violet, and Miss Oglethorpe. None of them had seen anyone else, and they had all been in different areas of the house. Amelie certainly did not seem frightened or anxious. Brave girl.

"Yes," she said. "A most unfortunate accident. But it is a lovely day."

"Bloody hell, that hurts!" a male voice bellowed from an open window above.

"It's a shame about Lord Sheffield, of course," she amended guiltily.

"Of course," he concurred, trying to appear subdued lest Amelie think him unfeeling. But everyone, including his uncle, agreed that though he'd received a nasty knock on the noggin, Grey had sustained only temporary damage. A day or so abed and he'd be right as rain.

In the meantime, Hayden had every excuse to hover close by his beloved Amelie. A wonderful day, indeed.

Overhead, dozens of swallows slipped through the air, somersaulting and diving in breathtaking displays of aerial artistry. A tabby cat the size of a small dog, lean and raggedy and missing most of one ear, lounged in the sun on the path ahead of them.

"I suspect there lies the author of Grey's headache," Hayden said.

"I wager you're right," Amelie said. "That's the carriage tom. Generally he stays off the balcony, because, well, Fanny chases him off."

There it was, then. A big old cat, playing where he knew better, and something startled him and he jumped, knocking into an urn and . . . Yes, an all-around satisfactory explanation.

"Do you really own a motorcar?" Amelie asked.

"Yes. A Milord Phaeton," he told her. "You will love motoring."

"I went with my father once, when we lived in London, before . . ." A shadow dimmed her radiance. "Before we moved here."

"Did you enjoy it?"

"Oh, yes! All the noise!" She laughed.

"I must add 'thrilling' to my list of things you like," he said, his gaze on her.

"You have a list of things I like?"

"Of course."

"I don't believe you. Where is this list?" she demanded pertly.

He looked down into her lovely, upturned face and was overwhelmed by a desire to kiss her again. Instead, he contented himself with squeezing the hand resting lightly in the crook of his arm. A man did not importune the woman he loved. With his free hand, he touched his chest. "Here. In my heart."

She dipped her head, adorably shy. He considered teasing her but resisted, pulling her gently back into step beside him.

After a moment, she asked, "Have you seen *Macbeth* performed onstage?"

He nodded. "With Ellen Terry as Lady Macbeth."

"Oh!" she enthused. "And I suspect you have seen the Eiffel Tower?"

"Indeed, I have had the opportunity."

"What is it like?" Her face shone, avid and entranced. "How did you feel when you saw it?"

At the time, he hadn't actually *felt* anything about the structure, his senses being otherwise engaged with an armful of the fair coquette who'd accompanied him, but he couldn't tell Amelie that. What *had* he thought? Surely he must have had some impression of the greatest engin— *Ah, yes.* "It is the greatest engineering feat since the pharaohs built the pyramids."

Amelie nodded, as if this were just what she would have thought herself. She would, of course. They were so perfectly in tune with each other. "I've seen pictures. And read about it. But it's not the same as seeing a thing for oneself, is it?"

"You'll see it someday," he promised. He wanted

to say more but he hadn't the right. He would have to speak to . . . well, he supposed he had to speak to his father to ask his permission to propose first. How convenient!

Still, it was agony wanting to ask her to marry him and not being able to. But this was Amelie, and everything must be done in perfect accordance with the rules of decorum, and those rules insisted that he speak to her guardian before asking her. She deserved no less.

He smiled at the thought. Who amongst his cronies would ever believe Hayden Collier could become such a stickler?

"I know I will," she said in an odd tone, and then abruptly added, "Do you think your father will invite me to live with him, under the circumstances?"

"I don't know," he said. "We shall have to wait until he returns. But I shall certainly advise it."

She smiled so warmly at him that his heart felt as though it were flipping over in his chest. "I should like that," she said.

He smiled at her pretty puckered brow. Poor lamb, she needn't worry over whether his father invited her to his home. She would live with him, as his wife.

"You've seen so much of the world, Hayden, and I so little." She sounded doubtful, as though she were wondering whether they could ever truly suit.

He couldn't have that.

"Yes, but you've seen magic," he reminded her, and it said much about the state of his heart that he actually meant it. "And I haven't."

"You have," she said, turning to regard him seriously. "The Eiffel Tower, motorcars . . . those are examples of true magic, the type of magic that transforms the world, not pictures falling from a wall."

With more animation, she went on. "Did you know that with something called the roentgen ray it is possible to see the structure inside the human living body without, er, opening it up?" She blushed. "I'm sorry. Of course you would. You'd be up on all these things."

Oh, dear. He'd never heard of the roentgen ray. "Ah, well . . ." He couldn't lie to her, but he could prevaricate. "Why would one want to do such a thing? It seems a little, well, vulgar, doesn't it?"

Her brow furrowed. "I suppose," she said. Luckily, she abandoned the topic, as they'd reached the big old tom. Amelie bent down and made a little chucking sound.

"Ought you to try to coax it to you, Amelie?" he asked worriedly. "It looks feral."

Amelie smiled. "I suspect it is, but I don't worry."

"Why not?"

"As I told you, animals respond to me. They would never hurt me. We have a sort of bond."

"You must have quite a menagerie of pets," he said.

"No. None," she said sadly. "Fanny . . . well, I don't think she actively dislikes them, but she can't abide being near them. She says they make her sneeze."

From the bedroom above came the sound of voices rising in a heated conversation. The cat swiveled its one good ear toward the sound and commenced purring. From underneath the shade of some bright green lettuces trundled a hedgehog, another in close pursuit. Very close pursuit. The one behind caught up to the smaller one and was— *Oh, my.*

Hastily, Hayden gripped Amelie's elbow and spun her around, heading back toward the house. She didn't seem to take anything amiss. Hayden glanced over his shoulder. Who would have thought hedgehogs would be such randy little blighters?

"Have you seen the cinematograph?" Amelie asked.

Hayden nodded. Here, at last, was a topic with which he was well acquainted, the topic of entertainment. "Oh, yes. Moving pictures. They're all the rage."

She gazed at him as though he were a god stepped down from Olympus to reveal the secrets of paradise. "Have you drunk a Coca-Cola? Have you ridden in the London underground electric rail cars? Have you been to the Waldorf-Astoria in New York City?"

He laughed at her eagerness. She was utterly charming, so fresh, so spontaneous, so curious about everything, so, well, so *inexperienced*. He frowned. She might be inexperienced, but she was certainly better informed than he was. Of course, what else was there to do here if one didn't fish or hunt? "No, no, and no."

She halted, regarding him in surprise. "Why ever not? If I were you and had your opportunities available to me, I would take full advantage of them to experience everything the world has to offer." She sounded, if not precisely critical, dismayed.

Hayden was unused to such a reaction. Generally, people were apt to praise him.

But for what? he wondered. Humor, urbanity, but mostly grooming. Not that grooming wasn't important, but perhaps he shouldn't be satisfied to be defined by the cut of his coat. Amelie deserved the best of him. In all things.

Yes. He would read up on the roentgen ray. Though

what it could possibly be any good— "Diagnostics," he announced, startling Amelie.

"Pardon me?"

"The roentgen rays. They could be used to locate breaks in the bone, the degree and severity of them."

"Oh, Hayden, that *is* clever," she said, her admiration shining in her face.

He preened a bit. He'd always had an interest in medicine. Maybe he would take it up as a hobby or something, or be an academician, since one might find practicing medicine difficult if one were to keel over every time some bleeding blighter popped into the surgery.

He'd think about it later.

Right now, he wanted nothing more than to enjoy being with Amelie.

Chapter Twenty-four

What an awful day, Grey thought morosely, staring out the window, where a battalion of chimney swifts dove in and out of his view. Not only had he been laid flat by a flowerpot and rendered incapable of navigating under his own power, but he'd passed out like a girl. When he'd come to again, it had been to find himself piled awkwardly into a highly aromatic cart, being transported down the hall by Violet and Ploddy.

As his demand that they stop had been completely ignored, he stayed there until they reached the bottom of the stairs, at which point it became evident even to the stubborn, iron-willed Juno overseeing their progress that they weren't going to get any farther with their prisoner.

With Ploddy's aid, he'd managed to struggle out of the cart, which was then hauled up the stairs ahead of him. Then, under *her* hard and unsympathetic eye, he'd pulled himself step by step up the seventeen risers before collapsing once more into the cart.

And now, *now* he lay between pristine linen bedsheets, a new bandage wrapped around his throbbing head, utterly and completely in the siren's clutches. He hated feeling so powerless. It brought back too many memories of arguments with his father, recalled too many episodes of impotent adolescent rage played out in reeking spiritualist dens.

Adding to his misery, he was now beholden to *her*. And she was nowhere to be seen. *Damn the woman.* Didn't she have a particle of human feeling? She ought to be here gloating, not flouncing about elsewhere. He would have been, had the situation been reversed. He would have been smiling down at him, smoothing back the hair from his brow, laying cool fingers to his cheek, and jeering.

The blazes with her. He didn't have time to satisfy her need to feel superior anyway. Because that urn *could* have killed Amelie Chase, and someone *might* be responsible for its falling, and, damn it all, she was right: It was *his* responsibility to ascertain where the threat came from—*if* there was a threat—which would be bloody hard to do lying in bed.

He'd been so certain Fanny had written the letter summoning him to Little Firkin. It made sense. She'd been trying to escape her prison without abandoning her charge.

But if the urn hadn't toppled over by itself, then his theory was wrong and Amelie stood in grave danger. But *who* would want to kill the girl? The throbbing in his head grew.

A light tap on the door interrupted his thoughts. He pushed himself higher on the pillows before calling for Fanny to enter. It had to be her. Everyone else pussy-footed around him.

It was.

She looked him over and then turned to someone behind her and motioned. A crone entered his room. There really was no better word to describe the small, wizened female festooned with an extraordinary array of what appeared to be old tablecloths. She looked familiar. Ah, yes, she was the old woman who'd challenged Amelie Chase to an incantation contest.

The crone sailed into the room with an exultant air, trailing crumbs and cat hair. She looked like a high priestess of some alien culture who'd just gotten word there was a human sacrifice available for the night's festivities. Violet followed her in.

"This is Grammy Beadle." Fanny spoke without preface. "She is here to see to your head."

Dumbstruck, Grey looked at Fanny. Her face wore a closed, uncompromising expression.

Grammy smirked.

"You have hired a witch to see to my wound," he said, just to make sure he had it right. "Knowing my views on witchcraft, necromancers, spiritualists, and the rest of the world's snake-oil salesmen."

"Snake oil's no good fer a cracked skull, young man," Grammy said with obvious disgust.

"I don't need her," Grey told Fanny. "It's not the first time I've been knocked unconscious. I know a thing or two about the signs of a concussion."

"You are the patient here. Be quiet," Fanny replied calmly, folding her hands at her waist like a schoolteacher dealing with a tiresome student. "Grammy is a talented herbalist."

"Don't you be callin' Grammy names!" Violet said sharply.

"Now, now, lass," Grammy said soothingly. "I'll deal with this."

"An herbalist is one who makes poultices and tinctures from herbs and green growing things," Fanny explained to Violet.

Violet snickered. "Ach. Any witch worth her mettle knows aboot sech things."

"And potions," Grammy put in severely, fearing her witchly light was being dimmed. "Don't ferget the potions. Not limited to salves and teas, I ain't."

"And potions," Fanny dutifully amended.

"She'll poison me," Grey protested, his head pounding like Thor's anvil beneath the hammer.

"Perhaps." Fanny didn't sound terribly concerned. "*Or* she might rid you of your headache."

"I'll need a pot filled with boiling water," Grammy told Fanny.

In turn, Fanny nodded at Ploddy, hovering uselessly by the door. "Have Miss Oglethorpe bring up a pot of boiling water," she said.

"Can't," Ploddy intoned. "The Oglethorpe left as soon as the witch crossed the threshold. Said one witch was enough, wouldn't stand two, and she's off to report yer doin's to the vicar. Says she'll be back when one or t'other leaves. Said that fer herself, she didn't care which witch went, but I was to remind you that the young witch might not be as set in her evil ways as the old one."

Fanny's composed demeanor showed a crack. She raised her eyes to the ceiling, muttering, "By all that's holy."

"Not exactly, mum," Ploddy corrected. At Fanny's

expression, Grey started to chuckle, which bloody well hurt and turned into a moan.

"Get me that boiling water, Ploddy."

The old man disappeared.

Apparently, the introductions were over, for with a quick, workmanlike clap of her hands, Grammy came to the side of the bed and leaned over him. She smelled of onions and cat.

Her small eyes, nearly hidden beneath the overhanging lids, grew smaller still as she peered at him. Before he could react, she reached out and stuck her thumb and forefinger above and below his right eye socket, wrenching his eye open as far as it would go. Then, grabbing his chin in a pincerlike grip with her other hand, she wrested his head around until he was facing directly into the brutal light. She leaned even closer, her gimlet eye inches from his.

"Look ta th' right," she commanded.

This was ridiculous. Gentleman or not, subjecting himself to the ministrations of the local witch was beyond what good manners demanded. The light seared his skull.

"My good woman—"

"Look ta th' right, ye great lummox!' Grammy said, bringing her point home by jabbing her elbow into his chest.

"Ow!" He looked to the right.

"Now left."

He looked left and caught sight of Fanny watching with imperious indifference.

"Up, then down."

"For the love of—"

"Up. And. *Down*."

Churlishly, he acquiesced.

She grunted, released her death hold on his head, and began poking his wound with sharp-tipped, shriveled fingers.

He endured with commendable stoicism, his gaze locked on Fanny. She would pay for this indignity.

Finally satisfied, the old lady turned toward her granddaughter. "Violet, fetch me some pussytoes and feverfew, a bit of greenswort, and a nice handful of St. Joe's weed."

With an alacrity Grey had yet to witness in the girl, Violet took off out the door. Grammy continued peering, muttering, and poking.

"I hope you are satisfied," Grey said to Fanny in his coldest voice.

She didn't look a bit intimidated. But then, neither had Grammy nor even that slip of a girl Violet. In fact, everyone in the damn house, including his own nephew, seemed summarily unimpressed with his bad temper. And he *was* in a bad temper. Very bad.

He hated being at the mercy of a little pain. She would think him weak, like the vapid Alphonse or that cold fish McGowan, men not of her caliber, unworthy of testing her mettle. That she didn't seem in the least disconcerted by his temper, his words, or his tone only made his case for him. She considered him negligible.

Bloody hell.

She didn't answer him, instead turning to leave the room.

"Where are you go— Ah!"

She glanced back. "Shouting will only make your head throb worse. I am going to get my sewing basket."

"Why?" he demanded.

"You are still oozing blood. If I do not stitch up that wound you will have a very nasty scar."

Dear God, the woman was going to poke him full of holes. Was there no end to her sadism? First the witch, now a needle?

"I assure you, ma'am, I do not have the least interest in whether or not I am scarred."

"I doubt that," she said primly, and before he could protest she continued, "I suspect you would like a big, mean, horrifying scar very well. But since you are in my house and under my care, you will abide by my decisions, and I have decided I do not want you to have a disfiguring scar."

" 'Vanity, thy name is woman,' " he paraphrased darkly.

"Why not? That's as good a reason as any I can come up with as to why I care," she said, and with that enigmatic statement she left, passing Violet.

The girl came in out of breath from running, her apron filled with forage. Ploddy followed her at a more sedate pace, carrying a china teapot, a tendril of steam rising from the spout.

"Here ye be, Grammy."

The old lady nodded, digging into the stained velvet pouch hanging from a cord around her waist and withdrawing a small mortar and pestle. Humming, she looked over the vegetation Violet held out for her inspection. She plucked a few leaves, shredded them into the mortar, and began grinding them into a paste.

Grey watched her, trying to ignore the bludgeoning pain in his head. "Do you really believe yourself to be imbued with special powers?" he asked after a moment.

"Aye, I am," she replied absently, then, "Marquardt Ploddy, set that pot down and get out of here before I turns you into a toad. Just trying to shirk some work is all you're doin' here."

Ploddy needed no further encouragement.

"You actually think you can cast spells, place hexes on people . . . make love potions?"

"Ayup." Grammy nodded. "A love potion'll cost ye a quid. Bit steep, I admit, but it's guaranteed."

"No. Oh, no," Grey said. "You misunderstand. I don't need a love potion."

"Never win her without one, not with yer lack of charm," Grammy said calmly.

"Win her? I don't want to *win* her," Grey protested, and then, because he didn't want the old biddy thinking he was thinking about Fanny, added, "Besides, I don't know to whom you are referring."

"Men," she muttered, then, "When ye're done playing blindman's buff by yer lonesome," she said, "you ken send word to me by Violet. And it'll still be a quid."

She took the lid off the teapot and dumped the greenish gray contents from the mortar into it. A sweet, pleasant-smelling steam rose. After a moment, she poured out a saucerful of the foul-looking matter and handed it to him.

"Drink the first 'alf now and the second 'alf in a few minutes after it's 'ad a chance to steep a bit."

"Really, I'm feeling—"

"Drink," she commanded, advancing on him with an outstretched claw.

He drank. Happily, it tasted better than it looked. He handed her the half-empty saucer and sank back against the pillows.

"Girl!" Grammy snapped her fingers.

At once, Violet darted forward, dragging a small fiddle-backed chair with her. Arranging her myriad tablecloth skirts with a waggle of her scrawny behind, Grammy settled down on it like a brooding hen. "Better yet?"

Astonishingly, Grey *had* already begun to feel better. The thundering ache in his head was still there, but more like thunder on the horizon, distant and less acute. He also felt a bit light limbed.

"What is in that brew?" he asked.

"Like I'd tell you," she scoffed. "Prettier faces than yourn have tried to pry me secrets from me."

"I don't have a pretty face."

She looked him up and down with a critical eye. "True enough."

Grey laughed. Once again, it was a mistake.

Chapter Twenty-five

After Grey finished moaning—bringing not a hint of sympathy to Grammy's raisinlike eye (what was wrong with the women in this town that they were devoid of every feminine impulse toward charity?)—he collapsed back on the pillows. Happily, the pain had been short-lived, and it occurred to him that in Grammy Beadle he had a font of information, in essence a star witness ready for cross-examination.

"Did you push that urn off the balcony rail?"

A look of astonishment spread over Grammy's face. "No," she said. "Are ye daft? Why'd I do a thing like that?"

"Because it is rumored that you want to be the only witch hereabouts," he said.

"That's right," she admitted. "And I will be, too. Once Amelie Chase leaves."

"Which is precisely why someone might suspect you of trying to hasten that day by upturning an urn onto the girl."

"Huh," Grammy said, and stared at nothing for so long a time that Grey became convinced that the notion of murdering Amelie was only just now occurring to her, and that she thought the idea might have some merit. Then, sighing, she shook her head. "Naw. In the end, it would only make things harder fer me."

"Because of the threat of prison," he suggested.

"Ha! Like a prison could 'old a witch of my stature," she scoffed. "No, because 'twould send the local lads into a right lather if I was t'kill the goose that laid the golden egg afore she's actually gotten on with the job of layin' it, if ya sees what I mean. Most folks 'round here lives right comfortable on the money they're expectin' to come into from that fortune what the colonel left.

"Course, I *could* spell the whole town into doin' me biddin' if I wanted to," she confided. "But Little Firkin ain't the only town I gots to oversee, and the sort of attention ye need to keep up a spell that big takes effort. Not to mention all them albino fox whiskers." She looked at him to see if he appreciated the degree of difficulty entailed.

"I can imagine." He nodded owlishly. That damn elixir had actually worked. He could hardly feel his head at all. In fact, his lips had gone a little numb.

She sighed tiredly. "Witchly empiring is a tricksy business."

He nodded sympathetically. He had no idea all of the considerations that went into cabal management. Who would have thought being a witch and a politician were such similar occupations?

"Do you know anyone who would want to harm Miss Chase?"

"Haven't you been listenin'? No one would harm a precious hair on her head, includin' me. What use is havin' a kingdom if all yer subjects is clearing out ahead of the dunners?"

Such logic couldn't fail to persuade. From a purely practical standpoint, no one in Little Firkin *would* want Amelie dead. But he'd known that. Which meant the urn must have fallen without the aid of a human agent . . . or the motive for the attempt was personal.

He hadn't realized he'd spoken his thoughts aloud until Grammy answered.

"Probably just a cat prowlin' about," she said. "We grow grand-size tabbies here. Besides, as well as her dad's fortune keeping her safe, no one here has gots much to say agin' Miss Chase. She 'n' Mrs. Walcott keeps to themselves, 'cept for Bernard McGowan and the vicar. And the vicar only comes 'cause the archbishop wrote 'im and told 'im he 'ad to."

Now, that was interesting.

"The vicar's sister works here, doesn't she?"

"She cooks," Grammy said, and leaned over to hand him the teacup. He accepted it.

"Does the vicar disapprove of her being here?"

"Vicar disapproves of everything aboot Quod Lamia, and Miss Chase scares 'im shitless, and like most folks that's scared shitless of something, he hates it fierce," she said simply. "And, twixt us, I think 'is sister's probably a witch, too. Ever taste her puddin'?" she asked slyly.

"Yes. It was delicious."

Grammy nodded in dark concurrence. "*Unnaturally* delicious."

"You seem to have a surplus of witches around here. Any others?" He took a sip of Grammy's potion.

Grammy gave the matter a moment's thought.

"Naw. That's just aboot all of 'em. I thought fer a while maybe Mrs. Walcott was one, but Vi don't see no evidence of it, and neither do I."

Grey almost choked on his tea.

Grammy leaped up, clapping him on the back, sending rockets of pain ricocheting through his skull. "Hold up a bit there, lad."

"Mrs. Walcott?" he sputtered.

Grammy sank back in her chair. "Now, that's one as ought to have gone into the witch trade, if you ask me. Never seen a more natural-born witch than Fanny Walcott."

If only she knew.

"What makes ye think someone wants to kill Miss Chase, anyways?" she asked, abruptly returning to the topic at hand.

"Someone wrote Lord Collier a letter to that effect."

She slapped her palms together, visually cleaning her hands of the subject. "Well, there you go, then. Ain't a half dozen folks in Little Firkin would even know where Lord Collier could be found to send a letter to." Her tiny eyes narrowed. "What about McGowan? He'd know where to send a letter. Yup, I fancy McGowan did it."

Grey shook his head. "McGowan was in Edinburgh speaking to a roomful of stamp collectors at the time of the initial attempt, and in the middle of the ocean on the second."

"Ach. That's too bad."

"You don't like the banker?"

"I don't like 'ow he treats them beasts of 'is," she said shortly. "Well, that's it, then, less you believe old Colonel Chase 'ad cause to worrit about them threats made agin'

Miss Chase when she was but a lass. And six years is a powerful long time between threat and deed."

He stared at her. He was certain what she said was important, but he couldn't reason out exactly why. The tea had clouded his thinking. Something flitted out there on the edges of conscious thought almost within grasp . . . and then it was gone.

Grammy leaned forward, shoving the saucer with the rest of its contents under his nose. "Drink up," she said companionably.

He took no further prompting.

It really was a remarkable potion. It had mellowed his mood and relieved his pain, though he admitted to feeling some floatiness. Nothing wrong with floatiness. Unhappily, something niggled at him, spoiling the experience. What was it . . . ? Oh, yes.

Where the devil was Fanny?

"Treating you well, are they?" Grammy asked.

"Yes, tolerably," he answered absently.

"Not you." Grammy jerked her chin toward Violet. "I'm talking to Vi. Folks like you always gets treated proper. It's folks like us 'as to always watch out so's we gets our due."

Not only was the old dame a doctor and a politician, but she was a philosopher, too.

"Well, Vi?" Grammy prodded.

The girl shrugged. "Fair enough, except they're always on to me aboot cleanin' up something or other. Use more soap on these floors inside a week than all Beadletown does on laundry in a year."

Grammy and Violet exchanged long-suffering looks of mutual mystification. "Well, you stick with it, lass. No reward worth 'aving is come by easy."

With a clap of her palm against the chair's arm, she tottered upright. Violet bolted to her side, as solicitous with her as any courtier might have been with the old queen. Arm in arm, they tottered toward the doorway.

"You're going?" Grey asked. He'd been enjoying their talk.

"Me and you both, lad," Grammy said with a wink. She turned to Violet. "Stay here and see as he don't try to get up, lest he goes head over arse like a pine pole at a caber toss. Dose him a few more times wit' the tea. That'll keep 'im off 'is feet. Should be fine by morning. But he ain't goin' nowhere afore then. Ta."

Violet shut the door behind her.

Grey tried to sit up but failed, collapsing back. *Oh, well.* Violet regarded him cautiously. "Yer head is bleedin' again, so don't you try nuthin' stupid. I already hauled yer carcass once today, and that was enough."

"Violet," Grey said with careful dignity, "I could no more rise from this bed than talk Fanny Walcott *into* it." Where the hell had that come from? Wherever it had, Violet seemed to accept his pronouncement as the last word in impossibilities, which did little to improve his mood.

"Good," she said, settling down in Grammy's vacated chair and crossing her arms over her skinny chest.

"If you don't like the work here, why don't you quit?" he asked.

"I will. Soon as I unlocks their secrets."

"Secrets? What secrets?" He was feeling blurrier and blurrier. Fanny had secrets? *Ah, yes. Of course.* And he was her confidant. *No, no.* That was wrong. She'd manipulated him so Amelie could . . . What was the word? *Inveigle.* So Amelie could inveigle Hayden.

"The secrets of Miss Chase's magic," Violet said, drawing his wandering attention back.

Poor child. Poor, deluded child. The pity of it was, she seemed a rather bright girl, really. Not clean, certainly. But with a native shrewdness that a little cultivation might eventually polish into intelligence. He felt an odd impulse toward charity.

"What magic?"

Violet rolled her eyes in exasperation. "*Her* magic."

"Yes, yes, lass. But what specific magic do you wish to be privy to?"

"All of it," Violet replied.

"So you wish to know how she flies about on her broomstick?"

"She can fly on a broomstick?" Violet whispered, wide-eyed.

"You'd know that better than I. I only just met the girl. You've lived with her—"

"Two years come June."

"Precisely. So, does she fly on a broomstick?"

"No," Violet admitted.

"Then she must summon whirlwinds and waterspouts?"

"No."

"No? Well, does she predict the future?"

Violet's face scrunched up. She shook her head. "Not to my recollection."

"At least she must cause the neighborhood cows' milk to curdle," he said in disgust.

"No," Violet protested loudly. "Miss Chase wouldn't—"

"*Couldn't*, Violet," Grey broke in kindly. "Miss Chase *couldn't*. Because there is no such thing as magic. There is nothing beyond the natural world, nothing beyond what we perceive with our five senses."

For the first time in his adult life he felt a tincture of sadness as he spoke the familiar litany. What had gotten into him? *Ah, yes.* Grammy Beadle's tea.

"It is all tricks and obfuscations designed to distract and disconcert while the magician makes fools of his audience."

"I don't 'alf know what yer talkin' aboot, Mr. Sheffield, but I ken what I ken, and I ken there's magic. Strong magic. And if'n I were you, I wouldn't go challengin' it with talk like that. Even you can't stand against certain rough magics."

Well, he'd tried. He closed his eyes.

"It looks to me like he can't stand at all," he heard Fanny say.

Chapter Twenty-six

At the sound of Fanny's words, his eyes opened. "You're not allowed to make quips," Grey said. "You snuck into the room while I wasn't paying attention and have an unfair advantage."

"Native intelligence and wit hardly qualify as an 'unfair advantage,' Lord Sheffield," Fanny said, masking her concern as she surveyed him. His pupils were enormous, the blue-green irises merely sparking rims around black pools. Good heavens, Fanny thought, alarmed, what had Grammy given him?

From the way he'd been denouncing magic and all its practitioners as she'd entered the room, she'd expected to find him on his feet at a lectern, not flat on his back, head lolling on a pillow, regarding her with a lazy, somehow sensual gaze that made her lips tingle with remembered sensitivity.

She was getting odd. She shouldn't be fantasizing about Greyson Sheffield. As she'd listened to him instructing Violet she'd been overwhelmed by a sense of disappointment and worse, distress. She'd felt as though she were standing on one side of a widening chasm, while on the other something irreplaceable grew farther away, and the ravine below filled with molten lava.

She blinked the disturbing image away. This was what came of living in the middle of nowhere with no contact with the outside world save printed material and Bernard McGowan. One lost one's reason.

She should be figuring out some way to hasten Grey's recovery, not be building daydreams around him. And yet, she could not stop thinking about how she'd felt in his arms or how devastatingly, ridiculously attractive she found him. He'd become the object of daydreams far more evocative and titillating than those involving chasms and rivers. Well, it was her imagination, and therefore private, and he needn't ever know how much she longed to feel him settling his body over hers again and—

"Damn, are all the birds in Scotland so bloody noisy?" Grey said. "Or is a cat raiding a nest out there somewhere?"

With a start, she came to her senses. *Oh, no.* What was she doing? She jumped up and went to the window. *That* was what she was doing. Reels of chimney swifts filled the sky outside in a flashing, chattering cloud.

"Not that I see," she said. She repositioned the basket she carried on her arm and pulled the window shutters half-closed. She turned around, smiling. "How do you feel?"

"Peculiar. Not unpleasantly so, however," he said. "Most unlike myself. I feel quite . . . nice. Must be the tea."

His liquid turquoise gaze traveled over her like

warm syrup, lingeringly on her mouth, her chest, her hips, and her feet. Even for Grey, his perusal was bold, but there was something missing in his languid gaze: the urgency, the raw vitality she'd come to associate with him. She missed it. Missed his fire and spirit and bluntness and brusqueness and—

Oh, Bedlam was too good for her!

"Perhaps you ought to dose yourself with it more often," she suggested.

"No. It's pleasant, but pleasant like warm milk. You'd be bored with niceness all the time, wouldn't you?" he asked seriously.

"I doubt it," she lied, and before he could question her further, she raced on. "How do you feel physically?"

"My head hurts, but it's pain at a remove. Like reports of a war on someone else's shore. And I think you're very nice but not in the least boring. I shall have to reassess my definition of 'nice.'"

She was pathetic as well as strange. Her pulse had begun fluttering at his faint praise.

"You called me Grey earlier," he murmured. "Out on the terrace."

"Did I?" She laid her basket on his bed.

"How do you think I look?" he asked.

She cocked her head, examining him. He looked wonderfully masculine, indolent, like the big tom outside. Self-satisfied, a little lethal, disreputable, and fully aware of the appeal of disreputableness to female cats. Especially the stupid ones.

"Aside from your enlarged pupils and a disconcerting tendency for your eyes to wander independently of each other, you look fine. Your color is good." She picked up his wrist. "Your pulse is strong and slow, and you've almost stopped bleeding. That will not last, of course, as you're bound to start again as soon as I begin stitching you up."

"There are lizards in the Americas that do that, you know," he said.

"Stitch people up?" she asked, flipping back the lid of her basket.

He grinned. "No. Their eyes focus independently."

"I don't recall saying anything about focusing." She picked out as fine a needle as she thought would pierce flesh and rummaged for a match. She struck it against the matchbox lid.

"I'm focusing," he said, affronted. "I see you quite clearly. You've rid yourself of the flower garden hat and changed out of that fetching white lacy dress into something severe and custodial."

"It's called a skirt," she retorted, squinting at the needle as she slowly swept it above the flame.

"Whatever, it isn't nearly as winning as the lace thing."

She dropped the hot needle onto a white kerchief, not bothering to hide her smile as she selected a skein of undyed silk thread. Whatever Grammy had dosed Grey with had rendered him less guarded in his comments. If one were not highly principled, one might take advantage of such a circumstance.

"So. You think I'm pretty?" she asked casually.

"I think the dress is pretty."

Her spirits unaccountably flagged.

"You're far too dramatic to be called pretty. I'm fairly sure Hayden would call you a stunner."

She missed the eye of the needle.

"Oh, come now, Fanny. You know how handsome you are."

"Well, yes," she said. "But I didn't know that you knew."

Once more, he grinned. "Good God, I could like you. Too well," he murmured.

"Except . . . ?" she prompted in spite of herself, and in spite of herself held her breath waiting for the answer.

He sobered. "Except you were a professional fraud. How can I forget that? I have spent my career seeing the results on unsuspecting fools of wiles such as yours, and now I find myself on the receiving end of those wiles, and I applaud you. They are damn near irresistible." His smile was sad.

"But I am not an unsuspecting fool. And you are keeping something from me. Hiding a secret. I would stake my life on it. But not my hea—" Abruptly, he bit off the last word and cleared his throat. "But nothing else.

"I cannot forget who you are, who you *were*, any more than I can forget that you had a part in making me the man I am. How can I trust what I feel for you when I don't trust *you*?" He sounded apologetic.

Ah, yes. That. Her secret. The thing that stood like a mountain or a bottomless chasm between them, separating them, just as it had separated her from everyone, always. Until here. Until Little Firkin. He suspected it. He sensed it. Yet he wouldn't have believed it even if she told him.

Nothing in the world would persuade Grey Sheffield that mysteries existed that no one would ever solve. She had no desire to do so. She'd had enough of people staring at her when she was a child. She understood too well the apprehension with which the world viewed mysteries, the isolation that the status of the unique bestowed.

Better a fraud than a freak.

"I know you're hiding something, Fanny. I just cannot figure out what it is," he continued.

Why must he see so clearly what she'd managed to hide even from Amelie?

"Grammy told me there aren't six people in Little Firkin who would know where to post a letter to Lord Collier," he said.

"Really?" she said.

"Really. And I imagine you are one of them." For a second, the fogginess clouding his gorgeous blue-green eyes lifted, allowing a glimpse of the shrewd intelligence beneath. "I will ask you straight-out for the truth, Fanny. Did you send the letter saying someone was trying to kill Amelie?"

She met his gaze, her heart racing. His brows dipped toward each other, but not in anger.

"Fanny?" he whispered.

"No. No, I did not." She turned to Violet. "Fetch Ploddy. I'll need him to help hold Lord Sheffield down while I sew up his wound."

The diversion worked as well as she'd hoped.

"No one needs to hold me down, ma'am," he declared.

"Good. I commend you on your fortitude." She advanced toward the side of his bed. Stained with blood, the pillowcase was already beyond salvaging. As was his shirt. His jacket, however, might be saved. "Violet, help me get Lord Sheffield out of his jacket."

His face closed into a cold mask. He tried to raise

himself up on his elbow, gasped, and collapsed back. The muscles at the corners of his lean, long jaw bunched. He clearly hated this.

His reaction seemed excessive. No one could fault a man who'd been knocked unconscious for being weakened by the event, except someone who had been rendered powerless before and learned to loathe the state.

She guessed it then, the roots of his abhorrence. He must have looked just so twenty-some years ago, when his father had dragged him from séance to séance to communicate with his dead sister, ruining his family's fortune and name, while all young Grey could do was watch, helpless and infuriated and incapable of preventing it.

Her gaze softened, and she looked away lest he see it. He would hate even more being pitied. She had learned that the other evening when Hayden had told them of Grey's past and she had masked her sympathy and won his involuntary look of gratitude.

"No, ma'am," Violet declared, breaking the tension of the moment with a mulish refusal. "I'm a respectable girl and a virgin, and I got principles, and no one ought to ask a virgin to 'elp a man get nekkid. You wouldn't ask Miss Amelie and you oughtn't to ask me."

"Violet," Fanny said, trying to find her patience., "I am not asking you to bed—"

"Don't never say no more!" Violet squeaked. "It ain't right and I ain't doin' it."

"At least ask Ploddy—"

"Ploddy ain't much better 'round blood than Lord Hayden. I'm thinkin' he's pukin his guts out right now after 'elpin' His Lordship once already. Why'd ya think he left Her Majesty's army with the colonel? No one else would 'ave 'im. Ye're on yer own."

"Violet, be reasonable."

"I am bein' reasonable. You ain't in the market for a 'usband like I am, 'less'n it's McGowan, and ye'd 'ave a better 'ope of landing Prince Edward, in my opinion. I gots a reputation to think on."

Heat erupted in a scalding wave up Fanny's throat. "That will be enough, Violet!"

But Violet wasn't through yet. "I'll 'ave Ploddy fetch His Lordship a fresh shirt, but as fer the rest . . . You're a widow. You've seen nekkid men afore. *You* do it."

And with that, Violet lifted her nose in the air and stalked from the room.

Chapter Twenty-seven

Fanny wasn't sure why she should be dumbstruck. Violet had acted completely in character: argumentative, incompliant, and outrageous. Behind her, Grey laughed. She faced him. At least Violet's overblown sensibilities had restored his humor.

"A witch who practices politics more shrewdly than many an M.P., and a scullery waif with as strict a sense of decorum as the Queen herself. Quite a fascinating household you run," he said.

"There's no 'running' about it," Fanny grumbled, eyeing him with trepidation she prayed didn't show. She was the only one left to get Sheffield cleaned up, stitched up, rested up, and out of here. And from the amusement he didn't even bother to hide, he knew it.

"I don't mind a little blood on my shirt, Fanny," he said, his tone gentle. "Or a scar. Really."

Had he challenged her, mocked her, or even dared her, she would have had grounds to leave him in his blood-soaked shirt, but his consideration undid any hope of that. She couldn't repay kindness with priggishness. And Violet was right: She had seen a naked man before. Just not one built like Grey.

"Don't be ridiculous." She advanced toward him and set the tray containing the water, sewing basket, and bandages on the bed beside him.

"First, I'll stitch that cut." She unwound the bandage from around his head and blotted away as much of the blood as she could. Throughout it all, he didn't flinch. His breathing didn't even alter its rhythm. Bless Grammy and her tea. Then she carefully clipped away the black, charcoal-streaked curls from above his ear, exposing the four-inch gash. "This will sting."

"No more than your tongue, I expect," Grey replied.

She upended a bottle of iodine onto a cloth and dabbed gingerly at the wound. Again, Grey remained stoically immobile. She blew out a deep breath and picked up the needle and threaded it. She took another breath and stepped behind him.

She'd never actually sewn flesh together. Perhaps it wasn't necessary. A second look destroyed this hope. Without stitching, the cut would reopen under the slightest provocation.

"I've been stitched up before," he said calmly. "Just go one stitch at a time. And really, the procedure will cause you more discomfort than me."

The unexpected reassurance melted some of her tension. "Thank you."

"You're welcome, Fan."

It was the second time he'd called her Fan. She liked it. She liked the way he said it.

She positioned the fingers of her left hand on either side of the cut and pinched the edges together. Then, biting down hard on her lip, she stuck the needle into the skin. The skin resisted. She pushed harder and still got nowhere. Tears sprang to her eyes.

This was horrible, far worse than she'd imagined. How could he just sit there like that?

"Tough, isn't it?" Grey asked conversationally.

"Pardon me?"

"Skin. It's a most extraordinary material: self-mending, waterproof, elastic and durable." He was talking to distract her. He was, she recognized, *comforting* her.

With a forceful thrust, she pushed the needle through the opposite side and pulled the stitched skin closed, tying a little knot and clipping it off.

"Indeed it is." She had to set the needle down for a second and close her eyes, thanking heaven she stood behind him, where he couldn't see how much she was shaking.

"I nearly fainted the first time I was sewn up," he said.

Blast the man for a mind reader.

"You're lying," she answered.

"Well, yes. I was hoping to bolster your confidence. After all, it's my skin you're impaling, you know."

She picked the needle up and, setting her jaw, took another stitch. Two down. The room began to wobble on its axis. She wasn't above asking for help. "Speak to me. Please."

"About what?"

"Anything. Please."

"Why did you marry him?" Grey asked.

"Marry him?"

"Brown."

Of all the things he might have said or asked, that was certainly the most unexpected.

"Because he said he loved me." She waited for a scathing reply. None came.

Rather than mocking her, he remained silent while she took another stitch, and then murmured, "I suppose. Yes." Then, "You must have been very young."

"Sixteen."

"Your parents agreed to the match?"

"No. Oh, no. We eloped. Alphonse was not the sort of young man a parent is proud to acknowledge as a son-in-law, and my family is a very proud one."

"Then why would you marry him?"

"Well . . ." She snipped off the thread. "I didn't *know* he wasn't a desirable sort. Daughters of the gentry don't generally go looking for a husband who'll bring shame to their family name."

She pulled the skin at the crest of his cheekbone more tightly together. "Certainly, I knew Alphonse was not as well educated nor as gently raised as I. But I thought he was atypical of his upbringing"—*like me*—"and misunderstood"—*like me*—"and unvalued. I didn't know any better. I hadn't been anywhere. I'd lived my entire life in the country until I met Alphonse."

She'd never spoken of this to anyone before. It was odd she should be doing so here, now, in these circumstances and with this man. And so casually, so easily, as if they always shared such things without fear of recrimination or judgment.

"Did you know, right from the start, his plans to hoodwink people with his spiritualist fakery?"

"Of course not," she said, taking another stitch.

"Again, a girl doesn't set out aspiring to a criminal career."

"But you knew soon after, and yet you remained a willing part of it?"

"Is that a question? I thought you knew all the answers."

He didn't reply, but he didn't need to; she wasn't going to go mute now. The words, bottled up for so long, the secrets held so close, the explanation she'd never been asked to give, poured out. "I knew it was all a fake. I knew it was rubbish, lies. I knew nearly from the first. Or soon enough after as made no difference."

"Why did you go along with it? Money? Notoriety?"

Of course, those would be the most likely reasons. They had nothing to do with hers, however. "I went along with the charade because I thought Alphonse believed his claims himself, and I didn't want him to be disillusioned." She waited for him to evince either incredulity or confusion. Once more, he disarmed her by exhibiting neither.

"You must have loved him, too."

"I loved who I thought he was." She could have added, *And I loved him for loving me as I was.* But that had proved not to be true.

"But you must have soon recognized the deceits he practiced," Grey prompted. "You must have wondered why he would contrive the nonsense with the violin and the disembodied voices if he really thought himself supernaturally gifted."

"At the time, I believed he had convinced himself that he was simply providing palpable evidence to aid his clients in believing what he *knew* to be true. You of all people should appreciate how much self-delusion a person is capable of when something is important to them."

He fell silent.

After a moment, he asked, "But you knew you possessed no otherworldly powers?"

She hesitated, filled with an inexplicable urge to tell him that she did possess supernatural abilities. But that would mean trusting him more than she already had, and this time with the truth of not only who she was, but what she was. She had once trusted Alphonse in the same way. And look how well that had worked. She would never make that mistake again.

"A person is capable of a great deal of self-deceit when it is important enough," she finally answered.

"But—"

"There," she said, cutting him off as she snipped the last stitch and standing back to look over her handiwork, noting that the bleeding had stopped. She also noticed a myriad of other scars on his face, small ones: a crescent-shaped silver line at the corner of his eye, a raised welt of shiny skin beneath the point of his chin, a crosshatch of faint hieroglyphics beneath one dark brow. How had the son of a marquess come by so many scars and, from the look of them, from so many different times?

What matter? It was no concern of hers. All she needed to do now was wait for his new shirt to arrive. Which, knowing Ploddy, might be some time yet. Still, she couldn't let him lie there in his bloody shirt.

"Now then," she said brightly, "let's clean you up a bit, shall we?"

"You sound like a nanny suggesting a nappy

change," he said dryly. "Just prop me up a bit on some pillows and I'll do the rest."

"Nonsense, let me help." She'd leaned over him, preparing to slide her arm behind his shoulders, and reeled back in a shock of recognition as her skin met his.

"Is something wrong?"

"No. No," she muttered, leaning forward and slipping her arm behind him. He was very broad and very warm and heavy. And that indefinable scent cloaking his skin inspired all sorts of heated images to flicker through her imagination.

"Are you really trying to move me?" Grey asked. "Because if so, you ought to commence a regimen of strenuous exercise at once. You're as weak as a kitten."

His words broke the spell holding her. She hauled him upright with a bit more force than necessary and shoved a towel over the pillow behind him. Weak she might be, but only in the head. Her arms were strong enough.

She picked up her scissors.

"You're going to *cut* my shirt from me?"

"The shirt is a lost cause. This will be easier." She didn't wait for permission, but angled the blade beneath his collar and began snipping, pulling away the sticky material as she went, carefully avoiding looking up, all too cognizant of his exotic blue-green eyes on her.

Her skin tingled and her bones felt rubbery. This was ridiculous. She was performing an act of charity. If she stayed very close and kept her gaze focused firmly on the scissors rather than on the muscular torso revealed with every snicker of the blade, she could keep it that way.

Grey didn't utter a word. Finally, she finished and tugged the ruined shirt from under him. There. That hadn't been so bad. She straightened, smiling victoriously, and her view of him, until then made up of disconnected snatches and glimpses, coalesced into a sudden, overwhelming whole. The sight hit her like a cricket bat.

He took her breath away.

She'd once thought of him as Ares, the Greek god of war. She hadn't known the half of it. The body she'd revealed had been fashioned on the anvil of time, tested and mended, knitted and reknitted of ever harder material.

This was no sleek youngster. His musculature was lean but dense, nothing superfluous padding the skin cloaking sinew and muscle that curved and bulged with each movement of his chest. His shoulders were broad, capped by thick muscles, his biceps prominent even when relaxed, his belly hard and flat. Silky-looking black curls covered his chest, thickening to a dark line that disappeared beneath his waistband.

"You don't look anything like Alphonse," she blurted out. "At all."

Grey, who'd been trying without success to reach the basin of water, glanced up and snorted. "I should hope not. Unless he worked driving spikes for the rails before he took to chatting up ghosts."

"You laid down railroad tracks?" she asked incredulously.

He laughed. "No. Not quite, though thinking back, it might have been the wiser choice."

"I don't understand."

His smile faded a bit. "I boxed."

"Boxed."

"I fought in fisticuffs matches."

"Fisticuffs?" she said, amazed. The memory of the felling blow he'd dealt Alphonse flashed into her mind. No wonder he'd made it look so effortless. And his comportment, the striking amalgam of gentleman and ruffian, now made sense. "Why?"

"Money." At her astonishment, he continued, "You can't make a fortune in the ring, but you can make enough. If you win."

"Enough for what?"

"Enough to pay for my schooling."

"But—"

"Come, Fanny, Hayden told you," Grey said, disconcertingly gentle. "My father bankrupted my family in his mania to find my dead half sister in some spirit world."

She looked away, the old guilt surfacing on a tide of self-loathing. How many families had been similarly affected by her and Alphonse's actions?

At the time, it had seemed innocuous. She'd even convinced herself it was charitable to offer comfort to those in mourning. Later, she realized the devastation caused by realizing that one's hopes were illusions. Like the illusion of her marriage. "Whom did you fight?"

"Carriage drivers, stevedores, farriers. Anyone who challenged me and whom I thought I could beat." Again, he lifted his shoulders, and the muscles bulged in response. "For the proper incentive."

"That's terrible," she said, searching his hard, supple form for signs of former abuse and finding them in a knot in the line of a rib, a star of scar tissue beneath his collarbone.

He laughed. "I agree. I must have been mad. As soon as I could do so, I stopped."

"Because you had a proper income?" she asked.

"Not entirely," he admitted. "I managed to track down the man primarily responsible for my father's financial ruin and sue him. He'd become quite wealthy, and I recouped much of the family fortune."

She nodded and began wiping the dried blood from the broad span of his shoulders, swiping his neck, then moving quickly on to finish off his upper torso.

And it was here she came undone.

She could feel the animal vitality of him coursing straight through the towel, soaking into her palm as it rode the even rise and fall of his magnificent chest, magnifying the heavy rhythm of his heart. She imagined it was like petting a lion, smooth and supple, but with readied power coiling effortlessly beneath the skin.

Her ministrations slowed, the dabs becoming strokes, the strokes, caresses. Beneath her touch, his belly muscles jumped and contracted like corrugated steel and sent a rush of light-headedness through her.

There. Finished. She began to step back, but spied a place she'd missed. A trickle of blood had followed the stepped ladder of his ribs toward the hollow inside the jut of his hip bone.

She swallowed. Gently, diligently, she traced the route. His breathing, so even and calm when she'd stitched him up, grew ragged and heavy. He shivered. Her mouth went dry. She was fascinated by the sight of tightening male nipples, his flesh pebbled and taut.

She ignored the powerful acceleration of his heartbeat, his bunching pectoral muscles, the sudden swelling of his biceps, and another heavy swelling lower, below his waistband. Completely ignored them.

"You don't really want McGowan, do you?" His voice was a purr, a husky sneer.

McGowan? Who was McGowan? She struggled to gather her scattered thoughts.

"Tell me."

"What?"

"That you don't want McGowan."

His voice was thick with satisfaction. And why shouldn't it be? She'd been ogling him like a starving cat did a bowl of cream. She struggled to find a shred of pride.

"Want? Of course I don't *want* McGowan. One doesn't want a person like one wants an ice cream," she said. "One wishes to further one's acquaintance— Oh!"

He'd grasped her wrist, stilling her ministrations and holding her hand flat against his stomach. She raised her face to his. He was smiling at her once again, gentle amusement in his expression. And once again the lightness of his clasp pierced her emotional armor as nothing else could have done. He must have been a dirty fighter.

"How is it that someone once married to what I presume was a man knows so little of the appetites of men?"

"I do!" she clipped out, stung. "Just because I choose to define liaisons less crudely than you doesn't mean I am incognizant of them."

He laughed, tugging her hand off his stomach and across his body, pulling so that she leaned over him, trapped. Startled, she looked down into his blue-green gaze.

"Fine. Then let's further our acquaintance," he murmured, and raised his free hand to cup the back of her head.

She could have broken free. He was weakened by blood loss and Grammy's tea. He wasn't even trying to hold her. Instead, he was persuading her, his fingers combing the pins out of her hair at the nape of her neck, his fingertips spanning her skull and coaxing her closer . . . closer. . . .

His breath, warm and fragrant, fanned her cheeks and eyelids, drifting them shut. His mouth touched hers in a soft caress that set her lips tingling and then was gone.

"Oh."

She felt herself falling, and he caught her, cushioning her against him before turning her deftly on her side. And then he was over her, above her, his mouth drifting down her temple, along the crest of her cheek, to the angle of her jaw, down her neck, and slowly, with excruciating purposefulness, to the shallow indention above her collarbone. The tip of his tongue swirled in a little circle there, dizzying her with the extraordinary intimacy of the touch.

"Oh!"

He chased moist, searing kisses back up her neck, touching his tongue into the corner of her mouth. She started, but he held her face for this new experience, languidly sliding his tongue along the seam of her lips, coaxing her mouth to open, to allow his slow, deliberate exploration.

His free hand moved down her arm to her waist

and drifted back up again, brushing over her breast. Beneath her prim white blouse, her nipples ached at the scant attention and her back arched.

She capitulated without consideration, without hesitation, one moment sighing in his arms, soaking up sensation like parched earth did a spring, the next, wrapping her arms tightly around his neck to deepen their kiss, tangling her tongue with his.

"Good God, Fanny," he muttered thickly, his hands bracketing her face, shaking with self-imposed restraint. "You're—"

Thud!

The window shutter banged against the inner wall.

Startled, Grey jerked upright, putting himself between Fanny and the window. She peered past him at a huge dark feline shape standing on the sill, silhouetted against the bright sky. It was the carriage house tomcat. With a sound like dough landing in flour, he dropped weightlessly to the floor and paced toward them, an ominous sound rumbling low in his throat.

"For the love of God, what the hell is that?" Grey asked.

"It's the carriage house tom," Fanny said, watching it in stunned fascination. The animal was wild. It did not come into the house. *Ever.*

"What's it doing here?"

"I have no idea. It's feral. It's never tried to come inside before!" She felt a frisson of trepidation at the creature's inexplicable appearance.

Grey shoved himself upright and swung his legs off the bed as Fanny scrambled off the other side. The cat paced slowly toward them, its gaze fixed and hypnotic.

"Fanny?" Amelie and Hayden appeared in the door. "What's going on?"

"Close the door and stay out," Grey said. "There's a feral cat in here."

Amelie looked around and spied the cat, who'd stopped and was eyeing the newcomers. Her face broke into a wide smile. "It's just the carriage house cat. It won't hurt you."

She hurried in, Hayden beside her, and would have dropped to her knees beside the huge beast had Hayden not stopped her with a hand to her elbow.

"No, Amelie!" Fanny cried out, rushing forward. "It's not safe."

Amelie laughed. "Oh, it's all right. The old puss has rather a soft spot for me, doesn't he, Lord Hayden? No animal would ever hurt me. Remember MacKee's horses? And remember only last week when we were having tea with Mr. McGowan, Caesar let me pet him?"

Oh, God. The girl had convinced herself she had some power over animals. The only reason Caesar had allowed her touch was because Fanny had been listening raptly to the sweet strains of violin music on a phonograph recording Bernard had brought back from Edinburgh.

"It's true," Hayden admitted, looking none too happy about it. "The dratted cat almost let her pet it down in the garden."

"Miss Chase," Grey cautioned, "have a care. It's growling."

Once more, Amelie laughed. "No, it's not. It's purring!"

Disbelievingly, Fanny bent her ear and strained to

listen. Good heavens, Amelie was right. It *was* purring, a deep, sonorous rumbling sound as rusty as it was oddly sensual. What was going on here?

She looked at Amelie. The girl smiled, confident and a little smug. She thought she'd bewitched the cat.

"Purring or not, that thing is doubtless a breeding ground for all sorts of disgusting vermin, and it is not allowed in this house!" Fanny declared. Snatching the blanket from the bed, she swung it out toward the cat with the flourish of a bullfighter.

Startled, the cat backed away.

"Git!" Fanny said, snapping the blanket toward it.

"Fanny, I can just—"

"No, Amelie. You cannot. This is a wildcat, not a pet. Don't deceive yourself otherwise!" she advised with another flick of the blanket.

The cat finally realized it was not welcome. With a sudden fluffing of its tattered pelt and one last baleful glance backward, it leaped through the window and disappeared.

With a sigh of relief, Fanny turned around just in time to see Grey sit heavily back down on the bed. He was still bare chested. Still battered and rangy as that old tom. Still just as dangerous to her.

And like Amelie, Fanny thought, hastily snapping open the blanket and settling it over Grey's all-too-obviously-male form, Fanny ought not deceive herself otherwise.

Chapter Twenty-eight

Grey cast a jaundiced eye at Fanny surreptitiously repinning a loose coil of luxuriant black hair. Then, without sparing him a glance, she swept up the tray and hurried from the room, pausing in the hallway only to intercept Violet with a sharp word that sent the girl on another mission. With that, she disappeared.

Coward.

Grey stared broodingly at the ceiling while at his side Hayden and Amelie began yet another long-winded conversation wherein they yet again discovered they enjoyed absolutely everything the other enjoyed, including, but not limited to, Gilbert and Sullivan music, American penny dreadfuls, long walks on misty mornings, quince jelly, badminton, and Jack Russell terriers. The only interruptions to this inanity were the breathless silences during which, Grey imagined, the pair stood gazing raptly into each other's eyes. Rather like poleaxed beef.

God, but young people in love were boring. Wasting all that valuable time exhorting one another's poor taste when they could be, well, tasting one another.

His body reacted at once to the carnal thought, and he shifted uncomfortably beneath the blankets. The problem was, instead of growing gradually inured to the effect Fanny had on him, with each passing hour he simply grew more sensitive to it.

His skin anticipated her touch; he grew warm at the distant sound of her voice; he vibrated like a tuning fork whenever she entered the room. Unfortunately, his senses were not the only parts of him to grow alert in her presence. All it took was a look from her, the scent of her lavender-washed hair, the sight of the light sliding over her skin, and he readied like a schoolboy at a peep show.

He'd kissed her only to spare her embarrassment. Her hand had been traveling too low on his stomach, and his kiss had been meant to distract her from seeing that portion of his anatomy that was becoming all too obvious. But once he'd touched her, higher motives collapsed under an avalanche of desire.

Oh, hell. What higher motives? He had no higher motives where Fanny Walcott was concerned. He never had. He simply wanted her—passionately, intensely, wickedly, wantonly, and frequently.

He supposed he ought to feel indebted to the damn cat for interrupting his near surrender to Fanny's wiles.

What was he thinking? *What* wiles?

The woman was about as capable of premeditated seduction as Hayden was of wearing mismatched socks. In the few days since he'd been here, she'd pronounced him rude, out-of-date, and old; tried to throw him out of her house; and called his nephew a ne'er-do-well. Gads, she was magnificent! But these were hardly the actions of a woman intent on seduction.

And, too, he believed Fanny's story about her marriage to Alphonse Brown and her subsequent involvement in his confidence game. He knew it was an inane belief on his part, another act of misguided trust, relying on emotions rather than facts, but ever since he'd come here, facts seemed to have lost their importance to him.

Besides, she had answered questions that had plagued him for years: If Fanny wasn't the young lady she appeared to be, where could she have learned to depict one so proficiently? And if she *was* a lady, how had she ended up married to a low-life poseur like Brown?

Her explanation *felt* true.

But the best liars often stuck as near the truth as possible, and certainly Grey was honest enough to admit he wanted her story to be true. The question was, how much did he want it?

He twisted irritably. He could torment himself for days with such nonsense, and to what good? There was no certain way of knowing whether she lied, told the truth, schemed toward some hidden end, or was simply what she appeared to be . . . and just what *was* that?

"Bloody hell."

"Oh, Lord Hayden, you're groaning! Are you all right?"

Damn, his rasp of frustration had drawn Amelie's attention.

"Fine."

"I'm ashamed. We didn't mean to ignore your discomfort," the girl said solicitously. She had swiveled around and was clasping her hands to her chest in an agony of self-recrimination. When the bloody hell had she and Hayden become a *we*?

"I wasn't groaning. I was muttering. Now, why don't you two toddle off and leave me to a good doze?"

"Oh, no," Amelie said. "Fanny made us promise to stay with you until she's returned."

"Impertinent wench. I am fine by myself. Better, actually, since I will rest more easily when it is *quieter*."

"Sorry, old man," Hayden said. "We'll be quiet as church mice."

And they were. They hovered at the foot of his bed, dividing their glances between pitying ones at him— oft accompanied by rueful shakes of the head—and longing ones into each other's eyes.

If he didn't still feel light-headed, he would have gotten up and thrown the young pup out by the scruff of his well-laundered neck. As it was, he endured for ten minutes and was just about to stop enduring— loudly and possibly physically—when someone called from down the hallway, "Miss Chase? Amelie!"

Bernard McGowan, flushed and disheveled-looking, appeared in the doorway. "Violet told me to come up here. She said there'd been an accident." His gaze found Amelie. "My God. I thought . . . I was afraid someone might be hurt."

Poor sot. Amelie had eyes for no one but Hayden and—only by reason of association—to some degree himself.

"Lord Sheffield risked his life to save ours. He saw one of the planters on the balcony above the terrace falling and shepherded us to safety," Amelie said.

"I didn't shepherd. I shoved," he said. "That's all."

"But he was *injured* in the course of *saving* our *lives*," Amelie asserted forcefully, ignoring his protestations.

She sounded like Fanny. He might like the girl after all.

"*Not* in the course of saving anyone's anything," Grey said. "Afterward. I was looking at the place from which the urn had fallen and was hit by another. Being felled by a flowerpot is hardly the stuff of epic poetry, Miss Chase."

"Lord Sheffield is modest," Amelie insisted.

At this, Hayden, taken aback by this obvious lack of insight on the part of his beloved, opened his mouth to correct her, but, upon witnessing the stubborn set of that same beloved's little jaw, he apparently thought better of it. "Modest, yes," he repeated.

"Bernard, I am so sorry not to have greeted you properly." Fanny entered the room, her face wreathed in tender smiles. "Violet seems to think Sheffield is having a salon up here rather than recuperating."

Twenty minutes ago she'd been on her back in his bed, returning his kisses. *Enthusiastically.* There was no possibility he'd imagined or exaggerated her response. So why the hell was she regarding McGowan so fondly? Maybe she thought she could retreat to safer ground. And who could be safer than McGowan? *Ha.* Let her try.

"Not at all, Mrs. Walcott," Bernard said, stepping to Fanny's side and taking the hand she spontaneously held out. He gazed warmly into her eyes. "I am afraid I didn't wait to ask questions but came straight ahead."

Why, the bloke was nothing but a cad, Grey thought

incredulously. A thin-blooded, overstarched, broody-looking, stamp-collecting cad. He probably thought he'd marry the heiress, then enjoy the widow.

"You are too kind, Bernard."

"I am just relieved no one was gravely injured."

"*I* was injured," Grey said.

Fanny ignored him.

Bernard raised his brow questioningly. A thin brow. Unmanly.

"Lord Sheffield will survive," Fanny said.

Bernard smiled. "If there is anything I can do, sir, please let me know."

Don't call me sir, *you little pipsqueak.*

"No, no, McGowan," he said. "You can return to your Yellow Camel Humps or whatever it is. No need to hang about here. I am in good hands." He cast a lazily proprietary look at Fanny. "*Very* good hands."

He waited, inwardly gloating and not caring the least that it was an unworthy sentiment, but Bernard, the dull-witted dolt, only nodded blithely. Amelie and Hayden had already returned to whatever little impenetrable sphere they currently occupied, oblivious of everything but each other. Only Fanny understood the innuendo. Her eyes widened and her mouth dropped momentarily ajar, then snapped shut.

"Ah, well, you'll let me know if I can be of any service," Bernard said.

Grey considered giving an even more provocative reply, but the quelling glare Fanny visited on him made him reconsider. The intent was to get rid of McGowan, not be asked to leave himself. "Too kind." He managed a smile.

Now that he'd seen the heiress was well and Fanny

was still doting, Bernard seemed inclined to stick around. At Fanny's behest—didn't the woman realize he was exhausted and did not want company?—Bernard took a seat and crossed his legs. "You say a planter fell?" he inquired seriously.

"Yes," Grey replied.

"From the balcony rail?"

"Yes." *Go home.*

"But those planters must be heavy. What do you think happened?"

"We don't know," Hayden awoke from his trance to say, his expression taking on the portentousness of the gravely concerned. "We hope it was simply an accident. There was no evidence of its being anything else."

"A cat tipped it over," Grey said. The moment the monster had made his ill-timed entrance into the bedroom, Grey's theory that the cat had knocked over the urn became a certainty.

Amelie shot a quick glance at him.

"You *think* a cat tipped it over," Fanny said.

Bernard looked from Fanny to him. "Am I missing something?"

"Mrs. Walcott believes someone might be responsible," Grey explained.

"Really?" Bernard asked solicitously. "I thought no one took the letter seriously."

"Someone wrote that letter," Grey said. "What they meant to achieve by sending it to Collier remains in question."

"Could it be Grammy Beadle?" Amelie asked, clearly nervous.

Grey reassured her. "As Grammy herself so deftly

pointed out, she wouldn't even know where to send such a letter."

"'Taint Grammy. She wouldn't waste 'er time throwing pots at ye. She'd hex ya and be done with it," Violet said, entering the room with the makings for a light tea.

"The vicar?" Amelie suggested, clearly distraught.

"The vicar wouldn't have the guts," Violet answered, setting the tray down.

"Succinctly put, Violet," Grey said.

"But then who wrote it?" Amelie asked.

Fanny was watching her young charge worriedly. He wanted to set her mind at ease.

"Anyone who knew about the odd terms of Collier's guardianship. A barrister, a banker, a friend, an acquaintance—Collier has a regrettable tendency toward indiscretion. Collier may well be the reason the letter was sent, not you.

"What if someone wanted to interrupt Collier's immediate agenda? What better way than to appeal to his sense of duty and force him to abandon his immediate plans by coming to Little Firkin? But instead of going himself, Collier sends me. Which means someone would be thwarted in his objective." Grey paused, thinking. "When is the next train due in Little Firkin?"

"Tomorrow," Fanny answered slowly.

Grey looked at Hayden. "We should be on it when it leaves. The more I think about it, the more I am convinced that someone was trying to disrupt Collier's travel plans, and since he is traveling to see to his various business interests, one of them is likely the target of whatever scheme is afoot.

"The authors of the plot may be revising their plan

even as we speak. If we follow your father to the Continent quickly enough, we might be able to determine who they are and what their objective is. But we won't be discovering anything here." He pushed himself up on the pillows. "Make arrangements to leave as soon as possible, Hayden. We owe it to your father to try to discover the intention of this letter."

"You can't go," Fanny said, her voice tight. "Your head. You may have a concussion."

"I don't," Grey said. "I've had concussions before. I know the signs of injury."

"You still can't go," Fanny insisted. "Even if that cat did upturn that urn, you still haven't done anything to determine whether someone in the town might want to hurt Amelie."

He was taken aback by her vehemence. "As I said—"

"I know what you said," Fanny cut in. "But you are making decisions based on assumptions. This is a town peopled with superstitious layabouts. Who knows what deluded thinking goes on in any of their minds? You haven't even asked any of the townspeople any questions. You only assume someone has some plot to discredit or defraud Lord Collier. You have nothing to base that on. One would think a man of your profession would utilize facts as well as fancy in formulating theories."

A palpable hit. He prided himself on his attention to fact. It was this attribute that accounted for much of his success in debunking spiritualists. But more important to him, she was still afraid for Amelie. He could not leave here like this. "Would it satisfy you if I spent another day interviewing the locals?"

"Yes," she said stiffly.

"One more day, but if I discover nothing, then my

time is better spent looking elsewhere for another motive for this letter. I have an obligation to my brother-in-law, too." He wouldn't discover anything. The more he considered it, the more certain he felt that the letter was a decoy.

"One more day," he repeated. "Then Hayden and I must leave." He looked at his nephew. Hayden nodded glumly. He might not like it, but he understood that his duty to his father came before his infatuation with Amelie.

"Thank you," breathed Amelie, looking so relieved that Grey felt his ire dissolve.

"I don't wish to be dismissive, but I can't help but think Lord Sheffield is right. No one would want to harm you, Miss Chase," Bernard said from the chair where he'd been quietly listening. "The idea is inconceivable."

The look he bent on Amelie was rife with longing.

Amelie didn't notice. She was too engaged in sending a similarly longing look at Hayden, who returned it twofold. Fanny added to this festival of pining, her face flushed with tender regard as she studied Bernard.

Had these people no pride?

Bernard turned toward Grey. "It's too bad you must stay through the morrow."

"How's that?" Grey said with ill grace.

"I'm going to Edinburgh tomorrow and would have enjoyed the company."

Bernard was leaving? Grey's spirits rose.

"But you've only just returned," Fanny objected.

"I know, but a wire came today informing me that a cover for which I've been pining has lately come up for sale in Edinburgh. I know you think me silly, but I cannot risk losing it."

The ass couldn't begin to imagine how silly Grey thought him. What red-blooded man pined for a stamp when chasing after it meant leaving behind a beautiful woman who wanted his company?

By God, he was jealous. He was jealous, possessive, greedy to recapture her attention. He wanted her to look at him in such a manner. He wanted her to play to him with those obsidian eyes. He wanted McGowan gone.

He was appalled.

"We'll miss you," Fanny said. She looked downright mournful. "But hope for your success."

"Thank you," Bernard said. He rose to his feet without tasting the tea he'd been poured. "I'd best go." His gaze flickered toward Amelie, then skated away. "I wish you a speedy recovery, Lord Sheffield. Lord Hayden." He nodded. "Miss Chase."

"Good-bye," Grey said. *Good riddance.*

Fanny followed McGowan from the room. He stared after her, every muscle in his body tensing against a primitive compulsion to rise from the bed, go after her, and fling her over his shoulder at the same time he explained (in what would doubtless amount to grunts and barks) that McGowan could visit her again only if he sought to have his blandly perfect features realigned.

Once more, he was appalled.

Because, he realized, he'd fallen in love.

Fanny walked Bernard to the front door and turned to him as he reached for the handle. "Bernard. Your friendship has meant a great deal to both Amelie and me over the years."

He regarded her quizzically. "Thank you. I value your friendship, too. I sincerely do. I hope you know that."

"I do."

"You sound as if you were preparing to say good-bye, Mrs. Walcott. Fanny."

She was. Not for herself, but on behalf of Amelie. The girl had tasted young love. Bernard McGowan, with his even good looks, sedate manner, and air of distinction, would never satisfy her now. She closed her eyes, trembling.

Poor Amelie. She'd tried to keep the girl from getting her heart broken, but she seemed determined to court misery. Lord Collier might be willing to be an absentee guardian to a girl purported to have supernatural abilities, but he would certainly not welcome her as anything more.

Poor Bernard. He'd have to give up his slow, persistent, though admittedly uninspired courtship. He would have made a decent husband, offering the peace of mind and calm sanctuary of a more mature man—though there were certain older men she'd lately become acquainted with whose affections, if offered, wouldn't promise a soupçon of either.

And poor me, Fanny thought, *who can't stop wanting a man who considers my morals only marginally better than those of a pickpocket*. A man who was impatient, imperious, rude . . . insightful, razor witted, sensitive, kind, and brought to life all her dormant passion.

"Not good-bye, Bernard. I just want you to know that we have appreciated all you have done for us."

He returned her steady regard quizzically. "Ah," he said. "Yes. I see. But I already understood as much."

She realized then that there were no stamps. Bernard was leaving rather than undergo the pain of witnessing another man taking the place he'd wanted.

He took her hand in his and gave her a weak smile. "It's for the best. He's far closer to her in age and temperament. Or so it seems."

"I do not assume anything will come of the association," she said, as kindly as possible. "In fact, I altogether doubt it."

"Yes. But you do assume nothing will come of ours."

She did not disagree.

He nodded. "I was too understated in my attentions, and too late in paying them. I will always hold Amelie—Miss Chase—in the highest esteem. I wish only for her happiness."

"I know you do," Fanny said softly.

"Thank you," he said, and left.

"The day after the morrow you'll be gone," Amelie said. Her heart would break. She knew it would.

"I'll be back as soon as I—" Hayden stopped, looking miserable. "As soon as I possibly can. I'll write every day."

A little burble of laughter escaped her, and she dipped her face away from him. He'd go away and whatever enchantment he'd felt would slowly dissipate. Yet, what could she do beyond embarrass him with demanding promises he was not yet prepared to make?

But she wanted to demand. She wanted to be reassured. She wanted him to stay.

"I'll look forward to reading them," she said, trying to smile.

"I love you," he whispered ardently.

Pride should have kept her from responding, but she couldn't be coy. No one had ever taught her that skill. She would have to speak to Fanny about this oversight, she thought on a burble of miserable hysteria.

"I love you, too."

Chapter Twenty-nine

Later that day, Grey lay in his borrowed bed, *The Iliad* lying open and unread beside him, the lamp's light casting shadows over the ceiling. Outside a veritable choir of nocturnal animals bayed, yipped, warbled, and screeched. In spite of the racket, he ought to be sleeping. A repeat dose of Grammy's brew had certainly been designed to render him relaxed, if not insensible. But he wasn't relaxed. He was unnerved. The terrible fact of having fallen in love with Fanny Walcott made sleep impossible.

Once he'd identified the emotion, he hadn't bothered arguing with his findings. Above all, he despised deceit, and that included self-deceit, which made his fall deliciously ironic, since he'd long ago deduced that love *was* self-delusion: a mother going into transports over a baby with a face like a three-day-old pudding; a man delighting in the braying laughter of his favorite mistress; a wife hanging on every word of her imbecilic husband's pontifications; and a beautiful, intelligent woman agreeing to marry a lisping, head-bobbing, white-faced flimflam artist.

There was no getting around the fact that love made a fool of truth. Love destroyed. It had certainly destroyed his father. Even the love he had for his three sons and they for him hadn't been enough to save the man his grief over the loss of Johanna.

But if one were fully aware of its pitfalls, vigilant in guarding one's autonomy, and strove to see beyond the haze this confounded condition engendered, one needn't abdicate one's reason entirely. He was still in possession of his faculties. He hadn't lost his mind, simply his heart. In fact, there was no reason anyone should know about it. Including her.

Which meant there was only one thing to do: turn tail and run. Only a fool rushed into certain danger. And Fanny Walcott was a veritable minefield. He knew she was hiding something, and he suspected she was plotting something, and he didn't care. He woke each day anticipating the next time he would see her, rehearsing in his imagination things he would say to win her look of surprised amusement, or consideration, or thoughtfulness, or indignation. Anything to secure her attention.

It was disgusting. He was utterly besotted. He did not want to leave here, and so, of course, it was vital that he did. It was the only reasonable, sensible, logical thing to do.

He stared at the moonlight streaming into his room and wished to God he were not a reasonable, sensible, logical man.

That same moonlight worked its alchemist's magic on Fanny's room, sweeping aside the colors of day and burnishing them with night-forged hues: silver and cobalt, black, argent and steel.

Her thoughts drifted in that netherworld between sleep and wakefulness. Fanciful notions courted her, thoughts she never allowed to surface found expression in fleeting images and whispered words. Here it was safe. Stripped of what she'd learned and what she knew, she was left with who she was. And Fanny was lonely.

Oh, she had Amelie and McGowan for company, and Violet, and even Grammy, but to some degree her secret would always keep her separate from others. Only in Grey's arms did she feel a sense of rapport, of bone-deep affinity. She understood him: the biting wit that guarded an all-too-sensitive heart, the pain that had fashioned him, the quest for justice that drove him, how lonely he was. How behind that sardonic mien, closed within that powerful body, was a man as desperate as she to touch and be touched. To love.

He was leaving and she might never again share that sense of belonging and homecoming she'd felt in his arms. Might never experience that ultimate union. And it wasn't as if she were a virgin or a young girl. She was a widow. She had no reputation to protect in that sense. Yet if she failed to act now, to seize the moment, all she would have would be regret.

Her eyes opened.

No. Not this time.

The door to his room opened, sending a puff of air over Grey's torso. But he must have dreamed the opening door and the freshening air, or experienced it as a hallucination, a by-product of the witch's dram. How else to explain Fanny coalescing out of shadows, silver-rimmed in moonlight? There was no other explanation. So he might as well enjoy his fantasy, let his hungry gaze linger.

A slight draft molded her thin nightgown to her slender body, revealing the lush weight of her full breasts, the graceful nip of her waist, and the swell of her hip tucking into the dark vee at the apex of her slender thighs—

"Grey?"

He froze, stunned. It wasn't a dream. Good God, didn't she have any idea of the havoc she was playing with his senses, the effect the sight of her was having on him? What was she doing here?

She moved closer. A diffused beam of moonlight touched her profile, brushing the high curve of her cheekbones with silver-blue and dabbing a pinpoint of light on the plump swell of her lower lip. Her hair drifted as she came nearer, swirling loosely around her shoulders and down her back.

She peered through the gloom to where he lay on the shadowed bed, heedless of any danger. *Foolish girl.* She was like the incautious princess in a child's tale, venturing near the ogre's den to investigate a curious sound. "Are you awake?"

"Yes."

He willed his arms to stay at his sides, even though she had positioned herself above him and was studying him with those black, fathomless eyes. A long coil of hair fell from her shoulder and swept across his taut chest.

She was on one knee on the bed, leaning over him,

her hair spilling across his naked chest, her hand fluttering over his face. "I was so alone."

"Me, too," he whispered, his hands rising and tangling in her hair as he dragged her mouth down to meet his.

Chapter Thirty

In response, Fanny wrapped her arms around his neck. Grey lashed her to him, his head raised from the pillow, his mouth hot and urgent on hers. She matched the hunger of his kisses with her own, her fingers digging into his shoulders, sending tremors through his big body.

He fell back on the bed, breaking the kiss, but his hands stayed in her hair, tugging her head back. She straddled him, bracing herself against his chest, her back arching, her neck thrown back in an attitude of vulnerability. He dragged scalding kisses down her neck to her collarbone and lower. She arched further, inviting him, opening to him. His mouth opened over the gossamer tissue of her nightgown, closing on her nipple, wet and ardent.

He stroked her nipple with his tongue, dampening the cloth, nipping away the fabric, and returning to dampen it again until, with a sound of urgency, he reached between them and dragged the neckline down, exposing her breasts to his sight. She gasped, and his fingers shivered in response as they coasted over the flesh he'd bared. His mouth closed with excruciating tenderness on a swollen nipple. Trembling, her hands clenched into fists against his belly, bracing her upright. A whimper escaped her lips, and she shifted her hips restlessly.

He groaned, tipping her over and onto her back. He shifted over her, bracing himself above her on his elbows. Lowering his head, he tendered hundreds of little kisses over her upper body, his weight holding her still beneath him. He murmured heated words, punctuating each erotic phrase, half-heard endearment, expletive, and prayer with long, deep, wet kisses.

"Please," she begged, her hips lifting up against the hard swell separated from her by the blanket and her gown. "Please."

He yanked the blanket from between them. His hands flowed along her flanks, his fingers finding the hem of her gown and bunching the fragile lace, rucking it up at her thighs. He tried to lift it over her head, but the ties and minute shell buttons held fast. So finally, with a sound of frustration, he simply rent the material down the middle and deftly slipped his palms down her sides to her hips and behind, cupping her buttocks.

His hands slipped lower between them, and his fingers touched her intimately, sliding between swollen, moist folds. . . .

"No. Please. Yes. More. Yes. Oh, *please*."

He couldn't answer. Had no voice to reply to the desperation in her face, the pleading in her eyes. Gently, he coaxed her legs apart, swirling his thumb lightly over her clitoris. She shuddered, the exquisite expression of disbelief on her face more arousing than any experience in his life.

And then he realized the truth: She'd never come before. Never achieved that unbelievable release of agony into pleasure. Damn Brown for a selfish bastard.

Ruthlessly, he clamped down on his own need, the driving pulse that ached in his loins. He would go slowly. He would take his time. He would make this last for her.

She was so damn vulnerable. So exposed. Her head was tipped back, her hair a silky black shawl beneath them, her eyelids half-closed, her lips parted, her breath a whisper of clove-spiked air. The moon shimmered over a tilted breast, the nipples dark and moist from his suckling. He would surely die of wanting her. He moved his finger lower, into her body.

Her eyes flew wide open, her arms gripping his biceps.

"Trust me."

He saw her anxiety fade, felt the tension ease from her body. He moved his hand, caressing, teasing, playing with her, and her gaze remained on his, the onyx eyes unfathomable, though her breath hitched and her heartbeat raced.

And finally, when his hand was slick and her body was trembling for release and his own felt as though he'd endured a century on a rack, he eased himself into her body, moving in one long, deep, slow thrust until he'd seated his full length deep within her. She shifted and he ground his teeth, clenching his eyes shut against the overwhelming sensation.

"Stay. A minute. I can't . . . I'm not . . . Stay."

She stopped moving, and he rested his head gratefully against hers, breathing harshly. The feel of her surrounding him was too intense, like a silken hot fist clenching his organ. He might die for wanting her.

Then die he would, if it meant pleasuring her first.

He rolled her over, seating her on top of him, her legs spread wide to accommodate him, still buried deep within her. She floundered, uncertain what to do. He felt a tender laugh rise in his chest, and he gently, firmly pushed her upright so that she sat fully upon him.

He caught her hips in his hands and gently bucked up into her. Her eyes widened in surprised discovery. He bucked again. Discovery turned to amazement, then eagerness. She began moving, awkward, delicious little pumps of her hips that set her ripe breasts bouncing, nearly undoing him but far from satisfying her. She whimpered, frustration supplanting her earlier eagerness. She'd clearly been teased with a hint of where this could lead before and left wanting.

Not tonight. He cupped her buttocks and lifted her, settling her against his upward thrust, lifting her, settling her again, teaching her the rhythm, the counterpoint of male and female in this exquisite dance. Her hands clenched and unclenched on his shoulders, the black satin hair sweeping down her back and brushing his thighs. Her lips parted in a sob. He pumped quicker now, a little harder. His jaw flexed with the effort of self-control.

Then, beautifully, richly, sweetly, she came. She cried out, her nails digging into his skin. And when she gasped, riding the last crest of passion, he pulled her down into his embrace and held her tightly, absorbing the tremors left over from her climax.

Grey stared at the night outside the bedroom window. In the indigo sky outside, a legion of bats whirled like dark confetti against the full moon. A chorus of owls, their haunting cry deep and bone-vibrating, echoed from the mountain and valleys.

He did not see them. He did not hear them.

His world had telescoped down to this one perfect moment, this one imperfectly perfect woman.

And then she started to cry. She wrapped her arms around his neck, holding on to him as though he were her last hope of salvation, and sobbed like a baby.

"Oh, God. I swear I was trying not to . . . Fanny? Please. Did I hurt you?"

She started to laugh at the same time she sobbed, and neither reaction seemed to want to end. "Yes, yes. I'm fine. I . . . I don't know what's wrong with me. It was just . . . It was so *beautiful*! I'm . . . It . . . It has made me . . . emotional. I'm sorry!" she wailed.

Beautiful? She was crying because their lovemaking was *beautiful*? *Dear God.* He had never felt so humbled. Never heard such honesty. Never felt such an answering accord.

For a long moment he was silent, absorbing her tears and gently stroking her back. Gradually her tears subsided, and then, out of the blue, she tumbled off of his chest and scuttled away, clutching up handfuls of the bed linens to cover herself.

"What?" he asked, desperate to understand what he'd done.

She began trying to wrap the sheet around her, but he was lying on part of it, and her nightgown was in shreds.

"You . . . you didn't . . . finish." Her cheeks scalded with a blush. "You are still . . . tumescent."

He had no idea what to say to that, so he answered, weakly, "Yes."

"Don't patronize me."

"Patronize . . . ?" he echoed numbly. "What the bloody hell are you talking about, Fan?"

"You feel sorry for me. Don't deny it."

"Dear God, Fanny," he said, anger rising in his voice. "You're a widow and you've never experienced a climax before. Only a sadist wouldn't feel sorry for you."

"Ah!"

She scooted off the bed and would have run, but he was too quick. He caught her arm and yanked, toppling her effortlessly flat on her back on the bed. She twisted, trying to roll off the other side, but he caught her wrists and dragged them up on either side of her head, pinning her.

"Let me go!" she said.

He shook his head, the dark locks tumbling over his forehead, his blue-green eyes ablaze. "Not until you see reason. You have no cause to lambaste me for feeling sorry for you."

"No?" she shot back, panting. "That's rich, coming from you. You, who would rather have hot tar poured down your nostril than have a word of sympathy directed at you."

His expression hardened with guilty frustration.

She saw it. "Ha!"

"It's not the same thing."

"It is. You would have the same reaction if I were

to . . ." God, she could barely bring herself to say it. "If I were to treat you to such charity."

Charity? She thought what they had just done had been *charity* on his part? She'd shaken the foundation of his world and she thought she'd been the recipient of his *charity?*

He began laughing at the absurdity of it, and her head snapped back around and his gaze slipped down over her face, her throat, to her breasts, rising and falling with agitation, and his laughter stilled.

"Here I was congratulating myself on my sensitivity, and you took as disinterest what was, madam, nothing short of a Herculean display of self-restraint." He chuckled again, releasing one of her hands and sliding his arm beneath her body. "Well, I certainly don't want to leave you in any mystery as to my *interest.*"

He dipped his head and his teeth closed on the point of her shoulder, nipping her as he pressed her deep into the mattress. She had no artifice in her. Without a trace of resistance, she wrapped her arms around his neck.

He kissed her from the point of her chin down her throat to her breasts, sending delicious, wanton pinpricks of pain shooting through her body. Abruptly, he shoved his hands beneath her buttocks, lifting her hips up, roughly kneeing her legs apart and settling himself between them.

She squirmed in a rapture of longing. Still, he didn't enter her. Roughly, he kneaded her buttocks, bruised her mouth with the ardency of his kiss. Breathing harshly, he pulled at the wrist he still held down, forcing her hand between them.

"Touch me," he said. "Then tell me I'm not interested."

He wrapped his hand about hers, closing her fist around him. He hissed as her hand slid over him, jerking back reflexively. "If I were any more interested, madam, I'd be spilling myself in your hand."

Then, gripping her knees wide, he thrust himself deep inside of her. His head fell to the lee between her neck and shoulder as he breathed raggedly in her ear. She clung to him, her knees wrapped tightly around his rock-hard flanks.

"Please," he whispered.

"Yes. Anything. More."

He rocked into her, urgent and feverish, his heart galloping against hers. She arched and he lifted his head, staring down into her eyes, watching her, licking the moisture from her temple, skating his teeth along her jaw, his expression intense and focused.

Pleasure danced like a mad dream through his veins, tearing apart his thoughts, pulsing, swelling, building toward a dizzying peak.

She closed her eyes and he called her back. "Look at me. See what you do to me. You utterly destroy me."

She stared up into his eyes, her own as deep and pure and inimitable as a drowning man's dream. His gaze never left hers, even when his body quaked and the air hissed through his clenched teeth. Even when she arched back and found her release again. Even when he pulled her against his hips, holding her tight to take one last, hard thrust deep. Even as the veins stood out on his neck and he found his own piece of eternity.

And when it was over and he rolled her to his side,

he nibbled soft kisses along her shoulder and upper arm.

"You're a fool, Fanny Walcott," he murmured. "How could you not have seen it? Even the old witch knows."

"Knows what?" she asked breathlessly.

"Why, that you have only to bend your finger to have me on my knees."

At the same time Grey was confessing Fanny's power over him, Violet was on her way out of Quod Lamia, heading to the terrace for her biweekly lurk. She was not hopeful. In fact, she'd pretty much given up on ever surprising Amelie Chase in the middle of doing some sort of magic. The lass was peculiarly cautious, which, while getting Violet's grudging respect, also deflated her hopes of winning Grammy Beadle's gratitude. But Violet was a persevering lass, if nothing else, and a duty was a duty, and this was her night to lurk about on the terrace, so lurk she would.

She rounded the house and stopped dead in her tracks.

There in front of her, lining the flagstones where the terrace met the meadow, were hundreds of eyes gleaming like effervescent fire in the darkness, fixed on Quod Lamia's second floor. Shadow cats, dozens of them, and other creatures, too, judging by the size and shape of the unblinking eyes: mice and weasels, fox, rabbits and hedgehogs, all crouching motionless on the terrace edge within a handbreadth of one another, staring at the house.

The breath caught in Violet's throat. Natural enemies lying quiescent in the shadows cast by a blue moon.

What could it mean? As she stood watching she realized something else: The night was filled with a low humming sound, rough and beautiful and hypnotic.

Violet's mouth dropped open as she realized what she was hearing: The animals, leastways all those that could, were purring.

She drew her breath in on a low whistle. A smile broke over her narrow, dirty little face.

Wait'll Grammy hears about this.

Chapter Thirty-one

Well, this was awkward.

The next morning, Fanny walked along the edge of the road leading into town, swinging her golf club as she went, using it as a sort of scythe, thoughtlessly beheading the heather sprouting from the verge. She barely remembered picking it up, and must have been so distracted she'd forgotten to put it down before she'd fled the house just before lunch, certain Grey would be feeling well enough to come down to eat. Last night had proved he wasn't in the least incapacitated. Not in the least.

She knew fleeing said little for her character, but she was not so much a coward that she wouldn't admit to the act. She'd fled, run away because it *was* awkward. Last night she'd felt so sure of herself. Of Grey. So certain that she understood him and that he understood her. But with daylight had come doubt. Neither of them had spoken of their feelings. This in itself was not unusual. They were both prickly and self-contained, wary of emotions.

She wanted to believe Grey loved her as she loved

him, but was that simply wishful thinking? He hadn't said as much, but there were other ways to speak aside from words. But again, always there was his suspicion of her, the well-founded suspicion that she was keeping something from him, which she was and would continue to do.

It was all very awkward and confusing. She needed to think.

She sighed, her golf club's arc slowing until the club rested in the dust at her feet. She looked around, startled to realize that she was at the end of Bernard's drive. Now she saw that the iron gate had been closed and a chain latched around it.

Bernard would have locked Caesar and Brutus in the house to guard his stamps. Grammy would be by later to heave a haunch of beef in through the front door. Grammy was the only person the poor brutes tolerated.

Except for Fanny.

She looked around. This was as good a place as any to think. The boulders guarding the bottom of Bernard's drive were flat-topped and sun-warmed. She clambered atop one and sat, swinging her golf club disconsolately at a thistle head below.

Should she return to Quod Lamia and tell Grey her feelings? Would he insist once more that she was keeping a secret from him, was planning something or concealing something? Yes. He would. It was his nature to abhor lies and demand truth. He had already demonstrated that he knew she concealed something. As long as they were in proximity to each other, he would not stop until he had revealed what she hid. Which meant, quite simply, that she shouldn't be near him. But . . .

She hesitated, frowning, for the first time in six years considering the unthinkable: What if she did tell him?

All her self-preservation instincts recoiled at the thought. Telling him could not end well.

He would think she was lying for some dark purpose or perhaps—marginally better—he would think she was crazy; or worst of all, he might believe her. Worst because then how would he see her? The answer was simple: just as everyone else she'd ever loved and confided in had seen her, as an oddity, a peculiarity, someone to be watched carefully. Even her loving parents hadn't been proof against that innate cautiousness that came when one was confronted with something abnormal.

Maybe she could write a letter. Damn, she wished she'd more experience with this sort of thing, but all she had to guide her was four years with a lying, conniving, dishonest fraud. Hardly good proving ground for future relationships with the opposite sex.

At the sound of a train's whistle, she lifted her head toward Little Firkin. Bernard's house was elevated above the town spread out below her a mile away, its twisted streets wending out from the center like an unraveling bit of lace. On the near side of town, the spur line had begun slowing as it approached the loading dock.

A single figure waited on the platform beside a pile of trunks. Ah, yes. Bernard. She was not the only one fleeing, she thought. She watched as the train pulled to a stop and a conductor jumped out, dragging out a short stack of steps leading into the single railway car. He then scurried forward to hoist Bernard's trunk to his shoulder, motioning for McGowan to precede him into the car.

At the back of the train, another worker hauled out a pallet and made quick work of unloading a few wooden crates before disappearing back inside. The whistle blew, and with a squeal of wheels, the train pulled away from the dock. And that was it. That was how easy it was to leave Little Firkin.

A savage outburst of barking coming from McGowan's house sent Fanny turning around again. Grey Sheffield was striding up the road from the direction of Little Firkin, bareheaded and without a collar, his sleeves rolled up over his dark forearms and his jacket slung over his shoulder.

He looked up at the sound of the dogs barking and caught sight of her. At once, he skidded to halt. For a long, awkward moment—she'd just known it would be awkward—they stared at each other, the dogs barking wildly in the background.

He didn't look like someone who'd been knocked unconscious and drugged a mere twenty hours ago. His hair had been carelessly raked back from his face, and his trousers were dusty. He looked entirely too virile.

A wave of yearning seized her, so strong that she had to clench handfuls of moss to keep from sliding off the boulder and flinging herself into his arms. Instead, she demanded, "What are you doing walking about?"

Her voice freed him from whatever paralysis held him. He started toward her, scowling. She didn't fear his scowls. Not anymore. They were simply his fallback expression, to be donned when he feared anything less would show vulnerability.

"I was in town," he said, stopping in front of the bolder where she perched. "Asking questions. Wasn't that what you wanted?"

"You should be back at Quod Lamia, lying in bed." As soon as she said the words, her face lit with heat.

She expected him to make some sort of rude comment. Instead, he answered by turning just as ruddy beneath his tanned skin. Oh, yes. This was all going to be excruciatingly awkward.

Too bad it didn't keep her from noting the curl of dark hair peeking from the vee of his open collar, or the dark down covering his forearm, or how that same forearm was sculpted of long, sharply defined sinew and muscle, and how strong his wrists were, and how elegant his long fingers—

No. No. No. She was not going to do this to herself. She looked up, determined not to spend a second longer rhapsodizing about Grey Sheffield's forearms. Doing so, she walked straight into the trap that was his eyes. Dazzling aquamarine eyes ringed by thick, sooty lashes, ensnaring her with their beauty, the heat in his gaze feeding the fire in her veins. She heard the golf club clatter to the ground as she felt herself falling forward, drawn by an irresistible force.

And then his arms were around her and he was snatching her from the boulder top, dragging her hard against him, his lips opening over hers. He plundered her mouth with hot, wet kisses, his tongue making salacious sweeps along the silken interior of her cheeks, his hands roving feverishly down her body to grip her buttocks and hoist her up against his body.

He moved forward to ease her against the bolder, his mouth never leaving hers as he whispered hot, ardent words against her lips. She dug her fingers into his cool, thick hair, tugging at him, wanting more, wanting to melt into him, dissolve into his body. Her reason evaporated under the sensual ferocity. She panted, wriggling against him helplessly, not knowing how to tell him without words what she wanted, needed, could not imagine never having again: him inside her.

With a low oath, he grasped her knee, urging her leg up around his hip. She struggled to wrap it around him, cursing her skirts. . . .

The sound of ripping cloth rent the air like a lightning strike, and with just as devastating an effect; Grey stopped kissing her.

He froze, his lips still tight against hers, one arm supporting her derriere, the other hand at his pants opening. Slowly, he withdrew his lips from her mouth and for a brief second rested his forehead against hers. His chest labored like a stevedore's. His eyes were clenched shut. Then he let her slip slowly to the ground.

Her sense of place, time, of how easily they could have been seen fell in on her with avalanche force. Yet still . . . still . . . a part of her wanted to say, *The hell with "could-be's,"* and climb once more onto Grey's solid, heavily muscled, perfectly masculine body. She didn't, of course. Instead, she stumbled back a step and touched her hair and fiddled with her collar. When she looked up, she saw Grey engaged in a similar activity, loosening a nonexistent collar and clearing his throat. He caught her eyes.

At the same time they both blurted out, "I'm sorry."

He smiled, and her embarrassment melted under the rare, gentle look. "I shouldn't have done that," he said.

She laughed, blushing like a schoolgirl. "And here I was under the impression that I'd been the one who'd 'done that.' "

"I don't think so."

"I do."

"Are we going to fight about it, do you suppose?" he asked. The idea didn't seem to upset him. His eyes glittered.

"Do you want to?" She fluttered her eyelashes.

Good heavens, they were *flirting* with each other, she realized incredulously. What was she doing? She had just finished outlining for her poor, senseless heart that any relationship between them did not stand a chance. Yet here they were, involved in some sort of bizarre mating ritual, the sort reserved for hedgehogs and porcupines and other equally prickly species. The thought made her smile, albeit sadly. Grey reacted by taking a sharp, involuntary step forward. He stopped himself.

"More than you can imagine, but this is hardly the place or time."

Her spirits collapsed in disappointment. "Of course. Did you discover anything in town about the threat to Amelie?" She struggled to find her dignity. She couldn't. Her heart was singing too loudly. "Not the place or time" meant there *was* a place and time.

"No. I saw McGowan before he left on the train, but he had nothing new to add. Then I spoke to a half dozen people, and then another half dozen"—his smile turned wry—"to appease you. No one knows anything about a letter. Most of them don't even know Lord Collier's title, let alone where to send correspondence, which leads me back to my original theory: Whoever sent that letter must be someone who wanted to keep Collier from whatever business he was attending on the Continent."

"I see."

And she did. Grey and Hayden would leave on the next train, at first light the day after tomorrow.

There was nothing else to say. What had she expected? Her heart felt as though it were being ripped to shreds, and her vision blurred. She turned her head so he would not see the threatening tears as Caesar raised his voice in a long, mournful howl, echoing the despair she felt. Brutus added his plaintive cry.

Oh, no. Not now.

She wiped her eyes with the back of her hand, willing herself to go numb, feel nothing, shed the emotions roiling through her. No good. Her heart contained a maelstrom of anxiety, desire, fear, and . . . and . . .

She had to leave, get away from him now, before others arrived and gave her turmoil a voice.

Gray looked toward the house. "Poor brutes," he murmured.

"Yes," she whispered. She had to leave. She could feel them, vague, sympathetic spirits drawn like metal filings to a magnet.

Grey sighed. "I hope McGowan made arrangement to have them fed." He was filling the void with words. But the void she foresaw was too large ever to be filled.

"Yes."

"Do you suppose they miss him and that's why they are baying like that?"

"No."

They are baying because they know my heart is breaking.

Chapter Thirty-two

Grey was missing something; he was certain of it. Something important. He just couldn't figure out what. The dogs were howling like the end-time was near. Fanny's eyes had dilated to enormous black pools, and she was staring at him with a completely unreadable expression.

"I have to go," she said. She sounded flustered, unnerved.

So was he. "Don't," he heard himself whisper.

Her gaze flew to his face. She looked startled. What was he doing? What was he thinking? He wasn't. He was feeling, always a dicey proposition, but damn, he was tired of fighting his emotions. He couldn't do it anymore. He didn't even want to try. He wanted to trust her. Trust what he felt as well as what he thought.

"Grey. You don't understand."

He laughed. "You're right."

"You don't. . . ."

"I don't," he agreed.

"Please."

"Whatever you want." *For however long.*

"You are making this very difficult."

"Yes. I know. I'm a bastard." He was. That she wanted to leave, ached to leave, couldn't be more apparent. She kept twisting around, her gaze darting anxiously. "I have never learned the art of pretense."

They were the wrong words. Her face blanched.

"Damn it," he said. "Fanny. Please. You must believe me, that wasn't a subtle gibe."

That brought a tremulous smile to her face. It was ridiculous how much pleasure it brought him. "It wasn't all that subtle. But you never are."

"I know. But let us both agree the past is over. I am sorry I judged you without knowing you."

She sobered. "You don't know everything about me now."

He shivered, controlling the impulse to sweep her up in his arms. He'd done enough sweeping for one day. "I know enough. You must believe me."

A fleeting expression of bewilderment and tenderness touched her face. "I do," she whispered.

He smiled. "Well, there's that."

"I wish I could tell you—"

Crack!

Whatever she'd wished to say was lost in the sound of a gun report. He swung toward the sound. It had come from the direction of Quod Lamia.

"What was that?" he asked.

"I don't know," Fanny said, frowning down the road. "Poachers?"

"No." She shook her head. "There are no poachers in Little Firkin. There's no need to poach. Anyone wanting to hunt has an entire mountain range at his disposal."

A tingle of apprehension touched his spine. "We have to go."

She didn't answer; she was already hurrying toward Quod Lamia.

They arrived at the house ten minutes later to find a breathless Hayden in the drawing room with Amelie collapsed in his arms, shaking uncontrollably. On the floor behind them a pool of shattered glass lay beneath a broken window.

"Someone shot at her!" Hayden exclaimed, his mouth drawn tight with shock and anger.

"From where?" Grey demanded, going to the window and looking out. "Did you see anyone?"

"No. I just got here," Hayden replied. "I was coming to see how you were faring. I must have been half a mile away when I heard a shot. I ran as quickly as possible and found Amelie huddled in the corner."

The girl began sobbing. Hayden's arms tightened around her.

"Thank God, thank God she wasn't hurt." The boy's voice shook, and in response the girl's cries grew even more heartrending.

Damn whatever coward had done this, Grey thought, frustrated. There was nothing to see out the broken window, except some more glass sparkling on the terrace below.

"Where is Violet? Ploddy?"

Hayden shook his head. "I don't know. I haven't seen either of them."

"No," Fanny said, her voice oddly harsh. "No. You will not suspect either of them. *I will not allow it.*"

She was breathing hard, her face as white as milk,

her eyes filled with suffering. But she hadn't moved from the doorway. She stood rigidly. "Tell us where they are, Amelie."

Her voice held a note of pleading. Grey understood. This was her family. She would be devastated to discover that one of them sought Amelie's death. Amelie finally lifted her head from Hayden's chest to look at her companion. Her eyes were huge, stricken, afraid.

"Violet went to see Grammy Beadle, who has taken poorly with a stomach ailment. Bernard asked Ploddy to drive him and his luggage to the train platform. He's still in Little Firkin."

Easy enough to check. Too easy. Grey mentally removed them from a list of suspects.

Amelie's words released Fanny from the tension holding her. She stepped forward, her hands outstretched toward her young charge, her eyes filling with tears. With a choked sound, Amelie left the shelter of Hayden's arms and flung herself into Fanny's waiting arms. She enfolded the girl tenderly, her cheek resting against the bright red hair, her eyes closed, tears seeping from their corners.

By God, he would find whoever was responsible for this. By all that was holy, he would. To think he'd almost left them here in such imminent danger. What if he'd gone yesterday? How could he have been so horribly wrong, and who would have paid the price for his error in judgment? Amelie? Fanny?

"Where did the shot come from?" he said.

Hayden, his eyes on Amelie, gave a short, frustrated shake of his head. "I don't know. Close. Near the house."

Grey nodded. "It would have had to be quite close if the shooter intended to hit his target," he said.

"Why is that?" Fanny asked quietly. Her eyes had opened, but she still stroked Amelie's hair.

"That was the report of a sidearm, not a rifle or musket."

Fanny's hand stilled. "I see."

"I doubt there are many sidearms in Little Firkin. We should be able to discover who owns one easily enough, and from there who has access to one," Grey said.

Amelie lifted her head from Fanny's shoulders. "Unless someone brought one in," she suggested softly.

Ah. Good. Her fear was subsiding. He'd already figured that Amelie had a sharp, analytical mind. It was a relief to see her using it.

"True. But at least it gives us a place to start."

"We must send for the constabulary," Hayden said. "At once. This is no longer a matter of speculation. Amelie's life is in danger."

"Oh!" At this reminder, Amelie buried her face once more in Fanny's shoulder.

Hayden's handsome young face collapsed in misery, and he looked as if he were an instant away from snatching her back out of Fanny's embrace into his own.

"Of course," Grey said. It was not in his nature to sit back and wait while others uncovered schemes and subterfuge. "But it might be some time before they arrive from Fort George. In the meantime, there is no reason I shouldn't try to discover things that might aid their investigation."

The reality of her situation had once again set Amelie's shoulders to shaking with fear.

"I swear nothing will hurt you, Amelie," Hayden said, coming closer and lifting a tentative hand toward the girl.

"Amelie," Fanny said softly, trying gently to disengage her. "Amelie. Lord Hayden is in *agony*."

It struck Grey as an odd thing to say, but the girl responded, allowing Fanny to unwind her arms from her neck. She clasped Amelie's wrists, lifting her hands between them. Tenderly, she kissed Amelie's knuckles and froze. It was only a fleeting instant, but long enough to catch Grey's attention. Then she turned the girl toward Hayden and stepped back.

Amelie took one look at Hayden's anguished face and began sobbing again. Hayden tried to put his arms around her, but she shook her head, backing away and burying her face in her hands.

Grey, whose well of unquestioning sympathy had just about been plumbed, grew aware of a frisson of impatience. He couldn't imagine Fanny going on like this, and was frankly becoming a little bored.

"She's overcome," Fanny gently told Hayden, who looked as though he'd just taken a dagger to the heart. She put a bracing arm around Amelie. "Come along, darling. You should lie down."

"Yes. Of course," Hayden said. "I've been insensitive."

Amelie wailed through her fingers.

Grey frowned, a terrible suspicion forming in his mind. *No. It couldn't be.*

Hayden blanched.

"You should begin your investigation," Fanny said. All her tears had dried up, leaving behind an oddly chill cast to her magnificent eyes.

"Yes," he said, his frown deepening. "I will."

Her arms still anchored firmly around the girl's shoulders, she led her from the room.

Grey watched her, troubled.

Amelie had just been fired upon, the house was empty of servants, and yet Fanny hadn't asked either Hayden or him to stay and act as a guard.

Why was that? What reason did she have to want to be alone in the house?

Chapter Thirty-three

Amelie gave in to the sobs racking her. She had never been more afraid, more miserable. She clung to Fanny, but as soon as the door to the bedroom shut behind them, Fanny's arm dropped from her shoulders and she stepped away.

"For the love of heaven, Amelie, wash your hands," she said in a hoarse whisper.

Amelie stared, startled. "What . . . ? Why? What do you mean?"

Fanny shot her a dark, impatient glare, turning the key in the lock. "You reek of powder."

"I'm not wearing any."

"Not that sort of powder. *Gun*powder," she said tightly.

Sightlessly, Amelie sank to the edge of the bed.

Fanny knew.

"You'd best just pray poor Lord Hayden was so overcome with fear for you that he didn't notice," Fanny continued, turning back around, "or if he did, that he didn't recognize the implication of the scent.

The poor lad, he had no idea why you wouldn't accept comfort from him."

Fanny knew. She knew about the gun, and she probably knew Amelie had written the letter, and . . . and *everything*.

"Oh, Fanny. I am so sorry!" she cried, rising and stretching out her arms.

"Hush!" Fanny said. She made no effort to come to Amelie. She stood listening at the door.

Amelie had never seen Fanny wear such an expression. She wasn't merely upset; she looked haunted, and her gaze held not a whit of warmth. She couldn't have lost Fanny's love. She . . . she depended on it, depended on her. She wasn't as mature and ready to stand on her own as she'd thought. She needed Fanny.

"Fanny, please! I had to. I was desperate!"

The coldness in Fanny's eyes melted beneath Amelie's fresh onslaught of tears. With a sigh of surrender, she came to the bed and sat down beside her.

"Why didn't you tell me?" she asked.

"I knew you wouldn't approve." Amelie gulped. "I knew you'd stop me. You'd never condone deceit in order to accomplish an end. You . . . you are too honest!"

"Stop." A spontaneous sound of anguish escaped Fanny's lips and she twisted away. Pain filled her face. "Oh, Amelie."

"I was careful," she said. "Except for the gun, and that was only because I had to improvise. Don't you see? He was going to leave unless I found some reason for him to stay, Fanny! You heard Lord Sheffield. He'd convinced himself the threat was against Lord Collier or his business or something equally ridiculous, and believing that, he would have told Lord Collier I was not in any danger. After that Lord Collier would never have asked me to come to London. And Hayden would forget about me!"

"That is the reason you shot the gun today. But why did you send the letter in the first place? And how did you manage to overturn the urn? Oh, Amelie." Fanny's skin paled. "Grey might have been killed."

"I didn't overturn the urn. The cat really did. It was an accident. I swear it. I would *never* risk anyone's life like that."

Fanny regarded her soberly. "And the letter? Why did you send it? Why now? Why all of a sudden?"

"Sudden?" Amelie cried, stung. "There is nothing sudden about it. We've been here more than six years, Fanny. A *third* of my entire life!" All the frustration, the injustice of her incarceration, came flooding back. "I was sentenced to exile without any say in the matter, just expected to sit here while the world races by, hoping that when I arrive in it, I'll be able to catch up."

"You should have told me you felt so strongly," Fanny said.

"I did. I told you all the time, and your answers were always the same: 'There's no sense grousing about it.' 'We must accept those things we cannot change.' 'No use complaining.' " She lowered her face into her hands.

"My dear . . ." The compassion Amelie had longed for Fanny to give her appeared. Having finally revealed the secrets she'd held so long, Amelie had unburdened herself. The relief was enormous.

"I didn't ever imagine this would go so awry," Amelie said plaintively. "I'd written Lord Collier a half dozen times, begging him to let us go to live with him in London, but he always wrote back refusing. Oh, politely, of course." Here she sniffed. "He travels too much with business and political concerns for it to even be feasible.

"But I thought that if the situation were dire enough, Lord Collier would be compelled to act and summon us to London. I never imagined he'd send someone to investigate. But even that didn't matter once"—her head dipped shyly—"once I met Lord Hayden. Oh, Fanny, I love him so much. I couldn't bear to lose him. I *can't* bear to lose him. That's why I had to come up with some reason Lord Sheffield would stay longer."

Fanny shook her head. "You didn't need to go so far. If Lord Hayden feels the same way, he'd have come back. And if he didn't return, then you were mistaking a fantasy for reality, and you are better served to learn it now, rather than later." Her eyes were shadowed with some painful recollection.

"Oh, he does!" Amelie averred. "He has told me he loves me."

"But he hasn't asked you to marry him," Fanny said somberly.

"No," Amelie said, drawing herself up. "But he must have reasons why he hasn't yet, and he will. He loves me, Fanny. I *know* he does."

"Then you should have trusted him," Fanny said flatly.

Amelie twisted away, her brow pleating. Fanny was not being very sympathetic. But then, she could not imagine Fanny ever being so in love that she would do anything to protect it.

"Perhaps I should have," she admitted. "But Lord

Sheffield decided he must leave, and he was going to take Hayden with him, and I was desperate. So I improvised. I might not have thought things out as well as I should, but the thing is done now, and you cannot tell Hayden, Fanny. Promise me."

"Amelie," Fanny said, exasperated. "If I have figured out your ruse, it is only a matter of time before Sheffield does."

"No." Amelie shook her head violently. "He was never close enough to smell the gunpowder on my hands. There's no reason for him to suspect me. This will work."

"Amelie. It wasn't that clever a ruse."

Fanny was wrong. "How do you know? Are you such an expert at ruses then?" she asked defiantly.

Fanny held her gaze. "Yes. I am." She did not explain this enigmatic statement further, instead sighing. "Look at the facts, Amelie, and you'll see you're the only one who *could* be responsible.

"You're one of the very few people who know where to send correspondence so it will reach Lord Collier directly. You weren't in the least concerned that an attempt had been made on your life when the cat overturned the urn yesterday. You didn't even try to dredge up a bit of a fret. You sent the servants conveniently away just before another 'attempt' on your life."

She continued with relentless logic. "But most important, there is no one in Little Firkin who has any reason to want you dead. And you are the only one in Little Firkin who has a motive to leave here—one way or another. Besides myself." She closed her eyes. "Which I am sure Sheffield is beginning to realize, if he hasn't done so already."

The thought of cool, self-contained Fanny going to such lengths for . . . well, anything brought a tiny smile to Amelie's lips. "No one would suspect you, Fanny," Amelie said.

Fanny smiled weakly in return.

"What am I going to do?" Amelie whispered, her head bowed over her folded hands.

"I suspect you should begin by telling Lord Hayden."

Amelie's head snapped up. "What? No. *No!* He'll hate me."

"No, he won't, Amelie."

"Yes. He'll hate me for lying to him."

"So," she said after a moment, "you prefer to punish him."

"What? No. What do you mean?"

"He is in agony, Amelie, thinking your life could be forfeit any minute and not knowing where the danger is coming from. This is torture for him. I know," she said. "It was torture for me just wondering if someone was trying to hurt you, and that was before there'd even been an 'attempt.' I can't imagine what he's going through now."

Amelie buried her face in her hands, too ashamed to meet Fanny's eye. She'd known, of course. She'd tried to reassure Fanny. She'd done everything to point out that the threat shouldn't be taken seriously. But she still knew how it had worried Fanny. She'd just been so selfishly in love, so relieved that Hayden, at least, had accepted her assurances, so willing to ignore the pain she caused others.

"And Mr. McGowan and Lord Sheffield and even Violet. All of them were concerned."

"I know. I am so ashamed. I am not a very good person, Fanny."

"You are. And a very young one. And a very heedless one. I understand. I know how easy it is to close your eyes to suffering you've caused. But now what are you going to do about it?"

"I can't tell him. I am not as brave as you."

Fanny flinched.

"Someday I will. I swear it."

"Amelie, you cannot build a future on lies."

Guilt and desperation made her sharp. "How would you know? Are you an expert on romantic relationships?" The expression on Fanny's face made her immediately regret it. "I'm sorry, Fanny. I have to be sure of him first."

"And when will that be? Next week? Next year? A decade from now?"

"I don't know!"

"Trust him."

Fanny didn't understand. How could she? She'd been married so briefly, and she wasn't in love. She didn't know to what lengths a woman would go to be with her beloved.

She grabbed Fanny's hand, clinging tightly. "It's my life," she said. "Promise me you won't tell him."

"This is a mistake."

"My mistake."

"I can't persuade you?" Fanny asked miserably.

"No. *Promise.*"

Fanny released her hand with a small distressed sound. "Yes, yes. I promise."

"You'll help me?" she asked pitifully.

Fanny raised her face to the ceiling, as though looking for answers. "I'll try," she finally murmured.

Relief washed through her, bringing with it tears. "Oh, thank you, Fanny! Thank you. Things will turn out. I'll marry Hayden and leave here . . . I mean *we'll* leave here. All of us. You'll see. There'll be happily-ever-afters all around."

Fanny regarded her somberly. "No, Amelie. There won't."

Grey went to the terrace to look for shell casings, thinking that the most likely place from which to shoot. Any shell casings would tell them the make and brand of the gun used, and from there provide a possible lead to its owner. He made Hayden come with him.

The boy was a mess. His late arrival on the scene preyed on his mind, making him feel impotent and ineffectual as both suitor and protector. It was useless pointing out that the shooter might not have even made an attempt on Amelie's life had Hayden been present, or worse, might have shot them both. Hayden didn't even hear him.

His miserable gaze kept returning to the house. "She didn't want me to hold her. She blames me for not being here to protect her."

"Nonsense." Grey might as well not have spoken.

"I should have been there," Hayden castigated himself. "I *knew* the threat was serious. I *knew* I should be on guard." He glanced irritably at Grey. "There was someone on that balcony, but I allowed myself to be persuaded differently."

Ah, yes. A little sharing of blame. Grey didn't care. If it made the lad feel better, he could lay the whole matter at Grey's feet. He wasn't sure he didn't deserve it. But there'd been a reasonable suspect—a cat—and rather than concentrating on Amelie's phantom menace, he'd focused all his attention on another.

"I should have listened to you," Grey said.

"Yes," Hayden clipped out, "you should have. Next time I will keep my own counsel."

"Always wise," Grey mumbled, barely listening. There was nearly as much glass outside on the terrace as had been spread beneath the drawing room window. He looked up. From the pattern of glass strewn on the flagstones, there was no clear indication from what direction the culprit had taken aim. Odd.

He moved farther along the terrace, his gaze on the soft ground beyond the pavers, looking for footprints, shell casings, *anything* that could help him discover who was responsible for the attack.

"What did you do with the gun?" A voice drifted down from an open window above, stern and reprimanding. Her voice. Fanny's.

All the breath left his lungs. What was she talking about?

"He's bound to discover it there. You'll have to rid yourself of it. Toss it in the river."

No. Please, Fanny. No.

He squeezed his eyes shut, straining to come up with some alternative meaning in her words.

"All right. What else?" he heard her ask, as if to herself. "We must manufacture a would-be assassin. Someone whom we can imply was mad and then . . . Not mad. Someone from your father's days in India, perhaps."

There was no alternative explanation.

He'd always suspected she'd written that letter. He was very good at interrogating witnesses, and he knew she'd been hiding *something*. But when he'd accused her of doing so and she'd looked him straight in the eye and sworn she hadn't, he'd believed her.

"No, no, and no," she was saying now. "That will never convince Sheffield. I'll have to think of something else." She paused.

She sounded stern and eminently practical. The woman who owned a voice like that would be devastatingly competent, formidably intelligent, and immeasurably desirable. A woman like that could make even a rude, unvarnished cynic fall in love. Could make him absurd.

And had.

Not surprising, really. When all was said and done, he was his father's child. As gullible and romantic and ridiculous as his parent.

"I'm sorry. I told you I had to improvise," he heard Amelie's voice, broken and tearful. "It was the only thing I could think of to convince him the threat was real so he would take me with him when they left. Lord Sheffield said himself that if something terrible occurred he'd take me with them." There was a pause. "I mean, take us with them."

Take her with him. So that had been the initial inducement, after all. It should make him feel better. At least Fanny's motives had not been entirely self-serving. It didn't make him feel one whit better.

This wasn't about motives and reasons, good or bad, whether she'd lied for her own purposes or for the sake of another; it was about his *heart.* He'd trusted her, and she'd lied to him. How could he ever trust her again? What if her excuse was reasonable, her motive pure? Next time it might not be so pure, or so noble, and the next even more impure and ignoble. How would he know?

He'd spent his life unmasking liars and exposing deceptions, cleaving to the truth like a lover. It was the one thing he'd always revered, could always depend on, immutable in a shifting moral landscape, definitive in a murky prospect, his compass in a tumultuous sea. It was as simple as that.

"This is not going to work."

"It will!" Amelie declared. "Hayden loves me. He'll never leave here without me."

"Grey?"

He turned. Hayden stood a few feet away, his face tilted up toward the open window.

"What did she mean?" Hayden asked in a voice Grey had never heard before from his nephew. But it was all too clear he understood. The expression on his face dissolved any impulse toward pity Grey felt for Amelie.

No matter how much Amelie Chase regretted her part in Fanny's plan, it was not enough.

Chapter Thirty-four

"There's a mistake," Hayden told his uncle.

"No."

"She wouldn't do this."

"She was under the guidance of another."

"I cannot believe it."

"You are not the only one deceived."

"If she did—"

"She did. They did."

"*If* she did, there must be extenuating circumstances."

"The circumstances are simple. I am her means out of here, and when that plan did not work, you became the means out of here. It did not hurt that you are the heir to a barony."

"No." Hayden shook his head, slowly at first, then gaining in force. "No. No. I cannot believe it of her. She loves me."

"You are not the only one who was deceived."

So it went for half an hour. Hayden paced up and down the drive leading into Quod Lamia. His uncle had been unable to convince him to go any farther from the house.

Try as he might, Hayden could not make any sense out of the words he'd heard Amelie say and for which Grey kept assuring him there was no other interpretation than that he and his nephew had been manipulated.

"We should go, Hayden," Grey said. "There is nothing for either of us here." He sat on the ground at the side of the drive, his back against a hoary old oak, his forearms resting on his knees. He did not look triumphant, as he had in the past when he'd exposed some shady plot. He looked grim, like a seasoned Roman centurion pondering his last battle.

The lines in his face, the weary slouch of his shoulders, even the hollows beneath his brilliant eyes only made him look even more like a ruffian fisticuffs champion than usual, and yet, rather than stay and fight, Grey kept arguing for them to leave without confronting the woman who'd so nearly duped him. . . .

Hayden stopped pacing, squeezing his eyes shut. The pain was more than he could bear. Amelie had duped him.

Her face appeared like a vision behind his closed eyes: her blossoming coquetry, her glossy red hair, her pretty eyes and neat little figure. She'd duped him with her unaffected manner, her unexpected bookishness, her infectious eagerness to experience everything he took for granted, her laughter, and her sweetness.

Amelie had *duped* him?

Inconceivable. He simply did not believe it.

With a roar, he punched at the air with his fist, swinging around to face Grey. "No. I will not leave until I've talked to her. She owes me that much, at least. *You* owe me that much."

"I?" Grey said.

"You. You invited me up here." He didn't care that he was being unfair. Being unfair was his due. "Had I not come, my heart would not now be breaking; my world would not now be shattered." He paused. "*If* it is shattered."

"Uh-huh." Grey blew out a deep breath and pulled himself to his feet, dusting his trousers. "Well, if you must, you must."

"I must."

Amelie lay on her stomach on the grass beside the river into which she'd tossed the gun and sobbed. She'd fled here, to her favorite spot, without thinking, unconsciously hoping to find some peace. She hadn't.

She was a coward and a liar. She was purposely putting Hayden through agony because he loved her, truly, deeply loved her, and when you loved someone you could not bear the thought that they were in danger.

Or pain.

She knotted her fists into clumps of spring grasses. If she loved Hayden she shouldn't be able to bear the thought that she was hurting him! But she was. How long could she allow him to believe she was in danger?

A week? A month? A year? Wasn't that exactly what Fanny had asked? Even if no one ever discovered her scheme and she and Hayden wed . . . how long before the constant upkeep of lies exhausted her and something slipped out? She'd kept this secret for only a little over two months and she was already worn out.

If only she could figure some easy way out of

this. . . . She went very still. There was a way, of course. She could simply confess all. Fanny might be right. If Hayden truly loved her—and he did—it would not matter when she told him, today or a year from now; he would still forgive her. And if he didn't? Well, in that Fanny *was* right. If Hayden didn't forgive her, he hadn't ever really loved her in the first place.

She recalled what he'd said that night on the terrace when he'd first told her he loved her. She'd described her connection with animals, and when he'd believed her and she'd expressed her amazement, he looked at her so tenderly and said, "That's what people in love do, believe in one another."

She *couldn't* let him suffer any more. She gathered her resolve and had just gotten up and started forward when a midge flew into her eye, causing her to stumble. She heard the loud sound of a branch snapping as she fell, tumbling down the bank. She came to a stop and rubbed the gnat from her eyes—

Crack!

She froze. That was no cracking branch. She'd been raised in a British outpost on the frontier of India, and she recognized that sound. It was the report from a rifle blast. Her heart began thudding thickly in her chest as a flash on the mountainside caught her eye. Someone was shooting at her.

Grey opened the door and led Hayden into Quod Lamia without bothering to stop and knock. Violet and Miss Oglethorpe were still gone, and he'd seen Ploddy disappear into the carriage house with a large bottle of whiskey. He didn't expect him to emerge until much, much later.

The door hadn't been locked or he'd be forced to break it down. Which, right now, he would be very happy to do. He would dearly like to destroy something. But he didn't. He kept his composure for Hayden's sake. He didn't want to be a poor example for the lad. One didn't go breaking down doors because one happened to be in a stew.

It wasn't working. Disparaging the situation as melodramatic or belittling his feelings with words like *stew* did not make it easier. He didn't want to destroy anything. Except his memories of her. Those he wanted obliterated. No. Those he wanted never to lose a single detail of: the cant of her eyebrow, the husky timbre of her laugh, the graceful way she held a teacup, the black-bramble hue of her hair . . . .

"No one's here," Hayden said.

"Yes, there is." He didn't question how he knew; he just did. He headed down the hall to the drawing room. It was empty, the breeze from the open French windows lifting papers from the overburdened tables and scattering them across the floor. The drapes billowed. The air felt chill.

"Fanny," he called. "The jig, my love, is up."

"I'm out here." There was no hesitation, no covert movements on the terrace. She sounded resigned, tired. He followed her voice out onto the terrace, Hayden at his side.

Her eyes met his. She looked ineffably weary, her shoulders bowed and her eyes clouded. She smiled sadly. She already knew they'd been found out. "I'm sorry," she said.

"No more than I," he answered.

"Where is Amelie?" Hayden demanded.

Reluctantly, her gaze turned to Hayden, who was exhibiting all the youthful outrage and hot-blooded thirst for confrontation Grey so notably lacked.

"She's left."

"Where did you send her? To do what?" Hayden snarled.

She recoiled at the venom in his voice, and Grey reacted, jerking forward.

"It's all right," Fanny said, holding up one hand. She looked at Hayden. "I didn't send her anywhere. She left. I don't know where she is."

"We'll be leaving in the morning," Grey said. "One way or the other."

"Yes."

"Yes?" Hayden demanded, quivering with indignation. "Is that all you have to say? *Yes?*"

She regarded him somberly. "What would you like me to say, Lord Hayden? It is obvious you have discovered that . . ." She hesitated.

Grey's eyes narrowed. She was editing her words, he realized, picking carefully. But then, lies required care.

"You have discovered that the letter asking for assistance came from her," she said, "and that there is no threat to Amelie's life. What more is there to say?"

"I want you to tell me why!" Hayden lurched toward her, his face red. *"Why?"*

Grey seized the boy and dragged him back. "For God's sake, Hayden," he growled, shaking the younger man. "Remember yourself."

"I want to know why," Hayden said plaintively. "I have a right to know the truth. If she's capable of it."

The blood drained from her face.

"I want to know how you coerced Amelie into agreeing to lie to me."

She clenched her hands at her waist and replied in a preternaturally even voice, "She is very young, Lord Hayden. And she wants to leave Little Firkin very much."

"You mean *you* want to leave Little Firkin very much, enough to use anyone and any means at your disposal. I heard you. I was just the alternative plan."

"No," she said. "No—"

"Yes!" All of Hayden's hurt filled that single word. "I heard her say that once Grey decided to leave she had to figure out a way to make us take her out of here."

"You misunderstood."

Grey slowly released Hayden, but remained nearby. The lad looked on the brink of either crying or committing murder. It was a toss-up as to which one.

They were never to find out, for at that moment, Amelie burst out onto the terrace, her red hair flying like a banner, gasping for breath, wide-eyed with fear, her dress stained with grass.

"Bernard McGowan just tried to kill me!"

Chapter Thirty-five

Amelie whirled around, her gaze searching the frozen faces around her. Why was no one doing anything? Saying anything?

"Did you not hear me? Bernard McGowan just shot at me! Twice! He could have killed me!"

"Oh, Amelie," Fanny whispered.

No. Oh, no. They knew. Hayden's face told the tale. She wheeled on Fanny. "You promised you wouldn't tell them!"

"She didn't have to," Hayden ground out before Fanny could answer, his voice hot with anger. "We overheard you plotting."

"Hayden, there was no plot!" She held out her hand to him. He spun away from her. Her panic fell before a new fear. "Hayden? Please. I need you. Bernard McGowan shot at me."

He made a sound of disgust, his back to her. She had to make them believe her. "I was by the river, and when I rose, I stumbled as I heard a shot, only I thought it was a breaking branch, and then I heard another shot and saw the muzzle blast and—"

"Stop, Amelie," Fanny said. "It won't work."

"But it's the truth." Her voice had dropped to a whisper. "The shots were close together, and I knew it had to be Bernard because—"

"Don't!" The word was torn from Hayden.

She stared at his profile, willing him to look at her, to see that she was telling the truth.

He wouldn't. He'd closed his eyes, the sight of her apparently as distasteful as the sound of her voice. "Please don't. I thought if you had a chance to explain yourself, to tell me the truth, you would take it. But you won't. You can't."

She bit back a sob. "It is the truth."

"McGowan left Little Firkin this morning," Lord Sheffield said. "I saw him onto the train myself and watched it pull away."

She didn't understand. She couldn't have been mistaken. "That's not possible. He's *here*, I tell you. He must have gotten off somehow." She knew she sounded as if she were grasping at straws. She was.

"Why would Bernard want to hurt you, Amelie?" It was Fanny.

"I don't know."

Oh, God. Even Fanny didn't believe her, and if she'd lost Fanny's trust, then she was truly lost. She had no one and nothing. She'd done this, she thought, looking at the closed, wretched faces surrounding her. She'd done this with her plans and her lies and—

"It's over, Amelie," Fanny said.

"Unless you'd care to try telling the truth," Hayden said coldly. And now he did look at her, his eyes hot and his mouth a thin line.

"That is the truth."

"Don't make this any more painful than it already is," Fanny whispered.

"Yes. No." She turned blindly and stumbled from the room.

Lord Hayden Collier lay with his arms crossed behind his head, staring at the water stain on the ceiling above his bed. Over the course of the night it had variously taken on the shape of an angel, a demon, and a siren, but eventually every incarnation had evolved into Amelie's face, wearing the same lost expression she'd worn when she'd fled Quod Lamia's drawing room yesterday.

He withdrew his hands from behind his head, clenched his fists, and pounded the mattress on either side. This act, too, had been repeated many times. As had the tossing down of too much whiskey, and staring for long moments at the same page in a book.

He just had to get through the next few hours. Then dawn would come and he and Grey would leave. The tavern owner, Donnie MacKee, had agreed to transport them the thirty-five miles to Flood-on-Blot, where the train was due to arrive in the afternoon. Grey was certain that for the proper financial consideration the conductor could be convinced to accept two passengers.

They had spoken little during the course of their dismal, cold supper. Images of Amelie kept appearing in Hayden's mind. The thought of leaving her, rather than offering the hope of relief from this torment, only made him more miserable. Confused, Hayden had suggested that there was no need for such a hasty departure. He'd explained that he was not so overwrought that he could not bear to spend another day in the same town as Amelie and Mrs. Walcott.

Grey had given him an unreadable expression and said, "Then you are a stronger man than I. We leave tomorrow."

His words had made no sense to Hayden, but nothing would dissuade Grey from his course. Consequently, their bags were duly packed and waiting in the front hall. The Twinningses would clean and close the lodge once they'd left and follow. Soon it would be as if they'd never been here.

Except for the scars that would never heal.

Hayden raked his hair back from his forehead. She'd looked so frightened. And she'd kept insisting that Bernard McGowan had shot at her. She must be a damn good actress. But what if she wasn't? What if she was telling the truth?

He groaned aloud, common sense warring with his heart and neither willing to cede ground.

He rolled out of bed. He simply could not leave Little Firkin without talking to her one last time. He didn't care that it was four o'clock in the morning.

They'd planned to leave town with MacKee by eight o'clock in order to make it to Flood-on-Blot in time to arrange passage on the mail train. There was no time to waste.

He arrived at Quod Lamia and tried the front door, remembering how Grey had simply walked in the house yesterday. Today, however, it was locked, so he skirted around to the terrace. There he paused and studied the windows above for any clue as to which one was Amelie's. All of the bedroom windows on the second floor had been left open, inviting in the unusually warm air. Except for one.

On a soft spring evening, no one shuttered their bedroom window—unless they were afraid something would come in. Something dangerous. It had to be Amelie's.

Hayden scooped up some shards of flagstone from the terrace. Aiming carefully, he threw the small missiles at the shut window and waited. Nothing. He found another handful and repeated the process. Again he waited, and was about to try once more when he heard Amelie.

"Who's there?"

Her voice did not come from behind the closed window, but from the dark rectangle of another window two down.

"It's Hayden."

A pale face appeared for just an instant in the window and, just as quickly, disappeared.

"You shouldn't be out there. It isn't safe. He might be watching." Her voice was a light, frantic whisper.

"I have to talk to you."

"Go home. It isn't safe."

"Not until I talk to you," Hayden replied stubbornly.

There was a long moment of silence. "Can you climb up onto the balcony? He might be watching the front."

"Yes."

"I'll unlatch the door to the balcony, but for the love of heaven, be careful."

He didn't waste any time in clambering up the thick vines coiling around the columns supporting the balcony and hefting himself over the rail. He had to wait a few moments before he saw her slipping carefully along the drawing room wall. She did not stand in front of the French doors, but to the side, reaching out to unlatch the lock. He stepped inside.

Her eyes appeared huge in her pale face. Her hair hung in loose waves around her shoulders. She had not dressed for sleep, but still wore the clothing she'd had on that afternoon.

For a second neither of them moved, and then he was sweeping her into his arms, holding her close, his lips against the silky crown of her head.

"I've been so scared," she said in a broken voice.

"Don't be. I'm here. I'll keep you safe."

"You think I'm lying."

"No."

"You don't believe me."

"Yes. I do." As soon as he spoke, he realized he did. The battle between heart and mind had been decided, and his heart had won. It didn't matter what she'd done, of which sins she was guilty, whether her story made sense or was even possible. He believed her because she'd asked him to. He loved her.

"But I did lie." She was weeping softly into his shirt, her hands clutched in fists against his chest.

"I know," he said. "Mrs. Walcott influenced you."

She'd pushed away from his chest and was staring up at him, her brows drawn together in confusion. "Fanny? Fanny didn't know anything about it."

Amelie was solely responsible? How was that possible? She was just a young girl. He looked for some way to shift the blame from his beloved's delicate shoulders.

"But the degree of planning, the machination . . . Surely she somehow inspired you . . ."

His suggestion did not have the effect he sought. Amelie drew herself upright, and sparks flashed in her exceedingly gorgeous eyes. "You do not think I am intelligent enough to scheme? That I haven't the wits necessary to machinate?"

"No, that's not it at all. I am sure you are capable of any number of nefarious intrigues. But you aren't *like* that."

He thought he'd handled that rather well. Amelie apparently didn't agree.

"But . . . I *am*."

At this, Hayden's mouth fell open, and seeing his flummoxed expression, Amelie's own grew baffled.

"Exactly what do you think I intrigued at?" she asked.

This was rather awkward. The heat rose to his face, and he was glad of the darkness that would hide his blush. "Ah . . . well, you know. Me."

"You?" She sounded stunned.

"Yes. My title. My inheritance. My . . . name."

A heartbeat. A second while his words penetrated. Then a volatile response. "You think I planned to *trap* you into marriage?"

"*Trap* is such an ugly word."

She gasped. "You do!" she thundered accusingly.

"Hush, hush." He grabbed her arm, pulling her close. She was adorably angry. "You'll wake the house."

"There is no one to wake. Violet is with Grammy. Ploddy is probably still sleeping it off in the carriage house, Miss Oglethorpe went to her brother, and Fanny's room is on the other side of the house, and you"—

she finally paused for breath—"you must be one of the most vain men in the world!"

Despite her anger, she did not make any attempt to move away from Hayden. He decided to take this as a good sign as well as to take whatever umbrage she wanted to visit on his head. Apparently, he—persuaded by Grey, he thought darkly—had gotten it all wrong. He was delighted.

"At least, I hope you are, because if you are an example of the young men the world has to offer, I may not want to leave Little Firkin after all. And that, by the way, is the reason I wrote your father and pretended to be threatened: to escape from Little Firkin. *Not* to marry you." She looked at him with a touch of disgust. "The idea! I didn't even know you."

"Well, we did think your original plan was only to escape here, but when that did not work and you met me, you went to an alternative plan."

"Because you are so irresistible?" Amelie said, her eyes blazing with indignation.

"Not at all. Because if I proposed, you would leave here with me."

Her face twisted as though she'd tasted something sour and hadn't decided whether to spit it out or not. Then the tension eased a bit from her shoulders and she sniffed. "Oh."

He released a thin, inaudible sigh of relief. "It was a frightfully clever plan."

"It was," she said, cheering up. "The idea came to me soon after Fan and I became so sick and shortly after I fell into the river. Fan said that if anything more happened, she'd begin to suspect we were being targeted."

"Very clever," Hayden repeated admiringly.

"It was." Her smile faded. "Except I didn't think I would have to lie to *you*. I only wanted to leave here while I was still young."

"I understand."

"But then things started to go wrong. Instead of summoning us, your father sent Lord Sheffield here. And no one but Fanny seemed to take the threat seriously, and then Lord Sheffield decided to leave." Her head bowed. "I couldn't bear the thought that you would forget about me. So I fired my father's gun out the window and screamed."

"I could never forget about you," he averred. "I love you."

Her head shot up. "And I love you! I should have trusted our love, just like Fanny told me to."

"Fanny?"

"She tumbled to the plan after I fired my father's pistol. She smelled the gunpowder on me. She was so upset! But I made her promise not to tell you anyway.

"I was so miserable, Hayden. I went down to the river to throw the pistol away, but I couldn't stop crying and thinking that Fanny was right, and that if I loved you, I would trust you with the truth, and if you loved me, you would forgive me."

"There's nothing to forgive," Hayden replied staunchly. "You are a creative, resourceful, and imaginative young woman who found herself in an unbearable situation and had the wherewithal and courage to do something about it," he said, and he meant it. By God, she *would* be the making of him.

He fell to his knees before her, startling her. "You must marry me. You have to marry me. My life will be meaningless if you are not by my side."

She gazed at him shyly, a dimple appearing in her cheek. "Of course I'll marry you. I was only waiting for you to ask."

"I wanted to do it all properly, and ask my father's permission first."

"Why?"

"That's how it's done."

She laughed, a sweet, soft sound. "Oh, Hayden, I am afraid I have a lot to learn about how things are done. Just look at the mess I've made of our courtship! I manipulated, lied, staged an attempt . . ." Her voice petered out.

"What?"

"I was not lying about Bernard McGowan. He tried to kill me."

She held his gaze somberly, and his own did not waver. "Why do you think McGowan shot at you?"

She nodded, appreciating the question. "I heard gunfire almost every day for the first ten years of my life. I know the sound of the different firearms: the pop of a pistol, the crack of a rifle, the sound of a carbine. I know how quickly various firearms can be reloaded.

"The man firing at me shot twice in a matter of seconds from a rifle. Only a bolt-action rifle can fire that quickly, and that is a military-issued weapon. Almost all the rifles in Little Firkin are single-shot breechloaders passed down from father to son. I doubt there's a bolt-action in town.

"And one more thing," she said quietly. "Bolt-action rifles are used primarily by sharpshooters. Bernard was a sharpshooter in India, and he has such a rifle. Both Fanny and I have seen it."

Gads. What a woman! "You pack. We have to get you

out of here. Then we'll rouse Grey and send for the constabulary and—"

"Lord Sheffield won't take me with you. Don't you see? He won't believe me. He'll think it's another ploy. He has no reason to trust me, and he'll think I have simply . . . beguiled you."

She had a point. "Not if you tell him about the rifle."

"Why would he believe that? I could have just as easily made that up, too." She gazed at him sadly. "No, I'm afraid my lies have caused me to forfeit the right to Lord Sheffield's aid, unless I can prove to him Bernard's involvement."

"What of Mrs. Walcott? Surely she will believe you?"

"She might eventually. But she is hurt right now. You should see her, Hayden. Her eyes are empty, her face devoid of all animation." The state of her companion obviously deeply affected her. "I tried to talk to her earlier, but she would not come out of her room. She only responded, 'Not now, Amelie. I am not angry, but not *now*.'

"Besides," she added, "Fanny can't decide that I should go. As my guardian's representative only Lord Sheffield has the authority to do that."

"Then I'll have to find some evidence to persuade him to take you with us," Hayden said with determination.

"But how?"

"I'll have to go to McGowan's house. If he's fabricated having gone away, he wouldn't risk staying there and being seen. But he might have left some evidence behind. Some explanation might present itself as to why he wants you . . ."

"Dead."

"Dead," Hayden repeated soberly.

She nodded. "Let's go."

He took a deep breath. He'd expected this. "You aren't coming along with me. You'll wait here."

"No, I won't," she said.

"It's ridiculous for you even to think of coming," he returned, growing a bit vexed.

"It's *ridiculous*," she replied carefully, "for you even to think of going without me. Have you forgotten Caesar and Brutus?"

In point of fact, Hayden had forgotten about the enormous, monstrous dogs. "Oh."

"Exactly. You need me. Caesar and Brutus won't hurt me."

"There's a great big difference between a mangy cat and two slavering, vicious dogs," Hayden protested.

She met his eye, absolutely certain of herself. "Hayden. You saw me with the carriage house tom. You saw the ravens in town. Our own horses were deemed unbreakable before Fanny brought them to Quod Lamia. Believe in me, Hayden. *Trust me.*"

He already had, with his heart.

Chapter Thirty-six

Dawn was a pale thread on the horizon when they arrived at Bernard's house. As Hayden had anticipated—he really was a genius—it stood dark and seemingly empty. But someone would eventually be by to feed Caesar and Brutus, if not Grammy Beadle, who had an unaccountable—and unrequited—fondness for the dogs, then someone else. They would have to work quickly.

All they wanted was one piece of evidence. The rifle would be nice. It would still hold the scent of its discharge. Barring that, perhaps there was something in his library or correspondence that gave a clue as to *why* he would want her dead. It still seemed unreal to her. Until a few days ago, she'd been weaving girlish daydreams around the handsome banker. Now he wanted her dead.

"There's a lock around the chain here," Hayden whispered from the gate.

"I have a key," Amelie said. "Bernard has us on standing orders to save his stamp collection in case of a fire when he is away."

She almost laughed. It sounded so absurd. Could dear, stodgy, stamp-collecting Bernard really want her dead? She unlocked the gate and slipped inside, Hayden at her heels.

"I will be watching those beasts like a hawk, Amelie. Should one of them so much as twitch wrong, promise me you'll run out of the house," he said commandingly.

"Yes, Hayden."

"I mean it, Amelie. While I trust your belief in this . . . empathy you have with animals, I am not certain every living creature knows it has one with you."

"They do," Amelie returned confidently.

And then they were at the door, peering through the unshuttered windows into a long hallway devoid of furnishings or ornamentation. At the far end slunk the gargantuan black silhouettes, heads lowered and hackles raised. The dogs had already heard them.

"You were right. Bernard isn't here," she said excitedly, then explained, "Bernard doesn't ever allow the dogs in the house when he's home. I think he's a little afraid of them."

"Well, I bloody well would be," Hayden murmured, his gaze riveted on the enormous beasts milling uncertainly at the end of the hall.

All she needed to do was shepherd the dogs into one of the smaller, unused rooms and shut them in. Then they could begin their search in earnest.

"Brutus! Caesar!" she called through the door. The dogs froze, Brutus, the larger, cocking his head toward her voice.

"That's it, boy. It's me, Amelie." She turned the knob and the door slid noiselessly open.

"He doesn't keep it locked?"

Amelie turned. "Bernard once told me that locks were more a psychological barrier than a real deterrent, and the dogs were both."

"I see."

"Wait here." She slipped into the hallway, shutting the door behind her. "Brutus? Caesar. It's me."

The dogs still hadn't moved. Caesar was audibly sniffing the air, and Amelie, despite herself, began to feel uneasy. A low rumbling issued from the dogs' vicinity. They knew she was uneasy. That had to be it. She had to master her uncertainty; it was making them uncertain.

She straightened her shoulders and smiled. "There, now, lads. What is all this grumbling about?" she said softly as she walked toward them.

Brutus's head lowered. Caesar's lips curled back, and in the chancy light of predawn, she saw the gleam of wickedly sharp fangs appear.

"Come back here, Amelie," she heard Hayden say. "*Now.*" He must have opened the door. No wonder the pair was reacting so aggressively.

"Shut the door," she said, without taking her eyes off the dogs. They'd begun to prowl closer, the light catching their black eyes and lending them fire. "They'll attack you."

"Amelie."

"Trust me."

She heard the door click, and relief made her knees go weak. She expelled a long, slow breath, smiling tremulously. "There. He's gone." She took a step forward, holding out her hand. "Come on now. We'll all go in the—"

One moment they were on the far end of the hall; the next they were bolting toward her, snapping and snarling, long ropes of saliva streaming from their open mouths, their nails clattering like a runaway train across the bare wood floor.

No! They couldn't be attacking. Not her! Animals loved— She stumbled around, amazed and horrified. Too late! Already, she could almost feel the damp heat of their breath. She flung up her arms to protect her face and was snatched out of the air and shoved aside.

She fell, sliding across the floor as she saw Hayden careen into the path of the dogs. He'd wrapped his jacket around his forearm, and Brutus's jaws tangled in it. Caesar fishtailed in midair and fell heavily as he skittered wildly, trying to come to the aid of his companion.

"Get out!" Hayden roared, pummeling the dog with his free hand as it savaged his arm. "Amelie. Get— Ah!"

Brutus's thrashing had torn through the cloth layers to Hayden's flesh. With a crash Hayden fell to his knees, rolling as he clutched Brutus's throat, holding the snapping maw bare inches from his face.

"Hayden!" she screamed. "Hayden!"

"Brutus! Caesar! Here! *Now.*"

At the whip-crack sound of the male voice, the two dogs froze. Brutus's head wrenched around in Hayden's grip and he whimpered, scrambling with his back legs to free himself. Caesar flung himself to his belly and crept into the shadows.

Bernard McGowan emerged from the stairwell, his face carved into lines of grave concern. He was carrying a bolt-action rifle.

"Good Lord," he murmured, his eyes traveling to

where Hayden sat, his back against the wall, the jacket in shreds around his bloodied arm. "Look at all that blood. Can't have that. My house must be free of evidence. Which means I have some cleaning up to do."

Hayden was breathing hard through his nostrils, his chest heaving up and down, his hair tousled, and his face glistening with sweat. Without thinking, Amelie ran to him and fell to her knees at his side. Hayden clasped her close with his good arm.

"Hayden, your arm!"

"It's not as bad as it looks." He gave her a wan smile. "Or at least, as I assume it looks."

He shifted, grimacing as he tried to rise, but Bernard's voice forestalled him.

"Please do not further complicate matters by making me shoot you." Bernard pointed the rifle at them, illustrating his point.

Hayden turned a glowering gaze on their captor. "We thought you were gone."

"As I should have been," Bernard agreed mildly. "I should have been miles from here by now, but Miss Chase's unfortunate clumsiness has delayed me. Although I blame myself for missing the second shot. I am clearly out of practice. And now I am in the unenviable position of having to improvise another plan."

He sounded merely pettish, like a librarian who'd found tea spots on a book jacket. It terrified her. "Why are you doing this, Bernard?" she whispered. "I thought you cared for me. I thought we were friends."

"I do. We were." He sounded surprised. "But as Mrs. Walcott was so instrumental in pointing out, friendship was as far as our relationship would ever go. Even if this young man hadn't come into your life.

Unfortunately for you, a short time ago something else came into mine, too."

"What is that?"

"A Two-Hump Yellow Wrong-Kneed Camel."

Neither she nor Hayden could think of what to say to this.

"It's a stamp," Bernard said primly. "*The* stamp. The stamp that will complete my collection, the work of my life."

"Aren't you a mite young to have completed your life's work?" Hayden asked with something of his uncle's caustic irony.

"No."

"When did this stamp show up?" Hayden asked. He was trying to buy them some time, Amelie realized.

"Months ago. That's the way with stamps. First there's a rumor, then a substantiated viewing. Then rumors of bids and counterbids . . . The proceedings can go on for months. Even years. I thought there would be plenty of time to woo Miss Chase, secure her guardian's consent, and acquire the beauty."

He was not speaking of her.

"But then . . . well, I am a realist. I saw the way things were going. So I began to make other plans," he said.

"Happily, Miss Chase, you had already laid the groundwork for me, claiming two attempts on your life that would have been impossible for me to have made, since I was in New York City on one occasion and on a ship in the mid-Atlantic another."

She'd forgotten her fear by now. She could not fathom how this man could be something so different from what she'd assumed. So cold. So calculating. But still just as pleasantly correct. "But how can my death benefit you, Bernard?" she asked.

"The Art Workers Guild," he said patiently. "They'll pay handsomely for the land Little Firkin sits on. It's not as much as your inheritance would have been, but with a loan or two, it will suffice for me to buy the Two-Hump Yellow Wrong-Kneed Camel."

"But you don't own . . ." She began shaking her head in confusion, but then it all came suddenly clear. "If the residents default on their loans, you'll own all their property."

"Oh, they already have. Nine-tenths of Little Firkin lives on credit. Credit extended to them. Sometime after your death—not too soon, of course—I shall insist they repay their loans. Since they will not be able to, their houses, and the land they sit on, will become mine."

"Why not demand they repay you now?" Hayden asked. Sweat beaded on his brow, but he still managed to sound reasonable, calm.

Bernard shrugged. "There are any number of people who would be willing to take over their debt on the merit of their future prospects. But with no future prospects, no one would be willing to extend them aid. And I own their land as collateral for their debts. Do you see now?"

"But that will take months."

"The crockery chap has already offered to lend me a great deal of money in exchange for co-ownership of the mortgages I hold on the land here." He smiled again, apologetically. "Now, then. Up you go, both of you."

Amelie's fear rushed back in. "What are you going

to do with us? You can't just kill us. People will be looking for us."

"Tsk, tsk," Bernard said. "Not at once. Especially since as soon as I leave here I will take the liberty of sending Lord Sheffield a wire, purporting to be you, Lord Hayden, telling him that the two of you have eloped."

"He won't believe it."

"Oh, I think he will. After all, the poor devil is looking for any excuse to leave."

"What do you mean? Why do you think he wants to leave?" Amelie asked, more to buy time than because she was interested in his answer. She knew why Lord Sheffield wanted to leave: He loathed her as a liar.

Bernard screwed up his face, studying her as though trying decide whether she was affecting ignorance or not. "Mrs. Walcott," he finally said.

His answer caught her off guard. Sheffield might despise her, but why would he hate Fanny? "What about Fanny?"

"He can't bear to be near her."

"Why?"

"What?" Hayden said.

Bernard looked taken aback. "You mean you two really didn't know? How could you not?" He shook his head ruefully. "Can there be a more self-involved creature than a young person in love?" He sighed.

"Lord Sheffield is in love with Mrs. Walcott," he explained with exaggerated patience. "But his nature is fighting against his heart for precedence in the matter, and he will not allow his heart to win. Having recently experienced something of the same problem myself," he said modestly, "I am most sympathetic to his plight. My heart, however, won out."

He was talking about the stamp again. Comparing it to Sheffield's love. Sheffield's love? The world grew more surreal with each passing moment.

"Now," he said, "we've chatted long enough. I've things to do, arrangements to make. Later, after night falls, we'll all take a walk over to Quod Lamia and pay a visit to the handsome Mrs. Walcott. Until then, you'll be my guests here."

He was going to kill Fanny, too. Because Fanny would never accept that Amelie would leave her without saying something to her, nor would she believe Amelie's death was accidental. Not after all that had transpired. Fanny, Hayden, everyone she loved was going to die because of her lies.

And a stamp.

She burst out laughing.

Bernard scowled. "Now, now. No hysterics," he cautioned.

She lifted her chin. "I wouldn't give you the satisfaction," she said. "I was laughing at how ridiculous you are, killing people for a stamp."

He nodded, his expression pained. "I quite agree," he said. "Indeed, I have thought exactly the same thing myself. 'This is ridiculous, Bernard! Have you lost your mind?' But then I think of that blank spot between the red camel and the blue and it doesn't seem to matter." He shrugged. "Now, into that room." He pointed the rifle into a small antechamber, which was unfurnished, like much of Bernard's house.

"And lest you think of trying to leave . . ." he added,

snapping his fingers. Brutus and Caesar, lurking in the shadows, leaped forward, their massive chests rumbling. "Please recall that the dogs will be waiting outside the door."

Without another word, Amelie wrapped her arm around Hayden's waist and helped him in. Behind them, Brutus and Caesar growled.

Chapter Thirty-seven

"Where are Hayden and Amelie?" Grey asked. He stood on Quod Lamia's porch, his hat in hand, and drank in the sight of Fanny like a man dying of thirst drank clear, cool water.

Except there was nothing clear or cool about her. The ultra-composed woman of a few days ago had vanished. She looked as exhausted as he felt. Dark circles bruised the delicate flesh beneath her eyes. Her hair settled like an ebony cloud on shoulders bowed by fatigue. Her skin held a grayish cast and her eyes were haunted.

"Fanny," he said more gently still. "Where did they go?"

"Go?" She sounded confused. "Amelie is still in bed. . . . I . . . What do you mean, 'Amelie and Hayden'? Why would you ask that?" She pinched the skin on the bridge of her nose, as though she were having trouble concentrating.

Wordlessly, Grey handed her the wire message. She bent her head over the single sheet, sweeping her hair back with one hand in an unconsciously elegant gesture. As forceful and opinionated as she was, there was still something of the woodland sylph about her, an otherworldly grace, an aura of fragility that everything else about her belied.

She looked up. "This says that Hayden and Amelie have eloped."

"Yes," he replied to her tone more than her words. "I don't believe it either. Even if he doesn't care whether or not he is disinherited by his father, Hayden has too much regard for the girl to jeopardize her reputation by eloping with her. I assume they are hiding here somewhere, waiting until I leave to reveal themselves. I also assumed you would know where they are."

She flushed. "No. I know nothing about this. But I intend to find out."

She turned, her hair whipping around lightly, her vibrancy returning as she strode along the corridor. He followed her, weaving through the cluttered hall, up the staircase, down another equally cluttered hall to a closed door. She pounded once on this portal. When no one answered, she opened the door. The room was empty. The window was closed, its drapes drawn, and the bed had clearly not been slept in.

Fanny looked, her expression concerned. "I don't know where they are. I swear it."

He didn't know what to think. His thoughts were too colored by emotion to trust them. Part of him wanted to believe she was as surprised and dismayed by this empty room as she seemed. The cynic in him suggested that her reaction had been prettily orchestrated to convince him she was telling the truth. The truth. It always came down to that.

"I don't care," he heard himself say. "Far be it from

me to interfere with whatever ruse you have plotted. Whatever it is, I am convinced Hayden is complicit. If he wants to stay here, so be it. He's of age. About the rest, I don't give a damn."

It was a lie. A terrible lie.

"Tell my nephew I wish him well." He began to turn away, but her voice stopped him.

"Wait. This is no scheme," she said. "At least, not to my knowledge."

"So, you are saying that McGowan really shot at Amelie yesterday?" he scoffed.

"No. I know Amelie made up the previous attempts upon her well-being and wrote that letter." She frowned. "And I don't think McGowan has done anything. But then, I also thought she was through lying before she said it."

"I don't care whether you know their plans or not. If Hayden is foolish enough to elope and the girl is foolish enough to agree, then good riddance to them.

"Who knows?" he said. "Were I younger, had I less knowledge of the world, and my history bore fewer abject lessons in deceit, I might have done the same thing in his situation."

He was speaking of her. Of them. And she understood. It was there in her eyes.

"Would you?" she whispered.

His tone, having begun harshly, dissolved into regret. "Yes. Oh, yes."

"But those days are long past," she said, watching him closely.

He wanted to deny it. Instead, he said, "Fanny? Aren't you tired? I am so tired of wondering what is and isn't the truth."

"I haven't lied to you. Not once since you've arrived."

Disappointment welled up inside him. "For the love of God, Fanny—"

"No," she broke in forcefully. "I haven't lied to you. The letter and the rest, it was all Amelie's doing. I just found out myself. And I didn't lie about anything else." Her gaze did not waver. "I cannot explain everything. There are things I haven't told you and things that are mine alone to reveal but I have not lied."

He turned away from her, his reason and his heart estranged from each other. He raked his hair back from his temples with both hands, closing his eyes, trying to concentrate.

She'd claimed she hadn't written the letter to Collier. Had Amelie? But Fanny hadn't corrected Hayden's charge that she had coerced Amelie into being part of a scheme she'd devised. She hadn't substantiated it, either. Had she been protecting Amelie? Why wasn't she now? He had never wanted to believe anything so much.

And now, finally, he understood his father's mania, his obsession, and how wanting a thing could separate a man from his reason and make him a fool. And, dear Lord, he would gladly, happily give anything to become a fool for her. To make a leap of faith and trust his heart.

But he couldn't.

He'd spent too many years revealing the truth behind the most cherished lies. He did not have faith; he needed proof.

"Will you tell me something?" He heard his heart in his throat.

She did not hesitate. "If in doing so I do not betray a confidence entrusted to me."

"I can't think that would be the case here."

"Yes. Then yes." It was a vow.

"In London. In Mayfair six years ago," he said, "how did you manufacture the sound and sensation of what others described as angel wings in"—he hesitated, unable to bring himself to say *your husband's*—"in Brown's séance parlor? What brushed so many of your clients' hair and cheeks?"

She actually shivered, briefly closing her eyes against his question. When she opened them, sadness filled them. For a long moment she looked at him, her gaze traveling over his features with a sort of hungry resignation reserved for a man embarking on a voyage from which he knew he would not return.

"Fanny?"

She sighed. Her shoulders lifted in a little apology. She smiled unconvincingly. "Bats," she said. "There was a colony in the chimney."

He regarded her in disappointment. "You can't train bats."

"No," she whispered. "You can't."

"Then how . . . ?" He let the question hang unfinished between them.

She lifted her hand in a gesture of entreaty, looked at it, and let it fall. She laughed and it turned into a soft sob. "What shall I call it?" she muttered aloud. "What word will make it palatable for you? What word will allow you to accept it? Accept *me*?"

"Fanny. What are you talking about?" he asked, profoundly concerned.

"Magic."

"Magic," he repeated. He could not believe she was saying this to him. He waited for her to explain, laugh, roll her eyes. She did none of these things.

"Magic," he repeated. "You are saying you conjured the bats?"

"Conjured? No. I simply called them to me. They . . . felt my purpose, I suppose."

Her gaze fluttered about the room. Whether she was seeking escape or inspiration, he couldn't tell. She looked on the verge of tears.

"Not just bats," she went on. "Every animal. If I feel something very strongly, if I feel the need of something very badly, they react. They answer that . . . inner communication."

"Dear God," he murmured.

A tear slipped from her eye.

He stared at her helplessly. He could not understand why she would do this. "Why are you saying this, Fanny? Why would you seek to provoke me this way? Knowing how much I loathe this sort of thing. Is it because I love you?"

"No." She shook her head violently.

He did not stop. His heart was breaking. "Is it because you have decided that anything further between us is impossible? That you wish to send me away without a shred of hope? Is that it?" A horrible thought occurred to him. "Is this, perhaps, your version of *kindness*? Because if it is, I beg you, be unkind."

"No!" Her voice was choked and hoarse. "It is because I do love you. Because you asked for the truth and I swore I would tell it to you."

He sighed deeply, wearily. Whatever her reasons,

she was not going to give them to him. "You are empowered with supernatural gifts?"

"Gifts?" Her laughter hurt to hear. "A curse. Yes."

"You have some sort of empathic relationship with animals?"

"Yes."

"You called the bats from the chimney in Brown's parlor to simulate the presence of spirits?"

"Yes." She nodded, a flicker of eagerness brightening her black eyes.

"Then call them now."

Her body jerked as if he'd suggested she shoot him. "I can't."

"Of course you can't."

"You don't understand," she cried plaintively. "It was never something I cultivated. Only those few years with Alphonse, and I never mastered it. I could call the bats, but only because they were so near already. It took every bit of my concentration to hold them there, and as soon as I let up, they vanished back up the chimney."

"Convenient."

"Grey, please. I didn't ask for this. I didn't seek this thing. I don't want it, and I have spent the last six years trying to suppress it. It isn't like whistling for a dog."

"It happens only when you are overwrought."

"Yes, yes!"

"Then it's too bad you can't manufacture up a bit of emotion, isn't it?" he said, gazing at her sadly.

For a second she stared at him, and then she tipped back her head, her eyes squeezed shut, her expression agonized. "It doesn't work that way," she whispered.

He took a step toward her. He couldn't help himself. She was so sad and so lovely, and she was everything he'd ever love and was fated to lose. It didn't matter whether she believed in this fantasy she'd spun or was simply trying to deceive him. Either way, she represented everything he could not believe in and everything he had fought against for his entire adult life.

He wished he could be angry. He couldn't. He'd felt similarly toward his father, wanting to despise him and being incapable of doing so. He didn't have the capacity to despise one whom he loved. It was his weakness; it was what made him vulnerable. He'd tried to protect himself, to hide the vulnerability beneath cynicism and caution. He'd done so well.

Until Fanny.

What hubris he'd possessed, thinking he could choose whom to love and when. But she'd swept into his imagination and then his dreams and finally his life, laying waste to all his self-assurance and peace of mind, destroying what he thought he knew and leaving him in a shambles.

"I love you, Fanny," he said, tenderly brushing a lock of black hair from her damp cheek. She trembled. "But I cannot betray who I am, even for you.

"There is no magic, just magicians. And amongst their stratum, my beloved, you are unquestionably without peer. I am utterly enchanted. I doubt I shall ever recover." He tried to smile. Failed.

"Grey . . . There is magic. I am sorry. I am so sorry. But there is."

"Hush." Gently, he cupped her face between his palms and lowered his lips to hers. Softly, sweetly, lingeringly, he kissed her. And when he finished, he rested his forehead lightly against hers until a shudder passed through him. He forced himself to step away and let his hand drop from her damp cheeks, tenderly bestowing a last caress as his fingertips fell from the soft curve.

"Tell Hayden—" He swallowed, looked away. "Tell Hayden I will wait for him until this afternoon, but I intend to be in Flood-on-Blot before dawn. I can't stay here. I can't. But if he chooses to stay, tell him—" He cleared his throat. "Tell Hayden to hold tight to his illusions. They are worth far more than reality. Good-bye, Fanny."

He did not look back.

Chapter Thirty-eight

So much for truth, Fanny thought, and started laughing and then sobbing and then laughing again. She dropped down onto a stack of books beside the hall table and buried her face in her hands.

A fresh onslaught of tears shook her to her very core. Grey had gone. He'd kissed her good-bye, and it had taken every ounce of willpower not to wrap her arms around him and beg him to stay. Thank God she'd managed to restrain herself. He already thought she was either mad or moronically committed to her own lies.

But in a short while, Donnie MacKee would drive him in his pony cart to Flood-on-Blot, and she would never see him again. She tipped her head back, and somewhere high on the mountainside a female fox wailed, Amelie's pony kicked in her stall, and a flock of starlings chattered at the windowsills.

"Oh, yes," she said through her tears, "*now* you show up. Where were you ten minutes ago?"

But what would have changed even if they had appeared? Grey would simply see a flock of birds, hear the results of a bee stinging a horse in its stall, and hear a vixen emitting a spring mating call. Nothing more. He was a professional skeptic.

She began weeping once more.

She had to stop this. It was accomplishing nothing. And it was important to accomplish something. Why? Because . . . ? She shook her head. There was no reason to accomplish anything more. She'd done quite enough for one day: lost the man she loved, lost Amelie. . . .

She stilled. Amelie. Where *was* Amelie? And Hayden? Like Grey, she didn't for a moment think they'd eloped. They had to be around here somewhere, relieved that Grey had left without further pressuring Hayden to accompany him or staying to glower at his nephew over his perceived idiocy in trusting a lying, deceitful woman.

Youth. Hearts' desires were not that easily come by.

There would be obstacles, not the least of which would be Hayden's father, especially after Grey reported Amelie's deceit. It would be far better for the couple if Hayden left with his uncle. At least he would be able to present a case for Amelie to Collier.

Fanny rose to her feet, wiping away her tears. If she stayed focused on the here and now, the jeering specters of the past and the pipe dreams of an impossible future could not find her, and she could buy some time to learn to live with regret. She would find Amelie and Hayden and convince the boy that he did more for his suit by leaving than by staying.

It would be nice to have some help looking for them, but Violet was still tending Grammy Beadle, who was still sick. Miss Oglethorpe was still in Flood-on-Blot delivering her monthly report on the dire doings at Quod Lamia to her brother. But where was Ploddy?

She hadn't seen him since yesterday afternoon, when he'd put the carriage away. She frowned, going to the kitchen and calling his name. There was no answer, so she climbed the back stairs to the servants' quarters. Ploddy's room, as befitted a former batman, was neat and tidy. The bed had not been slept in.

Was no one sleeping in this house but Fanny?

A touch of concern chased her back to the main floor. "Ploddy!" she called, looking in rooms and poking her head out windows. There was no answer.

Sometimes, when Ploddy was having a bad streak, he hid in the carriage house, in the loft above where they stored hay. But Ploddy hadn't been having a bad streak. A little setback here and there, but it had been months since he'd been so inebriated he couldn't function. And it had been at least a week since he'd even tippled and she'd found that bottle and upended the contents down the privy and then found Donnie MacKee and promised she'd be visiting his establishment with her golf club if he sold Ploddy one more bottle.

Still, there was nowhere else to look. She headed into the carriage house, where the big old feral tom greeted her with a sidelong glance of affront. "Yes, yes," she said distractedly. "I waved a blanket at you. You weren't mortally injured."

The cat abandoned his pose of indifference and came to her, twining around her legs. She hauled the huge creature up into her arms, burying her face into his dense, scarred pelt. Here in the safety of the carriage house she needn't fear being seen cuddling the savage animal.

Several small females appeared, members of the tom's harem, meowing questioningly. She set the tom down and brushed her hands lightly over their arching backs. She then found the rope that worked the trapdoor leading to the loft and tugged it until the door swung open and the ladder dropped down. Leaving the cats behind, she climbed up the steep rungs and poked her head into the loft's dust-mote-spiked atmosphere.

Ploddy lay flat on his back on a pile of loose hay. A half-empty bottle of whiskey—carefully corked—had rolled from his outstretched hand, the neck pointing accusingly at him.

"Oh, Ploddy." She hoisted her skirts and climbed into the loft, going to stand over him as he snored gently away.

She nudged him with her toe. "Ploddy. Wake up."

He grumbled and turned away from her, a line of spittle running down his chin.

"*Wake up.*" She used her foot to roll him onto his back.

"Ow!" he complained, finally opening his eyes. He peered up at her from eyes the color of cranberry jelly. His lips were cracked and caked, and the tongue he swiped over them looked just as dry and white. He groped with his free hand for the whiskey bottle.

She kicked it away.

"Tha's mine," he protested. "I earned it."

"Earned it, did you?" She would eviscerate MacKee when she found him. What had he talked Ploddy into doing? Sweeping out his bar?

"Mis-ser M'Gowan gib it to me," Ploddy mumbled indignantly. The wretch was still drunk. "Now, there's a g'enlman!"

McGowan? Fanny scowled. Bernard knew about Ploddy's drinking problem. He knew what a struggle it was for the old man to stay sober, and how hard they'd all fought to help him, Bernard included. Ploddy had to be lying to protect his cohorts.

"Are you sure MacKee didn't give this to you? Or one of his cronies?" she asked darkly.

"Nah," he sneered, trying to struggle to his elbows and failing. He gave up and flopped down flat on his back. "Pack of cowards. Scared shitless of a black-haired biddy. Not a pair o' balls amongst the lot of 'em." He flapped a hand at her. "Go 'way."

And with that, his eyes rolled back in his head and his mouth dropped open. In a second, he was snoring.

There was no reason to wake him again. It would be hours before he was lucid enough to navigate the ladder.

She picked up the whiskey bottle and was about to empty it out of the loft window when its label caught her eye. Fanny did not know a great deal about liquor, but she did know enough to realize the bottle she held came from the Lowlands. She could not imagine anyone in Little Firkin importing whiskey.

Except Bernard.

Why had Bernard given Ploddy a bottle of whiskey? Once asked, the question would not leave her alone. She dropped the bottle and descended the ladder, her thoughts racing. The only reason would be because Bernard had wanted Ploddy drunk. And the only reason he would want Ploddy drunk was so that Bernard could be sure that Ploddy was incapacitated.

She stood outside the carriage house, a choir of barn swallows chittering in agitation as they tumbled through the air above her. Where had everyone been yesterday soon after Bernard's train had left? Hayden and Grey had been confronting her, Violet had already left for Beadletown, Miss Oglethorpe was gone and . . . and Amelie was down by the riverbank, where she claimed someone had shot twice at her. Someone who knew her habits and that she often went there alone. Someone like Bernard McGowan.

Anxiety churned in her stomach. But why would Bernard want to hurt Amelie? It made no sense. He'd been courting the girl.

But Bernard had known Sheffield's plan to leave Little Firkin, and he had witnessed Amelie's reaction to it. It would not take much imagination to deduce that after such a disappointment a heartbroken girl would flee to her sanctuary to be alone. The perfect place to stage an ambush.

She could stand here wondering why Bernard would do such a thing, or she could act on her fear that he had. She decided to act. She swung around, quickly realizing that the first step was that she had to find Grey—

Grey was gone. So were Hayden and Amelie. Where *were* they? Panic sizzled through her thoughts, sparking dire scenarios in her imagination. Had Bernard— No. She would know if something had happened to Amelie. She would know it. She clung desperately to that belief. They were somewhere; she just had to find them.

Where would they go? She pounded her temples

lightly with her knuckles, trying to focus, to put herself in Amelie's shoes.

Amelie was shot at, and was certain it was Bernard, but when she told her best friend and guardians what had happened, no one believed her. For all intents and purposes, Fanny had locked herself in her room, leaving Amelie alone, unguarded, and afraid. Then perhaps Hayden arrived and was convinced, as Fanny should have been convinced, of Amelie's sincerity. What would they do? Where would they go?

To find some proof to convince others of Bernard's treachery. At Bernard's house.

But that would be insane. Bernard's house was guarded by two ferocious monsters—she inhaled on a hiss—that Amelie was convinced would never harm her, because she had a "connection" to all animals, wild or tame.

There was no time to go for help. No one to go to. No one who would believe her.

A shudder raced through her and she started down the drive, first walking fast, then trotting, then bursting into a dead run, her skirts held high. If anything happened to Amelie, if those dogs attacked her, it would be Fanny's fault. She'd been so intent on establishing herself as "normal," she hadn't done enough to dissuade Amelie from taking seriously what she believed was her recently discovered affinity for animals.

She flew along the road, barely aware of her burning lungs, her aching side, the cutting pain of the stones beneath her thin leather soles. Behind her, unnoticed, dozens of ravens slowly fell into formation in a long, wavering line, trailing her like a black banner in the sky. In the ditches, rabbits darted in frantic confusion, while ferrets streaked nervously through the woodland verge and foxes slunk anxiously amongst the shadows of pine and oaks.

She arrived at Bernard's house to the sight of an open gate. Heart thundering, she ran up the drive to the house and grabbed the knob, twisted it, and rammed her shoulder hard against the portal. It fell open without resistance, and she stumbled into the hallway. The first thing she saw was blood.

On the floor, against the wall. Amelie's blood?

A terrible sound filled her ears, and she swung toward it. It was the dogs, Caesar and Brutus, crouched beneath the stairs, their massive heads low, panting harshly. Dried blood caked the side of Brutus's neck and shoulder.

"No," Fanny whispered.

Brutus whimpered in response.

She didn't blame the dog. Brutus was simply a tool, fashioned by a far greater monster than himself to be a weapon.

"No," she repeated then. Raising her voice, she cried out, "Amelie!"

"Fanny!"

She spun around at the sound of Amelie's voice. With a sob of gratitude, she ran down the hall toward the door through which Amelie's voice had come.

"In here! Hayden is hurt!"

Fanny grabbed the handle, but it was locked. She looked around for something to use to pry open the door, but Bernard's home was as unadorned as a monk's cell. The only things he'd ever spent money on were his stamps and his clothing. The house, for the most part, was empty.

"I have to find the keys," she called out. "Do you know where they are?"

"I don't know!" Amelie answered. "Perhaps his stamp room. There's a desk. But be careful. The dogs are vicious, and Bernard is nearby."

"Where?"

"Why, right here, Mrs. Walcott," Bernard McGowan said.

Chapter Thirty-nine

"Dear Lord"—Bernard McGowan *tsk*ed coming through the open front door—"how much money must one pay nowadays for an adequate guard dog?"

Fanny froze, her gaze on Bernard. Behind her Brutus and Caesar had emerged from the darkness under the stairs and were slinking toward her, panting laboriously. For a second she wondered if she could somehow rouse them to turn on Bernard, but it was a short-lived thought. Animals reacted to her emotions, not her will, and right now her predominant emotion was fear. Like tuning forks responding to some inner vibrations she emitted, the dogs had begun shaking and anxiously licking their lips.

"Brutus! Caesar! Heel!"

Fanny jerked at the sharp, vicious crack of Bernard's voice. She'd never heard him sound like this before.

Caesar yipped but didn't move.

"I should just shoot the damn things," Bernard muttered, and now Fanny saw that he had a rifle with him. Her fear jumped to another level. He raised the gun and fear became dread.

"Don't shoot them!" she cried, terror-stricken.

As if she'd dropped the flag at Ascot, the dogs broke, launching themselves forward, streaking by her and through the front door past Bernard, who turned to watch them disappear down the drive in amazement, his rifle still leveled against his shoulder.

"When I find those curs, I shall ship their carcasses back to their breeder and demand a refund," he said.

"You scared them," Fanny said, trying to find a conciliatory tone. "They thought you were going to shoot them."

"How would you know that?" Bernard asked. "No matter."

He looked her over with a sigh of forbearance. "Well, Fanny, I must say I didn't expect you. Didn't Lord Sheffield have the courtesy to tell you your charge had eloped with his nephew? Admittedly he lacks polish, but he was raised as a gentleman."

She wouldn't tell him anything.

He shrugged. "Not that it makes any difference. The end shall be the same."

"What end is that?" she asked.

"Yours, I'm afraid. And Lord Hayden's. And Miss Chase's. Three." Now he looked saddened and a little perplexed. "I would so much prefer if it were only one. I tried. I did."

"You meant to kill Amelie."

"But only Miss Chase," he said. "I'm not a murderer. Well, I mean, I am a murderer. Or will be."

"You don't have to be," Fanny said gently. She dared not move. All she could do was hope to keep Bernard talking, to buy some time so that whatever madness possessed Bernard passed, leaving them all unscathed.

She'd known Bernard for years. He'd been a friend to them. He'd been one of the few sources of companionship they could rely on. He was not a murderer.

"Yes," he said. "I do. I have tried to think of some other way in which I might acquire the Two-Hump Yellow. I have spent countless hours devoted to the task. And there is none."

"Then maybe you don't need the . . . humps."

Her words clearly disappointed him. "No. You're wrong. I must have it," he said. "Mrs. Walcott—*Fanny*—have you never experienced passion?"

Her thoughts flew to Grey. "Yes."

"Then you understand. When one is in the hold of a passion, one is not accountable for one's actions."

"No, Bernard," she disagreed calmly. "The nature of a person should inform his passion, not vice versa."

His skin grew ruddy. His lips tightened. "I thought you would understand."

"I do. Let us go, Bernard. The Yellow Humps will wait."

"Two-Hump Yellow Wrong-Kneed Camel! *ONE-CENT!*" The words exploded from Bernard with a spray of spittle.

There would be no reprieve. No convincing Bernard to back down. He was gone from them. She hadn't been aware of when reason had ceded its place to this mania, but somewhere over the weeks and months it had.

"How will killing us get you your stamp?"

He was marching down the hall toward her, his face

twisted, the gun barrel bobbing with each stomping stride. She cowered back, and he grabbed her upper arm and jerked her in front of the door where Amelie was held. He shoved a key in the lock, gave it a twist, and kicked the door open, shoving her inside.

"Ask them!" he said, slamming the door shut behind.

"But why is he keeping us here this long if he intends to kill us?" Fanny asked. They had been in the bare room for what seemed like hours, and the light coming through the clerestory window was growing tepid with the waning day.

Amelie had bound Hayden's arm as best she could, but she had told Fanny sotto voce that the bite was deep and there was nothing she could use to clean the wound. She feared infection. Fanny didn't have the heart to point out that it was likely Hayden wouldn't live long enough for infection to set in. None of them would.

"Because he intends to take us somewhere else," Hayden said, shifting his injured arm and grimacing. They had huddled together against the wall, Hayden with his good arm around Amelie, Fanny on the girl's other side.

At Fanny's questioning look, he elaborated. "Because he doesn't want our bodies to be discovered here."

"He told you this?"

Hayden nodded grimly. "How could he explain the murder of two of his neighbors and a baron's son in his house? He couldn't."

Fanny leaned her head against her knees, trying to think of some way to subvert Bernard's plan.

"Where will he take us, do you think?" she asked, little expecting an answer. Hayden surprised her.

"He is going to take us all to Quod Lamia and burn the house down. With us in it."

Fanny's head snapped up. "Did he tell you this?"

Again, Hayden nodded. "He said the place is a fire-trap waiting to happen."

All those papers and books and journals and boxes, all the accumulated clutter of six years. Bernard was right: Quod Lamia needed only a spark to go up in a blaze.

"I have heard that being burned alive is a terrible death," Amelie whispered.

"We'll refuse to go. He'll have to shoot me," Hayden vowed tautly.

"No," Fanny disagreed sadly. "He'll have to shoot Amelie. Do you really think you could bear seeing her shot, not fatally but in some excruciating manner?" She didn't need him to answer. "Of course not," she said more gently. "We'll just have to do as Bernard says."

"Then we're lost," Amelie said.

Fanny did not answer. She let her forehead fall against her knees again.

"The dogs," she heard Amelie say.

"What about them?" Fanny murmured.

"Maybe I could turn them against Bernard. Maybe I could cause them to—"

Oh, God. This, too? Why not? A clean slate at the end of days—wasn't that what all sinners longed for?

"You can't make them do anything, Amelie," she said.

But Amelie had been inspired by the idea. She scrambled away from the wall, turning to face Fanny and Bernard. "I know I wasn't able to commune with them earlier, but I wasn't prepared. If I concentrate very hard, they might be made to—"

"You can't make them understand anything, Amelie. You never could."

"You're wrong," she said. "Donnie MacKee's runaway team, my pony, the ravens, they all responded to me—"

"They respond to me," Fanny broke in, and though she spoke quietly, her words sent a visible shock through Amelie.

For a second, no one spoke. Fanny felt Hayden's gaze, but she had eyes only for Amelie. A dozen emotions appeared and disappeared on the girl's face. She sank down off her knees.

"I don't believe it. You don't even like animals." She didn't speak with much conviction. Fanny could almost see the girl reworking various incidents in her memory, trying to ascertain Fanny's place in every scenario where she felt she'd communed with animals, and realizing that Fanny had been present at every one of them.

"I'm sorry," Fanny said quietly.

"You're sorry?" Amelie echoed, her expression unreadable. "You let me think I was special and it was you all along?"

"Special?" Fanny's lip curled around the word. "There is nothing 'special' about being a freak. You know what 'special' means, Amelie? It means being separated from everyone and everything you love. It means standing on the outside, looking in. I told you that you weren't a witch. I tried to convince you there was nothing unusual about you except your reputation. I never treated you as anything other than what you were," Fanny said.

"But don't you see? I *wanted* to be unusual."

"You don't know any better. You're young. The world hasn't dealt with you yet."

Amelie waved away her words. "You should have told me," Amelie said. "You should have trusted me."

"Yes and yes," Fanny said, each accusation a lash she accepted as her due. Fanny raised her hand imploringly. "As far as I know, I am singular," she said. "Everyone I have ever cared for is different from me. Including you. And everyone who has ever known about my difference has in one way or another distanced themselves from me."

Amelie continued regarding her coldly.

Fanny tried again. "You've always wondered why I didn't speak about my past or my husband. I'll tell you why now. My family lived in Surrey. I was just a toddler when they realized how animals responded to me. I think at first everyone was charmed. Until one day I was angry with my brother, so angry that . . . well, the dogs on the estate . . ." God, this was hard. "They were worked into a frenzy of rage. They attacked him and he was crippled. He's never forgiven me. I was afraid after that. I was afraid to ever feel anything too strongly. Until I met my future husband."

Amelie was watching her, wide-eyed. Hayden, too.

"He wasn't an army officer. He was a fake spiritualist. Alphonse had heard about my rapport with animals. He'd decided to court me before he'd ever even met me. Not that I knew that at the time. He told me I was 'special,' that I had a 'gift from God.' He asked me to make use of that gift in his séances. I did, because Alphonse said he understood what I was and loved me because of it. And that he could help me control it and we could in turn help others."

This was so much harder than she'd have ever imagined it would be. But then, she'd never imagined telling anyone. "Except he didn't really feel that way. The day he fled, he sent a message through his mistress, telling me that I gave him the 'heebie-jeebies.' Those were his exact words." She looked away from Amelie. "My dear husband, to whom I'd given my body and my heart, didn't want either. He had just been using me to help him defraud people."

She gave herself a little shake. She had to pull herself together. Confession might be good for the soul, but all she felt was defiled. "Six years ago, in London, Grey Sheffield exposed him, and me, as frauds. Alphonse fled the country and died shortly thereafter in a railway accident. He left me behind."

"Grey knew you? He recognized you?" Hayden asked.

"Yes." She bowed her head. "He thought I was perpetuating some sort of fraud here. He thinks I am lying now. Or mad." She inhaled a deep, shuddering breath.

"That's why I didn't tell you, Amelie. I didn't want to ever have anything to do with my 'special gifts' again. All I wanted to be was normal. Not mad. Not . . . 'different.' And living here with you in Little Firkin, for a while I was," she said with as much dignity as she could muster.

"I wouldn't have cared," she heard Amelie whisper.

Fanny looked up and met Amelie's gaze. And she believed her. She smiled and reached out to touch the girl's cheek. "I know. But I did."

"Very pretty." They swung toward the sound of Bernard's voice. She hadn't heard him enter. He stood just inside the room with the rifle pointed at them. "But now it's time to go."

Chapter Forty

Donnie MacKee drove a fine buggy, the seats well sprung and padded, the backrest high, and the wheels well-oiled. He liked his cart almost as much as he liked talking. And best of all he liked the money Grey had given him to make this evening ride to Flood-on-Blot.

Grey barely noticed him.

On the western horizon, the sun was rolling down the slope of a white-shouldered mountain, spreading a veil of pink and mauve behind it. To the east, the dusk seeped across the landscape like mist. Grey appreciated none of it. His gaze was fixed, his thoughts on Fanny.

He'd come to the conclusion that Fanny sincerely believed she had preternatural abilities regarding animals. But a man would have to be mad to share that belief just because he loved her.

Love should not rob a person of his integrity or reason. Yes, in a perfect world, love and truth should go hand in hand, but Grey knew better. Love guaranteed nothing. Certainly not happy endings. Look at his father, who'd loved a wife, then a daughter, then lost them both and finally lost himself in seeking to find them again.

"Whoo-ee! Will you look at that?"

Uninterestedly, Grey looked up to see where Donnie MacKee was pointing. Behind them, a churning cloud of black wings rose in a dark column above Little Firkin.

"Never seen so many ravens crowdin' the sky at one time like that. Must be a thousand. Strange is what that is."

"An omen?" Grey suggested with weary derisiveness.

Donnie rested his index finger alongside his nose, nodding sagely. "Aye. An omen fer a certainty."

Grey scoffed, his gaze on the black cloud. He might as well believe that Fanny had sent the birds spiraling up to the heavens like that. Hadn't she claimed animals reacted to her emotional state? If that were so, then those birds represented an emotional upheaval of epic proportions.

Just as it would take a leap of faith of equally epic proportions for him to act on that theory.

By both nature and choice, he was a man of science, not faith. The thought had never left him feeling so empty.

"What do you think, Lord Sheffield?" Donnie asked, slowing his team.

"I think they're migrating," Grey said. "Drive on."

In order not to risk anyone seeing him march Amelie, Hayden, and Fanny at gunpoint, Bernard walked them cross-country along the slope of the mountain, keeping to thickets of trees and down in the rills cut by the spring snowmelt. To further assure their cooperation, he kept Amelie in the back, with his rifle's barrel aimed between her shoulder blades. Around his torso, he'd wrapped a long length of sturdy rope whose purpose Fanny did not want to guess at.

Above them swirled an ever-growing flock of ravens. The heather and grass around them shifted and whispered with the passing of countless small bodies. But nothing impeded their progress. Fanny hadn't expected anything else. But both Hayden and Amelie clearly did. They kept looking back at her, their expressions desperate and questioning.

"I'm not their master," she finally said, the burden of their expectations too much to bear. "I'm not privy to their language. I can't direct them. They're just anxious and scared."

At this outburst, Bernard paused their march. "What are you talking about, Mrs. Walcott? To whom are you referring?"

"The animals!" Amelie swung around. "Have you not eyes, Bernard? Can you not see? We are surrounded by animals and they . . . they are all Fanny's *minions*!"

For the first time that day, Bernard looked truly startled. His gaze flew to the air, and for one brief instant Fanny held out the hope that Amelie's ploy had worked and that Bernard would be so unnerved by this unexpected avowal of witchcraft he would let them go, or at least drop his guard. It was a short-lived hope.

"Dear heavens, you both really believe you're witches, don't you?" He shook his head, seeming amazed and saddened. "Such madness. I never suspected."

His sadness was as brief as Fanny's hope.

"Soon enough ended," he murmured, and jabbed Amelie with the rifle barrel.

Hayden saw and jerked toward Bernard, his face livid.

"Stop, Lord Hayden, if you want Miss Chase's last hours to be painless."

Hayden stopped. But only just.

The boy was having a difficult time, torn by his inability to act and his fear for Amelie's safety. Thank heaven his native good sense had thus far prevailed. But if Bernard kept provoking him, Fanny had little doubt he would end up dead sooner rather than later.

Finally, they reached Quod Lamia. Once more, Fanny watched hope die in Amelie's eyes as it became apparent that no one was there.

They entered the house through the back door, Bernard looking about. "Do you ever throw anything away?" he asked after a second, smiling. He didn't seem to expect an answer.

He motioned them into the drawing room. "First you, Lord Hayden. Miss Chase, if you would be so kind as to tie Lord Hayden securely to the chair?" He cut a length of the rope he'd carried and tossed it to her. "Most securely. I will be checking."

Without recourse, Amelie complied. True to his word, Bernard checked the ropes and so discovered that she'd left a space between Hayden's wrists that might allow him to slip free.

Without a second's hesitation, Bernard swung the butt end of the rifle into the side of Hayden's face. Blood exploded from his nose. Amelie screamed and flung herself toward Hayden, but Bernard caught her by the arm, holding her back. Fanny edged sideways, but Bernard saw her and leveled the rifle at her.

"This is unconscionable!" Bernard shouted at them. "Do you think I want to do that? I hate this. *I hate this!*"

He shoved Amelie forcefully against Hayden, whose head was lolling against his chest. "Now, tie him up, and do it properly or I will break his nose all over again!"

With shaking hands, Amelie obeyed, sobs catching in her throat as she worked. When she'd finished, Bernard checked the ropes again. "Good," he said. "Very good. Now, then, upstairs, you two."

By now Hayden had regained consciousness. "What are you going to do with them? Where are you going with them?" he shouted, struggling against his bindings.

"Now, then, young man," Bernard said, his tone chill with offense. "Nothing untoward, I assure you. But if it is to be assumed that Miss Chase and Mrs. Walcott died in a house fire, they'd hardly be sitting about the drawing room while flames consumed them, would they? No. They'd be in bed.

"You, Lord Hayden," he continued, as if bestowing a great favor, "will be thought to have arrived too late to save them, but in the course of attempting to do so, you succumbed yourself. You'll be a hero." He actually waited then, as if expecting Hayden to thank him.

"Say your good-byes, Miss Chase."

Amelie stared at Bernard. All the defiance had gone out of the girl. She shivered where she stood, arms wrapped tightly around herself, slowly rocking, a ghastly cast to her skin.

Fanny had to do something, say something. She said the one thing she'd been clinging to, the one hopeless hope she'd been holding tight in her heart, proof against the madness and fear.

"Listen to me, Bernard." Her voice sounded shaky, even to her. "You must listen to me. If you hurt us, Grey will find out. He will burn down your house and every stamp in it. Then Grey will find you and he will kill you."

At this threat to his stamps, Bernard froze. His brows clenched together over the bridge of his nose. "Grey? Who is . . . Grey? You mean Lord Sheffield?" He laughed. "My dear Mrs. Walcott, Lord Sheffield is miles away from here. I waited until I saw Donnie MacKee drive him out of town before coming back and getting you."

And there it was, her final hope gone, disappeared like a conjurer's dove.

"Donnie MacKee turned around," said Grey Sheffield from the doorway.

Chapter Forty-one

Bernard swung around, already firing, and this time he did not miss. The bullet caught Grey, spinning him around and throwing him back into the hall.

"Grey!" Fanny screamed as Bernard snapped off another round. The bullet hit the doorframe, blasting it into splinters. Bernard dodged back into the room, grabbing hold of Fanny and dragging her in front of him. A sense of déjà vu seized Fanny. She'd been here before, shielding a craven while Grey stalked him.

Amelie had pitched herself onto Hayden and was working frantically to untie the ropes binding him. Bernard paid them no mind. His gaze was riveted to the doorway. Fear glided beneath his tense expression. "Lord Sheffield. Come out or I will be forced to shoot Mrs. Walcott."

"Didn't you hear her, McGowan?" Grey's voice was strong and sarcastic. "If you hurt her I will go to your house and destroy every one of your stamps; then I will return here and kill you."

"You wouldn't," Bernard breathed in horror.

"I would. I will. In fact, if you do not surrender

yourself this minute, I'll be off. You can watch the fire from here."

"No!" Bernard shouted. Sweat beaded his forehead. The veins stood out like cords on his neck, and a red film coated the whites of his eyes. "No. You mustn't," he sobbed. "You can't."

"Let her go."

"No!"

"Then good-bye."

Breathlessly, Fanny waited. She heard the sound of footsteps receding down the hall and a door opening and shutting. Bernard shoved her away, and she fell to the ground as he ran to the front window, tearing open the drapes and flinging open the casement. He leaned out with his rifle. "I'll kill him! I'll kill him!" he muttered feverishly. "Where is he? Where is he?"

"Here." Grey stood once more in the doorway.

Startled, Bernard jerked back from the window, firing randomly. Grey started forward, a look of fierce anticipation in his eyes. Bernard fired again, but he was rattled now, his hands shaking, and the bullet went awry. He fired again and the hammer fell on an empty chamber.

"Sloppy, Lieutenant McGowan," Grey said. "Six bullets. You're done."

With a growl, Bernard swung the butt of the rifle, aiming for Grey's head. With a low snarl, Grey caught it midflight. Bernard's eyes widened in amazement.

"No one threatens Fanny," Grey said, and for the second time in six years, he knocked a man clean out a window.

Hayden stumbled to his feet, feeling ridiculously light-headed now that the danger was past and he realized just how much of his blood was on the floor, on his shirt, and on Amelie's dress. He sat down again, cursing.

Luckily, Amelie didn't seem to find anything lacking in his attempted heroics. She kept weeping and touching his face and weeping again and declaring that a broken nose was no great matter if properly set at once.

Grey had fared far better. McGowan's bullet had hit him in the biceps but caused only a flesh wound that Fanny had grimly, and silently, bound. Afterward Grey had tied up the unconscious McGowan and left him lying on the front lawn. In the meantime, they would wait for Donnie MacKee. He had stayed at the end of the drive awaiting Grey's signal, per Grey's instructions, Grey having been concerned that the rotund innkeeper would be more liability than aid. Then MacKee could haul McGowan away to his bar's cold cellar for keeping until the authorities arrived.

"But, Grey, how did you do it? We all heard you walking away and the door closing," Hayden said, beginning to enjoy the cooing ministrations of his beloved.

"Ploddy," Mrs. Walcott said. Grey smiled at her admiringly.

"Ploddy?" Hayden repeated.

"Yes," Grey said. "I found him outside when I arrived, trying to decide whether or not to mount a rescue by himself. Would have done it, too, if I hadn't shown up. Grand old gaffer. Came into the house with me and stood right next to me the entire time. As soon as I said I was leaving, well, he left. Bernard made the proper assumptions and . . ." He shrugged.

"Ploddy, a hero," Amelie said wonderingly. "Where is he now?"

"He's guarding McGowan. I think he's settling in to enjoy his newfound hero status." Grey's gaze drifted toward Mrs. Walcott, who'd been uncharacteristically silent.

Hayden watched, trying to decide if there was anything to Bernard's claim that Grey and Mrs. Walcott were romantically involved. He didn't think so. They were both far too self-possessed, their natures too chilly and superior to ever know the sort of love he and Amelie shared.

Ah, well. He pulled Amelie closer.

Grey watched her, his heart, his only desire, and when she rose and left he followed. He found her on the terrace, looking out on the dark meadow. She must have heard his footsteps, but she didn't turn. Her eyes were raised to the night sky, a spangle of stars strewn across its black canopy.

"Bernard pushed the urn over," she said.

"So I assume."

"You *assumed* it was a cat." He heard the smile in her voice.

"For a while," he admitted.

She turned then, and he caught the glint of pearly teeth. "Why did you come back?"

"Enchantment," he said. "You cast a spell on me, and I was compelled to come to you, to find you, to remain at your side. It was a very fairy-tale moment."

She laughed, a full, throaty sound. "But you don't believe in magic."

He stepped closer to her, and damned if he didn't hear nightingales begin to sing sweetly from nearby. "Don't I?"

"No." She sobered a little. "But you should. Grey, I cannot be anything other than what I am."

He studied her face, falling in love all over again. "Fan, I do not know what you are, but I do know who you are, and that is a maddening, audacious, vinegary, and yes, *enchanting* woman whom I madly, ardently, stupidly love, and I would not change one thing about you. Ever."

She gazed deeply into his eyes, and whatever she saw there brought a shimmer of tears to her eyes. But she would not let them last long, lest he think he'd brought her anything but joy. "Not one?" she asked.

"Well," he allowed, "except for this strange obsession you have about clean-shaven men . . ."

And then he was pulling her into his arms and kissing her thoroughly, passionately, and deeply. And she did not protest about his lack of skill with a razor.

Not at all.

Chapter Forty-two

Lord Grey Sheffield was finishing his second cup of coffee and enjoying a lively account of paranormal activity when an enormous round shadow slid across his paper like a solar eclipse.

He glanced up and promptly did a double take.

"Good Lord, Fanny," he said, sitting back in his chair. "You've outdone yourself. I feel confident in saying no other woman in London is capable of balancing an entire table of ornamentation atop her head with as much sangfroid as you."

His wife, decked out in an extravagant hat and a lacy white dress that fit her form like a second skin, smiled. "So, you like it, then?"

"God knows why."

"Because it is chic," she said, shifting a small furry lump from one arm to the other, "and you, through your stubborn refusal to spend any time on your own appearance, must perforce delight in my elegance."

"Hmm," said Grey, his eyes falling on the whitish mound. "Is that another dog?"

"No. You told me no more dogs."

"Only because the howling at night has become a matter for some dispute with the neighbors. What is it then?"

"A rabbit. Quite quiet. I'll let it go in the garden."

"There is no garden. Your beasts have destroyed it."

"They're not mine."

"Yes, I tell myself the same thing about me."

She laughed and bent to set the rabbit on the floor.

"Amelie sent another letter yesterday. They are in Brazil now," she said.

"How many months is this honeymoon of theirs to last?" Grey asked.

"You can't blame them. Amelie's hungry to see the world, and Hayden is only too glad to show it to her."

She moved behind him and leaned over his shoulder. She knew he wasn't able to concentrate when she did that.

"What are you reading?" she asked innocently, her breath warm against his ear.

"An account of a man who claims to be able to move objects with the power of his mind."

"Do you think it's true?"

"Doubtful," he said.

"But not impossible."

"Not impossible," he agreed. "Though most of what we take for magic is simply a mystery whose answers have yet to be found."

"And which am I? Magic or mystery?" she whispered in his ear.

He turned and found himself looking up into her

eyes. Once more, and as always, time became suspended, his heartbeat stuttered, and time slowed to a long, liquid moment while he was lost in her gaze. "I don't know," he murmured. "I'm still working on it."

She wrapped an arm around his shoulder and slipped around to his front, sliding onto his lap. "Do you think it will take long to figure out?"

"A lifetime," he said, tucking her closer and inhaling the scent of her hair.

"You must be very committed," she said, and hissed with pleasure as his mouth prowled down her cheek to the curve where her neck met her shoulder. He traced her ear with his tongue, and she shivered.

"Oh, I am most resolute," he said, turning her in his arms.

"Perhaps I can prove my abilities," she said, a thrill of excitement shimmering in her eyes. "Would you like me to conjure something for you?"

"And only me."

She twined her arms around his neck and drew him to her. His mouth opened hungrily on hers. He'd never be able to kiss her enough, never be able to control the passion that erupted so spontaneously between them. When he finally drew away to give her a chance to catch her breath, a wicked gleam had entered her eyes.

"Yes, indeed," she murmured, pulling him back to her. "I certainly feel something stirring. . . ."

It was noon in Little Firkin. A perfectly lovely spring day. The sun glimmered on the river that danced happily along the town's boundary, and a breeze riffled the flags atop stakes delineating the site of a future pottery factory.

The people of Little Firkin leaned over their back fences for their daily chin-wag, enjoying the warm sun, while the shopkeepers swept the plank board-walk outside their shops. Children played Kick the Can in the street outside MacKee's Bank (formerly McGowan's), and a group of Little Firkin's finest young men flexed their muscles self-consciously as they unloaded building timber from the railway's loading dock, for a group of young ladies who pretended not to notice.

But when a capricious breeze nickered to life in one of the town's back alleys, kicking up a dust devil of leaves and halfpenny candy wrappers, and a voice like a strangled cat pealed through the town center, they stopped whatever they were doing and headed for Main Street.

An ancient crone with a face like a withered apple appeared at the end of the town amidst a swirl of dust, her ragged, multicolored skirts whipping around. On either side of her, legs braced and hackles raised, stood two enormous hounds, their lips curled back over huge fangs. The crone lifted a gnarled bole over her head and shouted, "Be there anyone here to dispute my claim to Little Firkin?"

Little Firkin turned its collective head, looking around hopefully, but no one appeared to accept the old dame's challenge. She glared about and then, sat-isfied, dropped her bole, dug into the velvet pouch hanging from her belt, and withdrew two bits of some-thing, which she then popped into the monster brutes' waiting maws to a chorus of canine lip smacking and tail wagging.

"Good lads," the woman muttered, and turned,

hobbling back down the street, followed by her two not-quite-so-ferocious-looking companions.

At the same time, a middle-aged representative of the Art Workers Guild let the curtain drop back down over the bank window through which he'd been watching.

"What in the name of all that's holy was that?" he asked, turning his bemused gaze to the rotund man sitting across the desk from him.

"That be Grammy Beadle," said Donnie MacKee. "Our witch."

Read on for a teaser from
Connie Brockway's

Skinny Dipping

Available from Onyx

Early September

Splat!

"For Chrissakes!" Eighty-two-year-old Birgie Olson lurched upright on the derelict swimming raft she occupied, setting it teetering precariously.

She looked around. Inches from her feet lay a broken blue balloon amidst a bright sunburst of orange tempura paint.

"What is it?" Her great-niece Mimi asked from somewhere alongside the raft.

"Some little shit launched a water balloon filled with orange paint at me."

"Splotchball," Mimi said.

"Huh?" Birgie rolled over onto her stomach, dipping her side of the raft a good six inches lower into Fowl Lake than its opposite. She was a large woman.

Below her, Mimi lay spread out atop an ancient, much-patched tractor tire's inner tube, her twin pigtails of dark hair floating amongst the duckweed. She wore a shapeless, faded Speedo swimsuit, much like the ones she'd worn when she was sixteen. Her eyes were shut.

"Splotchball," Mimi repeated calmly. "The kids made it up. It's like paintball, except no one here can afford the special guns and ammo, so they adapted slingshots and water balloons. Really, it's pretty enterprising."

Birgie ignored Mimi's admiration. "There he is!" She spotted a furtive figure plastered tight against the side of one of the six cottages that comprised the Olson family's ancestral vacation retreat, Chez Ducky. He looked like an albino spider monkey, all arms and legs, his towhead gleaming like a beacon. "Who is he? There. By Cottage Six!"

Mimi craned her neck to look around. "I think it's Carl Junior," she said after a minute. "Maybe Emmit. Could be Hal. Young Scandinavian males all look pretty much the same."

Birgie stuck out her arm and pointed at the kid, shouting, "You hit me with one of those things again and I will hunt you down and skin you alive, you odious example of unprotected intercourse!"

With a shriek of delight, the kid darted into the woods, a small motley dog dashing after him. Having dealt with the interloper, Birgie settled back and folded her hands over the field of blue hibiscuses printed on her bathing suit, a Lands' End double-wide, and stared at the beach.

"Who the hell are all those people?" she grumbled.

"What people?"

"Those kids. Emmits and Carls and Hals and God knows who all."

"Those would be the people staying at Chez Ducky," Mimi replied. Birgie could hear the smile in her voice.

"It's not funny."

"Well, it is sort of funny. Now that Great-Aunt Ardis has passed on, you're the matriarch of Chez Ducky. You oughta know the names of your loyal subjects."

Birgie sourly surveyed the domain that tradition was attempting to dump in her lap. At the edge of an old white pine forest, a series of derelict cabins spread out equidistant from one another, leading to the Big House, a white clapboard construction rising two stories high, its fieldstone foundation padded with moss and its oft-patched roof wearing a Jacob's coat of different-colored asphalt. A few scraps of the original gingerbreading still clung tenaciously to the upper eaves, but other than this initial stab at gentrification, no attempts had ever been made to gussy the place up. Named Chez Ducky by some wit, the compound had been built over a hundred years ago on eighty acres abutting a third-rate lake situated five hours north of the Twin Cities and half an hour west of the nearest town, Fawn Creek.

"Some kingdom," Birgie muttered, though in truth she was very fond of the place. She was fonder still of the fact that she could escape the summertime heat of her principal residency in Florida and spend the season up here for free. "If nominated I will not run; if elected I will not serve."

"No one's asking your permission. It's a hereditary position," Mimi replied. "Chez Ducky has always been run by the oldest Olson female."

Easy for Mimi to say, Birgie thought sourly. With a few silver strands just starting to appear in her dark pigtails, her peeling nose tip tilted and freckled, and faint smile lines permanently stamped at the corners of her mouth, Mimi reminded Birgie of a superannuated Pippi Longstocking. At forty-one, Mimi still occasionally showed up in mismatched socks or oversized sweatshirts turned inside out.

No doubt about it, Mimi had it good: no responsibilities, no obligations, no one to answer to. Birgie had it good, too—or at least she did before her big sister, Ardis, had up and died.

"Mimi," Birgie said, "I'm eighty-two years old, and I've learned as many new names in my life as I want to. Besides, most of the people here aren't even related to me."

She nodded toward Chez Ducky's beach. Little figures chugged up and down the shoreline, toting folding chairs, blankets, ancient TV trays, portable Weber grills, bags of charcoal, and cans of lighter fluid in preparation for the picnic later that afternoon. Birgie didn't know two-thirds of them.

Chez Ducky was like some petri dish experiment run amuck.

Seeded more than a hundred years ago with a few grains of expensive, indiscriminating, and congenial Olson DNA, the Chez Ducky population had exploded over the decades, devouring anyone with the slimmest association to an Olson. There were ex-wives and ex-husbands and new wives of ex-husbands and children of new husbands from former marriages and half brothers and sisters and their friends and . . . gawd! It made her head hurt thinking about it. She knew none of this was necessarily a bad thing, but it wasn't the same Chez Ducky she'd known growing up. And Birgie wasn't the only one expressing discontent with what Chez Ducky had become.

"Oh, I imagine you still have room in your old gray head for a few more names," Mimi said.

Birgie wondered whether Mimi would be so calm if she knew that certain family members, some of them the legal heirs to the property, were discussing selling the Chez.

If Chez Ducky got sold, that would be that. On the up side for Birgie, there'd be no family enclave to be the head of; on the downside, she'd be stuck in Everglades City year-round because she didn't have enough money to rent a place up here and she couldn't stay with one of her Minnesota relatives for more than a few days.

And where would Mimi go? As far as Birgie knew, this place was the only constant in Mimi's life. No doubt about it, they'd be screwed. But what could either of them do about it? Still, she supposed she ought to say something to Mimi . . . just let her know people were talking . . . but . . .

Beneath her blunt and blustery facade, Birgie knew herself to be a coward. She'd been too cowardly to get married, to have kids, to move into the head surgical nurse position at the hospital where she'd worked for forty years, or to tell someone bad news. She'd long ago come to terms with this failing in her character. She could, she reasoned, have had worse flaws. For instance, she could have been a Republican.

It wasn't that she thought Mimi would break down and bawl. Even when Mimi had been eighteen and the courts had declared her father legally dead, she hadn't blubbered. But Birgie never wanted to see that stricken look on Mimi's face again.

"What would you do with your summers if you didn't spend them here?" she asked as casually as she could.

One of Mimi's gimlet dark eyes opened. "But, I *do* spend them here," she said. "And I intend to spend them here. Always. Until they wrench the key to Cottage Six from my cold, dead hand. And who knows?" Mimi mused, closing her eyes again and grinning. "I might not even go then."

"What? You're going to haunt the place?"

"Maybe."

Birgie snorted. Mimi was a tele-spiritualist . . . or was it tele-medium? Birgie never could remember what the operators of Uff-Dead—Birgie's pet name for Straight Talk from Beyond, the paranormal hotline Mimi worked for and which catered to Minnesota's Scandinavian population—called themselves. Unlike the rest of the Olson clan, who, uncertain whether they should be concerned, conciliatory, or amused about Mimi's career and so opted to take the traditional Scandinavian route of ignoring it, Birgie wasn't above open scoffing. Not that she had many opportunities to do so.

The only time Mimi referred to her job was when someone suggested aloud that Mimi's father, John Olson, who'd disappeared when Mimi was eleven, was dead. Mimi would look the offender straight in the eye and reply, "If my dad was dead, I'd be able to contact his spirit, wouldn't I? But I can't, so he isn't." That generally shut down any further conversation.

Birgie didn't know what Mimi's mom, Solange, thought of her daughter's refusal to entertain the possibility that her ex-husband was dead, but she'd guess Solange didn't ignore it. No, sirree. Mimi's mom, So-

lange, was the anti-Olson, focused, insistent, and relentless. Not that Birgie considered Solange a bad
person. It must have about killed her to return Mimi to
the midst of her indolent former in-laws every summer
after the divorce. But she had. And she'd continued to
do so even after John's disappearance.

Solange and John had met in college at a Univer-
sity of Minnesota job fair—she was there for a job; John
Olson was there for the free hotdog. Solange hadn't
seen the carefree, wanderlust-prone young man as her
polar opposite. She'd seen a gorgeous Gordian knot
of potential she itched to unravel. John saw a pretty,
starry-eyed girl who hung on his every word and
enjoyed sex. No one had ever hung on any of John's
words before. They married.

When Solange finished unraveling John, a process
that took an embarrassingly short time, she realized he
wasn't ever going to amount to anything, big or otherwise, and that was exactly the way he wanted it. Sad-
der but wiser, Solange divorced John and swept their
black-haired baby girl off to her parents' palatial home
(Solange's great-granddad being Jacque Charbonneau,
the depilatory king, creator of Hair Today, Gone Tomorrow). There, Solange wasted no time trying to root
from Baby Mimi any suspected slacker tendencies she
might have inherited from her dad. Her fears, Birgie
conceded, were not without justification. As it turned
out, Mimi was a slacker of the first order. Unfortunately
for Mimi, it also turned out she had a sky-high IQ.

Solange, not one to suffer waste gladly, set about
"encouraging" Mimi with extracurricular activities,
handpicked play-groups, accelerated this and fast-
tracked that—at least that's what Mimi's dad, John,

had said. This encouragement met with mild success and probably would have escalated had not Solange remarried a decade later and forthwith produced two more bright little girls who, unlike their older half sister, not only *wanted* Solange's encouragement but actually seemed to benefit from it. And substantially, too. Mary and Sarah, Birgie recalled the girls' names.

Not that Mimi talked much about them. She kept her relationship with her Charbonneau relatives strictly separate from that with the Olsons. Or more specifically, her relationship with Chez Ducky. Since her dad had disappeared, Mimi had been living pretty much like she had a terminal disease. She had no responsibilities to anyone but herself and didn't owe anyone anything. Owning nothing of value, she had nothing to protect.

Except Chez Ducky.

That, Birgie thought sadly, was the hell of it. You couldn't get out of life without at least a few things sinking their hooks into you. And the fewer things that got to you, the deeper they set their hooks. For Mimi it was Chez Ducky. For Birgie, too, damn it.

She cleared her throat. "Mimi. You . . . ah, you got anything going on in your life?"

"Nope. I'm free as a bird. What do you want and when?"

"That's not what I meant. I meant, do you have a boyfriend? Or a girlfriend? Or anyone?"

"You are acting *so* weird today," Mimi said, wiggling her way up onto her elbows to peer at Birgie. "You feeling all right?"

"I just . . . you know. I want to you to be happy," Birgie muttered uncomfortably. Mimi's peer turned into a stare. Birgie understood. She was a little surprised to hear such maudlin crap coming out of her mouth herself.

"The thing is, things are changing so fast," she said, carefully feeling her way. "And, ah, they could change even faster."

"Birgie, I realize this is rough for you," Mimi replied, looking nauseatingly sympathetic, "but no one expects you to replace Ardis."

"Good. Because I'm not going to."

"And no one wants you to. You know that, right?"

"Right." She took a deep breath. "Look, Mimi, there's something you maybe ought to know—"

"No, there isn't," Mimi said quickly. Mimi had always seemed to have a sixth sense when it came to uncomfortable subjects and a successful tactic in dealing with them; she simply blew right past them.

"Really. I think—"

"I think we should go skinny-dipping!"

"Ah, geez, Mimi," Birgie burst out in strenuous objection, secretly relieved. At least she could tell herself she'd tried to warn Mimi of the way things looked to be heading. "You'd think you were a goddamn nudist. Look at the sky. It's broad daylight."

"So what?" Mimi said, dropping off the side of the inner tube into the water. "I'm suggesting skinny-dipping, not nude sunbathing. We're a hundred yards from shore and our lady parts will be discreetly hidden by the water. Come on. You can strip underwater."

Suiting action to words, Mimi disappeared beneath the surface of the lake, a circle of bubbles marking her descent. A minute later her fist popped out of the water clutching her blue Speedo. Mimi's head followed, water streaming down her face.

"See?" she said, flinging her sodden suit at the pontoon. It caught on the corner with a wet *thwack.* "Easy."

"Easy for you. Honey, I'd need a crowbar to get me out of this suit when it's wet." Birgie looked down. Shame. She liked skinny-dipping, too. It was a Chez Ducky ritual. Usually enjoyed after dark and for excellent reasons.

"That sucks," Mimi said.

"Yeah, well—"

She caught sight of the missile a second before it hit the side of the pontoon and exploded green tempura paint all over her. "Damn it!"

Birgie heaved herself to her knees and lurched to her feet, setting the raft rocking.

"What are you going to do?" Mimi asked.

"I'm gonna go find those little bastards," Birgie said grimly.

"I'm in," Mimi said. "Just let me get my suit back on."

"No. You stay. You'd only cramp my style by trying to keep me from killing those kids. I'm gonna put a moratorium on teenage boys at Chez Ducky. If I gotta be the goddamn head of this goddamn place I might as well get some satisfaction out of it. Unless you want to be the head of the place?"

"Ha. Ha. No, thank you."

She hadn't thought so. It was too bad. "Can I take the inner tube?" she asked. "I'm not as strong a swimmer as I used to be."

"Sure," Mimi said. "You sure you don't want me to come with you?"

"Nah," Birgie replied absently. She was thinking. What she needed was a replacement. But who? The Olsons of Chez Ducky had always been led by a matriarch, and the only other old ladies around were Birgie's dead brothers' widows, Naomi and Johanna. Neither would work. Naomi had been halfway round the bend for years and Johanna was so frantic trying to keep hidden the fact that she'd lately started shacking up with Charlie, her long-dead husband's twin, that she was on the verge of a nervous breakdown. But there was no reason *Mimi* couldn't head the family.

True, Birgie couldn't think of anyone more ill suited for the job, but she also couldn't think of anyone better equipped. Ill suited by virtue of her temperament, well equipped by virtue of her abilities. Mimi might deny it with her dying breath, but the fact was that everyone knew that during Ardis's last few years it had been Mimi who'd been the glue that had held Chez Ducky together. She'd sent in the taxes, arranged to have the septic tank sucked, kept track of . . . whatever needed to be kept track of.

True, Mimi might hate it, but she *could* do it. Hell, she might even keep Chez Ducky from being sold, and that would be good for her. Okay, *them.* Two birds, one stone.

True, Mimi would never agree, and she couldn't be pressed into service. Mimi had withstood her mother's demands to apply herself and do something—anything—for three decades.

But if Birgie was really good, really careful, and played this right, Mimi *might* be slipped into the position. Like an oyster slips down your throat.

Hell, Birgie thought as she dipped up and down on the corner of the raft, sending the pontoon rocking violently, it was worth a shot. She dove into the lake, causing barely a ripple.

Penguin Group (USA) Online

What will you be reading tomorrow?

Tom Clancy, Patricia Cornwell, W.E.B. Griffin,
Nora Roberts, William Gibson, Robin Cook,
Brian Jacques, Catherine Coulter, Stephen King,
Dean Koontz, Ken Follett, Clive Cussler,
Eric Jerome Dickey, John Sandford,
Terry McMillan, Sue Monk Kidd, Amy Tan,
John Berendt…

You'll find them all at
penguin.com

*Read excerpts and newsletters,
find tour schedules and reading group guides,
and enter contests.*

Subscribe to Penguin Group (USA) newsletters
and get an exclusive inside look
at exciting new titles and the authors you love
long before everyone else does.

PENGUIN GROUP (USA)
us.penguingroup.com